LEVI

THORNE BROTHER SERIES

AMBER ALLEE

Cover Design: Graphics by Stacy
Editing by: M.E. Carter & Andrea Barreiro
Formatting: Stacey Blake @ Champagne Book Design

For those who have the best of intentions with
your loved ones but get it wrong.
Here is your second chance.

FAMILY / FRIEND LIST

Levi Thorne
~ Lincoln (Linc) Thorne – Older brother
~ Everly Thorne – Sister-in-Law/Married to Linc
~ Reid Thorne – Cousin/Adopted brother
~ Daniel Thorne – Uncle/Adopted Father
~ Alice Thorne – Aunt/Adopted Mother
~ Eleanor (Ellie) Thorne – Grandma
~ Archie Thorne – Grandpa

Saylor Gentry
~ Adam Gentry – Father
~ Sharilyn/Glammy – Grandmother
~ Alan/Granddad – Grandfather
~ Halo Landry – Daughter
~ Everly Thorne – Best Friend

LEVI

PROLOGUE

Levi

I LOVE MY WIFE.

I do. There is nothing in this world that I love more. Not being an attorney or flipping the houses I own or all the money it makes. Not the wins I have under my belt in the courtroom or the fact that I was considered one of the hottest bachelors in the country alongside my brother, Linc. I used to think that all the extra digits in my bank account was what I wanted in life. What I was put here on this earth for. But it is not. Not by a long shot.

In fact, the moment a pair of the sexiest arms leaned over me to get the bartender's attention at the bar I was visiting with my brothers, Lincoln and Reid, the entire course of my life changed like the flipping of a coin. In a flash, I saw my future breeze in and it was in the shape of the most gorgeous woman I had ever seen. She smelt of sugar cookies and it made my mouth water. Her long brown hair floated down her back in curls. The most alluring chocolate-colored eyes captured me in a trance. When her arm brushed against mine, it shot tingles down to my core and I knew I was a goner. You could tell she had a big personality that drew people to her. Her sweet voice towards the bartender snapped me back into focus and I knew that I'd do whatever it took to be the one who took all her attention the rest of the evening.

She mesmerized me from that moment and something about her drew me in. It was like she had this aura around her, letting everyone in that bar know she was something special. My whole world stopped in those few seconds as I watched her giggle at something her friend was saying over her shoulder. Hook. Line. Sinker. Even her giggle set me on a dreamy path.

Reid elbowed me in the gut, just to get my attention, but I was not paying him any mind as she leaned past me, blocking my view of the guy next to me. Not that I was talking about the game with him anymore. My body jolted as our upper arms lightly skimmed each other. I was such a goner.

My mind exploded like the grand finale fireworks on the Fourth of July. No other touch from someone had made my body sing on contact. The beer bottle in my hand touched my lips to help with my dry mouth but my lips didn't close, as I was still staring at the most beautiful woman in the room. So, the alcohol slipped from my mouth and down the front of my shirt.

Classy. Way to look like a loser.

Reid had snapped his fingers in my face to bring me out of my trance. I knew then that she was something special and I'd be damned if she left here with some other loser, other than me. No, I saw her first and there wasn't any other outcome that would be acceptable. I just needed to work up the nerve to speak.

So, what did a good looking thirty-year-old guy who had the world at his fingertips do? I stared, waiting for the right words to say.

I was never one to seek out women, but this one was different. I had a feeling she was going to change my life forever. Normally,

I had a plan for everything I ever did. I was a scheduled person, structure was my life, but this little slip of a woman burned my mapped-out life up in flames. All it took was one look into her bright blue eyes and I knew she was mine. The look she gave me when we were almost nose to nose told me that she was just as captivated as I was.

"Are you just going to sit there and stare or are you going to actually talk, handsome?" she asked me.

The swig of alcohol I just had didn't do anything to help with my dry mouth. She leaned closer and the smell of sugar cookies made me want to nibble on her neck.

"How are you?" I asked and as the words left my throat, I wanted to slam my face down on the wooden bar top. *Who says stupid lines like that?*

She giggles and it's like music to my ears.

"I'm doing just fine, handsome," she counters. "You enjoying the game?" I nod because in my thirty years of living I've suddenly developed mutism.

"Don't be running off new customers, Saylor," the bartender says as he comes over with a tray full of beers. "It's twenty-five dollars."

"Just being friendly, Cal," she responds as she starts to dig into her purse.

My brain starts to finally function, "Add it to my tab," I say to the bartender.

"Sure," he says with an eye roll then walks off.

"You didn't have to do that," she tells me and places her soft hand on top of mine. The warmth of her hand sends tingles up my arm.

"It's my pleasure."

"What's your name?" she asks.

"Levi," I answer. "What's yours?"

"Saylor."

"Saylor is a very unique name."

"My dad was in the Navy so Mom thought it was fitting," she tells me. "You want to get out of here?"

"You're very forward," I say, never having a woman be so upfront.

"When I see something I like, I seize the day."

"I can respect that." I give her a smirk. She's a confident bombshell that just filled my weekend calendar up.

"Are you always this quiet, or have I just got you all tongue-tied?" Saylor giggles again and it makes me smile.

"You definitely have me tongue-tied," I say honestly. "But yeah, I'm usually the quiet one in the group."

"I'll crack your shell in no time." She winks at me and it's the sexiest thing I've ever seen; my entire life trajectory just took a sharp turn.

It was that simple. She and I went for a walk down the busy street of bars, talking and learning about each other. We found a small bench in front of a tattoo parlor and sat there for hours talking. If I didn't already think she was it for me, I definitely knew after conversing into the wee hours. She grew up as a military brat but lived with her grandparents in a small town, in northern California, near the Nevada state line. She's twenty-five, loves to bake and owns a successful bakery here in town. After that night, we spent every waking minute with each other, and three months later we said our wedding vows at the courthouse.

Now, here we are six months into our marriage and we have a little one on the way. Later this week we are finding out the gender of our baby and I couldn't be happier. Having Saylor by my side every morning when I wake is truly the best thing in the world.

LEVI

Some may think it all happened a little too fast, but I wouldn't change it for the world. Which is why I've dreaded today so much.

I love my wife and baby more than my life, which is why I have to end things.

Today I'm asking my pregnant wife for a divorce.

CHAPTER ONE

Levi

"Why would you file for divorce? That doesn't make any sense," Dr. Jordan asks shocked, which is exactly the reaction I expected. "I think you need to calm down and think this through, before you do something that can't be taken back."

"I don't care what you or Mitch have to say. I'm doing this my way and that's final. I don't need to be constantly babied, I'm a grown man who can take care of his family. It's my responsibility to keep her safe. Me! You know how hard it is for me to make sure Saylor doesn't even stub her toe under my watch," I practically yell at Dr. Jordan, as I pace the length of her office here in the building of our law firm. She keeps repeating the same thing over and over again, as if I'm not listening. I am, but that's not the route I need to take. I've told her and Mitch this multiple times, and it's like no one is hearing me. It's like they are ignoring all the warning signs flashing in front of our faces.

Five months ago, I started receiving the most disturbing packages at my office. The last one was a bone chilling threat against her and our unborn child. It contained photos of my mother lying on the floor of the living room, with a needle sticking out of her arm. Those photos were from a file taken by the Seattle police department decades ago, but what is the most disturbing part is that it's not my dead mother's face but Saylor's. How this psycho was able to retrieve this photographic evidence is scary. To say that I'm shocked is nothing new because we receive threats often, but this one has my entire P.I. team scrambling every minute of the day, especially because only a select few know she's pregnant. Then, I started to receive letters with photos that were practically right next to my wife at the daily places she visited. At first, I thought it was the usual hate mail but as time has progressed, they are getting more specific and horrifying.

Being an attorney and part of a large firm who gets the bad guys off, we get a lot of media attention that doesn't make us the most liked people. It's one of the reasons I've started to distance myself from the firm my brother started. I've never had any passion in this field anyway, but was pressured to feel like this was my only option. Growing up, I didn't want to disappoint my new family, so I did exactly what my older brother Lincoln did. He went to Yale, our dad's alma mater, and then went on to law school. My passion is working with my hands building things. In my spare time, I buy houses that need to be fixed then flip them. I keep some that I rent out, but mostly sell them for profit after I create the perfect home.

So that's why when I received the fifth package, I knew this wasn't some internet troll with nothing better to do with his time than send hate mail. No, these were turning out to be more personal and aimed solely towards my wife with a clear message. They were going to harm her. I've had people looking into this for months now, very discreetly, but we've gotten nowhere. I've told my brother, Lincoln, the very basic but haven't gone into details just yet. He just recently got engaged to Everly, who just happens to be my wife's best friend. I can't risk them finding out until I have a more solid lead. The last thing I need is to panic my pregnant wife and make her feel unsafe. Or worse, try to help and then something happens to her or the baby. I don't know if I would survive that.

"I don't care what you or Mitch have to say. I'm doing this my way and that is final. I don't need to be constantly babied, I'm a grown man who can take care of his family. It is my responsibility to keep her safe. Me! You know how hard it is for me to make sure Saylor doesn't even stub her toe under my watch," I practically yell at Dr. Jordan, as I pace the length of her office here in the building of our law firm.

Dr. Jordan has been with me since I got out of law school and started here at my brother's firm. I didn't want to live a life in solitude and tried to make a change. I felt better when I was alone and outdoors. But change is hard. She has helped in some ways, like opening up to my mom and dad and accepting them as my family. That was hard to do. Our biological parents died from a drug overdose when we were young, after our little sister was killed. We were orphans for a while, waiting to see if we had any relatives. Lincoln and I didn't even know that we had grandparents or about our father's brother, Daniel, and his wife, Alice, until CPS told us that we were going to live with relatives after several months in foster care. Even though Reid is our cousin, I do feel like he's a brother and we are as close as siblings are. I also use Dr. Jordan because dealing with some clients puts a strain on my mental well-being. I'm great at what I do but having to handle scum puts a toll on you. He gives me an outlet to let go of the smarmy things I have to endure.

"Levi, I know that you are grown but you have people in

certain areas that are there to protect you and your best interest. I agree with Mitch, and think you need to reconsider what you are about to do. Think long term and how this will affect you, your marriage, and the family you're about to start." Dr. Jordan tries to push, but I'm not having it. We pay her top dollar to help but this isn't helping anymore.

"Don't you think that I've thought this through! I haven't had a single night's sleep since this all began." I pause to get my anger and breathing under control. "You don't have anyone who looks after your family but you, correct? Why is so hard for you or Mitch to understand that I'm doing the same thing."

"Keeping her in the dark will help no one, Levi. She's a strong woman and I think you should tell her. She has a right to know; this is her life too. You can't just decide something like this and not include all parties. And to answer your other question, I'm not a mega millionaire that the world wants a piece of every moment of the day. You are because you take on high profile cases that the entire world watches from their televisions. They have very strong opinions about it sometimes and this is the fallout from that."

"It will be fine. Like you said I have the best people in place that will have this solved in no time. She will understand and we'll be back on track to start our family and not have to worry about this threat," I argue, sounding like a broken record. From an early age, I was told that talking to a therapist was supposed to be helpful, but I'm not seeing the vision any longer.

"Until it happens again, then what? You can't just play yoyo with your wife, women don't put up with that, especially your wife. And it's completely unfair to put her in that position. Levi, as your doctor and as your friend, I beg you to reconsider this. This act might have damning consequences for you and could blow up in your face. Think bigger picture. Things could go terribly wrong."

"I'll take it into consideration, Dr. Jordan." I appease her but know I'm dead set on doing things my way. "Thanks for seeing me on such short notice."

We shake hands and I leave her office. I've got a lot on my plate these days but my top priority is my four-month pregnant wife. Someone wants her and our baby dead. And by dead, I mean gutted on a fish hook. The letters alone will keep you up at night but then picture after picture started coming in of her daily routine. They've followed her and were even close enough to take photos of what was in her purse at her bakery. Now, the pictures are of her with a laser pointer, from a gun scope, on her forehead or chest or small baby bump.

That was the last straw for me, so when the letter came in about choosing between walking away from my marriage or losing her and my baby to a watery grave, I started making plans. My security thinks I'm nuts and shouldn't let some prick decide how to live my life, but I can't take that chance. What if I listen to them and this lunatic follows through with his threat. I'd never forgive myself if something were to ever happen to her or our baby. The team would go back home to their families and I'd be left alone losing the two most important people in my life. So, the decision was easy and after tomorrow I hope that I've bought my team some time to catch this loser, and then we can get on with the rest of our lives.

"We're here, sir," Mitch states startling me. I was so in my head I didn't realize that we left the office and are pulled up to the curb of the restaurant.

"Sir, I'm pleading with you. Please reconsider what you're about to do. I don't think you've thought about the affects this could have on Mrs. Thorne and your child," he pleads.

"I'll take that into advisement, Mitch." I try not to show my annoyance of him trying to change my mind, again, for the millionth time. "She'll understand once everything comes out, why I had to do this. She'll probably even appreciate it."

"Just remember that some things that are said can never be taken back, no matter if your intentions are honorable."

Tired of the same song and dance, I brush past him and walk into the restaurant before Mitch has a chance to hold the glass door open for me to walk through. I don't need another lecture and would appreciate for both Dr. Jordan and Mitch to keep their opinions to themselves.

The flirty hostess takes me to the table I'd requested in the middle of the packed restaurant, and she stays a little longer than necessary. After ordering a bourbon, I sit back and wait for my beautiful wife to arrive. She's the best thing that has ever happened to me and I thank the heavens that she walked into the bar that night.

The noisy restaurant quickly comes to a halt, and then mummers start. Looking up, I see exactly what caused the pause. My extremely gorgeous wife and mother of my baby walk in. She is glowing, and the pregnancy is bringing it out more, along with her feistiness. I never thought I'd find a pregnant woman attractive, much less fall in love and marry one, but the moment she looked into my eyes I was hooked for life. She is the most challenging woman in my life and puts me through my paces more than any case I've ever been through. Sometimes our arguments aren't fun, but I find that the way we banter back and forth is such a turn on. The other day I tried ordering for her at a restaurant because she had to have another bathroom break and when she came back, she not only put me in my place, but she also gave our waiter an earful. I fight the smile, trying to break free from thinking about that dinner. Saylor is truly one of a kind, and I'm a lucky bastard to call her mine.

We've only told our security and Dr. Jordan about the baby for now. I'm hoping this problem that we're facing will be over soon, and once we find out the sex of the baby, then we plan on making an announcement to the world and family. I know our families will be ecstatic and now that I've gotten over my panic, I'm overjoyed with becoming a father. I wasn't at first, but once I settled down and heard Saylor and Dr. Jordan out, I knew this is what I was meant to do.

I watch as she talks with the hostess and get a heavy rock in the pit of my stomach. The sunny sky is now turning to gloom in my gut. Saylor approaches the table in the middle of the room and people are starting to recognize us. We are usually shown to a private room or corner to keep out of the public eye but not today. Today I needed this to be public.

She has a breathtaking smile on and it makes me feel like shit.

"Hey, baby." She comes over and I make no move to get up from my chair. All the years of manners have just been thrown out, and my mother would slap me upside of my head for this.

Saylor gives me a curious look, then bends down to give me a kiss. Just as she reaches my lips, I quickly turn my head and give her my cheek.

"Levi?" Saylor gasps and a hurt look graces her face.

Showtime.

I gesture for my wife to take a seat but still make no move to help her in her chair. Her small four-and-a-half-month pregnant bump gets my attention. I swear her body changes every day, and it takes all my might not to touch her.

Focus on the goal, Levi.

She orders a lemon water and we give our lunch order. As

much of a prick as I'm about to be, she needs to eat before I follow through with this.

Saylor tries to hold a conversation with me the entire time, but I've only responded with short, clipped responses. After she's taken her final bite, she places her fork down with a clatter and throws her napkin across the plate.

Here we go.

"Levi, talk to me. What's wrong, you're not being yourself today?"

Taking a deep breath to steady my nerves, I place my napkin over my uneaten plate and steel my face toward my worried wife.

I'm sorry baby, please forgive me!

"I can't do this anymore."

"Do what?" She scrunches her face in the most adorable way.

Taking my finger, I wave it back and forth between us.

"This."

"W-what?"

"This. *We* are not working."

Her eyes are frantically roaming all over my face, but I keep stoic. Never showing any weakness. That's the first thing I learned in Law School. My heart is breaking right now as I watch her whole demeanor deflate. Her hormones have been all over the place lately and I hate to be the cause of any of this right now.

"I was having doubts the morning of our wedding but thought it was just nerves. I really wish I'd listen to Dr. Jordan about being engaged longer instead of rushing things. It was my bad."

The silence is deafening and I'm not sure how many minutes pass before she speaks but it feels like hours.

"Is this some kind of joke? Levi, this isn't funny."

Don't make me have to get nasty, baby. Just get mad then storm out.

"There's no joke. I want out. This isn't something that is appealing to me anymore. I liked my old lifestyle better." I shrug like it's not a big deal and toss back the rest of my drink and signal to the waiter for another. She sits there in shock as I take another sip of my newly poured drink, and try my damnedest to appear bored with this subject.

"Isn't appealing anymore? What the fuck's that supposed to mean?" Her voice raises, and I see people taking more notice of us. I knew this might be harder for her, to be blindsided. We've been so happy lately and there haven't been any warning signs for this to occur.

I'm sorry baby. This is the only way.

"Our lifestyle. It's just not enough now. I tried, but I'm not fulfilled. Blaire was right in that I needed way more than you could ever give me."

Please forgive me for saying that horrible woman's name.

"So, spanking the shit out of me isn't enough for you!" she spits back and now I know we've drawn a crowd. I'm pretty sure the meter maid heard her.

"Saylor," I growl in warning. "Watch yourself. I know that this is shocking but remember who you're speaking to." The lump in my throat only gets bigger and the acid in my stomach is burning my esophagus.

Just walk out, baby, then it can be over, and I don't have to keep going.

Her tears have flooded down her face and I think that she's about to get up and leave, but then something crosses over her face. A look of resolve, almost. Like a light bulb moment going off. She looks around the room and sees that all eyes are on our table. Saylor furiously wipes her cheeks with the backs of her hands. Her face hardens as she faces me again, and the glow she always has is missing. There is a fire that has been ignited in her that I've never seen before. I can handle her feisty side but this is something else completely. Maybe this wasn't the best idea to do this in public.

"You know what? You are nothing but a coward! You hide behind your expensive cars, yachts, and position in the community but you're a coward," she spews. She points her delicate, perfectly manicured nail in my direction. "Now, here we are not even six months later, and you want out." Another look of resolve flashes over her eyes. "Fine, have it your way."

She goes to stand, and I can see her struggling to straighten up because she is shaking. My instincts say to go to her and embrace her trembling body, but my mind is telling me that this is all part of my plan.

"You truly are the heartless bastard everyone talks about, but I thought it was because they just didn't know you. Today has shown me how blind I've been to that. You let those years dictate the rest of your life. Yeah, you had it rough, but there are others out there in the world who had it a lot worse than you did, and look what you did with it. Most people don't land families like your aunt and uncle, and they end up on the streets. Not some three-story mansion with private schools and luxury vacations. Instead of fighting for a better way to overcome it, you decided to help keep those people out of prison so they can do more damage to innocent lives, just like your dead parents let their drug dealer do." She tosses her napkin on the table then bends to grab for her purse.

There is a lump in my throat and I want to say something but the words are clogged.

"All that money in your bank account, along with a decade of therapy, and still you can't get a clue or come to terms with it. You work in a field that you despise just to please a family that should love you no matter what career choice you make. Ask yourself, after years with that escort woman, were you able to feel loved? Have meaningful relationships with people your age?" She's ticking a finger off on each argument and making my head spin as she puts me in my place. No one has ever spoken to me this way before, not even her. I feel heat on the back of my neck as she's calling me out. Each sentence is like a whip slashing across my skin, ripping me to shreds.

Saylor snatches her phone off the tablecloth and jams it down into her open purse. "The answer to all those questions is a big fat NO! For a smart man you sure are a dumbass. We were together, but for only a few weeks, and everyone told me what a different man you'd become—kind, caring and even started acting your age. I'm sorry no one was there for you growing up but I'm here. I thought we were moving forward in a loving relationship."

My chest is burning at her words, as if she's stabbing my heart with an ice pick, and I want her to stop but I'm frozen in place. I've never heard her speak like this before. Especially about my dead mother and father. Shit, she just aired out all my dirty laundry that only a few people know about.

She looks around the room that has all her attention. This isn't how I pictured my plan working. This isn't what was supposed to happen. She turns her attention back to me and my lungs refuse to let air in.

"Just remember when the time comes, and you want *our* life back, I won't be here. You remember this day and think about how badly you fucked up. You once said that you don't give second chances, well neither do I."

Oh, FUCK! I was referring to a legal case where I fired a new intern over making a slight mistake. She reaches for her purse and shrugs it onto her shoulder. I pray that she leaves quickly and the stabbing in my chest will ease. My hand automatically touches my chest to check to see if I actually have been stabbed, because the pain is brutal.

I need to stop this, to tell her that this was some stupid plan and it blew up in my face. I need to right this wrong. It was never supposed to turn out like this.

"I hope you continue to live a miserable life, Levi. That is exactly the way that you want to live, wallowing in your self-misery and 'woe is me' mentality. But just remember that the universe has a way of righting the wrong. What you put out is what you get back. One day, maybe not tomorrow or next week but one day, this conversation will bite you in the ass. Just remember, what goes around comes around, Mr. Thorne."

She turns to leave on her heels and I reach out to stop her. I can't let her leave. She is my whole world and even if this is an elaborate plan to keep her safe, the thought of her walking out of here without me is soul crushing.

Tightening my grip on her and pulling her back towards me has her off balance, so I stand to catch her. A gob of brown hair whips around and a hand crashes against my face, making me release her. Fuck, I don't think I've ever been hit like this before.

"Don't you ever put your hands on me again! You just lost the privilege to ever touch me," she seethes and corrects her shoulder strap.

Say something, you dipshit, before there's no going back.

Something catches her eye on her hand and she forcefully yanks off her engagement and wedding rings off her finger.

Oh god baby, please don't!

"Here, I'm sure the next dumb brunette will love to have this." She sinks them into my tumbler of bourbon with a splash. My voice is still mute, like it was when I first met her. "I'm sure your little side piece, Josie, will be happy to meet your needs once she's out of the nut house with Looney Linley. But let me tell you this one little thing, Levi. I am enough, maybe it's you that's not enough for me."

Saylor marches out and I'm left looking at her rings at the bottom of the glass. What the fuck just happened? It was supposed to be a light argument letting people see us, and questioning whether we're together, to give us a little more time to find the prick who's targeting us. Not this marriage ending fight.

The noise of people whispering brings me out of my thoughts and I see a mixture of judging eyes, along with some sympathetic ones. I don't need them. I need my Saylor, the love of my life. A hand touches my upper arm and I feel a burning sensation. Looking at the culprit, I see it's the little hostess. Shoving her hand away, I grab the tumbler of bourbon and pour the rest of the liquid on the table, then snatch the rings out. Placing the wet items in my pocket, I make my way to the front door where Mitch is waiting. The restaurant can bill me.

"Get the car Mitch!" I growl as we walk out onto the sidewalk. He leaves to retrieve the Mercedes and I try several times to call my wife. After six times I give up and climb in the back of the car when Mitch pulls up.

"Where is she?" I demand.

"Not sure, sir. Ryan was with her, but she took off in the car and left him at the curb."

"FUCK! How in the hell did my four-and-a-half-month pregnant wife overpower a six-four man? Tell him to find her or find a job mopping floors!"

I ring her again and the line picks up. *Thank god!*

"Hello?" I hear on the other line.

"Who the fuck is this?" I yell, not recognizing the voice.

"Oh, I just picked this up after a woman threw it out her window…" I hang up not listening to the rest of her annoying voice.

After tossing the phone in the seat next to me, I rest my hands on my face and try to gather my thoughts and catch my breath. She left. She left and thinks that she's not enough for me. I thought that telling her those things would send her running out and not explode into this earth-shattering public scene.

What have I done?

"Take me to work," I tell Mitch.

She needs some time to cool off and I'll give her a few hours, then go home and tell her everything. She'll understand once she learns about the threat, and then we can put this behind us.

"Yes sir," Mitch says begrudgingly. I know he wants to beat the shit out of me right now and I don't blame him. He and Dr. Jordan both warned me about putting her into this position, and I didn't listen.

CHAPTER TWO

Levi

"Hello?" I answer the phone as Mitch drives us back to the office.

"Mr. Thorne, a detective at LAPD has been calling for hours trying to get ahold of you," Carly, my secretary, informs me as I lean my head against the headrest. I can feel a headache brewing. "They have Blaire Hutchins in custody, wanting to speak to her attorney."

"Can you have Henry handle this?"

"Henry is on vacation, out of the country, until next Wednesday, sir."

I blow out a heavy breath, "Text me which precinct they have her at and I'll take care of it."

I hang up and immediately get the text from Carly. After telling Mitch the location, he puts his blinker on and we head in that direction.

Blaire is a problem between me and Saylor. When her best friend, Everly, was attacked and put into the hospital from one of Blaire's models, Pandora's Box was opened. Saylor learned that

Blaire hired out her models to wealthy men, to further their careers in the public's view. Blaire was my brother's first client after leaving our dad's law firm. There was an arrangement that was made long before I came on, after passing the bar. As time went on, Blaire started approaching me about letting the models take care of more than just photo opportunities at events. At first, I had no idea that she was offering sex after dates with her models but somehow it snowballed into that. Lincoln was using Blaire, so I thought it wasn't a big deal. Blaire and I had a few months of sex, until she paired me up with her newest signed client, who was wanting to become an actress. Josie was nice and from a small town in Iowa. She seemed to have some major goals and wanted to focus on them, in order to succeed. It was something I could appreciate since I'd rather be anywhere else than in the spotlight.

Over time, it was so simple to show up at events with one of Blaire's clients and play a role smiling at the cameras then mingling with potential clients that Lincoln was trying to snag. Then I'd go home; sometimes with sex at a hotel or in the back of the town car along the way. It was uncomplicated and easy to make a call and pick someone up last minute. Also, I have a hard time connecting with people on an intimate level. Sure, I can have sex, a lot actually, but there is no connection there. I have trust issues that stem back to my mother and father always picking their next fix over me and my brother. Their choices have fucked with me ever since they died, when I was seven years old. My aunt and uncle love me but, as a child and even now, I'm always waiting for the other shoe to drop. I like to keep people at a distance so that no one is able to leave me again, which is why I liked working with Blaire.

That is until Saylor walked in and changed my whole world. It was like I'd been waiting for her to show up and tilt my axis. She made me want to be a better version of myself. To connect with something other than money and winning. I stopped going to functions because I'd rather spend more time with her than a group of strangers. I learned we shared a love of the great outdoors. I opened up about fixing up houses and she urged me to pursue it. I'd taken her to a few of my projects and she fell in love with them. We'd work together in the evenings on a house sometimes, and it was then that I knew she was the one for me.

"Hopefully this won't take long," I tell Mitch, as he opens my door for me.

"I'll go and grab some coffee from around the corner."

I nod then head into the police station.

"Remove all phones and laptops and place them in the bin," an officer says, after I inform the desk who I'm here to see.

Once I've cleared the detectors, they bring me down to a small room with two metal chairs and a table. *What in the world could Blaire have gotten herself into?* A few minutes later, the door opens and in walks a very disheveled Blaire in an orange jumpsuit, with both her hands and ankles handcuffed. The female officer forces her down in the metal chair and then locks her cuffs to the table.

"No touching," the officer states firmly, then walks out of the room and stands with her back facing the door.

Blaire looks a mess. Her hair is all over the place and her eyes are almost swollen shut. *Shit, did someone work her over in there or what? Christ, I don't think I've ever seen her look like this.*

"Levi," Blaire bellows, "you have to get me out of here."

I've never seen her act so vulnerable in my life. Ever since I've known her, she has always shown a strong dominate, in control attitude with anything that was thrown at her. This person in front of me is not the Blaire Hutchins that brought me my first client, and who provided me dates to functions.

She tries to reach out for my hand, but a loud banging on the door makes her drop her hand mid-air.

"Blaire, what is going on? Why are you in here?" I ask, leaning on the metal table in front of us. Surely unpaid parking tickets don't result in this much disarray.

"I-I don't know how they found out or where to look but they got everything," she says rambling, but doesn't look at me in the eyes.

"What? What did they find?" Surely, she has been smart about her paperwork. She knows what the consequences are if she's ever caught on not being legitimate. *Maybe the Mayor wasn't happy about his companion? I haven't seen him with any arm candy in a while. Of course, I've not been to many events lately.*

"The police. They came to my home with a warrant to search my house on an anonymous tip or something. They made me wait outside and four hours later I'm being handcuffed and brought in here." Tears are streaming down her face now.

"What happened? Obviously, they found your kinky room but that isn't illegal. Who doesn't like a little kink?" I lower my voice, in case they are standing on the other side the two-way mirror watching our conversation.

She starts shaking and bows her head. Fuck, this can't be good.

"They-they found the room that had my safe hidden in the wall with all my files. They opened it and took everything in there."

"Files? What files are you talking about, Blaire?" I start to panic, knowing that she has helped me over the years in contracting my companions. Surely, she wouldn't have any evidence of my name, she knows how private I am. She's smarter than that. We're all promised anonymity when we pay for our model companions.

She starts to shake even more and she closes her eyes.

"Levi, they were my files of everyone I've ever helped. My

client list, my girls, the offers, videos—everything! Even the contracts that weren't a part of the companion side of the business." Christ, this isn't good. Doesn't she know how this will affect all her high society members, government officials, actors, and musicians?

"Me? Did you have a file on me?" She nods and bile rises in my throat. "What do you mean you have a file on me?" I slam my fist down on the table and she jumps. "Do you know what this could do to me and my wife, my family or business?"

"I-I'm sorry." In all my years of knowing this woman she has never apologized. "This wasn't supposed to happen. Everything was going as planned and we were about to cross the finish line," she mummers out the last part cryptically but I don't have time to analyze it right now. I'm trying to think of the damage control my firm is about to endure.

My anger is boiling over the top and I want to slap the shit out of her for this. My entire life could be turned upside down any moment, all because she was careless in keeping files of the upper echelon in our city. I reach in my pocket to contact Dean, but realize that I left all that at the front desk. Something flashes across my mind and I snap my face back to Blaire. She still hasn't answered my question.

"What are they holding you on?" I grit my teeth.

She bows her head again and I know it's bad. "I had a few photos of the model clients in compromising positions."

This doesn't make any sense. Who cares about photos as long as they are consenting adults. Adults...Adults...

"All of your *companions* are of age? Right, Blaire?" My hard look at her makes her shift in her chair.

"I-I had a few that might look young."

What the fuck?

"Look young or were young!" I try to calmly say. I could flip the table, I'm so furious, but the last thing I need right now is to lose my cool in a police station.

"This has to be someone out to get me. Someone who hates me," she rambles on and all I can think about is that she lied to me. She told me that everything was on the up and up. When I asked her about how this was legal she said that Lincoln had everything handled. I had this nagging feeling that something wasn't right, but I thought since Lincoln was okay with it that it was fine. *She lied! She lied! What else has she done? God help me!*

I start to shake and even though I'm looking at her, I don't see her at all. My vision is replaying everything that she's told me over the years. I start to feel like I'm the one imprisoned in here. Sweat starts to form on my brow and everything Dr. Jordan and Saylor have said come crashing down over me. *Not moral. There has to be more going on than just companionship. Possible prostitution. Taken advantage of. Manipulated.*

"How many, Blaire? How many are we talking?" I demand.

She actually has the nerve to shrug a shoulder. *Bitch.*

"Levi, you have to help me. I only helped further their careers and made most of them famous. You have to believe me." She reaches for my hand again, but I jolt away from her like she's trying to electrocute me. "This is going to ruin me."

My mind is reeling as I try to think back to the very beginning of our arrangement. All my companions were of age. Not one was under twenty-five.

Wait? Did she say she had videos?

"Were there videos of me or my brother in that safe?" I asked with clinched teeth.

It takes her several moments but the pale color of her skin tells me everything I need to know.

I stand up from the chair and button up my suit jacket. I can't be here. She is truly the vilest person my wife has tried to warn me about. Saylor said that she believed that Blaire was doing something other than companionship, but I argued until I was blue in the face that Blaire only ever helped her clients become famous. I defended that bitch over my wife, and we wasted our precious moments fighting over this horrible woman, who only ever wanted to further her status. Her little black book just might cost people more than all the fame and fortune she promised, and I foolishly thought there was nothing wrong with it until now.

"I'll have someone from the office get in touch with you." I throw over my shoulder as I walk to the closed door.

"Wait!" Blaire pleads as she tries to stand up, but is met with the chains keeping her in place. "You have to help me, Levi. Someone set me up to take this fall, to make sure I was placed here. No one knew about that safe but a handful of people." Blaire is desperate in trying to figure out who would've tipped them off, but what she needs to do is find out how she's going to survive in a jail cell. Her face is scrunched up tight as she narrows her eyes when I hear a screeching noise, which I assume is her chair scraping against the floor, and I turn towards her. "It was her," Blaire accuses trying to point at me. "It was that little bitch of a wife of yours and her cunt friend."

"You're crazy!" I admonish her. "Saylor has nothing to do with this."

"Are you blind? She hates me because we share something that she'll never be able to understand. That's why she demanded you hand off my account to an associate. She couldn't handle the fact that I had you first."

"*We* don't share anything!" I send a booming echo through the tiny room. "You did this to yourself. Only you are to blame here. You'll do best if you keep the name of my wife out of your filthy mouth."

I place my hand on the doorknob to leave, when a mocking laugh fills the room.

"She'll get what's coming to her, just you wait. You can't guard her forever. You can't even protect yourself, how do you think you can protect a wife and baby," she taunts and it cuts deep. "What kind of father can you be? Do you think once everyone knows your hidden secret life that anyone would let you be alone with a child?" She continues to laugh more as I'm frozen in place. I've thought the same thing and even spoke with Blaire about some of my fears in becoming a father. It was one night after we'd had sex after an event and we were drunk. "You'll do something to that baby and Saylor will leave you. She'll pick that brat over you and walk away without even looking back."

Wait… how does she know about us having a baby? I turn to confront her when the door opens and the female officer walks in.

"Times up for right now as we do a shift change and roll call. Exit and follow the signs back to the front to retrieve your items," she informs me, and I slowly step out of the room.

Behind me I hear Blaire's tone change.

"Wait! I'm sorry Levi, please help me. You know that if I go down then so do you!" The officer tells her to shut up, then the room falls silent.

Walking down to the end of the hall, I'm met with two men that I've had several meetings and charity events with, not to mention sat on opposite sides of the courtroom—Burt Buttons, the District Attorney, and Colin Banks, the Chief of Police.

"Mr. Thorne, a moment of your time, please," Colin says, but not really giving me an option. I can only imagine what this little talk will be about, and I hope my bank account can keep mine and my brother's name out of all the shit that's about to hit fan.

"Of course," I say and follow down a long hallway into a conference room that has papers stacked across it. Looks like it's going to be a long day.

Several hours later, we still haven't heard from Saylor since the restaurant debacle, but we know that she ditched her car at the local mall. Ryan has been in every store, but there isn't any sign of her. I know she's not there. Saylor hates shopping and it's just another hit to the gut. Tina, the housekeeper, has said that she'll call if Saylor shows up at the penthouse but I'm sure she's not going there any time soon. We've checked her bakery multiple times to see if she's hiding out there but so far no luck.

She is probably at my grandparent's house hiding out. I swear they love her more than me. Ever since I introduced them at a barbeque, they have clung to her. Shortly after the barbeque, my grandmother started stopping by Saylor's bakery helping her and then switching over to Everly's spa to have some treatments done to spend some time with her too. I'm pretty sure Saylor told them about the baby because I've received several texts from grandfather wanting to meet up with my attorneys to change his will. He wanted to include any future great grandchildren and Saylor. Mom says that grandmother has grown attached to Saylor and Everly. I know that my grandparents won't be here much longer and I need to make more of an effort to be with them. Hopefully, after this mess is cleared up and I'm not put six feet under for the stunt I pulled earlier by my wife, they will allow me to step foot in their house. Like I said, they prefer Saylor over me.

"Sir, Carly wants me to tell you to check your emails," Mitch tells me, as we walk down the steps of the police department.

I see a handful of messages from Carly saying the press has been having a field day with our scene at the restaurant. Dean, our private investigator, along with my PR team have been overloaded with calls and emails about today's earlier event. As much as I love technology, I really hate it when I'm the prime recipient. Another ping sounds off on my phone and I check it, hopeful that it's someone telling me where my pregnant wife is.

THE SLAP HEARD AROUND THE WORLD

YES FOLKS, YOU HEARD IT HERE FIRST. ONLY AFTER BEING MARRIED JUST SIX MONTHS, L.A.'S POWER COUPLE IS HEADING FOR DIVORCE COURT. THE COUPLE WAS EATING AT A LOCAL RESTAURANT FOR LUNCH, WHEN MR. LEVI THORNE BLEW THE LID AND DEMANDED THEY END THEIR SHORT-TERM MARRIAGE. SOURCES AT THE RESTAURANT SAY THAT THE ARGUMENT GOT PHYSICAL AND THEIR BODYGUARDS WERE NEEDED TO RESTRAIN MRS. SAYLOR THORNE...

Who the fuck writes this stuff and who even reads this? Fucking tabloids! Another ping comes through and I check the next one.

#DivorceCourt

Mega Millionaire and High-Powered Attorney, Levi Thorne, has ended his marriage in a very public manner. The couple, who have been dubbed America's Couple, were seen fighting at lunch. A witness overheard Mr. Thorne say that he wasn't happy in the marriage and wanted out. I hope he had an airtight prenup...

And another.

DIVORCES, ESCORTS, AND SIDE PIECES. OH MY!

MEGA MILLIONAIRE ATTORNEY LEVI THORNE ENDED HIS MARRIAGE IN A VERY PUBLIC WAY THIS AFTERNOON TO SAYLOR THORNE, AFTER ONLY BEING TOGETHER FOR A FEW MONTHS. IT WAS SAID THAT DURNING THE ALTERCATION THAT MRS. THORNE ADMITTED TO THE ROOM THAT MR. THORNE ASSOCIATED WITH AN ESCORT AND HAD A SIDE PIECE NAMED JOSIE. COULD SHE BE REFERRING TO SUPERMODEL JOSIE JAMISON? OUR REPORTERS ARE ON THE CASE TO FIND THESE TWO AND SEE IF THERE'S ANY TRUTH BEHIND IT. FROM RECENT PICTURES, WE'VE NOTICED A WEIGHT GAIN IN MRS. THORNE AND WONDER IF MAYBE MR. THORNE ONLY WANTS SKINNY WOMEN. UNTIL THEN, OUR COUPLE MIGHT BE ON THE 'SHORTEST MARRIAGE OF CELEBRITIES' LIST.

SEE THE VIDEO BELOW OF A WITNESS WHO WAS AT THE RESTAURANT WITH HER PHONE TAPING THE END OF OUR BELOVED COUPLE.

What the fuck! I launch my phone across the car and send it flying to the front passenger seat floorboard. This is a fucking disaster and I only have myself to blame. My phone has been ringing off the hook from my family, but I've sent it to voicemail. Reid tried coming to the firm's building but left when I wasn't there. I can't deal with their shit right now, I need to find my wife.

Mitch's phone begins to ring and I sink down into my seat as he gets behind the wheel.

"It's Olivia," he says from the front seat and motions for me to take it. "She says it's an urgent matter."

I take the phone and bring it up to my ear.

"What Olivia? I'm in the middle of something here," My voice sounds tired and defeated.

"Yeah, I know. I've read and watched the video a million times, you asshole. I thought you weren't going to go that route?"

Olivia knows everything about the threats we've been getting and has kept her mouth shut about what I should do. We met when my brother first started the firm; she is Lincoln's second in command and partner. She handles all the day to day business, while Lincoln handles all the big named cases and is the face of the firm. She runs a tight ship and he wouldn't have it any other way.

"It seemed like the only option at the time and I'm trying to fix it. What's the urgent matter?"

"San Diego needs you down there now. The deal is going south fast. Today is the day on the expiration paperwork and it will hurt our chances of the Chambers Co. opening a base company in Singapore. This isn't an account we want to lose if Lincoln is trying to branch out into representing international businesses." Fuck! We've been dealing with this company for over a year and if we don't sign today, then we'll lose the account to someone else. We can't have a large company like this leave us and take their business to one of our competitors. Or show that our firm can't handle that type of business dealing. "I'd go but most of the planes are being grounded here in New York because of weather. I'll never make it in time."

"I'm on it. Tell Hall that I'm coming and that he better not have screwed this up."

Two years ago, we opened satellite offices in New York, Florida, Dallas, and San Diego. They've all worked out really well and we're in the process of opening a firm in northern California. Tom Hall is over the firm in San Diego, and I'm starting to wonder if we shouldn't find another guy to run the firm there. I've told Lincoln in the past that being an attorney wasn't what I wanted to do, and after today and all of its events I think I'm going to pull out. Saylor and I can live on my real estate and her bakery business.

After agreeing to head down there, I hang up with her and

let Mitch know of our new plans while handing him his phone back. Hopefully this will only take a few hours, then I can get back here and explain everything to my wife. Linc usually takes a helicopter down to San Diego and back, which makes the trip not as long and boring.

"Mitch, I want to…apologize for not listening to your advice. I see now that it was a mistake to follow through with my plan."

"Mmhmm," I hear him grunt.

I knew this was going to be hard but damn throw a guy bone.

"Do you think she'll be back at the apartment when we arrive home tonight?"

Small talk with my employees is not something that I've ever done before meeting Saylor. She's the one who is friendly with everyone and wants to include them in everything we do.

"Not sure, sir," Mitch finally says. "If it were me, I'd cut all the break lines on the cars and set the apartment ablaze."

Well, fuck!

"Then I'd take you to the cleaners during the divorce. A very public divorce that exposed you for everything that you'd *ever* done." He never moves his eyes from the front of the car and now I wish I hadn't asked.

Shit! Talk about pouring salt on an already opened wound.

"You think she'll di-divorce me?" I gasp and almost take my hands off the column. I won't let it happen, no matter if I have to tie her to the bed until she gives birth.

Birth.

Christ, what if she was so upset that something happened with the baby and she's at the hospital? Panic is starting to set in as we approach our office building.

"Levi!" I hear from the front seat. "Everything will work out just fine. The team and I will make sure Saylor understands what was happening. She's going to be pissed and you're going to have to grovel. A lot. But she'll eventually understand."

"Th-thank you Mitch." I whisper as my heartbeat slows to normal. "I promise to listen and take your advice from here on out. I've definitely learned my lesson."

"I hope so," he murmurs and I think that I wasn't meant to hear it. "Marriage is hard and not rainbows and lollipops all the time. It's about making decisions with another person and including them in your life. You're still learning and so is Saylor. It'll take some time but you'll find your rhythm."

"Thank you, Mitch."

I feel one hundred percent better after hearing Mitch, and my gloomy mood is starting to lift. Just as we stop at the red-light in front of our building, I start to hear a ticking noise. It's faint at first, but as the car idols the louder it seems to get.

"Do you hear that?" I ask, making sure my ears aren't thrumming by themselves.

Mitch turns his body then leans closer to the console. "Get out of the car!" he yells, then scrambles to open his door.

I do the same and right when both feet hit the pavement I start to run away from the car, but there's a loud boom and it shatters my eardrums and a force has me thrown on the concrete street. My head hits something hard as screams are heard off in the distance. Pain is overtaking me as my last thoughts flash of deep blue eyes and a giggle that could bring an entire stadium to their knees.

Saylor.

I love you, Saylor. Please watch over our baby and never forget me.

CHAPTER THREE

'm sitting next to the stark white bed, holding the hand of my battered and injured husband. Well, soon to be ex-husband, I guess. He looks like he's been put through a meat grinder but thankfully he survived. I only found out about the incident through the news at the hotel I was staying at. I'd thrown my phone out the window after leaving the restaurant and never looked back. As soon as I saw the news and heard his name mentioned, I rushed over and haven't left his side. His parents, Daniel and Alice, were on vacation and should be here soon. Their plane should land any moment. Reid has been in and out of the room all day, bringing me food and hovering over me. I guess when your life is played out on the internet and TV you can't really pretend that nothing is wrong.

Levi has a broken leg and wrist, he had internal bleeding but the surgery to remove his appendix and spleen stopped that. The most important is his head injury and neck. He and Mitch were thrown away from the explosion and into construction machines by the curb. The doctors won't know the extent of the damage until all the swelling goes down. They have a stint in to drain the blood and to relieve some of the pressure to the brain. The doctors are hopeful but I can tell that they aren't sure if he'll wake soon, or at all for that matter.

Mitch is two doors down on the ICU floor with Tina, our housekeeper, by his side since he doesn't have any family to watch over him here in California. He has both legs and a collarbone broken. He too was thrown from the blast but didn't incur as severe of injuries as Levi did. He hasn't woken up yet either, but the doctors aren't as concerned as they are with Levi.

I try to avoid leaving the room if I can help it. Every time I do, I seem to get the sympathy look or pitiful eyes from everyone around me. It's either from my husband being in the hospital or the fact that our entire marriage ending argument was played out for everyone to have a front row seat.

Of all the times for both Everly and my grandparents to be out of town, right now is terrible timing. I've contacted Everly and she and Lincoln were in London celebrating their engagement. And my Glammy and Granddad didn't answer. I suspect that they are either hiking or at a place in Montana with no signal or service.

"How's he doing?" I'm pulled out of my own self-pity for the moment when I hear Reid's voice. He and Lincoln really are good brothers and we've become close since Levi and I announced being married. Being an only child sucked, until Everly came into my life when I was eleven, so having Reid and Lincoln to lean on also is great.

"Same. They check on him every hour but his vitals haven't changed."

He nods and takes a seat on the other side of Levi's bed.

"You know that my brother is the dumbest bastard alive for what he did at the restaurant. I'm sorry you had to be put through that. I have no idea why he did what he did, but I know that he adores and loves you. Obsessed, even. It doesn't make any sense."

I let out a heavy sigh.

"Sometimes we just aren't enough for someone else. We should've gotten to know each other a little longer before jumping into marriage. I think we both rushed it because this was our first real relationship, for the both of us, and we skipped over a bunch of steps before we made that leap down the aisle." Even saying the words is like swallowing acid. I don't believe them but I sure as hell don't want any pity from his family, or anyone else for that matter. I'm doing a good enough job of that all on my own.

My hand immediately goes to my stomach and a knot forms. How are we going to raise our child? Does he even want to be in their life, or does he want to cut ties completely?

"I don't believe that at all, Saylor. I've never seen two people who are more in love than you two. It kind of makes the rest of us look bad for not having such a strong connection like the one you both share."

"I'm not going to argue with that but sometimes maybe love just isn't enough." I shrug and can feel the tears in the back of my eyes.

We sit there in silence for a while, letting the beeping from the machines take up the noise in the room from the lack of conversation.

"Who is the escort, Saylor? Is it someone we know?" Reid asks after a beat. I know the Thornes have no idea about the Blaire situation, and I hate that my temper got the best of me at the restaurant. Levi had confided in me and I broke it. Even as mad as I am at Levi, I never wanted to be the one to tell someone else's secrets.

"Reid…" I start to say but his phones goes off.

"Hello…you did, okay…okay see you guys soon." He hangs

up and turns his focus back on me. "That was Mom, they just arrived. Dad got a call and needed to make a stop first and then will be here."

I nod, then the door flies open and a handful of nurses come in. Reid's phone goes off again so he walks out to answer.

"Dr. Richards wants to update some scans. It should only take an hour tops." The older nurse says, as she connects his IV bag to the bed along with all the other portable machines that are making Levi comfortable. "Honey, go have some caffeine and stretch your legs. Fresh air is always recommended."

Taking her up on the suggestion, I walk out of the room and spot Ryan standing across the door. We make eye contact but don't say a word. I know he searched for me when I caught him off guard and sped away. I bypass him on my way down to Mitch's room. With a light knock, Tina answers looking about how I look, I'm sure.

"Any updates?" I ask after pulling her into a hug.

"About the same. How about Mr. Thorne?"

"Same. No changes."

"Don't worry, dear, they are strong and will pull through this."

I nod. I've been numb since yesterday. I'm not even sure how one is supposed to act in a situation like this. I've cried so much since yesterday that my tear ducts are dried up.

"Let's go and get something to drink, Mrs. Thorne. I'm sure the baby needs a break and a good stretch," Tina says and leads me out of the room. We go down to the cafeteria on the first floor and I grab some juice and a banana, while she gets a coffee and muffin. Ryan follows close behind and pays for our items, since neither of us thought to bring our purses with us.

Walking off the elevator, we are met with the entire Thorne family. Grandpa and Grandma, Eleanor, and Archie Thorne, are seated by the nurse's desk and stand to greet me. I notice that Daniel, Levi's Dad, is standoffish and eyeing me as though I've killed their dog.

"How are you doing, sweetheart?" Grandma asks, as she ushers me over to her seat. "Everything okay with b-a-b-y?" she whispers the last part.

"We're as well as can be expected, given the circumstances."

"Don't worry, sweetie, those Thorne men can pull through just about anything." She winks and a small smile pulls at the corners of my mouth. The first I've had in over the last twenty-four hours. No one must've told her about what happened yesterday.

"I know. Levi would never willingly leave the ones he loves." Even if I'm not included in that statement, I know that he'd fight tooth and nail to be here for the rest of his family.

The bell of the elevator dings, and out comes Levi's bed and his nurses wheeling him to the room. Two police officers and a man in a cheap suit follow as well, behind the nurses. As they approach, we all stand and start to make our way over to Levi's room but stop when the officers block the door after the bed enters the room.

"Excuse us, we'd like to see our son." Alice, Levi's mom, stands toe to toe with the officers and almost pushes past them.

"Sorry ma'am, but there has been a development."

"Well, don't just stand there like a statue, tell us what the hell is going on!" Grandpa demands.

The young guy, probably around my age in the cheap suit, steps forward and flashes his badge. Detective Ford.

"After receiving a preliminary report, we've found some footage of our suspect tampering with Mr. Thorne's vehicle." Detective Ford tells us.

Gasps set off all over the place and my knees go weak.

"Wait, it was Levi's car that exploded? Not the car next to his?" Reid asks the same question I just thought. All these hours we thought it was the car next to theirs at the light that blew up. "You mean the bomb was meant for my brother?"

Grandpa grabs ahold of me to keep me from landing on my ass. Out of everyone, Daniel doesn't look one bit surprised and I wonder if he knows more.

Who would want to kill Levi?

"Who would do something like this? Do you have any leads?" Reid asks the million-dollar question.

"Yes, we have a suspect and are about to bring them in. We feel very strongly about it and think we have our person." Detective Ford assures us.

"Well, then what are you standing around here for. Go do your job and take this asshole down!" Reid yells and all movement and chatter stops in the hallway.

"We are on it," Detective Ford says, then turns to the officer to his left and nods. They both step to the side of Alice and take a few paces over, until he is close to Grandpa and myself. "Saylor Thorne, you have the right to remain silent. Anything you say can be used against you in a court of law. You have the right to an attorney…"

Shocked.

Numb.

Dream-like state.

Foggy haze.

Is this some kind of joke? When did we enter the Twilight Zone?

"…do you understand everything that has been said to you, Mrs. Thorne?"

I'm not even sure I can respond. Is this man serious? I've never even had a ticket, much less tried to hurt another person.

All hell breaks loose when the man tries to place handcuffs on my wrist. Grandpa shoves the officer and Grandma gets in Detective Ford's face. My body is shaking like a leaf, as Alice tries to steady me while yelling that they've made a mistake.

"You are out of your minds!"

"What are you talking about? This is his wife!"

"Is this a joke?"

"What kind of rent-a-cops are you?"

The berating and yelling continue until Detective Ford screams out.

"ENOUGH!" Everyone stops. "Let us do our jobs or I'll haul every one of you in."

"You are not laying a finger on Mrs. Thorne," Ryan dares and steps in between me and the officer. For the first time in my life I'm thankful to have Ryan. He looks menacing at six-four, towering over the others. The second officer, on the right side of the Detective, catches him off guard and subdues him against the wall. "You're making a big mistake. Mr. Thorne will make sure to have you shoveling shit at a circus when this is all over!" he yells and tries to break free from the hold, but is tasered into submission.

I feel the cold metal against my wrist and it burns as they clink them into place.

This is not happening. This is not happening.

Slowly, I'm escorted out of the ICU and down to the front of the hospital, where the paparazzi have been camped out since news broke of Levi's car bomb. The flashing from their cameras start going off and blinding me, even as the officer tries to shield me from their cameras. I still haven't been able to form a single word and just follow as the officers lead me to the police cruiser. He opens the back door and places a hand on the top of my head to help me into the car. The questions that are being asked are just as ridiculous as me being arrested. We pull away from the curb and head out into the street.

I'm not exactly sure how long the drive was to get us to the police station, because I'm pretty sure I blacked out after everything that has happened within the last twenty-four hours. Once we've entered the building, I'm taken to a dark room and placed at a metal table where they lock my hands onto it. Then I am left in the empty room alone.

That is where I sit and wait. And wait. And wait. For what, I have no idea. I place my forehead in my hands and let the waterworks flow. I thought the well was dry but this has turned into a different level. Ever since meeting Levi, my life has been turned upside down between Blaire, the psycho ex-escorts, being held at gunpoint, the quick marriage, getting pregnant, wanting a divorce and then the bomb. And now this. I'm definitely all tapped out at this point.

The door finally opens, after what feels like hours, and Detective Ford struts in with blue folders in his hands. After depositing them on the table in front of me, he scrapes the metal chair out and takes a seat.

"Sorry to keep you waiting Mrs. Thorne, but the station is jammed packed today with criminals." He smirks. How can anyone find it amusing when you're being accused of something like this?

He reaches in to his jacket pocket and pulls out a recorder and sets it on the cold table. It looks just like the one that Everly and I used to play with as kids growing up.

"Listen, I was just promoted to Detective and this is my first real case. I plan on making a big splash out of the gate, so it would be in your best interest to cooperate. Make this nice and easy for everyone involved." He reaches out and strokes my hand with his fingers and I try desperately to yank them away from his touch but the handcuffs bite into my flesh, keeping me in place.

"This is ridiculous, you can't talk to me like that and get away with it," I say and flick my hand over to the corner, where a camera is mounted on the wall. "My family will have your badge for saying that to me."

He chuckles like there is some joke I'm not privy to. "Well, I guess it's my lucky day since the cameras in this room aren't working. Hence our trusty old-school recorder." He waves his hand at the tape recorder, and my heart drops into my stomach.

He presses play, and then starts to talk again.

"This is Detective James Ford questioning the suspect, Saylor Thorne, on the suspicion of her husband's, Attorney Levi Thorne, car bomb and attempted murder." He looks up, making eye contact. "Mrs. Thorne, have you had your Miranda Rights read to you?"

Trying to pull any type of wetness into my dry mouth, I come up empty.

"Y-yes," my voice comes out as a whisper, feeling like sandpaper, so he pushes the recorder up to my face to say it again. "Yes."

"Good. Now, Mrs. Thorne, there seems to be a number of videos of you threatening your husband after what looks to be a heated argument at a restaurant yesterday around lunch time. You have one hell of a slap on you." He chuckles and opens the folders. "It seems to me that a woman scorned, such as yourself, would have motive in causing the demise of her husband. Especially without a prenup involved."

I've seen all kinds of police shows and movies where they interview the suspect and their lawyers tell them over and over to not say a word or answer any of their questions, but I truly have nothing to hide. But with being married to an attorney, I've learned a few things along the way.

"I didn't do this. I love my husband very much and would never try to cause him any harm. Yes, we had an argument but that didn't mean that I'd try to kill him."

Wait? Do I even have a lawyer? Can Daniel be my attorney, being that he's family? Should I call Lincoln or Everly? How does this even go? The movies aren't even real but they make it seem like this. Shit, I don't even know where my dad is to try and get ahold of him. I don't even know if he'll have phone service to answer my call. My grandparents haven't called me back yet so I know that they haven't gotten my messages.

A knock on the door has Detective Ford turning the recorder off, then up from his seat and opening the door.

"Ah, just in time. We were just getting to the fun stuff," Ford says, and opens the door wider to let whoever is on the other side in.

Thank god, Daniel walks in with a briefcase.

"I need a minute alone with Mrs. Thorne," He informs the detective.

"Sure."

"Can you uncuff her?"

Detective Ford strolls over to me with key in hand and unlocks the cuffs. I rub my wrists to try to get the blood circulating, as he walks out the door.

Daniel has yet to make eye contact with me and is fidgeting.

"Daniel, what is happening?" I plead.

"I don't know, Saylor, you tell me," he says. "Alice and I get dragged back here from vacation to find out that someone has tried to kill our son and you're the prime suspect," he snaps at me.

"You can't possibly think that I had something to do with this!

This is nuts!" How could he think, or even suggest, something like this? Daniel and I haven't been on the same page ever since Levi and I eloped and he brought up having a postnuptial agreement since we didn't get a prenup, but I at least thought we had formed some kind of understanding over the last few months.

He shrugs and takes out a folder from his briefcase. *What is it with everyone and folders?*

"Seeing as how my law firm representing you is a conflict of interest, I suggest you retain a good attorney. You seem to have put yourself in some hot water."

Is this really happening right now? My mind can't even compute everything that is being thrown at me. I wonder if Olivia is back from New York yet. Maybe she can help me out.

"What? You're not going to help me? Like in, at all?"

Mind. Blown.

"No, I'm not. But I am here to represent the best interest of Levi." He takes out some papers from the folder, and slides them over to me with a pen set on top.

One thing I've learned about Levi is that you don't just sign papers without thoroughly looking over them. Picking up the pen to look over what these papers are, causes my heart to stop beating.

Divorce Papers.

CHAPTER FOUR

Saylor

Divorce Papers.

I knew this would be coming but maybe not *this* soon. Did Levi have these drawn up before lunch yesterday? The last few days we've spent together showed no indication that this was where our marriage was heading. I thought we were happy and blissful; we have a baby on the way and in two days we were going to find out the gender of our baby.

Is it the baby that is scaring him away?

When I first told Levi about being pregnant, his reaction was less than stellar. It took the first two weeks to convince him that he was going to be a great father. Between Dr. Jordan, Mitch, and myself, we finally were able to show him that everything was going to be okay. When he embraced becoming a father, he whisked me away to a secluded island as an apology for his actions. He even made me recreate the moment of telling him that I was carrying his child. I thought he was crazy when he handed me a sack full of pregnancy tests to take, to make it even more real. We laughed and cried and made promises all night, while holding each other tight.

His words from the restaurant come back in my head as I re-play yesterday's event. I felt as though he cut me to the bone and I was exposed to everyone in the room. How can someone tell you they love you hours before, then rip it all away in a matter of minutes? He had never spoken to me that way or treated me so poorly before, even in the beginning stages of our relationship. He was cold, and his eyes were pleading with me, almost as if he wanted to say more. Did he really want to do this or was there something else? Looking at the pages in front of me tells me everything I need to know.

A throat clears and it brings me back to the reality that is now my life.

"Just sign next to all the blue arrow tabs and then we can be done with this," Daniel says, pushing the pen towards me.

"Why are you acting like this? I'm family—"

"In a matter of a few signatures and around sixty days, that won't be the case." He leans back in the cold, hard metal chair. "I saw the videos. Hell, the entire world apparently saw what went down yesterday; let's try to move this along and then you can," he swings his arm around the room in gesture, "resume your new life, shall we."

"I'm not signing anything until I speak with Levi, and that doesn't look to be anytime soon," I grit out. Our marriage might be over but I want a face to face with him if I'm going to write off the last eight months of my life, six of which we were married. "How are you even able to file something like this while my husband is in the hospital, basically on life support? You have to have his signature to make this legit." At least that's what I'm hoping. Maybe Levi and I can talk this through and work something out?

"You're not going to get any more money out of him, if that is what you're thinking. This has been in the works for some time apparently. Levi was just merely trying to give you the courtesy of saying it to your face, instead of finding out through a messenger." He seems as if he's enjoying this. "As for how, I'm simply acting as his proxy. In the event that he is rendered incapacitated, I'm the one who makes all his decisions if needed. I was also informed that he recently spoke with Lincoln about a divorce, a few months back."

My heart sinks, and I'm losing the will to fight for our marriage after hearing this. If that is true then Levi and I need to have another conversation, because it's starting to sound like he has been lying to me about our *happy* relationship our entire marriage.

The smug look on my father-in-law's face makes me want to throat punch him.

"I don't give a flying fuck about *our* money." I jab about it being half mine, since I didn't sign a prenup.

"Listen here you little gold-digger, you are going to sign these papers and then my family is going to wash their hands of you. When he came to me and started asking about advice on divorce, I knew he was trying to find a way to undo what he'd so carelessly done. I always thought Levi was too good for you, and I plan to rectify that today."

"And what are you going to do about our *baby*? Can't wash your hands of this little one so easily, can you?" I place my hand on my barely there stomach.

His eyes widen briefly but then he erupts in laugh.

"You can't really be so naïve in thinking that faking a pregnancy will keep Levi in your clutches? I can see where the apple doesn't fall far from the tree."

Is he talking about my mother? Bastard!

My mother met my father while he was on leave during one of his deployment tours. They had a quick romance and before he left on his next mission, they found out she was pregnant with me. They married the next day and were together up until she died from cancer, when I was ten.

"Fuck you, Daniel!"

"Ah, there's the trailer trash I always knew was hiding under that poor, quiet, small-town girl, looking for a handout. I know for a fact that Levi never had any interest in becoming a father, and even made a point about it never happening to him. I also know he never wanted to get married so, after yesterday's events, I plan to help him rid himself of you."

"At least I never made him think it was okay to have escorts for years!" I admit, letting my tongue slip for the second day in a row. I can almost bet the farm that he's used Blaire's services in the past. His face falls, and a confused look crosses his face. "Parents of the century if you ask me. I wonder what Alice would think if she knew all about Blaire? Or your parents, for that matter," I smugly say. I know that Daniel knew of Blaire and her business. He used to represent her before she left his practice then signed with Lincoln at his firm. There's no way he didn't know that both of his sons had arm candy that often at events and couldn't put two and two together. And how dare he talk about my mother that way. You hit below the belt and so will I. He doesn't want to get me started about how they raised Reid, who's a borderline closet alcoholic, but thinks no one knows about it.

A knock on the door keeps me from reaching across the table and throat punching my father-in-law. Detective Ford waltzes in and stands at the top of the table, as Daniel and I are both in a stare down.

"I must've interrupted something life shattering with the way you both are eyeing each other." His cocky voice is like nails on a chalkboard.

"No, we're finished here," I say, and shove the unsigned papers back over to Daniel. "I think I'll take my chances in front of a judge."

Is it possible that Daniel is setting me up?

"Well, sorry to break up this family reunion but I've been called out, so I'm gonna need to put you in a holding cell until I get back."

I stand, making the chair fall back tumbling over onto the floor, and make my way over to the Detective. I need to get away from Daniel before I do something that will make things worse for me and put me away for something that I've actually done. He cuffs me once again and we walk out. We head down a long corridor and through several heavy metal doors before the jail cells come into view.

"Aren't you supposed to finger print me or something?" I ask, as several catcalls burst out and indecent gestures are made as we reach the end of the hallway.

"We'll get to that when I get back. The DA wants to speak with you first," he informs me as we slow our pace. "Try not to cause any trouble while I'm gone," He says as he uses a key to unlock the metal door and uncuffs me.

The clinking of the metal sets in the reality of what is truly about to happen, and out of desperation I grasp for his shirt. "Please, you have to believe me, I didn't do this. I would never harm anyone, much less the man I love," I plead and the waterworks start again.

He pries my fingers off his clothes and gives me a shove away from him. The jolt sends me flying, and I almost lose my balance.

"That's what they all say, sweetheart." He slams the door shut and I'm left holding on for dear life to the bars as he walks away whistling.

Sobs wretch from my chest and I feel the walls closing in on me.

After what feels like hours, I finally get myself under control. I wipe my wet face and turn to find a seat, and wait until Detective Ford comes back so that I can call my dad or Everly to help me. But what I find when I turn around is like being in a horror movie.

Blaire Hutchins, and two other women are seated on benches watching me. The smirk on her face is one that I'd love to wipe off if we were in a different setting.

"Well, well look what we have here ladies. Part of LA's golden couple," Blaire boasts. "What in the world could you have possibly done to land yourself in a place like this?"

"I could ask you the same thing, but I think I already know the answer to that one," I retort.

Her face morphs to one of hatred and she stands to her full height.

"I knew you were the little snitch that put me in here," she accuses.

"I have no idea what you're talking about. Leave me alone and I'll do the same."

This woman is delusional. How my husband had anything to do with her is beyond me. You only have to be in her presence for a short time to want to shower off the ick that seeps off of her. We have had so many fights and wasted so many hours on this gutter-ball that it blows my mind. At first, I wanted to give Levi an ultimatum picking her account or me but I knew deep down that that wasn't what people who loved each other did. Sadly, I thought he'd come around to see the way love is supposed to be, but I'm not sure he was ever meant to. I tried to plant little seeds about her business and how there was no way she was just sticking to the legitimate side of business. Every time he would mention her business the word 'prostitution' rang in my ears. It was like he had blinders on and it didn't matter that he was filthy rich, he just kept wanting more. I've always wondered what he and his shrink, Dr. Jordan, talked about when she was brought up.

That is what everything boils down to; no one understands him. Or the life he had to endure before his aunt and uncle stepped up to raise him. Such a shame; a wasted life with so much potential.

Crossing the cell, I sit down on the furthest bench away from everyone and cross my arms over my body. How in the hell did I get put in a cell with a prostitution ring leader? I've never even jay walked in my entire life, yet here I am in the same vicinity as someone who makes money off of operating in the sex trade industry. What is she even in here for? She probably propositioned a cop, not realizing it.

I hear the whispers from across the room, but ignore it. There isn't anything I want with that woman, or the other two locked away with me. Keeping my head down and my eyes on the floor, I don't realize that something is terribly amiss it until it is too late. Three sets of feet line up in front of mine. Looking slowly up from the ground, I'm met with Blaire and the other women. Her smirk this time is almost evil.

"Let's welcome our new cellmate, ladies," Blaire cheers.

Before I can respond or move, a muscled fist lands against my face making me see stars.

The sounds of beeping startle me awake, and I'm dumbfounded as to where I am. The walls are white. The chairs are white. The curtains are white, but no windows. God, please say I'm in a dream and the last few days haven't happened. Something tickles my nose and I'm aware that I have a breathing tube connected to my nostrils. Pulling it away, I try and sit up but my body aches. Immediately my mind goes back to the last thing I remember.

Blaire.

That bitch.

I reach for my stomach and feel a round speaker device tied to it. The swooshing sound to my left indicates the heartbeat and from the rhythm, the baby sounds fine. Out in the hall, a loud voice is screaming and berating whoever is close to my door.

"She was never to be put in a cell with anyone else!" the voice yells. "Do you know what could've happened because of your brainless—"

The large metal door opens and a woman in green scrubs walks in with a clipboard, taking my attention from the loud man to my new visitor.

"Oh good, you're awake," she gleefully says.

"Where am I?"

"The infirmary at the jail. We're like a hospital, but we are equipped to handle the small stuff." She checks my vitals and writes down the results before addressing me once again. "Mr. Buttons will be here at any moment to speak with you."

"Who?" I ask. "Is my baby okay?"

"Everything is normal and your baby is doing great." She smiles and feeling relieved, I finally let a breath out. "The District Attorney, Burt Buttons. He was just beside himself when he got here to find you in this state."

"What?"

Just as she's about to answer, the door opens and in walks a man in a very expensive suit. He has blonde, thinning hair, and a round potbelly.

"Mrs. Thorne, I'm the District Attorney, Burt Buttons. First, let me apologize on behalf of this department and the city of Los Angeles. As soon as I saw the report on the news, I knew I had to get down here as fast as I could. The Detective has been dealt with and won't be bothering you again. You should have never been put into a jail cell."

I don't say anything because I don't know if I can trust anyone here. What if they're trying to trap me into saying something that will incriminate myself?

"I've personally sent for a doctor to come and check you over, and they'll be by again before we leave here."

"Leave. I get to leave, as in walk out of here?"

"Yes, of course."

I truly must still be in my bed back at our penthouse, in a non-stop dream. None of this makes any sense, and as the day wears on it's becoming more absurd.

"There are still a few things I need to get in order before you leave, but by the time the doctor has done the final checks I should be finished."

"What things?"

"Mrs. Thorne, I know things have been turned upside down right now, but I can assure you that I'll make it my life's mission to see that you are sent somewhere safe, and away from all of this."

I'm not sure if I hit my head but I have no idea what this man is talking about. He sees the confusion on my face and drags a rolling stool over to the bed.

"I know that you had nothing to do with your husband's car bomb. I've spoken to your bodyguard, Ryan, and he filled me in on what has happened." Okay, but that doesn't explain much. "I am also aware that your father-in-law just filed divorce papers at the courthouse a few hours ago, along with a restraining order to stay at least one hundred yards away from your husband."

So this *is* really happening. He filed for divorce and now I can't even go and sit next to him by his bedside.

"I—"

Well, I don't really know what I can say right now.

"Listen for just a second, Mrs. Thorne. I think that you have two options here, and I'm offering two sets of doors for you to leave through today. One, you stay here in Los Angeles and hash out the media that will follow you around, harassing you until they find the next story. You'll have to deal with whomever tried to kill your husband, and have them possibly go after you and your unborn child. I know that you have bodyguards, but even they can't protect you at all times."

He's right. Whoever did this to Levi was able to slip through Mitch, or Dean, and his men. They almost succeeded in killing him. What if I'm their next target? I feel like everything is up in the air at the moment.

My hand lands softly on my belly, and my heart lurches. I can't let anything happen to my baby. This baby is my responsibility, and I plan to protect them with everything in me.

"What's the other option?" I croak.

"Door number two will be a big adjustment. It will mean uprooting your life and not looking back," he pauses letting it set in. "At least until the person or persons are caught who tried to kill your husband. Once that is done, then you'll be able to come back."

"Uprooting? Like Witness Protection?"

"Kind of, except I'm not putting you in the system. But in a sense, yes. You'll get a new identification and live somewhere else entirely. You won't be able to contact anyone for a while, in order to ensure your safety."

"Even my grandparents?" I gasp.

"Even your grandparents. You could write them a letter, letting them know about the circumstances, but you won't be allowed to tell them where you are or contact them after you leave here. I'll make sure to get the letters to them."

The thought of not being able to contact anyone is devastating. And I'm pregnant. What about the baby?

"How-how long do you think I'll be away?"

He shrugs one shoulder. "It's hard to tell, Mrs. Thorne, but I can assure you that I'll contact you the moment we are able to bring you back, and that it is safe for you and your baby. If then you want to return and contact your loved ones, then you're more than welcome to and if not, that's your choice. I'm not sure if Lincoln, or your husband, have told you this but we've had to do this on multiple occasions."

"You have?" I ask.

"Yes. The three of us always work together, to make sure our clients are safe and secured, when something horrifying happens during cases," he informs me. I've never heard Levi talk about something like this before, but Levi usually just gives me the CliffsNotes version of most of his cases. "I can tell that Levi hasn't told you of this before. Let me assure that you'll be in safe hands."

"And I have to make this decision right now?"

"I've got a few errands to run to get some things in order but yes, I'll need an answer when I get back," he adds and stands to leave. "I know that this is a lot to deal with but I hope that you know that whatever you choose, the District Attorney's office is on your side and so is the police department. Things might be a little rocky with your husband right now but he'd want to make sure you were somewhere safe. I've spoken with Lincoln and he seems to think that this is the best option."

He's spoken with Lincoln? That changes things slightly. Lincoln is one of the most well-known and sought-after attorneys in the country. Everly is always telling me about his wins and everyone he gets to work against, within the courtroom. Mr. Buttons seems like a nice man, and it sounds like he and Lincoln work together. Maybe Lincoln is trying to extend a helping hand without alerting his dad that he is helping me?

With that, he leaves me alone to the sounds of beeping once again.

What in the hell am I going to do?

Do I stay and fight for a marriage that my husband clearly doesn't want, or leave for an unknown amount of time to start a fresh new life, while the threat is taken care of to keep my baby and I safe?

CHAPTER FIVE

Saylor

I'm huddled in the backseat of Mr. Buttons' Cadillac SUV, hoping to avoid the sleazy paparazzi. He was able to pull into the underground garage and move me out of the building without anyone knowing that I left.

Dr. Hampton came and did his last and final check up on me and was able to access my file from Dr. Ren's office. He printed them off in case I needed to take them with me, if I decided to choose option two. He was very informative and thorough when he examined me. After what Blaire and her two jail mates did, I wanted to make sure there weren't going to be any long-term effects or surprises later on. He was able to see the gender, but I refused to be told what the baby was. It was supposed to be a special moment to share with Levi, but now I can't let myself go there. Maybe at the next appointment. Dr. Hampton's advice was to stay stress free, exercise and to make sure to eat a healthy diet.

Once we've hit the highway, my nerves have wound me up tight. Is this the right decision? Should I go with the other option? Would anyone even care if I stayed or left? I think about my grandparents and Everly, and a sadness hangs over me like a rain cloud.

"You can sit up now," Mr. Buttons says and changes lanes.

I move to sit behind the passenger seat and buckle in.

This is it. No turning back once I tell Mr. Buttons my decision. He said that I could let him know once he got me safely out of the police station, and somewhere on the outskirts of the city.

We pass a sign for Burbank. After we bypass the airport, Mr. Buttons pulls into an older looking shopping mall and parks in the back of the building. He gives a nod, then exits the car and opens my door in the back.

"We'll be here for a little bit."

I follow him as he opens a metal door, and the smell of shampoo fills my nose. *Where are we?* He continues through the hall to a door at the end. Once we are in, he closes the door and has me seated in a small sofa chair in the corner.

"I know this can be a lot to take in within such a short amount of time, but you aren't the first to go through this, Saylor," he tells me, and I watch him wipe sweat from his forehead with his handkerchief. "The time has come, I need your answer. Remember that whatever you choose, the DA's office and police department are on your side. Our goal is to get you away from the on-going problem."

I sit there, for what seems the longest minutes of my life, warring with myself at the decision in front of me. Both are equally heartbreaking and leave knots in my stomach. If it were just me, I know the door I'd walk through but having this little one to consider makes it even harder. Having weighed every pro and con, I set my mind and don't waver in my answer.

"Option two, Mr. Buttons. I'll leave for now to give this a chance, but once the situation is contained, I want to come back to my life here. Even if there may not be one to come back to."

"Okay, Saylor. Let me make a call and set everything in motion. You'll be leaving within the next two hours."

He pulls out his phone and walks out, leaving me there in silence. It isn't long before a knock startles me, and a little blonde and purple haired lady comes in.

"Hello, my name is Nettie. Burt said to come and escort you to have your hair redone." She bounces on her feet.

"My hair?"

She looks confused and turns when Mr. Buttons comes back into the room.

"Nettie, can you give us a minute?" She nods, then leaves, closing the door behind her.

"You want me to change my hair?" I ask incredulously.

He takes a seat across from me and steeples his fingers at his chin.

"Saylor, you have to know that the entire world knows who you are. If we are going to keep you safe, we have to put in place some safety measures to ensure that most people won't recognize you. What would be the point if someone were to see you, then sell a picture to some sleazy magazine?"

He makes a good point, but I hate that I have to change my appearance. He places a hand on mine and gives it a light squeeze. Mr. Buttons has made this transition easy and has treated me so delicately since coming into my room at the jail infirmary.

"You can change your mind right now if you want. I won't be upset or mad if you do. This is life changing, Saylor," he says. "But please know that everyone thinks this is for the best, for now." There is something in his tone and eyes that shift. I can't quite put my finger on it but something isn't sitting well with me. I'm not sure if it's because everything is happening so fast or if I'm truly exhausted from the last few days.

"I know," I whisper, looking down at my feet. "Okay, let's do this," I say with a little more determination this time.

An hour and forty minutes later, Mr. Buttons walks into the small room and has several large envelopes in his hands, just as Nettie is finishing up my cut and color.

"Here you go. Once you are in the car, I'll need you to read over and learn your new life, and the history that comes with it. The point is to be as believable as possible, if you are to have any chance with the locals." He hands me the sealed documents, and Nettie turns the chair to face the mirror for me to see the finished product.

Tears well in my eyes as I see a different person staring back at me. My hair, that was once light brown, is now midnight black and the length that once almost hit the top of my butt, is now barely resting on my shoulders. A sob leaves my throat, and my hand tries to stop it by clamping down over my mouth. Nettie has covered most of my bruises with light makeup, but there is still some dark purple shading throughout my face from the pounding I took earlier.

"You don't like it? Oh gosh," Nettie says, with disappoint in her tone. It's not her or her work, it's me.

"She just needs a minute Nettie. Can you let the gentleman in the back room come in, and ask him to bring the bags with him?" Mr. Buttons asks.

There is no way to find my voice, much less say any coherent words. He kneels down, the best he can to my level, and gives me a sympathetic look.

"You can still change your mind, honey. Nothing is set in stone yet, but once you walk out the back door, then there's no going back until you hear from me again. It could take months before you get that phone call from me."

"I understand. I think my hormones are all over the place. It's been a long few days, you know?"

"I completely understand."

A knock on the door reveals a tall, muscular man in a button-down shirt that fits him tight across the chest. He stands in the door frame in jeans that were made for him, and his light brown hair is spiked in the front. His green eyes are assessing every inch of me. I might be married but I'm not dead. *The married part not for long.* He looks like a bear ready to attack at a moment's notice.

He comes in and heads straight for me, holding his hand out for me to shake.

"Brody Jackson," he introduces himself with a deep baritone voice. "You must be the beautiful woman I get to help." Do not swoon. Do not swoon.

"Saylor."

"Now that introductions have been made, let's give her some time to change and then you two can be on your way. Saylor, there are several bags of clothing to get you through until you get settled into the new town," Mr. Buttons says, and pushes Brody out the door.

I see the clothing store bags, and to my astonishment they fit perfectly. There are even some clothes, for when my belly gets bigger, as I'm further along in the pregnancy. A tap on the door reveals Brody and Mr. Buttons, who seem to be finishing up on a heated conversation.

"Ready? The ride is going to be a long one, and I'd like to head out as soon as possible," Brody states, as he reaches for my clothing bags.

"We'll meet you at the truck," Mr. Buttons informs Brody and sends him away. "I know at first, this will be difficult but put your mind at ease in knowing that this is the best option for you and your little one. Brody will take excellent care of you and protect you with his life. I've known him for a long time, and he'll do anything that is needed to protect those he cares about."

"Thank you." I reach to the small table, by the salon chair, and hand Mr. Buttons five sealed envelopes with names for each person who I'm contacting for the last time. "Can you make sure that each one is delivered?"

"Of course, Saylor." He places them inside his jacket pocket, and then hands me my travel papers I'd set down while I changed clothes. "Remember to read over the notes and try to be in the shadows for a while, until the news dies down."

We walk out of the room and out the back door, where a black four door Chevy truck is waiting. Brody is leaning up against it, typing away on his phone. He must hear us because when he looks up, he puts the phone in his back pocket and walks to us.

"Ready?"

"I think," I hesitantly say. Am I?

"You're in good hands, I promise," Brody reassures me, then walks me over to the passenger side and helps me into the truck.

Before the door closes, Mr. Buttons places a hand on my arm.

"I'll contact you the moment it's safe. Just know that the District Attorney's Office is doing everything it can to ensure your safety." He taps the pocket of his jacket where my letters are securely placed. "And I'll send these out in the morning. It's to give you a head start."

"Thank you."

He closes the door, and after he and Brody exchange a few words, they hug. Brody gets in and fires up the engine. Brody eases the truck back and pulls out of the shopping strip and onto the road heading towards a highway. We sit in silence for a long while before either of us speaks. In a way, I like the quiet but in others I want to know what's going to happen and where we are going.

"Do I get to know where we're going? Or is that something I'll find out when we get there?"

"No, you can know. We're headed to my place in Montana. I just bought some land on the outskirts of this amazing town. We'll be there while we wait. It's gorgeous and the weather is great; we just don't have access to beaches." His smile is infectious and I find myself sharing in his happiness. Maybe this won't be so torturous after all.

"What a small world? My grandparents and my husband's grandparents also have a place in Montana."

"Really? What city?" he asks as he changes lanes.

"My grandparents live in Dillon, and Levi's grandparents have a place in Twin Bridges."

He nods, "My place is South of Helena. It's right outside Whitehall."

"Do you have a storyline also, or do you get to play yourself until I'm allowed to come back? Am I a friend visiting or long lost relative?"

"You haven't read through the paperwork, have you?"

I shake my head and reach to open the large envelope. I find a booklet and open it to reveal a passport and driver's license. Upon further inspection, I see my new name and an updated photo. *How did they get that so soon?*

Sadie. My new name is Sadie. My heart skips a beat because that is my mother's name.

"Sadie Jackson?" I cannot believe this. "This can't be right." I'm going to be one of his relatives?

"Oh, I can assure you that it is." He winks, and it makes him even more attractive. I hate myself for even acknowledging it.

"Jackson? As in you?"

"Yep." He pops the 'p' between his full lips.

"There has to be a mistake. This isn't right."

"No mistake, Wife."

Wife?

The name on the papers isn't what sends my heart into a race to leave my body. It's the official paper behind it that almost has me passing out. I whip my head over to the driver's side and see Brody glance over at me with a mega smile.

What in the living hell have I gotten myself into? Before I can stop it, the damn bursts as the tears flow and there is nothing that can stop it plummeting down my face.

Wife.

CHAPTER SIX

Saylor

We've been on the road for hours as I continue to read over the papers of my new life. Hoping that if I read it again, the words might be different and that the life I'm going to be living for the foreseeable future isn't hitched to this man seated next to me.

Who in life have I pissed off to earn everything that has been thrown at me the last few days?

There are pages of back story and pictures of us photo shopped to make us seem like we've been together for years. YEARS! How in the world could they have pulled all this together in such a short amount of time? The pictures are of Brody and I at the beach, of our 'wedding,' at a Halloween party, at Christmas, dancing. There are so many I can't wrap my head around this, it looks so real. Like, we really are this couple who are so in love with each other.

How do families in Witness Protection handle all these changes?

"I can hear your brain going into overdrive over there. I've sat in silence a while to give you some time to adjust but now we need to talk," Brody says as he pulls off an exit.

"How did all this happen?" I wave the photos and paperwork over for him to see.

He shrugs, "It's the government. They can do pretty much anything and in a short amount of time if you know the right people."

This boggles my mind and it makes me wonder if Levi's team is as good as those who did all of this. This is a good thing though, right? It means that the police department will be able to catch this mentally disturbed person quickly and we'll be able to resume our lives soon.

"Where are we going?" I ask as to why we're stopping if we just stopped thirty minutes ago to fuel up.

"Starving, how 'bout you?" The moment he says that my stomach makes a growling noise that makes him smile. "What does the little jellybean want? Burger, fries, chicken, shake?"

"Mmm." I haven't had fast food since meeting Levi. He always deemed it unhealthy and bad for the body. "Burger, fries and a large chocolate shake." I actually moan as I say the words.

"Done."

We pull into the drive thru and place our orders. Brody gets double what I ordered and it makes me wonder how he can eat so much and still have a body like that. We eat on the road in comfortable silence, which surprises me.

"So, are you having to live a lie also? I mean with the military background and all." I point down to the middle console at the folder.

"No, I served my time and just recently got out. I've read over the file and it matches up to my life pretty much. Joined the Marines right out of high school and up until a year ago, I was an active member for twelve years."

"So that makes you thirty."

"Yes, just had a birthday three months ago. Don't you remember? You planned this big trip to the beach. What a bad little wife you are. Being married for three years and you still can't get my birthday right." He gives me an astonished look like I really knew when his birthday was. It makes me giggle and I start to relax a little more being in the same close quarters with him.

"It's going to take while for me to get on board with all of this, you know that right? I've never had to lie or try and make something up on a whim." I've looked over the file and most of it seems easy enough but I still have my doubts.

He throws me a genuine smile.

"No worries little lady. I'm a patient man." He winks and focuses back on the road. "Look, the town we are going to be in is not large in size, and with you being pregnant it makes sense for us to be 'married' so as to not raise any questions. People will just think we are settling down to start a new life and we'll keep mostly to ourselves."

"Little lady?" I scrunch my nose at his endearment, but his reasoning is spot on. I am trying to stay under the radar and not draw too much attention to myself.

"Yeah, I'm trying to work out what pet name works best for you, sugar."

"Ugh! Definitely not sugar!"

"Pooh bear?"

I shake my head at the direction this car ride has headed. Brody has definitely made the tension leave, and it's as if we've been old friends bickering for ages.

After another hour and my belly full of greasy food, my eyelids start to grow heavy. I can feel my head bob and a soft pillow catches my chin.

"Here." Brody places the pillow on my shoulder and grabs in the backseat for a blanket.

"Thank you, Brody," I say as I lean my seat back slightly.

"Anytime, Momma Bear," I hear him whisper before sleep takes me under.

I feel the truck come to a stop and hear the gear shift pull to the park position. My eyes are still so heavy, but from the small sliver through my eyelids, I can tell we're at his ranch.

My door opens and I feel Brody unfasten my seatbelt and pull me close to his body.

"We're home," he says, but I still can't muster the energy to wake up.

I feel myself being carried and then placed on the softest material. Letting out a small moan, a warm blanket is placed over me once again and I drift off to dreamland.

Waking up in a panic after hearing the loudest scream, I tuck my knees up to my chest and gaze around at my surroundings. I'm in an unfamiliar place. The door across from my bed swings open and the hall light shows Brody in a pair of pajama pants. Only pajama pants, holding a gun surveying the room. He spots me and quickly glides over to the bed.

"Are you alright? I heard the scream from across the hall and came as quick as I could."

"I heard it too," I say, but then realize that I'm covered in sweat and Brody is looking at me with a confused expression. "It was me, wasn't it?" I whisper almost ashamed, remembering what I was dreaming about.

"Hey," Brody sits down beside me and wraps a comforting arm around my shoulder. "Things are going to work out, you'll see."

I nod as the tears fill my eyes. How am I ever going to move on from Levi? He was my whole world; it began and ended with him. Even if this is over soon, will he forgive me for the awful things I said to him at the restaurant? I didn't mean half of what I said. I was just mad and reeling from his confession. We may not be married after this, but we will need to work on co-parenting for this little one.

"Are you okay, or do you want me to stay until you fall back asleep?" Brody interrupts my thoughts. I'm completely embarrassed about needing to be comforted after only meeting this man hours ago, but something tells me that Brody is someone I can lean on.

"I'm good, thank you Brody."

"I'm here if you need me." He gets up and walks out, but leaves the door slightly ajar.

Hours later, I wake to the smell of bacon and coffee. Stretching out in the cloud-like bed, I walk down the hallway as my nose sniffs out the direction of the kitchen. I was asleep last night when we finally arrived, so I have no idea where any of the rooms are located.

Finally, reaching the large open kitchen, I watch as Brody glides around the room like he's been doing it his whole life.

"Good morning," I say, not wanting to sneak up on him and make him spill the food.

"It's a great morning," he replies back and plates the food. "Coffee or juice? I don't know too much about pregnancies and the dos and don'ts yet."

I smile at his thoughtfulness.

"Juice please."

He nods and gestures for me to have a seat on a barstool, as he pours some juice in a glass for me.

"After breakfast, I'll show you around the place so that if I'm not here you won't get yourself lost."

"Lost? How big is this place?" I ask. Surely it can't be any bigger than the penthouse that I lived in with Levi.

"Well, we're sitting on fifty acres and with you being pregnant, we should have some kind of plan in case something was to happen and we needed to get you some help."

"Fifty acres? Are we out in the middle of the woods in a cabin or something? How far is the town from here?" I question.

"We're on the outskirts of Whitehall. I have some guys who help me out with the up keep of the place. We've got cows, horses, and goats."

"How long have you owned this place?" I ask.

"I just bought it a little over a month ago. When I got out of the service, I wanted to get out of the city and away from the hustle and bustle. Montana looked like the perfect place to escape. This is only the third time I've been here since buying it. When I got the call about you, from Burt, I thought it was the perfect time to make the move. I'd planned on coming out here in a few months, but this was a good excuse to get up here sooner."

The sound of tapping across the wood floors draws my attention, and I turn my head to see what is making the noise.

A large red and black German Shepherd comes to a stop at the entrance of the kitchen, and bounces when he sees Brody, but quickly gets in a defensive stance when I catch his eye.

"Zeus, come here boy." Brody gets on the floor at eye level with Zeus and greets the enormous animal. I've always been a small dog person.

Brody scratches both ears and says encouraging words to his friend.

"Sadie," Brody looks up to me as he holds the collar of Zeus. I guess the pretending has officially started as he addresses me by my new name. "I want you to meet the other half of me. Zeus has been with me since I left the Marines. We have the best security system in place, but Zeus is my main deterrent."

He pats him on the side of his tummy and runs his hand down the spine, all the way to the tail.

"Sadie," he continues to use my false name, "place your hand out to let him get a good smell of you."

I do as I'm asked, and Brody brings him over, and I fidget a little as Zeus sniffs the heck out of me.

"I need you to trust me so that Zeus understands what you are to me."

I give a quick nod and watch as he walks over to me, and he engulfs me in a tight big bear hug. His arms are ripped and he could easily toss me around like a ragdoll with those things. Zeus whimpers, not getting any of his attention, and Brody scoops me up and carries me over to the large oversized couch. He sits down with me in his lap, and Zeus follows his master but stays at our feet. After a few minutes, Zeus leans forward and plants his chin on my legs where my hand sits.

"Give him a scratch around the ears."

I make a move to do just that, and it startles Zeus, as he whips his head back quickly.

"Slowly, Sadie."

With the movement of a snail, I reach for the top of his head and when my fingers graze over his hair, his look of apprehension fades in his eyes and he leans in once again. It doesn't take long before Zeus and I are best friends, and he is following me around everywhere.

After giving me the grand tour of the spacious ranch-style house of four bedrooms, six bathrooms, gym, a media room, and man cave, he and Zeus show me the outside part of the property. As far as the eye could see is green grass and large trees. There are several large barns throughout the property, and men who are busy with the animals, tractors, and fixing things.

"We have six men who work on the property," Brody tells me as we leave the cow barn, where two men help deliver a baby calf.

"We?" I wonder if he has a partner who helps finance a place like this.

He gives me a side smirk.

"Yes, Sadie, *we*. As in you and me, remember? We are married after all." He nudges my shoulder as we walk towards a shop.

A man in a cowboy hat walks out of the shop, wiping his hands of what I suspect to be grease, and finds his way over to us.

"Brody, you're here! I didn't think we would be seeing you for a few more months." They shake hands and turn their attention to me. I watch as this man gives me a once over, taking in my injured face from being assaulted at the jail.

"Patrick, I'd like to introduce you to my wife, Sadie. She's the reason we decided to come sooner. She just couldn't wait another day to get out here in the great wild." Brody's smile makes me smile and Patrick reaches out to greet me, only to be stopped by Zeus who has now put himself between me and Patrick. Zeus bares his teeth until Patrick returns his hand to his side. "Easy Zeus," Brody commands. Brody must've noticed Patrick's looks so he adds, "Sadie was attacked in the mall parking lot before we came here. It's also one of the reasons we wanted out of the big city. We didn't want our little one raised in all the hustle and bustle." He places his strong arm around my shoulder, then places his large hand on my stomach. I flinch at his touch, as only Levi touches me this way, but I remember we have to do this if I want to stay hidden, so I lean in playing the part.

"Well, that makes greeting a little harder." Patrick chuckles as Zeus sits his bottom at my feet, but is still on high alert. "I'm Patrick. I'm in charge of the workers and making sure the ranch is running smoothly around here." He reminds me of my dad. I can tell from the wear on his face and hands that he's been working outside his entire life.

"Sadie." I finally greet, but make no move to touch him for fear Zeus might remove his hand from his body.

"I hope everything is up to your standards, ma'am. We've been trying to get this place move in ready for the last three months, since she's been deserted almost three years."

"It's beautiful out here and everything looks amazing. Please call me Sadie." I tell him and brag of his hard work.

Off in the distance, Patrick gets called away and Brody, Zeus and I start to walk over to the horse corral to check out the new ones who were bought at auction two weeks ago.

"What is it that you do? I mean, how do you afford a place like this?" I say before thinking, and want to kick myself for being so nosy. "You don't have to answer that. I just know that my dad never received a payment to afford a place like this when he left the service, but maybe times have changed." Again, the filter has been opened. But surely the government wouldn't put me with some drug trafficker or some crazy person, right?

"It's okay, Sadie, you need to know where *our* money comes from." He shrugs as we lean on the pipe fence as a black stallion trots in a circle. "After I got out of the military, I had no clue what to do with my life. Being a Marine was all I knew. A few months later, I was out at the shooting range and a thought came to me about the guns we used out on one of our tours. I always said it would work better if it had a better type of scope, and we were wearing a better type of glasses out in the field. Thus, came the grand idea of trying to create a new scope with goggles you can wear for both day and night time. Even if a person has a prescription."

It sounds impressive and Brody seems like the determined type; if he puts his mind to it then it will happen.

"Three months later I had a prototype. I contacted an attorney to patent it and they were able to get me in contact with someone who knew how to get a government contract, so I could have them distributed to our men and woman in the service."

"Whoa. That's amazing, Brody."

"So, we're millionaires," he says casually. "Anything you could ever want is at your feet, Momma Bear." He smiles as big as the Grand Canyon.

After lunch I'm exhausted, even though I just slept for almost twenty-four hours, and decide to take a nap while Brody heads out to discuss some things with Patrick. Zeus, of course, is with me laying down at the foot of the bed, keeping a careful watch of the door.

Brody had given me a tablet to keep in touch with the outside world, as long as I didn't communicate with anyone from back home. I pull up the news back in Los Angeles, to see if there was any news on what Levi's current condition was, and found several videos outside of the hospital. Clicking on the top one makes my blood boil, as I watch Daniel Thorne come to the top of the steps to make a statement.

"Thank you all for your support during this difficult time in my

family's life. Right now, there haven't been any changes to my son's condition but we'll let you know as soon as there's any improvement."

After a pause, the reporters start their assault of questions.

"Mr. Thorne, is it true that your daughter-in-law is responsible for the car bomb that almost killed your son, and is being held at the police department?"

"We are not allowed to comment on that right now, as the investigation is ongoing. But I will say that everyone who is family and loves Levi is by his side, and it will stay that way for the time being. Thank you all, and we'll update you as soon as we know anything."

"Mr. Thorne, is it true that your son, Levi, has filed for divorce from his wife, Saylor, of only six months?"

"Yes, that is true and hopefully it will be quickly resolved. That is all for now, thank you."

He walks back through the sliding doors of the hospital, and the feed ends. I toss the iPad across the bed and let out a mournful sob. It's over. It truly is over with a simple snap of the fingers. I turn on my side and cry into the pillow. I cry for the woman who loved a complicated man. I cry for the woman who thought she was enough for a man, who professed before me and God that he'd love her until death due them part. I cry for the little girl who had big dreams of marrying her Prince Charming and living happily ever after. I cry for all the silly books I loved to read that showed me that your true love really does exist. I just… cry.

I feel the bed dip and a cold, wet nose lands against the skin of my neck. Zeus has half of his body on top of me in some sort of comforting position, almost like he's trying to give me a hug. I give in and throw my arms around his body, and sob into his hair. He never once moves as my body finally tires out and I fall asleep.

CHAPTER SEVEN

Levi

Los Angeles, California
3 Months Later

BEEP…*BEEP…BEEP…*
The constant buzzing in my ear is making my head hurt. It feels like the morning after an all-night drinking binge. God, I wish someone would shut off that stupid alarm. Where the hell is Saylor at? She must hear it too.

Trying to open my eyes is like lifting a car up by the bumper using only your upper body. Christ, what did I drink last night?

BEEP…BEEP…BEEP…

I let out a groan and hear voices from afar.

"He's waking, call the doctor."

I'm barely able to open my eyes. When I finally do, I see I'm in a dark room and the smell of disinfectant spray hits my nose. *Tina has truly gone overboard on the cleaning.*

"Call everyone and let them know," I hear a voice again, and then the sound of a door latching shut.

"Levi? Levi, it's mom. Please baby boy, wake up. Come back to us."

Mom? What is she talking about? I'm right here trying to wait out this annoying hangover. I really want to sleep some more, to maybe bypass the excruciating pain I'm suffering from right now.

BEEP…BEEP…BEEP…

I groan and try to call out for someone to shut off the alarm.

"Saylor," I try to say, but it comes out a whisper as my throat feels like sandpaper. "Saylor!" I try with a little more force.

"Oh dear," I hear mom gasp.

The door opens and I vaguely see a blur of a person in a white coat.

"Mr. Thorne, I'm Dr. Legend. Can you open your eyes for me all the way?"

Doctor? What doctor? Why is there a doctor in my face?

I try to force them open, as they sting, but a bright light flashes into them, forcing them shut to stop the shooting pain. "Okay, I'm going to order some tests and scans to be run, and then we'll be able to tell where we're at. Can you squeeze my hands?" I do the best I can. "Good, now can you feel this?" I feel a sharp object against my feet and jerk away. "Great, great."

"Saylor," I say again, wanting to find out what the heck I'm doing here and why I can't feel her presence like I always do when she's in a room.

"We'll get to that in a moment, Mr. Thorne. I need you to open your eyes again and focus on my finger."

With the strength of Hercules, I open both eyes and see a hazy man in a white doctor's coat with Mom standing at the end of the bed. I follow the finger and sip out of a straw before addressing him and mom. The cool liquid is exactly what I need at the moment.

"Mom, where's Saylor? Where am I?" I see my mother look ashamed for some reason and then look down at her feet. "What's wrong?"

"Honey, you're in a private wing of the hospital—"

"Mr. Thorne, can you tell me what the last thing you remember is?"

I bring my eyes up to the ceiling and try hard to think back to last night, but I don't get the chance because the door bursts open with Dad, Lincoln, and Reid all rushing in and pushing each other to get closer.

"It's good to have you back, Bro. Three months is a long time to not see your scowling face," Reid jokes.

I'm not in the mood to deal with him, as my head feels like it's on fire. Wait. Did he say three months? My eyes frantically search the room but don't find my blue-eyed beauty. Where is she?

"Three months? What the fuck happened to me?" I demand, now that I'm able to talk a little better.

"Mr. Thorne, I'm going to need you to calm down and try to remember the last memory you had," the doctor repeats again, but my mind is racing all over the place.

I try to rack my brain. Saylor. I remember having amazing morning sex, then meeting with Dr. Jordan, and then after that was seeing that horrible bottom feeder, Blaire. My brain is a little hazy but I continue on.

The threat. My stupid plan. The meeting at the restaurant with Saylor and it turning to shit. She left and I had to leave for a meeting in San Diego with Mitch. Not finding Saylor. Being in the back of the car. The ticking and the heat.

The explosion.

I was in an explosion.

"Saylor. I need to see Saylor, right now," I say, and everyone stops as if they're frozen in place. *Did my world just hit a pause button?* No one says anything, but everyone slants their eyes over to dad. Lincoln looks pissed and crosses his arms over his chest.

"Yeah, *Dad*, why don't you answer that one," Reid hisses.

"Reid don't you start that right now. Your brother has just woken up and doesn't need the added stress," Mom chides him, but he's not having it.

"What the fuck do you think is going to happen when he finds out, *Mother*?" He shakes his head. I've never seen Reid speak to our mom like this before. "Can't you see he's already worked up wondering about her?"

"Where is she?" I ask interrupting their hateful banter like I'm not in the room.

"Son," my father starts, but there's a hint of remorse in his voice. "There was a big misunderstanding and I'm afraid—"

He's interrupted as the door flings open, and a woman wheeling in a wheelchair comes barreling in. I notice right away that it's Tina, and Mitch is the one in the chair.

"Mr. Thorne, we came as soon as we heard," Tina says, a little out of breath like she just ran here. She maneuvers the wheelchair past the others and catches my father's foot as she comes up to the side of the bed. My father winces and does a small hop. Tina doesn't even acknowledge anyone else in the room, which is odd.

Am I having a crazy dream? What the hell is going on and where the fuck is Saylor?

"Mr. Thorne it's good to see you finally awake," Mitch comments.

"Thank you, Mitch. Is everything okay with you?" I nod at the wheelchair.

"I should be good as new in a few weeks. Physical therapy is helping build my muscles back to normal." He pauses and looks around the room at my family. He leans in and tries to quietly talk. "We need to speak as soon as you're able, sir."

"Speak now, Mitch." It seems important.

"I'm not sure you're going to want an audience for this one," he nearly whispers again.

"Can you give us the room?" I ask, not giving them a chance to respond.

"I'll have the staff come by in twenty minutes to collect you for a few scans." The doctor informs me, and then turns to leave the room.

"Son, there is something I'd like to say first, before you hear what Mitch says. I need you to understand where I was coming from."

What could he possibly have to explain?

I look over at Mitch and Tina, and see them shooting daggers at him. They aren't trying to hide their distaste for him at all.

"You have to understand, when we got that call to come back home, it was the worst thing a parent could go through. Finding out that their child could die before you can even get a plane ride home was the most helpless feeling in the world." He loosens his tie from around his neck. He looks like he's aged ten years. "We landed here in LA and I received a call from one of the partners at the firm. They had someone from the police tell them of the arrest that was going to be made in connection with your car bomb. When I found out who it was I didn't believe it at first, but then they sent me the videos of the fight you had at the restaurant and my mind started to go all over the place. No one ever wants their child hurt, and when it does happens they want to hurt the person right back. I am so sorry and you have to know that I'd take it all back if I could."

What is he talking about? What does the fight Saylor and I had at the restaurant have to do with who put a bomb in my car?

"Okkkkay?" I'm still confused.

"What he's trying to say is that he did nothing when Saylor was arrested as the number one suspect for the bomb, right here at the hospital, in front of your room," Tina spits out while continuing to stare holes into my father.

"WHAT?" I yell, despite my sore throat. My chest begins to hurt, and I move my heavy hand to try and relieve some of the pressure.

"They handcuffed her and paraded her out in front of the press before driving her to the police station." Tina seethes, not trying in the least to curb her distain for him.

The guilty look on my father's face says it all.

"I...you..." I can't even form words, much less a sentence. "Where is she now? Still not there, I hope. You better pray to God that she better not still be there!" I grit towards my father. How in the hell could anyone think Saylor would be responsible for something like that?

"She's not there, son. She was...released," He solemnly states, and then hangs his head.

"Oh, thank god!" I say, and let out a deep breath.

"Tell him the rest Daniel Thorne," Mitch pipes up. He's never used my family's first name before, and he's been with me for many years.

"There's more?" I question. How can there be more? What in the ever-loving hell is going on?

"Oh, there's more, little brother. A lot more." Lincoln chimes in.

"I... I thought she was the one who set this entire thing into motion. I wasn't thinking clearly. You have to understand, I was in a really bad place thinking that you were never going to wake, or even make it through the night." He tries to justify his actions. "The Detective said they had enough evidence, and it was a solid motive."

"Just say it."

He huffs then starts, "I went to the station and she was just starting to be questioned by Detective Ford, so I interrupted them and got the room cleared. I…we spoke for a few minutes and then I told her that I couldn't represent her, due to a conflict of interest."

"Okay but you could have had one of your other associates be her attorney," I say, trying to move this along so someone can bring her to me. "Or Lincoln could've had someone from our firm handle it."

"I couldn't do that because we were representing you."

I know I just woke up after three months, but none of this is making any sense. Why would he represent me when I have my very own law firm with my brother?

"The firm couldn't because we were handling your side of the divorce proceeding," he says the 'D' word, and a white flash covers my eyes and my head starts to throb.

"The d-why in the fuck… who said anything about…"

The beeping from the machines start to go off, and my body is heaving from my breathing.

"Calm down, Levi or you'll pass out," Mom says as she rubs my arm, but right now the only thing I can think of is throwing my father out the nearest window.

I close my eyes and start to count to ten, but end up at two hundred and fifty-five. The machines have quieted back down and I train my eyes back on my traitorous father.

"Son, I saw the videos and thought that was what you wanted.

You basically implied it and I wanted to protect you. The Detective said he had enough motive to start the arrest process."

My ears are burning from listening to him try and justify his actions regarding my pregnant wife being tossed into a jail cell like some criminal off the streets.

Pregnant. Oh god, the baby.

"So, you left her there to fend for herself? Did she look like someone capable of causing a car to explode, Dad?" I spit so much venom out of my words. "She was four and a half months pregnant. Do you think she could've made the bomb in the back of her bakery, in between baking cookies and cake?" I scream.

Gasps fill the room.

"Are you fucking kidding me right now?" Reid starts to shake his head. "That's just great Dad, I can't even believe I defended you at the beginning," Reid yells. "You can officially say that you've ruined another one of your children's lives."

"Pregnant?" Mom asks. "Saylor is pregnant?" She looks between myself and Dad.

He drops his head to his chest and I know that he knew she was pregnant.

"You knew, didn't you? She probably told you at the police station and you didn't care that your grandchild was in danger. Or that something could've happened to them," I accuse. "How could you do something like that you bastard!"

"No, your father would have never left her in that place, had he known she was carrying a baby," mom speaks up in his defense. "Tell them Daniel, that you'd never do something like that," she urges Dad, but from the shameful look on his face it tells a different story. "Daniel, no that can't be!" You can hear the devastation in Mom's voice as she shrieks and shakes her head. She looks horrified, then strides over a few steps to where he is standing. Mom reaches out and grips his upper arms in both her hands. "How could you do something like that? She's our family—" She swings her arm out and hits Dad in the shoulder, startling all of us. Never has she lifted a finger in anger towards anyone. She continues to hit him until Reid and Lincoln pull her off as he stands there and takes every slap and punch.

I'm in my own hell thinking about what Saylor went through that day. Being hauled out of here and then having Dad turn his back on her. And our child.

"If you didn't get her out then who did? Olivia? Everly, or their grandparents?" I look over from face to face to find answers. Wait, where is Everly at? She's usually attached to Lincoln.

"We don't know, sir," Mitch says. "There is no record of her being booked in and there has been no trace of her since."

"The fuck's that supposed to mean? No one's seen her in the last three months?" I counter. How can that be? She couldn't have vanished into thin air.

"Dean is working on it, sir, but it appears that the camera footage from that day has been deleted." Mitch tries to explain. There is something holding him back from telling me something else, and from the angst in Mitch's eyes I know it's a doozy.

"Just say it, Mitch," I snap. My patience is no longer intact and if I could move around, I'd break every bone in my dad's body.

"We were able to finally locate Detective Ford, and he was able to tell us that there was an incident in the jail cell that Saylor was put in," he pauses, as I'm sure steam is billowing out of my ears. "It seems that three inmates roughed up Saylor and a doctor was called in to examine her."

"Is she…was the baby hurt?" I stammer. My life would end if something were to ever happen to Saylor or our baby. This was the entire reason I put my stupid plan in place.

"According to the doctor's report that Dean was able to obtain, she was bruised heavily but the baby was fine and healthy at the time of being examined."

I let out a sigh of relief, but it does little to cool the flame lit in me. I'll make each and every one of them pay for this. Starting with…

"We'll find her, Son."

"Get the fuck out of here and stay the hell away from me," I spew to my father. "You let my pregnant wife stay at the police station where she was assaulted and could've lost our baby. I'll never forgive you for that!" I yell.

"Wait, don't let him leave without telling you the other fuckup he did while you were in a coma," Lincoln speaks before Dad has a chance to try and defend his actions. He seems to hold his own personal hatred toward our father, and I wonder if it's about Saylor too.

"Lincoln, not now," Mom, who has finally calmed down, tries to cut him off but it's too late.

"What else could there be?"

From the look on Lincoln's face, I know it has to be bad. And a rock drops in my stomach.

Dad lets out a sorrowful sigh, and I know this can't be good.

"I-after I left the police station, I filed the paperwork to start the divorce process and also obtained a restraining order," he tries to whisper the last part but I heard every single word.

"You filed for divorce of MY marriage without even consulting me? How the fuck were you able to file without my signature?" My heartrate monitor goes off again and I feel my chest starting to hurt again. "Did Saylor know you did that? What the fuck did I need a restraining order for? She's barely over five foot and falls over when the wind blows!"

"It was all over the news within minutes after he filed," Tina growls.

"I signed as your proxy, in the event you were incapacitated. I'm still listed as your power of attorney. I thought I was doing the right thing—"

"Did. Saylor. Know?"

"Yes, I made sure she found out," he admits in a defeated tone. This will forever change our relationship. Even if I had really and truly wanted out of my marriage, it would have been my decision and mine alone. I've never asked my father to fight any of my battles for me, and why he thought this was okay makes me question everything I've ever known about him.

The fire in my head ignites further, and my weak arms and legs are shaking out of control, and it feels like I'm starting to convulse.

"Call the nurse in here," I hear Mom say, but I can't take my eyes off of the man I used to look up to. How could someone you love betray you in the worse possible way?

The door opens and an older woman comes through with a needle and sticks something into my IV. Immediately my eyes grow heavy and before I can fight it any longer, I'm lost to the darkness once again.

A cold cloth stretches across my forehead, jolting me awake. I push the cloth and the hand away, trying to get my bearings about me. In the corner I see Lincoln next to Reid, with his feet propped up, playing some game on his phone.

The nurse tries again to swipe the washcloth over my face and I'm not having it. Only Saylor ever gets to touch me.

"Get. Out." I grit. She takes heed of my warning and high-tails it out of there.

"Oh good, you're awake. I thought we'd have to wait another three months to hear your voice again," Reid says as they make their way over to the side of my bed.

I groan, thinking about earlier. I'm still having a hard time grasping that all this actually happened. What the fuck has my life become?

"I need to get out of here. I need to find my wife." I try to locate the IVs, ready to yank on them, but Lincoln grabs my hands.

"They won't let you, and if you try to pull these out then they said they would tie your hands to the rails," Reid states. "Your guys are working around the clock to find her, Levi. Let them do their jobs while you recover. Your body has been through a lot. They said even after you leave here, you're looking at a month of physical therapy to get your muscles back functioning, like Mitch is doing right now."

I huff. I've never been one to sit around idly.

"Why are you so bitter towards Dad?" I finally ask after a few silent moments.

"Your relationship isn't the only one Dad has put a strain on." A sad regretful expression crosses Lincoln's face.

"What happened Lincoln?" I genuinely ask. He looks about how I feel right now. Miserable.

He lets out a long-drawn-out sigh, then runs his hands through his hair like I do so often.

"We didn't know that Dad wasn't helping Saylor until the next day. Everly started asking where she was after he came back from the station, but he kept it very vague and said not to bother her until she contacted us. Said that she was fine but needed some time to herself to sort all this out. We believed him, but then as

Everly tried on several occasions to call her and didn't get an an-swer, she started to get worried. Then Sharilyn, Saylor's grand-mother, called not long after and told all of us about the divorce filing, and everything went to shit after that. He told us that the police had hard evidence against her and that they wouldn't release her. He had said that filing the divorce papers was your idea, and even if you were incapacitated that he was doing it on your behalf.

"Everly flipped the fuck out and slapped the shit out of Dad. He'd made a low blow comment about making sure your money was secure, and that none of your hard-earned money would be placed in her hands. I had to literally pull her off of him. I stupidly jumped to Dad's defense, saying something ridiculous to the effect that it might be plausible for Saylor to tamper with something after the restaurant scene you both made." He looks shamefully over at me, and I wince thinking that Saylor could never have done anything harmful to anyone, much less me.

"But we were too late to right our wrong. Everly got ahold of Saylor's grandparents, Sharilyn and Alan, after leaving here tell-ing us that we'll regret standing by Dad. Everly wasted no time trying to clean out her things from our apartment. She said she couldn't be with someone who'd jump to conclusions before know-ing all the facts, especially about Saylor. We both said some really harsh things, so she left. By the time I was calm and started to think rationally, I couldn't locate Everly for days. By then, Mitch woke up and he set us straight as to what really was happening." He pauses, rubbing his face with his hands as if reliving those moments. "Everly's Dad came down here to help her and Saylor's grandparents find Saylor but they were having no luck. When I finally found out where Everly was, I begged on my hands and knees, in front of the entire city, for her to forgive me. A few days later, she agreed to meet with me, and I've been trying to make things right ever since. She's put a pause on our engagement until we work through all this."

"I'm sorry about all this, Lincoln," I tell him, seeing how torn up he is.

"It's not your fault, bub," he says, grabbing my hand.

"So there's not a single bit of evidence of where she might be? Nothing?" I ask.

"Everly's Dad is trying to locate Saylor's father, to see if they can pull some resources together from their government connections to find a lead. He's been out of contact for almost a year, and Tommy didn't know if he was out of the country or not. It seems like her dad just disappears all the time. But I'm not sure they'll be sharing that with us if they do, seeing how we're enemy number one at the moment."

He has tears in his eyes, and he's trying hard to blink them away. I know this is hard for Lincoln. I'd gone with him to pick out her ring just a week before he proposed. Lincoln was never one to settle down, like me until I found Saylor, but he truly is so happy with Everly and I know she's the one for him.

"Is that all that's been going on?"

"When Mitch woke and told us about the threat to Saylor's life, and how you pulled the scene at the restaurant to draw the guy out, we knew our lives would never be the same. Even Mom and Dad aren't in a good place after Mitch uncovered what Dad did at the police station. I can only imagine what this will cause, now that he knew she was pregnant and left her there. Grandma almost had a nervous breakdown so Grandpa took her to their place in Montana."

God, so many lives have been ruined because of this.

"I hope once I bring Saylor home, we can work on getting

your life back on track with Everly. I love you and will do everything in my power to help get you there."

The door opens and reveals Mitch, Ryan, Dean and another guy I don't recognize. They have stacks of boxes in their hands, and Tina is behind Mitch wheeling him in.

"Thought you might want an update of what we know so far, sir." Mitch says at the end of the bed. "This is William, he specializes in security and has a lot of connections in the government."

I nod and look at my siblings.

"Go home and get some rest. I need to find my wife and baby."

"Did you know what the gender is of your baby?" Reid asks hopeful, but I just shake my head.

"No, we had an appointment at the end of that week to find out the sex. The baby was being difficult, or really shy, and not showing us anything." I give a little chuckle, thinking about how we did everything to get it to turn or move, but then frown. "Saylor should be," I pause adding the time, "almost eight months now. I bet she knows since we only have a month left."

Shit, I've got a month to find my wife to be there when my child is born. My heart sinks, thinking about not being there to see them born. Will Saylor be alone? The thought causes my chest to tighten and my pulse to race.

Don't go there, Thorne. You'll find her.

Reid and Lincoln leave with the promise to be back in the morning. Now it's time to get down to business.

"First, what is the status of this divorce that my father pushed?"

"Sir, once we heard that your father filed it and the press were all over it, Lincoln put a stop on the filing and had the document sealed from the public," William says, as he pulls some papers out of a folder and slides them over to my tray for me to see.

So, it didn't go through. Thank god!

At least that is one problem solved.

"Was there a correction sent to the press?" I ask.

"No, we didn't know how to proceed, Sir. You usually never comment on your personal life to the press, and we were waiting for you to wake so that you could make that decision. We knew you were trying to keep her safe from the threat so we did nothing." I'm annoyed, but understand where they are coming from. I've never been one to comment on my private life, but I'm afraid Saylor thinks I really want us to end our marriage.

"What do we know about her whereabouts so far?" I ask around the room.

"Our thoughts are that DA Burt Buttons is the one who was able to get Saylor out of the station without being noticed. We recently believe that he came and offered to help Saylor, to get away from Los Angeles, and away from the person who was truly behind your accident." William answers.

"Okay, and have we spoken with him? Where did he put her?"

I know that he has knowledge of me being one of Blaire's clients, and hope that he handled her with care. He and the police chief stopped me at the station after my meeting with Blaire, to discuss my files being part of the evidence they found in her safe. My bank account took a hit to keep mine and Lincoln's name out of the press, and those files were to be destroyed as the money made it to their accounts, the little crooks.

"We think he placed her in Witness Protection," Dean states.

Witness Protection? Why in the hell would he do that?

"What did he say when you spoke with him? Surely he understands that we're all on the same page."

I wait for a response, but it's slow to come.

Christ, now what.

"We haven't talked with him."

"Why the hell not? Shouldn't that be the first thing to do?" I demand.

"Uh, well you see," Dean stumbles.

"Sir," Mitch interrupts the stammering of the firm's most trusted employee. "DA Buttons can't be reached now. He is no longer here for us to question."

"Okay, find out where the hell he is and get someone over there." This isn't that hard to figure out. What is wrong with everyone?

"Sir, we can't communicate with Mr. Buttons."

"Why the fuck not?"

"Because he died sir, four weeks ago arguing a case against your brother."

CHAPTER EIGHT

Saylor
Whitehall, Montana

I feel like I'm the size of the cow barn that stares at me right outside the back window. Brody thinks I've swallowed the basketball from the backyard that went missing around the time we moved in, but I don't find it as funny as he does. I continue to ask the doctor if I'm carrying twins or even triplets with how big I feel, but Dr. Ellis assures me that this is a single birth.

I'm two days to my due date and everyone on the ranch is on baby watch. Brody has made sure everyone is overly prepared in case my water breaks or I go into labor. He has gone way overboard in the 'daddy' role. He knows that this isn't his baby, but he is making sure that I'm not missing out on any of the moments that the father of the child should be doing for the mother. We've gone to birthing class together and even took a parenting class at the small local hospital. We do prenatal yoga classes every Tuesday and Thursday morning, then head over to the diner to have a large chocolate milk shake. Brody even sent out a certified person to teach everyone on the property the correct way to perform CPR for both infants and adults. I truly am lucky to have him in my life. It was like the world knew I needed someone like him.

The nursery is done in neutral colors because I wanted to wait until the baby is here to find out if I'm having a boy or girl. A part of me was hoping to be back home in Los Angeles by now and have Levi by my side, but I think reality has set in that he doesn't want to be a part of mine or our baby's lives. I was ordering some things for the nursery online last month when an article popped up about him being sent home from the hospital. I couldn't bring myself to click on the page to read the full article, but at least I know he's recovered for the most part. I can't let myself go back to that dark place once again.

After watching the video of Daniel on the steps of the hospital, I had a complete breakdown over everything that happened in those few days. Brody had to force feed me and I rarely went out of my room. Zeus was my only comfort. After three weeks went by, Brody busted through the door and drug me out. He said that I'd wasted enough time on that loser and that I had a little person to think about, and I needed to focus on that. He was right, and after that afternoon I haven't thought much about my life back in LA. Every now and then a thought will creep in, but now I see that my future is with this little jellybean.

"Ready to walk that baby out?" I hear Patrick yell, as Zeus and I step off the porch for our morning walk from the cow barn to the horse stables. Brody has made sure all the guys know to keep a watch out for me while I'm outside. He learned early on how I'm not the most balanced person to walk this earth. Now add thirty pounds to the front and I'm a walking disaster.

"I'm hoping today is the day," I yell back.

Zeus keeps in step with me as we start our morning routine. Brody had a call come in as we were walking out and will catch up when he's done. As we approach the final leg of our walk a sharp, tight pain lances over the front of my belly and it has me doubling over from the pain.

"Ah, ouch that really hurt."

Zeus whimpers, as if he can feel the same pain and is going through it too.

Ever so slowly, I continue walking back towards the house when another jolt almost brings me to my knees. I scream out this time, and Zeus starts howling in a tone I've never heard before. He continues until I hear yelling and watch as Brody comes shooting out the back door at lightning speed.

"I gotcha, Momma Bear," he says as he kneels down in front of me. The other guys come running over to check on me, but Zeus gets in between them and me, warning them to stay back.

"It hurts, Brody. It came out of nowhere and then this awful pain shot—" I don't get finish that sentence because a gush of liquid flows down my legs and pools at my feet. "Oh, shit."

"Okay, we got this. Focus on your breathing," Brody says in a calm manner, then turns to the guys. "Patrick, get the truck ready, her bag is by the front door."

"You got it Boss," he replies and runs off.

Brody picks me up bridal style, and carries me over to the truck that Patrick is now loading with my bags. He places a thick towel down on the seat right before Brody carefully sets me down on it. He closes the door, and is on the phone with the doctor and tells her that we're heading to the hospital.

Four hours later, I'm in the final stages of pushing and I regret not getting the epidural. I feel like my insides have been wrung out

like a wet towel, and I think I've depleted all of my water supply from all the sweating I've done.

The doctor came in five minutes ago and said we were almost there. *I swear they said that an hour ago.* I'm tired and all I want is to go to sleep and wake up in a week. My eye catches my left hand and I see the two beautiful wedding rings Brody gave me a few weeks after arriving here, but my mind goes back to that dark place and for some reason I can't focus on the doctor's directions.

"Okay, Sadie, when the next contraction starts, I need you to bear down and really give me a push," Doctor Ellis instructs, but I can't hold back my emotions any longer. Turning to Brody, who has been by my side and coaching me through this, I wail and burst out.

"I can't do this. It's not right, he should be here. He should want to be here," I sob. The nurse on my other side wipes a cold cloth over my forehead.

Brody releases my leg, keeping a firm grip on my hand, but moves up close to my face so we are almost nose to nose.

"Momma Bear, you are the strongest woman I know. You are all this little baby needs in this world and you are going to be the best mother a child could ask for. I'll never leave your side and will be here through everything with you." He pauses as I fight the next contraction. "We need you to push, Sadie. Be strong for this little one and let's welcome little jellybean into this world."

I nod and wait for the doctor. On her command, I dig deep through the burning and push as she tells me to. After three of the longest counts to ten, we are rewarded with the sound of the most beautiful cry.

"There we go, little one," Dr. Ellis coos as the tears stream down my face. "Do the proud parents want to know what this little, and I mean little, bundle of joy is?"

Brody squeezes my hand and kisses my temple. The pain's suddenly gone, and all my focus is at my feet where I can see a head full of brown locks.

"Yes, yes please tell us," I cry out.

"Mommy and Daddy, I'd like to introduce you to your sweet little girl," she exclaims, and both Brody and I burst out in a yell-cry. "Daddy, you want to cut the cord?"

Brody whips his head to me and I can see the uncertainty in his eyes. He may not share the same DNA with my little girl, but he's been here every step of the way, and it doesn't look as though that will be changing any time soon.

I give him a firm nod, and he wipes his eyes with the back of his hand before taking ahold of the medical scissors to cut the cord. Once he's done, Dr. Ellis passes my baby girl over to the nurse as she starts to clean her up, weigh her, then check her breathing. Brody comes back over, taking my hand and kissing it.

"Thank you, Sadie." He places his face in the crook of my neck, and I grab him like he's my lifeline. "I know she's not mine, but I'll protect and love her for as long as she needs me. And you for that matter," he whispers in my ear.

I know this is an emotional time for all of us, but in a way Brody and I have become a family. We may not have that sexual context to it like a normal husband and wife, but he has fulfilled every other aspect of meeting my needs.

"Thank you, Brody." I kiss his cheek and we share a moment over everything that has transpired on this amazing day.

"Who wants some snuggles with this little princess?" the nurse asks, coming over to the bed.

My eyes fill with tears again as my little girl is placed on my chest. Skin to skin. Brody wraps a thin blanket over us to cover us both up.

"Here, let's get the first family photo," the older nurse suggests, and Brody digs for his phone in his pocket.

After a million photos, everyone leaves the three of us to have some bonding time as a family after the little princess took right to the breast without any problems. I should've known she'd be a total boob monster like her father. *No, don't think about him right now.*

"Well, she definitely takes after her momma in the food department," Brody jokes of my healthy appetite.

My eyes are growing heavy after the exhausting day, but I don't want to miss a single second with this little girl.

"Have you thought of a name?" Brody asks as he takes a seat next to the bed.

I look down at my princess and can't help the smile that has taken up permanent residence on my face.

"I have thought of a million over the last few months but none seem to fit."

"Maybe someone close to you? Or a family name?" he suggests.

I pause and think it over, there's no one on either side of my family that comes to mind. Wait, I know of someone who thought this would be the perfect name. She has come to mean a lot to me before all of this craziness happened.

"Halo," I say as she lets out a content sigh, making me think I made the right choice.

"Halo, that's a beautiful name for this little one." Brody lightly touches her head.

"I was thinking about having Landry as her middle name, if it's okay with you." Brody's full name is Brody Landry Jackson, and I wanted to somehow honor everything he has sacrificed in taking us in and making sure we are protected.

The smile spreads across his face and I'm concerned he'll split in half if he keeps it up.

"Halo Landry. I love it, Sadie, thank you."

We sit there in comfortable silence, just watching her sleep. I didn't think you could love something so small so fast but I do.

I can't fight the sleep as I doze off, but Brody is right there to lift her up as he cradles her to his naked chest, wanting to continue with the bonding the nurse said was important for both parents.

"Brody," I sleepily say getting his attention. "You may not be her father by blood and if something were to ever happen and this situation were to change, I still would want you to be in our lives." He nods, patting Halo gently on her diaper.

"Wild horses couldn't keep me away from either of you now. No matter where this life takes us, you will always be a part of my life at any capacity."

"I know when we leave here her birth certificate will say that you are the father and it will be a fake document, but I really and truly want you to be her Godfather."

"Oh, Saylor." I gasp as he uses my real name. "I'd be honor to have such a title." He leans down and kisses the top of her pink beanie. "Get some sleep before your next feeding, Momma Bear."

Brody

I lean back in the lounge chair as little Halo Landry quietly sleeps on my chest. Never in my life did I think I'd end up like this. Looking down at this precious baby girl makes me think that having a family is just what I need in my life. Halo and Sadie have become my whole world in such a short amount of time, and I'm not focused on the task I was given.

When I received that call from my Uncle Burt, I almost said

no. I hadn't seen him in almost three years since my Aunt Genie passed away, but we spoke regularly. They were never able to have children so they more than latched on to me when the time came. They were the last of my family, since I lost my parents towards the end of my senior year in high school. I stayed with them in Los Angeles until I graduated, then shipped off to the Marines the day after I walked across that stage. Uncle Burt always supported me in any venture, and even helped get me with some contacts when my patent for my scope and glasses came through. He and my dad were close.

The call I received a few months back rocked my world. It was his secretary, Judy, calling to say that Uncle Burt had a massive heart attack in court and they weren't able to revive him. He was the last of my family, and that was a tough realization. I flew over to Los Angeles to handle the funeral arrangements, but told Sadie that I had a business meeting for a potential company wanting to license my goggles. I hated lying but I didn't want to upset her. We'd just gotten her out of her depression and I didn't want her to relapse or set her off again.

I was in Los Angeles for two days, then flew back as soon as I could. I hated being away from Sadie and it was then that I realized that I was alone, and the only person I had left was her and the little jellybean she was carrying. I'd read up on Levi Thorne, his entire file and the one I was able to obtain through my contacts, not to mention watching the videos of the restaurant was horrifying. Uncle Burt brought me up to date on Thorne being one of the many who was sucked into the web of Blaire Hutchins, who was caught as the leader of a prostitution ring. My uncle also told me that Levi had become just like Blaire, in following her into becoming one of her clients, but from the files I thank my lucky stars I was able to get Sadie away from that asshole. If he could throw something so wonderful and perfect away then he didn't deserve to have them. He was still in a coma when I was there handling everything. None of my uncle's colleagues mentioned any pending cases, so I know Sadie is safe now. My uncle always had a backup plan for everything, and he told me that this was one time he didn't want anyone to know about securing her away. She is now my responsibility, and I plan on keeping her and this precious little one safe and hidden.

A month later, I got another call from Uncle Burt's estate attorney, wanting to have a sit down to go over the will and his assets. I left once again telling another lie, but I did promise this was the last time I'd leave her alone until the baby was born. When I arrived at the attorney's office, we spent three hours going over his estate and signing over all of his accounts and properties to me.

When I was leaving the office, I was approached by two bulky men wanting me to come with them for a chat with their boss.

"What's all this about?" I question as we exit the SUV and walk into the hospital.

"You'll see," one of them says, and guides me into a conference room.

I sit there for at least twenty minutes before the doors open and a nurse wheels in a man. The closer he gets, the more that I recognize him.

"Mitch? Mitch Howard, is that you?" I ask in disbelief. He doesn't look anything like himself. He's lost a lot of body mass and has thick, angry red marks across his cheeks, and looks nothing like that last time I saw him.

"Brody Jackson. It's good to see you brother," he greets, and I stand to welcome him. We shake hands and I feel the hard grip from it.

Mitch Howard and I go way back. We were Marines together

when I first joined, and he was on his way out of the service many years ago.

"Man, what happened to you?" I ask. Was he in a car wreck?

"I had an accident a few months ago but I'm recovering," he admits. "But that's not why I've called you here."

"Okay, what can I do for you? I'm not in the military anymore, if that's what you need. Got out over a year ago."

"No, it has nothing to do with that. This has to do with your Uncle, the District Attorney," he says, and I notice both men who escorted me in the hospital are still in the room.

"Uncle Burt? He passed away a month ago. I came here to finalize his estate," I tell him. Where is this interrogation going?

"My boss's wife was taken and put into hiding by Mr. Buttons and we were wondering if you'd know anything about it," Mitch implores.

Then, it hits me like a ton of bricks. Thorne's file. Mitch's name never registered that it was him who is his head of security. In the service, we address everyone by their last name and he left five years before I did. He's looking for Sadie and the baby. Is it safe to tell Mitch about them? Could this be a trap and I'm leaving the door wide open for the fox to get into the hen house? My hen house. Uncle Burt said that no one knew about his move to secure Sadie. Am I putting her in danger if I mention this to Mitch? Can I even trust him?

I'm about to answer when my phone goes off on the table and the sound fills the room. Looking down, I see Sadie is calling me. Peeking up, I watch as Mitch sees the name across the screen.

"Excuse me for a second," I say, and place the phone to my ear and discreetly turn the volume down. "Hey Momma Bear," I use her endearment and receive a light giggle, making me smile.

"Sorry to bother you but can you bring home those chocolates like last time you were there? I can't stop thinking about them and the baby wants them too!"

I snort, remembering her inhaling them in one sitting. I should get double this time around.

"Yes, dear. Is everything alright? You feeling okay today?" I question and look over at Mitch, who is eyeing me. I hold a finger up, telling him I'll explain in a minute.

"Everything is perfect, but Zeus has barricaded the doors and won't let anyone in the house. Oh, and can you pick up some ice cream on your way in driving through town. I'll be done by the time you get home."

"Really? You had two pints when I left."

"I shared with Zeus," she whines her explanation.

"Alright Sadie, I'll see you tonight."

"You're the best!" I hear her squeal and tell, who I'm presuming is Zeus, that I'm getting her requests. It's the little things like this that makes me happy. It's why I'm more than determined to keep her and the baby safe. I can't even imagine a life without her in it, so I decide right there that I'm keeping the cover that was established all those months ago.

We hang up and I return the phone back to the table.

"Got a woman?" Mitch smirks. He only knew me as a love'em and leave'em type in the military.

"Oh yeah." I hold up my wedding band and Mitch looks shocked.

"When did this happen? The Brody Jackson I once knew would never settle down."

"Until the right woman came along. We've been married three years, and have a little one on the way."

I tap my phone and show him a safe photo of Sadie. She's turned to the side that shows off her pregnant belly in a long flowy dress. She's out in the backyard feeding the goats, and her hair is covering her face. She looks beautiful and Zeus is, of course, right next to her in the picture.

Mitch briefly examines the picture, then hands it back.

"Congrats, man. Never thought I'd see the day. Always thought you were a blonde man. When is she due?"

"Thanks, we're due in almost two months. It's exciting but scary as shit." I try to convey. I don't want to give anything away. Mitch was always good at determining when someone was bullshitting. But I was trained just like him to pass any interrogation. I've always had a thing for blondes and Sadie is the furthest there is.

"Sorry to hear about your Uncle, but he has something I need." Mitch cuts back to business. He makes it sound as though Sadie is a possession instead of a person, further proving to me to keep quiet.

"I wish I could help you, Mitch, but I have no idea what he did as the DA," I become just as serious. "I hadn't seen him in a long time and we only spoke on the phone every so often." I shrug. "Never was any of it about his work or anything like that."

Mitch nods and sits back in his wheelchair.

"I need to find the boss's wife. Your Uncle pulled some shady shit and he's about to reign hell on all of LA and his family."

"I wish I could help but I don't know anything about what you're talking about. Who's your boss anyway?"

"Levi Thorne."

"No, shit. The attorney from all the gossip articles." I chuckle and so does Mitch. "I'm pretty sure everyone saw the video of them at that restaurant. Didn't he ask her for a divorce or something?" I play dumb.

"Deep down he's a good man but a little misguided at times."

"Well, my Uncle kept records of everything, even when I lived with him and my Aunt. He had boxes of records for every little item that went on in his life. Maybe his office has some paperwork with a lead?" I suggest, knowing that this was probably the only time in my Uncle's life he didn't jot down his plans or have paperwork drawn up. He wanted to make sure I wasn't named in any of his business.

"I'm working on it as we speak, but you know all the red tape the government throws at you."

I nod and check my watch.

"Sorry to cut this short but I've got some chocolates to collect for a very pregnant wife and a plane to catch." I move to stand.

"Of course, Brody. Please contact me if you think of anything, or come across something of your Uncle's."

"You got it."

We shake hands and I walk out of the room and out towards the exit. I dodged a bullet today, and hope that I won't have to face him or his goons ever again.

I was determined when I got home to keep my focus on the task of keeping Sadie and the baby safe, but every day she chipped away at my focus. She is the most fun, loving, sassy, cheerful, silly person I know. She accepts everyone and is truly genuine when she meets them. Everyone on the ranch fell in love with her within a day. Especially, when she started baking and sharing all her desserts and treats with all the men. It's intoxicating and I'm finding myself falling for her every day. I know it's wrong, but the more time we act as a family the more the lines of fake and real are starting to get blurred for me. When we go out in the town, we are a married couple who holds hands and orders for each other, and it's the exact life I've always wanted for myself. I know that this has heartache written all over it, but I can't help the way she makes me feel. I'm in deeper every day and now that little Halo is here, I can't see the line in the sand anymore.

The door opens and our nurse come quietly in.

"I was just wanting to check on baby girl and Mommy before my shift ends," Nurse Peggy says.

"They're great. Sadie just wanted to rest for a bit."

"That's perfectly normal. Have you changed the little one's diaper yet?" She asks.

I shake my head. She shows me on the diaper where the picture changed colors, indicating that Halo needs a new one. After not waking her on three failed attempts, I finally mastered the diaper change and got her back on my chest. When I practiced on the dolls at the birthing class, it never said that as soon as air touched the baby's skin she'd pee. Definitely wasn't ready for that.

"When your wife wakes, she's going to want a shower. You can call for a nurse to help, or do it yourself," Nurse Peggy whispers, not wanting to wake either of my sleeping beauties.

"Okay, thanks."

She leaves us alone to our quiet room. I finally turn off my brain and recline back in the chair, almost lying flat. The smell of Halo is the perfect balm for relaxing. Before long, I feel my eyes begin to droop. I place a protective hand on Halo over the soft pink blanket I bought at the gift shop, then let my eyes close for a little while and dream of the life I'm going to have with this family, and how I'll do anything to keep them.

CHAPTER NINE

Levi

Los Angeles, California

I wake with a start, as my fingers fall on the keys of my piano and send a loud noise echoing through the room. Right before Saylor and I eloped, we started a *'New Adventure Jar'*. We wanted to start doing activities that were new to us as a couple. We each placed five activities, written on a folded piece of paper, in a jar and once we completed the task or adventure, we'd pick a new one. We drew "learning to play the piano" when the threats against my love started rolling in and I made the biggest mistake of my life. I bought us this beautiful grand piano to learn on, here at home, after I refused to return to the class she signed us up for. She and I were the oldest in the beginners' class by two decades. After that, I found a nice lady who came here to teach us.

My hazy eyes try to adjust to the bright light from the floor to ceiling windows. I see another large empty bottle of liquor sitting on top of the piano, with the tumbler missing. It's either shattered against the wall somewhere in the corner, or I bypassed it all together and drank straight from the bottle. *Again.* Saylor loved this piano and played all the time. Sometimes I'd bring my work home with me and sneak in so that I could hear her play when it was her time for a lesson. She was getting to the point where she didn't need to look at the sheets to play the three songs that we'd learned because her fingers moved to their own accord. She is truly a priceless gem.

I can't keep going on like this. It's been a month since Saylor's due date, and we still can't seem to find her. I can't keep drinking every night, hoping I don't have nightmares of my beautiful wife laying on the cold floor next to my dead child. The thought makes me vomit in the trash bin next to my piano. Tina knows my routine by now and it saves her time and clean up if she just places it there in the early mornings.

We haven't been able to find one trace of where Saylor has been sent. Not one piece of paper shows where that asshole, Burt Buttons, placed her. Dean has hacked the government database and found all the Witness Protection placements, but with over ten thousand to look through, it's going to take a while to find my family.

The penthouse has become command central as William, Dean and others are now camping out here, working around the clock. Reid has taken one of the guestrooms and stays here as often as possible. Lincoln comes by after work most days. He calls several times a day checking in. Things are still on shaky ground with him and Everly. My mother comes by every day, before or after she's heading to work, to check on me to make sure I'm eating and to make sure I'm still healing properly. Daniel has been banned from coming within twenty feet of my building, and I haven't seen him in a long time. After what he did, I don't think I could ever get past his actions, even if he thought he was doing the right thing. Mitch mentioned that he has hired his own PI to find Saylor and our baby, but I don't care at this point. He could find the cure for cancer and I'd never bat an eye at him.

My father-in-law blew into LA not long after I woke up. Adam Gentry is the scariest motherfucker I've ever experienced in my life. He looked every bit military but there was something about him that felt off. Saylor had mentioned his time with Everly's Dad, Tommy Bryant, when he was in the service and the trauma they experienced. She'd said that he'd go missing for months on end, leaving her to Glammy and Granddad to look after.

Adam didn't take too kindly of how his daughter was treated when he was told why she took off. Everly and Tommy had finally gotten ahold of him after many attempts of trying to contact him. He was up in Alaska, deep-sea fishing for two months, and came back with hell beside him. I'll never forget meeting him for the first time.

"Where is my daughter?" we hear roared down the hall. I'd just gotten back from physical therapy and was exhausted. My family was here, all waiting to hear if tomorrow was the day that I got to go home. Lincoln had stopped by with Everly's dad after they went to lunch to discuss some things.

A man storms into the room and the temperature dropped to freezing. His eyes were wild, and only when they locked in on Tommy did they focus.

"Where is she?" Adam asked.

Tommy went straight to him, speaking in a hushed voice. Every muscle was locked into place on his body the more Tommy spoke with him.

"Mr. Gentry, I'm Daniel Thorne, Levi's dad—"

"I know who the fuck you are. I know all about you and your family," Adam sneers over Tommy's shoulder, looking Dad straight in the eyes. Mitch and Dean had some questions for Dad of his time when

he was at the police station with Saylor, and just happened to be there during all this. "Which one of you is responsible for all this, this time?"

There is a lot of activity outside my hospital room, as I see multiple hospital security guys hovering close. Apparently there was a famous movie star giving birth and was in my private wing of the hospital, so security has been tight the last day or so.

"There was a slight misunderstanding when Levi—" Dad didn't even get the chance to finish his sentence before Adam lunged past Tommy and nailed him with his large fist. The room erupted after that.

He not only laid out my father, knocking him on his ass, but every security personnel in his wake. I watched, mesmerized, wishing I was the one who knocked Dad's ass out. He didn't spare me any favors either, and knocked my ass out even in my wheelchair, at the time. I deserved every stitch of pain he landed across my face. He was furious, and promised that if he found Saylor then he'd make it his life's mission to keep us apart. Mitch, of course, has someone on him following his every move to make sure he can't find her first, then take off with my family. God only knows what he'd fill her head with since he hates me, and I'd never get my chance to explain the reasons behind that horrible scene at the restaurant.

The day after he whirled in, we received a call that Blaire Hutchins was dead. According to the Police Department, she hung herself with torn sheets from her bedding. Everyone chalked it up to her upcoming trial, but something in the back of my mind didn't add up to me. It wasn't until the day before she died that I learned that it was that rancid bitch who was the ring leader, who had Saylor assaulted in jail. Mitch and Dean put me on lockdown to keep me from leaving the hospital and choking the bitch dead with my own two hands. Lincoln confessed to the family, shortly after, about Blaire and all that she was involved in. Of course, dad went into lecture mode but Mom shut him right up.

Olivia is holding down most all of my cases at work. Lincoln thinks that it's best until further notice, and doesn't want me to be bothered with anything business related until my family is back safe and sound. I spend a lot of time working with my hands at a new property I just purchased. It's a gut job and I love nothing more than taking a hammer and destroying everything in my wake. Nothing else matters.

Mitch has exhausted all his leads and is following up daily with new ones. I wanted to go to the public and have a news conference about finding Saylor, but was strongly advised against it. Since I didn't listen to their advice the first go around, I'm much more dependent on sticking with their opinions these days. We haven't heard from our suspect, who made the threats against Saylor and our child since before the bombing incident, but it might tip him off if I was to make a plea for her to return home. Also, the crazies would come out of the woodwork trying to find Saylor, and then we'd be putting her in a hostage situation. I'd sign my entire life's worth over to have her here right now.

As for Detective Ford, let's just say that he will have a problem collecting a paycheck anywhere here in the states. Between Lincoln and Olivia, they had him blackballed here, Canada, Mexico and anywhere else they have pull. *Good luck at the North Pole, fucker!*

As always, I head to the nursery and sit down in the rocking chair beside the crib and stare around the room. I found the perfect room decor online one night I couldn't sleep, before I started to drink to fill the void. I had Tina organize someone to come and recreate it except for the crib, I felt like that is what dads are supposed to do as parents; a rite of passage. There are neutral colors throughout the room, and small little animals fill the walls and corners of it. It's like a miniature zoo in here. Mom went crazy and has the first years' worth of clothing, for both a girl and boy, in the walk-in closet.

Christ, I don't even know if I have a son or daughter.

Automatically, I touch the chain around my neck that holds Saylor's rings. I do this often. They never come off, I always want to feel them against me. I was lucky that I didn't lose them in the bombing, or at the hospital, when I was transported.

Next to the chair is the worn-out envelope with the letter that was sent to me, from Saylor, while I was in a coma. She sent out six letters to her family letting them know she was going away for a while. Myself, Grandma, Adam, Glammy, Everly, and Tina were the only ones who received them. The only one I haven't been able to read was Adam's. Reaching over, I unfold it for the millionth time as my heart clenches.

Levi,

I'm sorry for everything that has happened over the past eight months since we've known each other. I wish I could go back and decline taking your offer to hang out at the bar that night, then maybe we'd never be in the state we're in right now. We'd have never crossed paths and your life would go on as it was. I'm sorry for ever wanting more from you and taking you out of your cold, little bubbled life you've constructed and made you into a person you can't live with. But, I'd like to thank you also. Thank you for showing me that even a small-town girl can have it all, even if it's just for a short amount of time. I do love you, more than I care to admit, but after the last few days, our story has come to an end. I'll sign whatever paperwork you need once you are awake to end this marriage; I just wish it'd been you who presented it to me instead of a third party. I wish you all the happiness in the world and hope that someday you'll look back on this very short amount of time and not have regrets but smile.

Me leaving was the hardest decision I've ever made. Even though we aren't in a good place, I still wanted to be by your side. Mr. Buttons said that, for the sake of our baby, it might be better to leave for a bit, until the person responsible for your car bombing is found. He'd said that you and Lincoln have done this numerous times, and that this is what you'd want. I'll keep our baby safe until the authorities are sure it's safe to return. I only hope you accept this child with open arms, even if we aren't together.

I know that I said some horrible things to you at the restaurant and regret making public what you had told me in confidence, but I want you to know that I will always love you, Levi. Even though we are closing the book on our story, you will always hold a piece of my heart and soul.

Love Always,
Saylor

I finally let out all my frustration that I've been holding in all these months and let the flood gates open. I grab the sonogram picture from our first time seeing our baby and hold it tight to my chest. I hear the door creak open and see my mom standing there in her business suit. She sees my distraught face and the tears and rushes over to me.

"Oh, baby boy let me hold you," she pleads. No one has been able to touch me since I've been home from the hospital. I don't want to be touched by anyone except Saylor, but right now I need someone to lean on. Someone who will be the strong person for me in my time of need.

"Mom—" I choke out. "Where did they take her? She hates me Mom, and I did this to us. I was the reason she was alone to give birth to our child. Me." I wail like the seven-year-old boy who lost his parents.

I've never cried like this. Not even when the cops told me that both of my parents were dead. This is much worse than the marks I bare on my skin from the burning I received because of the bomb, I feel it to my core.

"It's okay, Levi." I think I've shocked my mother with this behavior. She's rocking me as if I were a baby. "We will find them and bring them home. Saylor and the baby are safe, don't let your mind go to a dark place. Your family needs you to stay strong."

"I can't, Mom." I admit. "I need her, she's my everything." I continue to cry.

I must've fallen asleep because when I open my eyes, I have my head on Mom's lap and she's resting up against the wall. Feeling ashamed that I've broken down in front of my mother, I lift up.

"Sorry," I murmur, and rub my sore eyes.

"Nonsense. Don't you ever apologize for needing your mother.

I only wish I'd been there when you needed it," she says solemnly, referring to this whole mess I've created.

"Don't start this again, we've been over this and we promised not to look back," I remind her. "How are Grandma and Grandpa doing?" I change the subject.

"They've decided to stay out at their Montana home for a while. Mother hasn't been dealing well with not having Saylor around," Mom says. "She went up to that Police Station every day for a week, demanding to see Saylor. She was devastated when she learned about her son's betrayal. I swear she would've had Daniel over her knee and a wooden spoon in her hand, had she been twenty years younger." She chuckles sadly. "They don't know the whole story about everything, just that Daniel didn't help her and the baby when she was taken in. They both have been depressed about her being gone and the "pending" divorce. I told them that once the dust clears that she'll be back and you guys would work it out. That seemed to relax them a little."

I can only imagine the strain that all this has put on her marriage to Daniel. As much as I love to see him suffering, I hate that it's at the expense of my mother. I had heard Lincoln and her talking about her and Daniel separating for a little while.

"You and Daniel will work things out, mom." I try to sound genuine, but I could care less for him. He wouldn't leave anyone unscathed if someone were to try and break his marriage up to Mom, and I feel the same. Family or not.

"I know you are only being nice but thank you anyways." She knows how I'll never forgive him for what he's done. "Have you thought about telling Grandma and Grandpa the truth and letting them know everything that is going on? Grandpa might be able to help in some way."

"I've thought about it but think it's best to just let them be at their vacation home and not bothered with all this mess I've created. I know that they don't need any more stress with what Lincoln and I are going through."

They are truly heartbroken about Saylor and the baby, and I don't want to add any more stress to them. I don't think I could bare hurting them too.

"Has Lincoln heard anything from Everly lately?" I know the answer, but ask anyways.

"They are working things out slowly. I can only imagine that she's a bit gun-shy to be part of this family after everything. I know that her dad has been around a lot lately. We've spoken a few times."

"I've got to get to work; I was supposed to be there an hour ago." Mom slowly rises up from the floor and I follow up with her. "You should have Lincoln and Reid over to stay with you some time. I know that they'd love to be able to spend that time with you."

"Sorry for making you late," I say. "I'll give them a call."

"Nothing is more important than family. Now stop drinking so much; your skin looks horrible and you don't want to kill your liver before your wife and child come home."

I crush her in a hug, and almost start to weep again. She has always been my biggest champion.

"Love you, Mom."

"Love you too, baby boy."

"Sir, we have something." Mitch rushes into my home office with an envelope two days later.

I hold my breath as he passes it to me, and I stare down at it like it could be a bomb or contain the Holy Grail. The side has been cut open since all mail and packages have to be scanned and opened for security purposes. My hands shake and I feel a bead of sweat form on my forehead. I know this handwriting. It belongs to *her*.

"You're going to want to see it, sir," Mitch pushes, with a slight smile on his face. He knows what it contains.

Not wanting to wait anymore, I reach in and pull out several pictures, along with a small note. The first picture is of a small baby girl with a bow on the side of her full head of brown hair. Her eyes are closed and she looks so peaceful. My fingers run over her little face, noticing she has my nose but Saylor's perfect lips. The next one is of her in a basket surrounded by a pink blanket, wearing pearls while she's looking at the camera.

A small sob leaves my throat. She has my eyes and she's the perfect mixture of Saylor and I. I can't believe for one second that I had any doubts about being a father. One look at her and I know I was meant to be a dad to this little one, and any other babies that Saylor and I have in the future.

I pull the next one forward and see her tiny feet, which are probably as long as my pinky finger, and smile. She is the most delicate thing. The last photo I have is of her in a pink bow as big as her head and a matching pink tutu; Mom would definitely approve.

I look over the photos multiple times, taking her all in and memorizing every detail of her precious form. I know everyone says they have the most beautiful baby in the world, but I know for sure that it is true in this case. Christ, when she gets ready to date, I'm going to have to beat the boys off with a stick. Maybe Mitch will teach me how to shoot?

The small paper floats from the desk to my lap, and I tear my eyes away from my daughter to read it, hoping that Saylor left me some clue as to where she and my baby girl are.

Levi,

I hope all is well and that you have healed from your injuries. Our baby girl was born last month, and I thought you'd want a photo of her and know that she is perfect. She came into this world quickly, arriving after only four hours of being in labor. She weighed barely six pounds and was nineteen inches long. Don't panic about her size; she is healthy and strong. From the pictures, I hope you can see that she was gifted your eyes and nose, and was left with a ton of hair on her petite head. She is healthy and growing every day. She has the most beautiful name because the moment I saw her I knew that she was an angel.

I want to say that I understand. The family life and the bachelor life are two completely different lifestyle, and I'm not judging you for it. It only solidifies that we are truly over. I guess I was still holding out hope for us. After seeing pictures of you around town recently, without your wedding band, I know that you've moved on and I will try to do so as well.

As hard of a pill as it is to swallow, I realize now that if the great Levi Thorne had wanted us then he'd move mountains and leave no stone left unturned. I'll wait for a call from Mr. Buttons, letting me know when it's safe to return. Then I'll contact you, if you'd like to meet our daughter.

Saylor

"NO!" I scream out. I'm sure the sound bounces off every wall in the apartment.

I bang my fist on the desk after re-reading her letter for the hundredth time and swipe everything off, only leaving my baby girl's photos and the letter there. She thinks I don't want her. She thinks that Buttons is alive and will call her when the coast is clear. Shit, this is such a mess.

Your father did turn her away and try to force her to sign divorce papers. Not to mention the restaurant scene.

My body is shaking with rage, this is all my fault. I look down at my naked left ring finger and want to beat the shit out of myself. The hospital had to cut mine off when I was brought in with all my broken bones. I've been so worried about finding her and the baby that it didn't dawn on me to have it replaced. My hand immediately goes to my neck to clutch her rings that are around my neck. I breathe a little easier, but I still can't control the flash of anger.

We are being set up and are running around chasing our tail, trying to follow any leads. We can only assume that's it from the psycho who tried to murder me or threatened to harm Saylor. Mitch went to confront Norman Weeks, the new DA, but he doesn't seem to have any idea what Buttons was up to.

"MITCH!" I bellow, knowing he is on the other side of the door. He comes in quickly and sees the state of the room, with all my desk items scattered on the floor.

"Sir."

"Did you read this?" I hold up Saylor's letter.

"Yes, sir."

"Call Franklin at Courtier and have the same wedding band made as the one Saylor designed for our wedding. Christ, she thinks I wanted the divorce and that I've moved on." My voice hitches as I say those words.

"Already called and it should be here by the end of the week. He's putting a rush on the ring."

"Good. Get Dean and William here. There still are photos of me floating around," I say as he types on his phone, probably texting them to get here now. "Also," I pause and pick up the photos of my daughter. I can't help but smile. "I have a daughter," I say proudly.

"She's a beauty, sir," Mitch says as he returns the smile.

"Have Tina change the room to match the princess that she is," I say proudly as he types away on his phone.

A knock on the door interrupts us, as Dean and William walk in. Mitch must've had them on standby after security checked the mail. They have a seat in front of the desk and I sit down, still holding my pictures.

"We need to comb over the birth registry across the country. Saylor gave us her weight and height; that should give us something to go by."

I can't stop smiling at her name. Grandma is going to be thrilled that Saylor and I have a little girl. I knew they had gotten close those few months and treated her like a true granddaughter. I only wish we all could've been there when she gave birth and wasn't alone.

"Sir, I've already compiled a list. We will run them through the registry and see if we have any hits in the U.S. alone that were birthed last month. That's if she even had the baby at a hospital. She could've had a home birth and not filed any paperwork. Also, if she is out of the country, we'll have to go by each individual one as they all handle birth certificates differently. Not gonna lie, but it might take us sometime to sift through the list."

Shit! Not what I wanted to hear but at least we have something to go by.

"I don't care what you have to do or what laws you have to break but find my family!" I demand, then dismiss them.

I walk over to the window and look out over the gloomy sky. There is a break in the clouds and the sun shines through. Hope. I feel as though all is not lost. Picking up my phone, I call the one person who I want to share this incredible news with. It rings twice before the call is picked up.

"Hello?"

"Lincoln…"

CHAPTER TEN

Levi

Two Years Later…

"Sir, I think we've found something." Dean and William barge into my home office. Dean has been with the firm since the beginning; he researches and is a computer guru when cases come in, and we need to find hard evidence that will help our cases out. William was brought on when I screwed things up with my wife.

Papers are scattered everywhere across my desk at my penthouse. Mugs of coffee, coke cans and tissues are littered on every available surface. Tina, my housekeeper and cook, always tries to sneak in here to clean up, but I'm always pushing her out so that something doesn't get moved or lost in the organized mess I've created in my home office.

"What do you have for me? Did you find her? Did you find my family?" I shakily ask. I've been running on caffeine and rarely leave these four walls.

"We aren't a hundred percent sure but it's the best lead we've had all year. We've sent our P.I. to check it out and confirm our suspicions," William answers.

"Where are they?"

"Montana, sir. A little town south of Helena," Dean says. "They are with Brody, Burt Buttons' nephew, who is retired from the military and was interviewed after Buttons died."

Montana? My parents and grandparents have a place around there. So do her grandparents. How could she be right under our nose and not know it? Did Sharilyn and Alan know this entire time?

Dean passes me the grainy black and white photos of a woman and child entering a Mom-and-Pop grocery store. She has on a hat and sunglasses to shield her face, but when I look at her from head to toe, my body gives off that tingling spark whenever she and I are in the same room. It's her. It's the woman who has turned my world upside down for the past two and a half years. As I examine each photo, I take notice of the man beside her. The one who is continually touching her and my child, as if they belonged to him.

"MITCH!" I bellow, he appears in the room within seconds. "Call and get a jet ready, we are headed to Montana."

"Yes, sir," he responds, and whips out his phone as he makes his way out the door.

I leave the office and head to my bedroom, which has gone untouched since my world fell apart. Walking into the closet, I start to find some clean clothes when I catch a glimpse in the mirror. I look so ragged. My beard has filled in, since I haven't bothered with it in months, and the dark circles under my eyes show how I haven't been sleeping. How can I? I've lost the two most precious things in the world.

Deciding that I don't want to scare them, I grab for my jeans, polo shirt, and boxers while making my way to the bathroom to clean myself up. Grabbing for the shears and razor, I step into the hot steaming shower and start to groom my body, and rid myself of the beast that has consumed me for so long.

After a very long, hot shower I step out and put on my clothes before looking into the mirror again. Looking back is the man who once had it all, but foolishly sent it away thinking it was for the best. I just hope she will forgive me. Forgive for everything that I've done. I hope that I haven't ruined everything. The man looking back at me is slightly different from two years ago. After everything I've been through, I'm definitely a changed man.

"Don't worry sweetheart, I'm coming to bring you home."

I'm sitting on the plane, heading for Montana to get my family. *Family.* A word I'm proud to say out loud. Years ago, I thought it was something that didn't have a lot of meaning but now I can almost taste it. My knees bounce with anticipation, and I think it's the cause of the plane shifting and not the turbulence leaving California.

The flight is only two hours and forty minutes, but it seems to take all day before the wheels come down on our private chartered jet. Mitch has been in the front with Dean, William, Jacobs, and Colbert, our new security on this trip, going over the town and any information we might need once we head in to get my two girls.

I've dreamed of this day for the last two and a half years. I've made so many mistakes that I can only hope Saylor will forgive me for. The first, being a dick at the restaurant that fateful day. Dr. Blake, my new therapist, says that I need to start from the beginning when opening up to Saylor, even if she doesn't want to hear it. She needs to know that I'm no longer going to keep her in the dark on anything anymore. Tell her the smallest of things, even if I think it doesn't matter. Trust is going to be the key factor and the foundation of our relationship once Saylor is done pelting the hell out of me verbally. She might even decide a good beating is in order and I'd take every lick she offers, as long as she comes home with me.

Turning my phone on once we are taxiing down the runway, my phone starts to blast with text messages, voicemails, and missed calls. All from my mother and Linc. I hear the panic in her voice from a voicemail, and don't finish listening but call her immediately. Something has happened.

"Mom, what is it? What's wrong?"

"Levi." She sounds relieved to hear my voice but I can tell she's trying to muffle her talking. "I need you to get on a plane and come to Grandma and Grandpa's vacation house. Right now."

"I just landed in Montana for some business, Mom. Is Grandma okay? Did she fall?"

I haven't been in contact with my grandparents in a long time. Once I came out of my coma, they came out to their Montana home after they all learned Saylor had left. I've seen them a handful of times over the last two years but most have been quick visits. They don't know everything that happened and that everything was a ruse to catch the person responsible for the car bombing. They took it very hard when Saylor was taken from the jail without a trace and came out here for some solace. They've invited me out here multiple times, but I always give them an excuse that I'm working on a case, even though I haven't stepped foot in the firm in almost two years.

"No, but you need to get here immediately," she stresses with a whisper into the phone. Her voice is almost panicked and it makes me take a pause. "Please hurry."

"My plane just touched down here in Bozeman. We'll be there as soon as we can."

Is it a coincidence that Saylor is possibly near the same town as my grandparents or hers?

"Good, good. I…" there's some voices in the background but mother tries to cover it up, placing her hand over the phone. "I can't talk but get here."

The phone call ends and I'm on alert as to what is happening right now at my grandparent's vacation home. I let Mitch know, and after discussing it for a minute, we decided to take a quick detour before checking in to our rooms at our hotel.

An hour and a half later, we pull up to my grandparent's ranch style home and see all the lights on in the house. The sun has been down for a few hours and the stars are shining bright tonight. The front door opens as we all pile out of the SUV, and Mom comes hurriedly towards us, putting us all on high alert.

"Baby boy, I need you to prepare yourself for what you're about to walk in to."

"Okay," I say slowly, wondering what my grandparents have gotten themselves into. A dead body, maybe? Mitch would definitely need a raise if that were the case.

"Come." She grabs my hand and yanks me in. I glance a peek over my shoulder and see my security looking around for any threats.

Walking into the rustic décor of their home, I first notice the smell of wood and outdoor scent; I always do when I visit here. Nothing has changed much over the years except for updated photos on the walls. Security spreads out in the room, looking things over, when both of my grandparents walk into the open floor plan house and spy me in the living room. They both gasp, and so do I.

"Lev—Levi, what are you doing here?" Grandma asks, but

doesn't take a step to greet me. I don't blame her because I'm planted right where I'm standing.

"Alice Renee, I told you not to contact him yet!" Grandpa scolds my mother.

"He has a right to know," she remarks, defending herself.

No one has moved a muscle, including security. Time has stopped as I view the prettiest little girl I've ever seen in my grandmother's arms. She's holding two dolls in her hand while trying to give them her pacifier. The books I've been reading say that she should've already been teething by now, but some toddlers simply enjoy putting things in their mouth to comfort themselves.

The phone in my hand drops to the floor, taking her attention away from her toy and to the sound. She sees a group of us on this side of the room, and abandons her toys to the ground while grabbing ahold of Grandma and burrowing her face into her neck. A thought comes to me in my jumbled thoughts.

"She's here," I say in astonishment. "Is my Saylor here too?" I ask, looking around hoping she'll come out from down the hall.

"She's not here, son," Grandpa says. He checks his watch, and I can tell he's trying to figure out something.

I feel my shoulder jolt forward, and realize that Mom just pushed me towards my daughter. The one I've dreamed of almost every night since I received those newborn photos from Saylor. My feet sway over to them, as I sit down next to Grandma and my baby girl on the couch. She's still being shy and not looking at any of us. I drop down to my knees in front of her, and lightly run my fingers over her head and down her back. She's so small and delicate, like a little China doll. She is the perfect mixture of both Saylor and I. She finally turns, and it's like I'm looking at myself in her eyes. Our matching blue eyes sparkle in hers, and I can't help but smile so brightly and big at her.

"Halo, can you say hi?" Grandma pats her tiny back.

Halo. My baby is named Halo.

Recognition hits as that was what my Grandpa called Grandma. She hated when he called her his angel because she said she was anything but an angel. So, he started calling her Halo because when she was younger she had almost white hair when they met. I remember Saylor swooning when Grandpa explained his moniker for her.

Tears well up in my eyes as I think about my wife naming our daughter after someone on my side of the family. It's also a reminder of how much I've screwed up all of this and all the time that has been wasted from the biggest regret I've ever made. Not wanting to focus on that dark path, I turn my mind off and give all my attention to my little love.

"Hello, Halo. I'm your daddy," I finally find my voice and a small crack comes at the end. This is the moment I've been waiting for, to meet my little girl.

"She doesn't take to strangers very well…" Grandma starts to say, but Halo surprises us all and reaches out for me. Like she's been waiting for me too.

I pull her into my arms and try not to squeeze the ever-loving shit out of her. My face goes to the crook of her neck and I inhale, smelling her baby scent. I feel the moisture leave my eyes as I realize I've been through hell to get to this moment, but everything that has happened in the last two years has been worth it. She wiggles in my embrace and I know that it's a sign to let her go. As much as I hate it, I ease up on her tiny body and set her down on the ground. Halo straightens, then turns to go to the corner of the room, where she has an entire section of toys for her to play with. I watch with fascination as she plays and busies herself. I never paid much attention to children before, but now I can't seem to tear my eyes away from her and every little move she makes.

"Levi, why are you here now?" Grandma asks, breaking my tunnel vision.

"What do you mean? I'm here for my daughter and wife," I say, sitting back on my heels.

Grandpa tenses next to Grandma.

"Why now and not when you first woke up from your coma?" he snaps back at me, and I take a seat opposite of them. "You never mentioned looking for them." I realize now that I should've had my entire family in the loop as I tried tirelessly to locate Saylor and our baby.

The next twenty minutes I lay everything out for them. I tell them about someone trying to harm Saylor while she was pregnant, and how I orchestrated the entire restaurant debacle to buy us some more time. About the car bomb and how we think it was connected to the threats against Saylor. I tell them about Daniel giving Saylor divorce papers against my wishes, and all the events that happened after that. When I'm done, both are in tears but also very mad at me. I can't blame them for it but I thought I was doing the right thing by keeping some of these things from them. There was no need to worry them when I had a massive team to solve this situation, but I can see now that this is just another mistake to chalk up with all the other ones.

"Damnit Levi!" Grandpa yells, and it makes us all jump. "Don't you see what all those secrets have caused? If we had known... then Saylor would never have..." Grandpa looks over at Grandma, and a flash of regret passes through their eyes, making me wonder what their unspoken conversation is about. "This is going to be so devastating." He scrubs his hands over his face, then through his salt-colored hair.

I'm about to ask what they are talking about when I feel a small amount of weight touch my knee. Looking down, my precious baby girl has a toy in her hand, showing it to me.

"Pay ball?" Halo asks in the softest gibberish I've ever heard. All conversation forgotten, I get on the floor beside her.

"Of course, baby doll."

We roll the bouncy ball to each other and I do some silly moves that make her squeal in laughter. I catch Mitch recording the event, and will have to get him to share those with me. I've never been around children before, especially this young, but it feels…right—natural.

An alarm goes off on Grandpa's phone and he quickly turns it off before standing.

"I'm sorry Levi but they'll be here soon to pick Halo up."

"Well, I wasn't planning on seeing Saylor until the morning but I guess we'll see how she takes seeing me."

"Not here Levi. We've spent the last year being there for her and Halo. She'd be devastated if we ambush her like this. She doesn't know everything that you went through, and her version is not a pleasant one with you," he informs me. I can't believe they've known her whereabouts for a year and not said a word. "I'm asking you to not be here when they get here. This might turn into a huge confrontation, and you wouldn't want to do something you'll regret in front of your daughter."

"I'm not leaving," I start to say, but Grandma interrupts me.

"You can stay but you must keep out of sight. All of you," she demands, shaking her finger at all of us. "You've created a shit storm and it's going to take some time to get out of it. Right now, you're the enemy in Saylor's eyes and until she can calm down and listen to what really was going on, she won't hear a word out of your mouth and might try to hightail it out of here. This conversation needs to happen when Halo isn't around in case things get heated."

After a long moment, I concede.

"Fine."

Mom, myself, and the security all make our way to my grand-parent's room to wait until after my wife and daughter leave. I want so badly to come out and surprise her, but deep down I know Grandma is right. Saylor doesn't know the entire story and only thinks I've been living the single life.

We hear the front door open, and my wife's angelic voice rings out in greeting our little girl. There are several voices in a conversation but I can't make out what they are discussing. Mom and the security are waiting in the bathroom, while Mitch and I wait in the closet, with plantation bi-fold doors that you can see out of through little slits.

A man's voice rings out in laughter and it grates on my nerves. It must be Brody Jackson, the man who's been hiding my wife and daughter for the past two and a half years. A tightness forms in my chest, knowing that they've been under one roof longer than mine and Saylor's entire relationship. I hate it. And him. My hands ball into fists as I want to punch the life out of the little fucker.

Dr. Blake has warned me that Saylor may have moved on since not knowing the whole truth, but I can't bring myself to think about that. I know after the last letter she vowed to move on, but I'm hoping and praying that it's not the case and that by some miracle she's still mine. *What am I saying, she'll always be mine.*

The door to the bedroom opens, and my heart stops. My body is frozen as I hold in my gasp. My beautiful wife slowly walks in and takes in the room, as if she's looking for something. Our daughter is on her hip, playing with her short black hair. She's still just as beautiful as the day I first met her, if not more holding our baby girl. She's wearing a pair of short black athletic shorts and a team jersey with the name, 'Bombers,' across the front. Saylor walks to the middle of the room next to the bed and scans the room. Something catches her eye and she lazily walks over to the bookshelf, next to the closet where Mitch is all but holding me back.

My grandparents are very proud of their family and display photos of all of us over every wall in this house and in the one in LA. I have the perfect view of her and it wouldn't take much to reach out and touch her. Her chocolate eyes look over every picture and when she comes to the one of me outside of my first completed flip house, she runs her fingers lightly over my face. I long to have those fingers run over my skin, just to feel her again. I see a wedding band and engagement ring on her left hand and my throat starts to close up. She can't be married, we aren't divorced. *She doesn't know that; the documents have been sealed.* I don't think I could recover if she was ever married to anyone but me. *Please God, don't let her have remarried.*

"Dada!" my perfect little girl says, looking at my photo, and my heart grows two sizes bigger.

Saylor gasps, then squeezes her a little tighter.

"Yeah, baby bear, that's Daddy," she whispers in her ear like it's a secret, then kisses her temple.

A small gasp leaves my throat that I know she couldn't have heard but suddenly Saylor looks right at me. She can't see me, but it's as though we are staring at each for the first time. Saylor takes two steps and is directly in front of my door. All she has to do is open the door and we'll be reunited again. Slowly, I watch as she reaches up with her free hand that isn't around our little girl and places it on the door level with where my heart is.

Does she know I'm here? Can she feel me like we used to every time one of us walks in a room?

My hand automatically reaches up and is placed against hers. Only a flimsy piece of wood separates us. I haven't touched her in so long that my body is yearning to be pressed against hers. My hand presses harder on the door, wanting to feel her again and our eyes meet, locking into the wood as if it were glass. We both are holding our breath, and at the exact moment we both shudder from the top of our head down towards our toes. She goes to open her mouth but our moment is broken.

"Momma, you ready to head home and get our girl to bed?" A man walks into the room and steals my woman's attention. She reluctantly turns to face him, taking her away from me. Mitch placed a hand over my growling mouth when that dick said *our girl.*

"Sure." The man, that I assume is Brody fucking Jackson, takes my daughter from my wife's arms and cuddles her close.

"You okay?" he asks. "Grandpa said the SUV in the driveway was a rental since he put his in for a check on the motor." He tickles my baby's side and she lets out a squeal. "I told him to let me know next time their car needs anything and I'd have one of my guys look it over, or we could replace theirs with a new one for Christmas."

Fat chance you family stealing fucker. You won't be around for Christmas! Get your own family.

"Mhmm." She's not listening. Something is distracting her, and I know it's our connection. She feels the buzz just like I do when our bodies are this close. He doesn't even pick up on it because he's too busy with my daughter, and I want to burst out of this closet and snatch Halo out of his arms. She's mine! Not his.

"You ready? I could use a good rub down after that awesome game tonight." He winks at her, and bile rushes from my stomach up through my esophagus. *NO! Please don't.* I scream internally.

She smiles at him, then nods. He reaches out with his hand

and she willingly places hers in his. They both start to walk out of the bedroom, but when they cross over the threshold Saylor looks back over her shoulder. She stares back at me with wonder, then bites her plump lip likes she's inviting me to take ahold of it between my teeth. I actually groan and thankfully she is out of the room before she could hear it.

"Mitch, I want everything you've got on Brody Jackson and I want it as soon as we get to our hotel room." My voice is a whisper, but it comes across with harsh authority.

"Yes, sir. Already in the works."

I know Mitch is going to beat himself up for missing the signs with Brody, but I can't blame him. He had only just woken from his coma and had been tirelessly working to find Saylor. Tina and Mom had said that he pushed himself too hard and ended up almost relapsing before I woke up.

Moments later, we hear the front door close, then foot steps down the hall. Grandma comes in and looks around the room.

"Come on out, they're gone."

We all step out and I feel like the weight of the world is pressing on my chest. I just allowed my wife and daughter to walk out of my sight while I stood by and let it happen. This will be the last time that ever happens.

"Do they live far from here?" I ask when we all come back to the living room.

"About thirty minutes at a ranch a few towns over. It butts up to the forest area," Grandpa informs me. "We've never been out there. She's always come here to us."

We sit in silence for a while, and the quietness has the walls closing in on me as I think about my wife and daughter with another man.

"How did you find her?" I ask.

"It was the craziest coincidence, really. We had just gotten here on our long drive and decided to make a grocery run before it got too dark. I needed something on the baking aisle and there she was. I knew it was her, even in a ball cap. She was looking over a can of something and I called out to her. She immediately looked over and it was like time stood still. Her face showed so many emotions before we embraced each other. The sound of a little baby drew us back and that was when we saw our precious Halo. After many hugs and tears, Saylor told us not to say anything about seeing her and that she'd come by in a few days to talk with us. That was when we met Brody."

"Are they together?" I finally ask after a beat, not letting the pain from the words consume me.

"Son," Grandpa heaves a long breath. He looks over at Grandma, and I can see it in their faces before the words are ever confirmed. Fuck!

"She came to us about two months ago, wanting to have a conversation. At the time, we didn't know everything that had happened with the two of you; only the bits and pieces before we left Los Angeles and Saylor's version of what went down between you two. She told us about what Daniel had done on your behalf, and then how she sent you letters and pictures of Halo and how you never came for them. At the time, we saw everything from her side since you never told us you were looking for her. We didn't want to rock the boat that might hurt us from seeing Saylor and Halo. We thought she might leave and go somewhere else if she thought we were going to blow her cover that Mr. Buttons had put into place for her and Halo's safety." Grandma takes a deep breath, and I know the next part is going to be hard to hear. "Brody explained to us that everyone was in on her location, and that this was something that Mr. Buttons and your firm had done multiple times in the past."

"She came over with Halo around naptime and once our little angel baby was asleep, she asked us to sit down. We thought she was leaving, I did at least." She looks over at Grandpa and he takes her hand in his. "She asked us what we thought of Brody. He'd always been polite and generous and was great with Halo. She seemed to really take to him and he was always there for Saylor. I knew then what she was there to ask. She wanted to get our blessing, to move on from you, to be with him." Grandma places her free hand on the side of her face and rubs her temple.

"Son, you have to remember that we didn't know the truth of what was going on back in LA. Even though you and Saylor only had a short amount of time together, she was so torn up about the thought of moving on from you. We tried so many times to get you to come here for a visit to speak with you and the few times we went to California, but you never would show up." I can hear the disappointment in her voice. "Had I known our son had gone rogue in starting the divorce, we'd have told her right away what was happening."

My body shudders as I lean forward, placing my face in my hands. What have I done to us?

"She sat right there, on that same couch, and was wrestling with whether she was doing the right thing, and accepting that her marriage was really over, even if you had moved on. Brody had helped her pick up those pieces that were shattered when everybody's life imploded over two years ago."

My mother grabs my hand and tries to release the fist that I've made after hearing how Brody wormed his way in. He's known for the last two years that his uncle was dead and that this situation should've never have happened.

"So, she moved on." I simply say, and stare at the corner where my daughter's toys are arranged.

"Don't you dare blame her for this, mister. You were the one who didn't let anyone in. You kept secrets from everybody and this is of your own making," Grandpa tells me straight. "We have only been in contact with her for the last year, and she is slowly trying to put the pieces of her life back together. I can only imagine what that poor soul had to endure while she was pregnant, then raise our perfect angel with no family around. I, for one, am glad she had Brody to lean on. Well, not now that we know how he's lied to her, to keep her for himself."

He's right, this is of my own making. We are only here because I thought I knew what was best for her. I did this. Me. I've lost my family on the decisions I made, and didn't listen to others.

"Don't you go and start that self-loathing." Grandma shakes her finger at me. "I've known you since you were eight years old and the moment Saylor stepped into your life something woke inside of you, like chains were released. I've never known you to give up so easily, and I don't expect it to happen now. Not when your family is on the line."

"But you just said that she moved on two months ago," I counter.

"She didn't know that there was another option. She didn't think you ever wanted her again. Is it going to be easy? Hell no, but if you don't want that precious angel calling Brody, daddy, for the rest of her life then I suggest you pull yourself together by your boot straps and fight for what's yours."

Hearing Grandma say that, I immediately tense and my brain starts to work up plans on how to get my woman and daughter back, but a dark thought clouds my mind.

"What if I've truly pushed her away though? What if she wants nothing to do with me, even after I tell her everything?"

"Levi, there isn't a time that goes by that I don't catch her in our room looking over your pictures in there. She doesn't know that I watch her, but I see her every time. She opens the door and takes Halo in there, she points to you and then whispers in her ear." My heart aches when she says this because I know what she's saying, my name to our daughter. "I don't think she'll ever be over you. She's going to need some time to process everything, but you can't give up hope."

I nod and try to formulate a plan.

I check the clock and see that it's getting late, and knowing that my grandparents like to turn in early, I stand.

"I'll see you both tomorrow. Thank you for taking care of my family when I couldn't," I say and grab them both in a tight hug, crushing them to me.

We say our goodbyes and my security and I drive away from their house. My mind is racing, and the farther we get from my family, the more I can't stand it.

"Jacobs, take us to Jackson's ranch," I say in the quiet car. He cuts his eyes over to Mitch quickly and then back to the road, thinking I didn't catch it, but I did.

"Sir, I think it would be best to go back to the hotel and regroup in the morning. Today was draining, and I think you might have a better head on your shoulders once you've had some rest." Mitch tries to coax.

"I know you mean well Mitch, but there's no way I can rest knowing that my family is in the same vicinity of me. Take me there."

"Yes, sir."

We drive for a while; in the dark it's hard to decipher what's around but the black top road ahead of us. Finally, we pull over a cattle guard and then follow the path up to a large ranch style house, from what the headlights reveal. My heart is ready to leave my chest at the thought of seeing her again, but this time she'll know that I'm here.

We park in front and I think how this is only the second time in my life that I am a complete and utter nervous wreck; the first was asking her to marry me. Mitch must sense it, so he turns to face me.

"Levi, Brody Jackson is a military man and if he is anything like what I remember, he'll protect them with his life." Why is he telling me this? "If he's backed into a corner, we'll need to proceed with caution so that no one is hurt." He must see the questioning on my face, so he explains more. "For the last two and a half years, he's been playing *family* with your wife and now daughter. I'm sure he'll see it as you coming to take his family from him." I nod, now understanding. "And for the love of God please keep your temper under wraps. This isn't going to be a walk in the park for anyone."

I nod and take in what he's trying to convey, then inhale a deep breath.

We exit the vehicle and walk up to the porch with Mitch, Jacobs and Colbert flanking me. One more deep breath, and I knock steadily on the thick wooden door. It takes a while, but I can hear voices on the other side, and wait before I knock again. The door flings open and Brody Jackson stands tall, with both his shirt and belt unbuttoned. He looks disheveled, like we just interrupted something intimate. I swallow the bile that is threatening to come up, at the thought of what we just stop them from doing.

"Sorry guys, but we already know about Jesus," he candidly says, and moves to close the door.

Fucker! He knows exactly who we are.

Before he can close it completely and before I can stick my hand up to stop it from shutting, Mitch shoves his boot in the doorway. He presses his chest right up against Brody's chest, so that they are both nose to nose.

"I think you can make some time to hear what we have to say, then depending on your answers, we might need to have that talk about Jesus," he says, punching Brody in the gut, making him double over, and it causes him to back up a little, allowing the rest of us to walk in. *So much for keeping our cool.*

I take a quick look around the living room and find it cozy. I can smell that she has recently baked some of her treats. There are pictures of my girls all over the room; Saylor definitely added her touch to this house. Without thinking, I pull off one of the pictures of Saylor and Halo riding a black horse, and hold it in my hands. They are both smiling so brightly and laughing. Mitch and Brody take a seat on the couches. He's breathing heavily from the blow to the stomach and fidgets slightly, looking over at the hall-way that I assume leads to the bedrooms, where my girls sleep. It must be only a matter of time before Saylor comes in.

"Why Brody? Why did you lie and keep her hidden, even after your Uncle passed away?" Mitch starts questioning. I know they go way back, and Mitch has been kicking himself for not follow-ing up after he questioned Brody over two years ago.

Brody gives a shrug and leans back in the cushion, looking bored at the conversation.

"I was given a job and I did what I was expected to do." He looks over at me and smirks. I want so badly to knock his teeth in, then that smile won't be so pretty. "I think it worked out for everyone involved, don't you think. He," Brody points over to me, "got to move on with his life of being a bachelor, and I got the family I've always desired."

Putting the photo in my pocket, I turn, giving this piece of shit my full attention.

"There's just one problem with that, you little fucker. That's *my* family and I have no intention of letting anyone else fill my shoes. I'm husband to that beautiful woman living here temporarily, and that little angel has my blood running through her precious body. Mine. This is *my* family and no one is taking my place," I growl out. Is this guy for real? Does he really think any man with a woman like Saylor would give her up willingly?

"It seemed easy to throw them away over two years ago," he retorts, pushing off the cushion and placing his arms on his thighs, leaning in.

"I didn't throw them away and you know it. The truth is about to come out and the only person to be thrown away is you!" I seethe.

The baby monitor goes off and the small cry from my daughter fills the room. My heart aches as I hear a creak from a door, then my beautiful wife's voice. "Momma's here baby bear, don't worry." Saylor starts to hum, and I can almost picture her swaying with our baby girl in her arms. I need to see them, to be with Saylor to comfort my daughter.

We are all distracted for a brief moment when the front door bursts open and five men barrel through, all armed with guns in their hands. *What the fuck?*

Jacobs and Colbert all draw theirs as Brody shrugs off Mitch, then bangs on the end table, making a drawer on the side shoot out. Brody reaches in and produces a gun, and stands up with his guys. Mitch stands in front of me as Brody aims his gun at us.

"I think it might be best if you and your goons leave my house and property before this gets out of hand. Patrick will see you out," he says and flicks the gun towards the door. "Sadie and Halo have everything they need right here."

Sadie? They changed her name to hide even more from me.

"I'm not leaving without my family," I growl out and buck up. "I've been waiting too long to get them, and I'm not going anywhere."

A voice down the hall comes into ear shot, and I'm worried for her safety with all the guns drawn.

"Brody, I thought you were coming to bed?" Saylor asks before she comes into view. She's wearing a short silk robe and her short hair is pulled up half way. "I've got the shower ready." She stops when she sees the room filled with men, who are all pointing guns at each other. She gasps, and both of her hands cover her mouth to keep her from screaming. She takes in the room, and her eyes finally find mine. "Levi," she whispers. It's as if our bodies are magnets; she takes a step in my direction and I do the same.

Of course, that shithead and his rat pack try to block us, but it's the growl of a monster at the side of Saylor's leg that has me at a complete halt. A very large German Shepherd is now standing between me and the love of my life. He's baring his teeth and his ears are pointed straight up, ready for battle if need be. Saylor leans down and pets him between the ears and speaks to him. He follows her command and sits at her feet, but doesn't take his eyes off of me or my men.

"Sadie stay back," the fucker says, and maneuvers to her. He bends down and whispers something in her ear and she goes ramrod stiff. Her eyes widen, but she never turns them away from me.

"Baby," I start to say, but she cuts me off.

"What are you doing here Levi, and all of you put your fucking guns down, there's a baby in this house," she demands, and for the first time in forever, I'm as hard as a rock. Not from only hearing her voice say my name, but how she commands the room. All of Brody's men holster their guns, as does Mitch, but Jacobs and Colbert are unsure if they should do as she asks. Mitch nods and they follow suit.

I clear my throat, hoping not to sound like a frog.

"I've come for my family," I say, not taking my penetrating eyes off her. "You're a hard woman to find."

She huffs, then crosses her arms over her chest, making the round tops of her breast sneak through.

"I find it hard to believe that *The Levi Thorne* took all this time to find me. With all the resources at your disposal, now you come? I don't buy it," she challenges.

"It's true. We've been looking since before I came out of the coma." I look over at Mitch to confirm, and he nods to her. Her eyes widen again, and they flick back and forth over mine to affirm her suspicions. Brody grabs for one of her hands and secures it in his, making me want to rip it from his shoulder.

"You can't have her, she belongs with me." Her voice betrays her, and I imagine Brody has filled her head with more lies regarding the reason I'd be here.

"Baby," I calmly say with both hands up in surrender stance. "I'm not going to take her from you. I came to get you both."

She looks even more confused, and I hate how lost and uncertain she looks right now. She's always portrayed a sassy, confident sense of personality, and this isn't that.

"Why now and not two years ago? What's changed? Tired of the single life, or ran through all of Blaire's escorts? I've seen the pictures with you and that brunette. You can't lie about that."

This is not the place to have this discussion. I want to explain everything to her but alone, and away from these men so they can't turn things around or twist my words.

"Come with me and I'll explain everything. We can talk and you'll know exactly what has been going on for the past two and a half years. Please, give me a chance," I plead. "There is so much that you don't know that has happened."

"So, you can brainwash her? Not a chance buddy," Brody pipes up, giving his unwanted opinion. He wraps his arm around her shoulder and my body goes rigid.

"If you knew anything about that woman beside you then you'd know that no one makes decisions for her *but* her," I chide him. "And we both know who the brainwasher here is."

"I—" she sounds unsure and not as confident as earlier. "I— think you should leave," she staggers out, and shifts her weight from one leg to the other.

"Saylor, please give me the chance to explain. I've waited years to see you and meet our daughter." I hate using our daughter as I way in, but I'm desperate right now.

Saylor closes her eyes at my words and I can't let her reject me again, my heart couldn't take it.

"I'm staying at the Arvon Hotel in town, come by anytime. I'll be staying there for the foreseeable future." I notice a pen and pad on the coffee table, and lean down scribbling on it. "Here is mine and Mitch's numbers, if you need to reach me." I walk over to her but Brody's goons try to step in the way, and that damn dog shoots up and bares his teeth. I stretch out my hand, and to my pleasure, she extends hers to take it. I deliberately graze my fingers over hers, and that explosive tingling shoots through my body. From her gasp I know she feels it too. *We still got it.* Looking into to her brown eyes, I can't help but get lost once again, like when we first met. "Please give me a chance, baby."

I reluctantly drop my hand and take a step back. I need to leave here before I level out every man and animal in this room.

As I walk out, I can feel my heart splinter as the distance once again forms between me and my loves. I need to get myself under control before I send her running again and this time, I'll probably never find her.

Once in the car, we head out towards the hotel and I whip out my phone. It only takes two rings before she picks up.

"Yes, sir," she answers quickly.

"I'm having the jet sent for you. I need you here with me, Sarah," I vaguely say. She knows what I need and what I'm referring to. Saylor was right about me having another brunette in my life. She's been with me for the last two years and I've leaned on her for most of it. I can only hope Saylor will understand, when it all comes out, and not hate me even more, with all of my fuck ups.

"Yes, sir, I'll be ready and waiting."

"I'll send you details as soon as they are made. We might be here for a while so pack accordingly."

I hang up, ending the call, and tell Mitch to make the arrangements for her to arrive as soon as possible.

CHAPTER ELEVEN

Turning over for the fiftieth time in the last hour, I check the blood red digital clock at five past six in the morning. Not wanting to lay here any longer, I scoot over avoiding Brody's arm and leg, so as to not wake him. I need to be alone with my thoughts so I can figure out how I'm going to deal with this *Levi* situation. I wanted to sleep in my room last night but Brody insisted that I not be alone in my thoughts; I'd be up all-night worrying. Too bad that's exactly what I did anyway.

It would be so easy to ice him out, take off and run away again, but is that what I want for my daughter? I've been her only parent till now; what gives Levi the right to come charging in? He says that he's been looking for me, but I find it hard to believe with his resources and Mr. Buttons having knowledge of my whereabouts. Mitch, who I had once gotten to know well when I was first married to Levi, has always been truthful with me, but my pessimist side tells me that my ex-husband pays him to do as he wants and says. So can I really rely on his word?

Ugh!

Another side of me says that I need to let him be a part of Halo's life, even if he is only there popping in and out of it. It seems that his attention span lasts only three to six months at a time. Can I really put Halo through that? A part time dad? She deserves to have the best, everything her little heart desires. It would be so easy to get wrapped up in his charm and mesmerizing eyes, and his sex appeal. The whole package really, but can I emotionally survive the next time he walks away to find greener pasture?

No. No I can't. Brody is the safe bet and my safety net, who has been there through everything. Sure, this was an assignment to him at first, but what he confessed to me last night, before the bottom fell out, has my mind in a tailspin.

We just put Halo down in her crib, and I'm laying across Brody's body as we make out like teenagers. My thoughts from earlier, about feeling the electricity that only Levi can make me feel, are almost gone the more I'm concentrating on nothing but Brody. But something is nagging me in the back of my mind. When we were picking up Halo tonight at Grandma's house, she smelt just like Levi. She had his scent on her clothes and I swear a hint of his aftershave lingered on her body. It's weird because I haven't smelt him in years, but as soon as I picked her up, I knew that smell right away. Of course, I chalked it up to maybe Grandpa changing his cologne, but still something was there and I can't quite put my finger on it.

Our bodies are rocking against each other and our hands are roaming. It wasn't but a few hours ago that he was inside of me, thrusting and enjoying our climaxes, before having to pick up my baby at Grandma's house. Brody pulls back from my swollen lips and looks deeply into my eyes. I can see everything through them; happiness, future, security, family.

"I love you, Sadie," he professes, and I gape at him. "I don't want

you to say it back, but I just couldn't go another minute with you not knowing. The way we came together was unconventional, but I knew shortly after you'd change my world. I see a future when I'm with you and Halo and when you are ready, I want to take that next step with you." He leans in and covers my mouth with his.

We pull away to catch our breath and let me gather my thoughts. Is this too early to love each other? Do I love him? We have been dating for almost two months, and have been 'married' for the last two and a half years. He's been there for me and seen me at my worst. He loves Halo like his own. What more could I ask for in a man? Do it Saylor, leave the past behind and don't look back. Stop waiting for someone who is never going to come back or love you again. But can I love him when my heart clenches every time something reminds me of Levi?

"Brody I…" The sound of car doors slam, bringing us out of our bubble.

"Go start the shower and get all lathered up, I'll be there shortly. Patrick and some of the guys stayed late to do some inventory," he says as we stand, so he can open the door that was just knocked on. We both head in different directions but he halts me before I make it to the hallway. "And don't you dare touch yourself before I get there, or I'll tan your fine ass."

"I guess you better hurry up." I twirl and head down the hall as he opens the door. His delicious threat is just enough to get my head back on straight. I've come to miss being touched and loved on that only a man can give me.

A blanket is magically placed across my lap, as Brody sits down in the other rocker on the porch, bringing me out of my thoughts from last night. He places the baby monitor on the side table, along with my morning coffee. When Halo was born, tea and water wasn't cutting it anymore with the long nights of feeding, and I needed something with a little more kick. Coffee has been my savior to survive.

"Thank you."

"Did you get any sleep at all last night?" He asks as Zeus makes his way through the doggie door and nudges my leg, while looking out at the pasture. "I see that the workers are going to be enjoying all your treats from your lack of sleep," he says. Baking has always been a passion of mine from a young age.

Glammy taught me how to make simple cookies when I was five, and by the age of ten, I was providing desserts to our town for special events. She and Granddad helped me open my bakery in LA, down from their spa. I didn't think it was going to be as successful as it was when it first opened, because of the competition around the big city, but it caught on like wildfire. I was able to pay back all of their investments within the first six months. At first, they refused the money saying that it was their pleasure to jumpstart my dreams, but I wanted to show them that I was working hard and able to make it all happen.

"Not really. My mind wouldn't turn off."

"We can go and leave this place behind. Just tell me what you want, and I can have us out of the country in a matter of a few hours." Brody snaps his fingers. He is such a good man; any girl would be lucky to call him husband. "I mean it, in fact, let's go on a little vacation, just the three of us. We can go to the beach, Halo can play in the sand and ocean for the first time. Our own little family vacation."

"I wish it were that simple." I heave out a long breath.

"It can be, just say the words and I'll make it happen," he assures me. We sit in silence for a while as I replay the last two years of my life here on the ranch. I reminisce about my childhood time with my grandparents and occasionally my dad; being out here on this acreage of land has its healing abilities. Country living is the best medicine. Halo loves it here, with all the animals and being around people. Everly and I used to get lost out in the forest back where we grew up in Janesville, California.

We rock for a while, waiting for Halo to wake so that we can start our day, but I feel a cloud covering us today. Eventually Halo stirs and I'm about to stand, but Brody puts a hand on my knee, stopping me from rising.

"I don't want to lose you and I feel like ever since last night, you're pulling away from me. I don't want Thorne to try and taint your view of me by telling you things about me that aren't true," he cautiously states. "I still stand by what I said last night. I love you and I want to take the next step with you. We can have the fairytale life, Sadie, you me and our little bear in there."

I place my hand over his, "Brody, no matter what happens you will always be a part of mine and Halo's life. I wouldn't be here right now with that beautiful, healthy little girl if it hadn't been for you. You aren't losing me. I'm just not sure why *he's* decided to come now. And what in the world did he mean that he's been looking for me and Halo this entire time. Mr. Buttons hasn't even tried to contact us so doesn't that mean the threat is still out there? Is Levi putting us in danger by coming here?" My mind won't stop running a mile a minute, but I need to focus on my baby. I squeeze his hand and lean over and peck his lips before standing and making my way to Halo's room. Brody looked lost in thought, so I leave him there while I take care of my girl.

After breakfast, Brody and I take Halo over to the barn to feed the chickens and cows. She loves chasing them around their pen, trying to give them food. When all the food is given, I take her over to her little jungle gym some of the workers and Brody had built for her when she started walking. When the temperature starts to rise, I bring her inside for a snack and juice while Brody checks in with Patrick. I'm loading the dishwasher as Halo plays with Ginger, our newest German Shepherd that was a birthday gift from Brody, and Zeus in the living room. She rolls all over them and they just sit there and take it like champs. There is no doubt in my mind that they would die before something ever happened to that little girl.

The backdoor opens, as Brody walks in on the phone talking. He winks when he sees me, then passes the phone over to me. I give him a questioning look and he just smiles before striding over to Halo, and wrestles with Zeus.

"Hello?" I answer.

"Saylor, dear, you're still coming over to help with the baking for bridge club tonight, right?" Grandma asks.

I slap my hand over my forehead and mouth a curse.

"I'm sorry Grandma, I completely forgot. Yes, I'll be there shortly." I check the clock and it's after ten. "I'll be there in thirty minutes with bells on," I joke.

"Great. Thank you dear, I don't know what I'd do without you and that little blessing in my life," she says, and I feel the same about her. I'm about to hang up when a thought crosses my mind.

"Is Levi going to be there?" I don't know if I'm ready for round two yet, but I should at least ready myself if he is.

"Not that I know of dear. He called this morning and said he had something to do at the hotel till after lunch."

"Okay, thank you."

We hang up and I rush off to the bedroom to change into some jeans and a shirt with my sneakers. I do a side braid, now that my hair is growing out from when I first arrived here, to make sure no loose strands are going to get dipped into any icing, before walking out to the giggles in the living room. Brody is at the bottom of the dog pile with Zeus on top of him then Ginger is across Zeus with Halo, of course, on top. I swear she's going to be a cheerleader at the top of the pyramid, with the way she's always on top of the pile.

"Okay, party people it's time to tame this down a notch before a little person or dog gets hurt," I joke, because I know not one of them would let Halo fall.

"You heading out to Grandma's house?"

"Yeah, I forgot that I agreed to help her with the baking this week for her bridge club."

"Is *he* going to be there?" Brody asks, with a look of disgust on his face.

"I asked, and she assured me that he wasn't. Grandma might be a lot of things, but a liar is not one." I see Brody slightly flinch, but doesn't say anything.

"I can go if you want. I'm not much help in the kitchen but I can be there in case *he* does show."

I gently place my palm on his cheek.

"Thank you, but I can manage. Don't you have the vet coming today anyways?"

"Ugh! Fine, do you want to leave Halo with me? She can be my sidekick and order the guys around." He tickles her sides, sending a wave of cute giggles throughout the room.

"I've got her. You know Grandma only has me over so that I'll do all the baking and she plays with Halo the entire time anyways. And I think Glammy and Granddad might be back from their cruise. I can't remember if it's today or tomorrow but they'll want to see this little one the moment they arrive."

He turns his head slightly, and in such a loving manner, he kisses my palm.

"I'll be home later, kay," I say, leaning over two dogs and pucker up to his pouty lips.

"Kay," he says against my mouth, then I scoop up Halo making Ginger whine like I'm taking her toy away from her. "When you get back, there are some things I need to tell you after we put this little one down for bed." Usually that means that Brody did or bought something he shouldn't have. I can only imagine what it can be this time. Last time, it was in the form of Ginger, our newest German Shepherd addition to the family.

Once we get to Grandma's house, I hear voices in the kitchen then see a woman I haven't seen in a long time, Alice Thorne.

"Oh Saylor." She cries as she rushes over to me and Halo, and pulls us into a tight hug. I'm frozen in place, unsure of what to expect from her. The last time I was in a room with the Mr. Thorne, he was hanging me out to dry. Does she think I was capable of hurting her son too? Why is she here and why didn't Grandma give me a heads up?

Halo wiggles down and out of my arms, before heading over to Grandma for treats she only gets here. *Thanks a lot kid, I needed you for a shield against these people.*

"Oh Saylor, we've been so worried about you. There hasn't been a day that has gone by that we haven't tried looking for you," she gushes, still holding on to my upper arms like I might bolt.

I want to roll my eyes, but my good manners kick in, although I'm sure she saw my eyes narrow a little.

"Mrs. Thorne," I say tersely. This isn't my house, so I know it would be rude of me to ignore her, but this is so awkward.

"Saylor?" She looks confused, but covers quickly. "Please call me Alice, we have so much to talk about, but I think you need to discuss everything with Levi first. He'll fill you in on the events that happened and caused all of this to be set in motion." She continues to fill me in like I know what the heck is going on around here.

Now I'm the confused one in the group, but remain stoic. I'm not letting my guard down with her or her son any time soon. They've put me through the ringer over the past two years, and I'm not about to be led down the road to destruction again.

I give her a nod of acknowledgement, then walk into the kitchen where my daughter and Grandma have migrated to. Looking on the counter, I see pans filled with sweets to feed an army.

"I thought you needed some help, Grandma?" I question, with a raised eyebrow.

Grandma at least has the decency to look guilty, then uses Halo as a shield by picking her up and cuddling her, all the while her great-granddaughter is stuffing her face with a cupcake.

"Oh well, I might've exaggerated slightly." Her cheeks pinken and the tip of her nose blushes. This woman will be the death of me. "Besides, I needed to see my precious baby."

"You just saw her yesterday," I say deadpan.

"Yes, but Sharilyn and Alan are about to be back from their trip and you know how I hate to share my playtime with her," Grandma says, waving her hand around. She's lying so hard because both sets of great-grandparents love spending time together. They even vacation together, and are even looking to buy a large piece of property and build a small compound, so that they can both have a house near each other.

"So, what is the actual reasoning for having me come over?" I have a pretty good idea, but don't want to presume anything.

"Well," Grandma pauses and taps her finger against her lip, as though she's deep in thought. "I guess while Halo and I decorate all these desserts, you can have the long-awaited talk with

Levi." She peeks over my shoulder, and I know that this was her and Alice's plan all along. I just don't know if I should be mad at her for pushing me.

"I-I'm not sure that I'm ready to talk to him yet," I weakly say. What I really want to do is beat the shit out of him for just showing up without any notice.

"Yes, you are. You've wanted to yell at him for the past two years and this is your chance," Grandma urges.

"Ellie!" Alice gasps.

"What? The girl has been put through hell and she deserves to have all that frustration put to good use. I'd even recommend a few good whacks with a wooden spoon." Grandma shrugs, then pops a bite of a chocolate chip in her mouth. "Go and speak with him, Saylor, and then let him tell you his side of things. Either way, you two are going to have to work together as a unit to parent this little one. She deserves to have both parents in her life, even if they can't be married anymore."

"We aren't married anymore," I snap back, not meaning to take out my anger on her. Alice takes in a quick breath and caresses her hand to her chest. "Mr. Thorne made sure to publicly file the paperwork while I was being beaten by that horrible woman in jail. Remember?"

Alice starts to shake her head, "No Saylor, it's not what you think. You two are still…"

"Alice, I think it would be best if Levi was the one to tell her." Grandma pushes, then turns back to me. "Go and talk with him." She gives me a knowing look. "Give him a chance."

"Fine," I throw my hands up in the air. "But don't ambush me again like this Grandma," I scold her.

"Promise," she says while crossing her heart, then forcing us into a group hug with Halo in the middle.

I turn and see Alice with the biggest smile on her face and bouncing on her feet. She still looks a little unsure and would love to join in on the hug, but I'm not ready to receive any kind of affection from the family who kicked me to the curb so easily.

Grandma is right. I need to push my own issues with this family aside and try to get along with them, to some extent, for Halo's sake. Taking Halo out of Grandma's arms, I set her down and walk her over to Alice. Squatting down to her level, I point to Alice.

"Baby bear, this is your other grandma, Alice. Can you say hi?"

Halo is a loving child, but only to ones that she knows. She hugs me tight and burrows in my neck. Standing up with her in my arms, I need to set some boundaries with her and the rest of the Thornes. After everything I've been put through, I'm the one who's in charge.

"I don't mind you spending time with Halo, but it has to be in the presence of Grandma and Grandpa, myself, my grandparents, or Brody. If I find out that you and Mr. Thorne have taken her somewhere, without one of them, you won't like what happens," I threaten. I've never been a violent person in my life, but when it comes to Halo there's nothing I wouldn't do to protect her.

"Saylor, I'd never do anything to hurt or bring harm to my precious grandchild," Alice says affronted, but I don't care about her feelings. I'm not going to let them take my child away from me, and possibly turn her against me. I've seen firsthand the poison that Daniel can spew, and I won't have it in front of Halo.

"And I bet you never thought your son would pay for escorts either," I snap, then realize what I just said. That is between her and her two sons, not me. "Those are the rules. I know firsthand how cruel you all can be, and I won't have that bleeding over onto my daughter and have you poisoning her. Take it or leave it. I sure as heck don't want Mr. Thorne alone with her at any point."

"That won't be a problem, dear. Grandpa and I will make sure to abide by your wishes," Grandma says, rubbing my arm. She gives a stern look over to Alice, then takes Halo over for some more sugar.

I go to leave the kitchen, but Alice blocks the doorframe.

"Saylor, I'd never hurt her or you for that matter. I'll do as you ask and earn your trust again. Daniel won't be a problem," she pauses for a moment then continues. "We separated a while back and…" I hold my hand up, not wanting to hear about their marital problems. She obviously must understand and stops talking. For the last two years, I've stayed drama-free and the peace I've felt is something to cherish and cling to.

It's hard to be like this to Alice because she'd been nothing but kind to me since I was first introduced to them, but things are different now and the well-being of my daughter comes first and foremost. It seems as though everyone has an agenda these days, and I want to make certain that Halo isn't a target or used to manipulate me.

The drive over to the Arvon Hotel is longer than expected. My mind is all over the place and I'm ready to jump out of my skin at the thought of being in the same room as Levi. Alone. Last night, I was in a room full of people and he still made me feel as though it was just him and I. There was still that spark from when we first met, and when he reached out to hand me the piece of paper, the jolt shot to the deepest part of my soul. How can he still hold that kind of effect over me after all these years?

Dig deep, Saylor. You hate him. He left you and instead of letting you leave the marriage with dignity, he publicly humiliated you for the world to see.

Parking the truck in the front, I check the mirror one last time before exiting the vehicle. *Why do I care what I look like? He can just shove it where the sun don't shine!* Walking in, there are a few people ahead of me at the front desk. It gives me a minute or two to calm my nerves and get my thoughts under control. I should make sure Mitch, or one of the security guys, is in the room so that things don't get out of hand. Lord knows I hope the hotel bolted down most of the furniture so that I can't use them as weapons when Levi tries to use some lame excuse for his absence all these years.

I'm brought out of my inner thoughts, when I hear Levi's name being used. Turning my focus on the person at the counter, I'm struck in the chest.

"Yes, Mr. Thorne is expecting me. He called ahead to make sure I had access to his room," the lady in a flowing dress tells the receptionist. Her brunette hair is up in a French twist as she taps her heels against the tiled floor. Stepping to the side slightly, I take in her profile and all the breath leaves my lungs. It's her. The woman who's been photographed with Levi at several functions. "The name is Sarah."

I take a step back forcefully, trying to put some distance between us. He's moved on and the last shred of hope I've been holding onto in my pathetic being makes me want to curl up and die all over again.

She's given a key card and told that Levi's suite is 209, up the stairs and to the right at the end of the hall. She grabs her rolling suitcase and makes her way towards the stairs.

I take the empty seat next to the entrance door, and try to wrap my head around the last twenty-four hours. This is it. I can walk right out the door, go pick up my daughter and try to co-parent the best I can, with a man who I'll never have again. Or, I can pull my bootstraps up and confront the man who's been tormenting me the last few years. Get everything off my chest, then head home to Halo and Brody and go back to my quiet, safe life here.

I'll be accommodating when it comes to Halo, as long as he abides by my rules and only my rules.

Releasing a sharp breath, I stand with a new-found determination and march my resolved ass up those stairs to confront my ex-husband and his new woman. Hope she knows what she signed up for because momma's not holding back, just like the restaurant all those years ago.

CHAPTER TWELVE

With each step on the stairs, my anger fuels my body to climb higher and higher. How dare he say he's here to bring me and Halo home when clearly, he's got someone else. Why can't he just leave me alone like he has for the past two years?

Marching down the hall, I see someone sitting down in a chair at the end of the hallway, checking his phone. They must hear my footsteps and rise the closer I get. Guess it must be break time for security. Good thing I didn't have a gun, I'd already taken this slacker out before he saw me.

"Can I help you, miss?" Levi's security asks.

"I need a word with your boss," I snap, and cross my arms over my chest while tapping my sneakers on the wood flooring.

The door across from 209 opens, and Mitch walks out but stumbles when he sees me standing in front of him. At a closer look, I can see some light scaring that wasn't there before.

"Mrs. Thorne," he says surprised. Yeah, well that makes two of us buddy.

"Saylor," I demand, correcting him. As soon as possible, I plan on legally getting my last name changed back to Gentry, now that I know I can come out of hiding.

"Saylor," he smirks when he repeats my name. "Are you here to see him?" He looks over at the closed door that will lead me to Levi.

"That's the plan. I think it's time for some answers, don't you?"

He sighs, as if in relief, and it confuses me.

"Of course. I'm so thankful we were able to find you. Besides Mr. Thorne, we've all been searching frantically for you. I hate that you were able to slip through my fingers. I take the blame for this long gap."

I'm not sure I believe this, but I bite my tongue. Why would it be Mitch's fault?

"How's Tina?" I change the subject.

"Great. She can't wait to see you and meet baby Halo," he says with a mega smile on his face, then he turns serious. "I know you have a lot of reservations but please hear him out. There's a lot that you don't know about, and some things are going to be a little hard for you to hear, but please be patient and give him a chance. I can see the fire in your eyes and I know you want to cut him up, and it might cloud your judgement on what Mr. Thorne has to say."

"I think I already know what's been going on but thank you anyway, Mitch."

He nods, then retrieves a key card from his pocket and walks me over to the door of 209.

"Then I wish you luck, Saylor." He swipes it above the handle and a green light signals that the door unlocks. He holds down the handle and opens it. Stepping aside, he motions for me to enter.

I stroll in and hear the door close, then relock. Around the corner, I can hear voices and it makes me falter and almost trip over the future Mrs. Thorne's suitcase. All the anger I was feeling, as I was stomping up the stairs, has taken a back seat and my legs are now jelly.

"Yes, I understand." I hear a woman's voice before hearing a thud, then silence.

I'm not sure my heart could handle walking in on a sex scene with that woman and my husband. *Ex-husband.* Shaking my head and steeling myself, I turn the corner. Levi is pacing the room by the window, and my new replacement is on all fours in front of a wingback chair, a good distance away from each other. They both haven't noticed me, until Levi turns to re-pace in the opposite direction. He freezes and looks as though there's a ghost in the room. The woman looks up at his stopped movement, then turns in my direction.

"S-Saylor," Levi whispers like my name is a prayer.

"Levi," I toss back, and I'm pleased at how firm my voice is.

"I...didn't think you'd actually come here."

"Is that why she's here?" I snap and point to the woman still on the floor. "Really Levi, you should be more discrete unless you want the world to know where I've been stashed away."

He looks to the woman, then back to me like he forgot she was there, then shakes his head.

"She's not what you think. I needed her here with me to get through this."

I raise my hand, not wanting to hear about his *needs.*

"I don't really care what you do these days, but I came here to discuss Halo." I cross my arms over my chest and wait, but then see the lady grab the phone that I didn't notice before on the floor and put it to her ear.

"I'm gonna need to call you back, sir." She ends the call. So, was she not referring to Levi as sir?

"Mrs. Thorne, it's a pleasure to meet you." The girlfriend rises from the floor and stalks over to me, with her hand outstretched. "I'm Sarah Blake."

I look between her hand and face a few times, then over to Levi, who is still standing in the same spot as earlier.

"Does she really need to be here, or can she come back after we finish discussing our situation. I'm sure she's great and all, but I think this is between the two of us," I say, ignoring the woman.

"Saylor, Sarah is—" Levi starts, but I interrupt.

"I don't really care at this point. She can be the Queen of England, but I want it to be made clear that when we iron out some type of visitation that any of your flings are not to have any contact with my daughter." I shoot a death glare to the woman, then back to Levi.

"Mrs. Thorne, I can assure you—"

"It's Saylor, or hasn't Levi told you that we're divorced? I'm sure that the title might be yours if you play your cards right." I can't seem to stop myself at the pelting that keeps coming out of my mouth. My filter has long since left the building, but years of hurt and anger have festered for too long, and I'm on a rampage.

"Saylor stop it!" Levi yells from across the room, and makes his way over to us. "Sarah is not anything like that, she's been my shrink for the past year."

He pauses, and lets that settle in.

His shrink? Shrink. What happened to Dr. Jordan? Although, if he'd listen to me from the start, then he'd have dumped Dr. Jordan right after we married.

They both must see the confusion on my face and help me out.

"Mr. Thorne came into my services as a referral from Dr. Jordan," Sarah starts. Her demeanor is really professional and calm. *Too* calm for me.

Well, shit, color me surprised. Then my mind flashes back to everything I just said to her, and I'm ready to jump out the window at how I've been towards her.

"But the photos online?" My mind is reeling, trying to make sense of this information. Am I being made to look like a fool, or is this real?

"We both were at the same charity functions a few times and were talking when those were taken. They were very harmless and what they don't show is my husband standing right next to me in all of them," she confirms, and I take the moment to look down at her ring finger to see a wedding band set. She then presses a few buttons on her phone and swipes over a ton of photos of her and her husband. He's older than her and balding. *Don't judge, Saylor! God, I feel one inch tall.*

"I'm sorry for the things I said earlier, I thought—" I trail off.

"Apology accepted." She looks over at Levi, then nods in my direction to get him to engage in our conversation. I've never known Levi to be so quiet before, and it's a little weird. "Mr. Thorne, would you like for me to come back, or stay while you and Saylor have this discussion?"

"Alone. I'd like to have her alone," he answers, never taking his eyes off of me. His intense stare causes me to squirm slightly, and I'm tempted to ask her to stay as a shield.

Sarah picks up her notepad from the side table and walks out the door. We are both still standing in the same spot, not moving. I've waited for this moment for a long time and now that it's here, I can't remember what I wanted to say, or yell at him for, that matter. Everything has been thrown out the window and my mind is blank. I was expecting one thing, and now that it wasn't what I thought, the lack of wind has deflated my sails.

"What happened to Dr. Jordan?" I ask as the door closes

behind Dr. Sarah Blake. The woman who I thought for the last eight months was my husband's new shiny trophy.

"She wasn't working for me anymore. The more I saw her, the more I knew that she wasn't helping. Sarah, or Dr. Blake as she prefers, has really helped me deal with a lot of past issues."

There is silence and only the hum of the room's air conditioner fills the void.

"She specializes in abandonment and early childhood traumas," he blurts out, and my eyes widen. Levi never wanted to admit that he had issues of abandonment and trauma as a kid, and it shocks me that he was admitting it now. "When I first met with her, she was able to breakdown a lot of my walls because I was so broken, with not being able to find you and Halo, that I spilled the beans to a complete stranger."

Levi lets out a slight chuckle.

"Dr. Blake likes to keep things very professional, and decided to take me on as I conquered my past."

Swallowing hard, I can't help but feel my cold heart melt slightly after hearing that.

"Linc and I even moved our parent's grave here and found some of my mother's family. I haven't contacted them, but I have their information if I wanted to. It was something that I wanted to do with you when we found each other."

"That's great Levi, really. I'm glad that someone was able to help you overcome that trauma. I know it couldn't have been easy," I softly say. He shrugs as if it's no big deal, but for Levi who bottles everything up and hates to talk about himself, this is huge.

After my mom died from cancer, my dad and grandparents made sure to get me some help. I was a preteen who didn't understand how to we went to seeing her every day to never seeing the person you loved the most ever again. Everly came along, shortly after her passing, and we latched onto each other and never let go.

Levi didn't get the same help. I think that the Thornes thought he was too small to have any issues or trauma from his parents dying, ultimately from the guilt of his sister's tragedy, to see that he needed someone to talk with. Yes, his brother Linc was there, but he was a kid too and they shouldn't have had to carry that weight around all by themselves. Levi internalizes everything until it boils over. His brother has always taken the brunt of anything that ever popped up, but it made it to where Levi wasn't processing and overcoming the hurdles he was facing, just tamping them down further. I always thought Dr. Jordan placed Band-Aids over Levi's internal battles. When I tried to bring up moving to a different therapist, he squashed it. So I stayed quiet, because at least he was seeing someone.

"I knew that I had a daughter out there and if I was going to be the father she needed me to be, then I needed to get my shit together and put to bed all of my demons."

"You're going to be a great dad, no matter about your past. Halo only needs to be loved and cared for. Everything else comes day by day."

He lifts one side of his mouth, and I find myself doing the same.

"Would you like something to drink?" Levi offers, breaking the silence.

I nod, not trusting my voice until I can get my backbone in order again. It's a little early to be drinking, but I have a feeling I'm going to need it.

Levi walks over to a cart, and fills two drinks with an amber colored liquid. He quickly tosses one glass back, then refills. I finally will my legs to move, and walk over to the large window of his suite that overlooks the little town.

"I've waited so long to finally have you in the same room again. I think I might be dreaming," Levi says as he comes to stand behind me. "I know you don't believe me, but I have been looking for you from the moment I woke up from my coma."

I roll my eyes, and a goofy grin spreads across his face, as he sees it in the reflection. He really expects me to believe that.

"I find that hard to believe, Levi. With your resources, you could find anything, at anytime, anywhere. Please don't try and fill my head with bullshit. I was born at night, but I wasn't born last night."

"It's not bullshit, baby. I've looked for you and Halo the entire time; ask Mitch or Dean. They've been with me the whole way. Linc and Olivia can confirm it too. They've been running the law firm while we've been dashing all over the world with tips on your whereabouts. Every time William or Dean found something, we jetted off, no matter how small the lead was."

What? That makes no sense.

"Levi, come on, Mr. Buttons knew where I was. I was a phone call away."

"Burt Buttons died a week before I woke up from my coma," he fiercely states.

The words echo in my ears and my knees go weak, making me almost drop my drink. That can't be true, we would've known about that. Brody would've heard something and told me about it. Surely the government is more organized than that.

I start to shake my head and stumble to the sofa to sit down. I need some space to think about this. He's mistaken.

"I promise I'm not lying. Mitch has all the paperwork to prove it. Brody Jackson came to handle the funeral arrangements and then made another trip to finalize his estate weeks later."

My head snaps over to Levi, who is seated on the sofa with me, but at a safe distance.

"No. No that can't be. Why would Brody handle those arrangements? Only family deals with that," I counter. He must be mistaken, or is trying to pit me against him. My anger builds in the silent pause. "I hate you Levi. You'd do anything, or say anything, to get what you wanted. I mean, it's your job to persuade people to believe what you tell them."

He looks as though I've slapped him, and if he were any closer I might. How dare he try and turn me against Brody. A man who's been with me this entire time. Brody has been nothing but kind, and honest, and loving to me and my daughter this whole time.

"Saylor, I'm not lying, I promise on our daughter. Brody is the only nephew of Burt Buttons, the late District Attorney of Los Angeles. I can show you the proof. Mitch even met with and interviewed him while I was still in the coma." He whips out his phone and texts something. "He and Brody know each other from their time in the military. Burt Buttons hates Linc and I because we always beat his ass in the courtroom. He and Linc have had a horrible rivalry since graduating law school. I think he saw my bombing as an opportunity to try to retaliate against us."

My mind is having such a hard time focusing, that I don't even hear Mitch and Dean come in with boxes of files. They place them in front of me, and I jump up out of my seat. This is a set up. Surely, they are wrong about this.

"No, this is all bullshit. How dare you come in after two years and try to ruin things for me. You've ended our marriage and moved on and so have I," I yell. "You really are a piece of work. What, Blaire run out of prostitutes for you to give you the perfect public image, and now you think you can come here and ruin what I have with Brody? To think that I'd believe some made up paperwork you had your guys falsify?"

"I've never moved on from you Saylor. I've been holding vigil, looking for you and our daughter. I received those two letters and almost went mad when I read that you thought I'd moved on. It was only the newborn photos that kept me from losing my mind. Seeing her finally gave me the hope to continue to live and continue looking for you."

He looks so sincere. This is not the strong, confident man that I dated and married all those years ago. Wait, what about the other photos?

"What about the other photos?" I ask. I sent pictures of Halo every few months, updating her growth.

"What other photos? We only received the one letter about you leaving and the one about Halo's birth." Levi snaps his head over to Mitch and Dean, and they both look just as confused.

"Saylor, we only received two letters in the mail from you. I personally made sure to check the mail before anyone else did," Mitch says, and my stomach bottoms out. I have to set my glass down on the table to free my hands, so that I can wrap them around my body.

"I-I sent one every few months updating you on her. There were several photos included. Her first birthday, I sent an entire roll of film," I say but don't recognize my voice. Brody made sure to run into town to send them off to his contacts before making their way to LA, to throw off where we were located, in case the person responsible was watching or intercepted them. "You promise you didn't get them?" I ask, losing the battle as a sob leaves my throat. Why would he lie? Or Mitch or Dean for that matter?

Levi shakes his head and stands to walk over to me. I know

if he touches me right now, I'll fall apart. Holding up my hands, I stop him.

"Please don't touch me," I whisper, and he nods but doesn't move from in front of me.

"Baby, I love you and our daughter more than anything in this world. You have to believe me."

I brush the back of my hand against my eyes to keep the tears from falling. What in the hell is going on and why are there so many interferences?

"Then why did you throw me away? Why did you humiliate me in front of the world and then send me divorce papers?" I begin softly, and am yelling at the end.

He lets out a long sigh and goes back over to the sofa. He pats next to him, and I follow him without second guessing. Once he's sure I'm not going anywhere, he slides off the cushion and onto his knees in front of me. His shaky hands bolt down on my knees and he looks up into my eyes. The spark that is always there when we touch ignites through my body, but I try to ignore it as I brace myself for what he's about to reveal.

"Let me start off by saying that I'm the world's biggest asshole, and I'll never forgive myself for putting you or our daughter through that. I can only hope you'll forgive me and let me make up for the lost time I've created between us." He leans down and places his forehead on the tops of where his hands are attached to my legs, then turns and looks me straight in the eyes. "I am truly sorry for that day at the restaurant. At the time, I thought I was doing the right thing by you and our child. I was warned not to go down that road, but didn't listen. During the lunch, I immediately knew what a horrible decision I had made, but couldn't find you to make things right after you had left."

"You're not making any sense."

"A few weeks before the restaurant…"

Levi goes on to tell me how the baby and I were being threatened. He has Mitch and Dean show me the letters and photos that were sent to Thorne Law Firm, and I can't believe that someone could do something so horrendous. The fact that this person was able to get this close and go undetected sends a shiver down my spine. Then they show me the files on the car bomb; they were able to cross match that it was the same person who sent the threatening letters along with also sabotaging the car.

"Did you find out who did this?" I ask.

He nods, "It took us a while but we finally found out who it was, and he won't ever be a problem for our family again."

I blow out a breath I didn't realize I was holding.

"Who? Who would do something like this to us?"

Levi looks over to Mitch, and Mitch gives him a firm nod.

"Kevin Jenkins. He was a Senior Associate at the firm while we were dating. He was fired but Linc thought he went away quietly. We were horribly wrong."

"But why?"

"We think that it had to do with firing him after catching him falsifying some documents on a case he was working on. What I didn't tell you is that it got physical and I stepped in with a beat down. The more we looked into him, the more disturbing things we found on him. He also had a big dislike for the Thornes, so that might have pushed him even further over the edge." Mitch speaks, up but doesn't elaborate any more than that.

"So, he's in prison?" I ask, wanting to make sure no harm can come to Halo.

"Kevin Jenkins is dead. When the police finally closed in on his location and had him surrounded, he blew himself up before they could get in there and retrieve him. The medical examiner did a thorough job and did the test twice to confirm it was his body," Mitch explains the details to me.

We sit there quietly for a while, just taking everything in. I definitely wasn't expecting to hear all of this when I came over here. It put things in a different perspective, but I still need to keep my walls up. Levi has the ability to crush me and all my resolve, with a simple look or touch, and I need to be strong. I've lasted being away from him for over two years, and I don't want to look back.

"Why Levi? Why didn't you tell me about the threat? We could've avoided all this… heartache if you'd just let me in. Look at this mess you created."

He drops his head and looks at the floor towards his bare feet. If it were possible, he'd curl up into a ball.

"I was scared," he whispers. I must've heard him wrong.

"Scared? Of what?" The Levi Thorne I knew was never scared of anything or anyone for that matter. He was always on the quiet side of things, but that didn't mean he was a pushover and would let someone steamroll him.

"My whole life I've only had to take care of myself. Me. If I messed up, I always had Linc to rely on to help me fix things when I was hurt or in trouble. Then I met you, and you turned my entire world upside down. You became everything to me. Every breath I took was in some way to make sure you were taken care of. I lived, ate, slept and breathed for you," he pauses. "I realized that I was walking in everyone else's shadow and doing what they thought I should be doing. It was like waking up for the first time in my life. You gave me a purpose, and I promised myself that I'd do whatever it took to be the man you deserved and the best version of myself for you." He turns and finally looks at me. "When I first received those letters and then the photos, my mind went to a dark place. A place I hadn't been to since I was a child. The thought of losing you and then our child turned me into another person. You didn't know this but I had six guys watching you at one time. Four of them while you were in the apartment. Every photo had my nightmares coming back and I wasn't thinking clearly at the time of our fight in the restaurant."

The sound of his voice tears open my heart hearing his struggle. I try to put myself in his shoes and it breaks me apart.

"When I got the letter demanding I leave you, I made a rash decision. My thought was that we'd have a public argument, and that would give us some time for the team to catch the guy, or guys, behind all this. Never did I think that the next time I saw you would be two and a half years later. I know now that it was truly wrong, but at the time the thought of someone taking you away from me, because of one of my cases turning someone into an enemy, had me going into overdrive. You are the most precious thing in my world, and if something were to ever happen to you because of me, I'd die. And then to add Halo in the mix, it sent me over the edge. Dr. Blake and I have been working on what I can and can't control, and I think I've made some real strides."

"You could've just told me and I would've played along, Levi. We were supposed to be partners. We made vows to be one," I sharply say. "I get that everyone has catered to you since you were a kid but when we got married, we became team. When you hurt, I hurt, that's how a marriage works."

His sad eyes make me ease up on my anger, but I'm still mad that he shouldered this alone and brought us to this point.

"I know that now, and after you left the restaurant, I knew I'd blown it and made the biggest mistake of my life. I thought you'd come back home after a few hours, and then we'd discuss it and I'd tell you everything and then we'd make up and come up with a plan. I had no idea the downhill snowball that started after it."

"Well, you should've known you can't make decisions for others Levi. It's like playing Russian Roulette," I snap. "Everything would be different and now look what you've caused. Your daughter doesn't even know you but what few pictures she's seen at Grandma's house," I fume. "I haven't seen my best friend in years and she doesn't know my daughter!"

"I know, don't you think I know that?" His voice is shaky and he pulls at his hair. "Every day that went by, I wanted to go back to that horrible moment and choose to do things differently. I drank myself stupid for weeks on end to pass out, just so I didn't have to replay everything and live with the consequences. Your father made sure to rub it in, don't worry."

"My father?" What did dad have to do with this?

"Saylor, your father has hated me from the moment I met him and is a constant thorn in my side," he sneers.

"That is not true Levi, and I think you need to watch what you say about him or I'll walk out that door and we won't speak again. You've never even met him," I demand, pushing his hands off my knees and get up from the sofa.

"It's true," he defends. "When he came to the hospital, after I woke up, he told me how I wasn't fit to be in the same room as you. That I'd never equal up to the man you deserved. I knew he was right but I at least wanted to try, the thought of not being with you wasn't an option for me. Adam told me that one day you'd wake up and leave my pathetic ass for a real man who didn't have such fucked-up issues. That if I couldn't even take care of my biological parents, then how could I handle someone as precious as you." His voice cracks at the end, and my heart clutches.

I'm speechless. Why would dad say that to Levi? Dad had been out of touch for almost a year when I met Levi. When I tried to phone him, he never answered any of my messages or sent any correspondence to me. I've grown used to it over the years but I have my grandparents, Everly and her dad as a support system.

"I thought when the threat came in that I was man enough to handle your care and safety, and thought my plan was the best. I wanted you out of the spotlight for a while to secure the threat, then I'd be able to show you that I truly was the man you deserved and could count on. I handled major court cases with people's lives on the line. You'd think I could keep my wife and child safe." He looks as though his heart is breaking in two, right in front of me.

"Levi—" I say, but can't finish. I need some distance to think everything over. I can't be in this room any longer with this man. I need to process all these details that have been thrown at me.

A thought crosses my mind. "Why the divorce then? If this was just an elaborate plan to lure out the culprit, then why did your father come to the jail and serve me divorce papers, demanding I sign them?"

A flash of anger crosses his face and his eyes narrow at my questions.

"Saylor I never told him to do any of that. I was just as shocked to learn about it when I woke up three months later. I never told him that I wanted a divorce from you. He did that all on his own without my permission. Daniel and I have not spoken since; I told him he was dead to me at the hospital after what he did. There was no coming back from him knowing you were pregnant and didn't help you. As far as I'm concerned, I hope to never see or hear from him ever again. Everyone feels the same and has little to do with him. After a while, Mom couldn't be under the same roof and separated from him. He's lucky I didn't run him out of the state and ruin his career."

"So, you didn't want to divorce me?" I sound pathetic asking, but I want to hear the words.

"Never," he breathes out. "Saylor, we aren't divorced. You are still very much my wife."

"What? But I saw the papers and was told they were filed. Brody said—"

"Dean and William found out and put a stop to them immediately, then had the documents sealed. They never made it past that point, and I had the courts erase every bit of evidence of those documents from their mainframe when I woke up."

Now this is too much.

"We're still married?" I screech.

"Yes baby, we are. You are still very much my wife and I'm still very much your husband." He closes the distances between us and places a hand on my hip as I chew on my thumbnail, thinking about what he just said.

My head was already about to explode before this, and now I can't even begin to comprehend this new information.

"But me and Brody have—" I stop before I say we've been together intimately for the last month. This is a straight up nightmare for all parties involved.

"It's okay, Saylor. I realize that you thought we weren't together. Dr. Blake has helped me tremendously about the realization of that. I don't blame you for trying to move on when you thought I did." Why is he so calm about this? The Levi I knew before would level this room if another man even looked at me with lust. I'm so confused about all this. He helps me sit down in the chair that is located next to my wobbly legs and bends down on the floor again.

A thought crosses my mind and I want to bang my head against the wall. I've slept with someone when I was still married. Neither Levi nor I were virgins when we met, but when I made those vows at the courthouse with him, I meant it. A sickening feeling boils in my stomach, making me want to vomit.

I stand quickly without saying a word, grab my purse and make a bee line for the door. I hadn't even noticed that Mitch and Dean left the room. As my hand touches the knob to open the door, Levi's hand comes up from behind me and presses against the door to keep it closed.

"Please stay, baby. Don't walk out that door," he pleads, and I feel his chest at my back, making my legs wobble. My body comes alive when he's near and I almost give in. But I can't stay, not when I've had so much thrown at me. This isn't what I was expecting to hear when I came here. I thought he'd moved on and that he truly didn't want me in his life anymore.

"Maybe you should've thought about the consequences before you set all this in motion." I shove his hand off the door, ignoring the zing from our touch, and rush out and down the hall towards the stairs. I can hear him pleading with me in the distance, but my legs don't stop even though my heart wants me to turn around and run back into his waiting arms that will never let me go.

When I make it out of the hotel and into fresh air, I feel dizzy. How did this get so messed up? One decision changed the course of everyone's life and shattered my world. Can I fault him for wanting to protect me and Halo? Is it fair to hate him for what Daniel did at the police station, making me think this is what Levi wanted?

Alcohol. I need alcohol, and a lot of it. I make my way past my truck and towards the bar across the street. I can't go home right now, Brody has got a lot of explaining to do. Would Levi and I be back together if Brody had told me his uncle died? What else could Brody be keeping from me? Why didn't he tell me that Mr.

Buttons was his family? When did he go back to LA? Was it one of his trips for 'business'?

I hear a female's voice screaming my name right before I enter into the bar.

"Saylor!"

I turn to see who it could be and am engulfed into a warm hug. Dark hair covers my face and the tightness around me is almost suffocating.

"I thought I'd never see you again," the smell of vanilla wafts in my nose and my muscles release all the tension from the last few hours. I hear a sob and my body shudders against hers.

"Oh Everly!" I cry against her neck.

We hold each other under the awning as we cry our sorrows out. Finally she pulls back at arm's length.

"I'm getting you microchipped," she tells me, then pats my shoulders and cups her hands against my cheeks. "I've missed you so much. Where is the baby? What is her name? Have you been here this whole time?"

"Wow, slow down," I say as she peppers me with a ton of questions all at once. "How are you here?" I ask once our tears have stopped flowing.

"Levi called Linc last night and we got on the first plane we could," she explains. "This whole time you've been here close to Glammy's town?"

I nod.

"Brody has a ranch outside of Helena."

"Brody?"

"Yeah, I think we might need some drinks and I'll explain everything," I say, and lead her into the bar. We pick a booth, off in the corner, and I immediately start a tab for us.

"Keep them coming, please," I say to the bartender as she comes by.

"By the way, I let Dad know last night after Linc got the call. Your dad has been AWOL for a long time. So, you should reach out if you can to let him know about all this. Now, spill," she says as our first round of drinks gets quickly delivered.

As I tell her what I went through the day I was arrested, she sits and listens, holding my hand as I relive one of the worst days of my entire life. Losing my mom at such a young age was the worst, but this was up there. I explain about Mr. Buttons and how he'd said that Linc and Levi work with the courts to relocate people until it's safe to return, and bring her up to date with Brody. Drinks have never stopped flowing as I tell her everything that led up to this morning. I show her pictures of Halo and she cries even harder at how big she's getting. We talk about everything, trying to catch up on the last two-and-a-half years.

"I can't believe that Glammy and Granddad kept this from me," Everly says above a whisper, and I get up and walk to the other side of the table, engulfing her in the tightest hug.

"Please don't be mad at them. When they and Grandma and Grandpa first saw us in Helena about a year ago, Brody made it clear that if they told anyone then we'd have to relocate."

"This is all so crazy, Saylor."

"I know. It's like a spider web of bad decisions and regrets all weaved together."

"What are you going to do, now?" Everly asks as she licks the salt off the rim of her margarita. "If what Levi is saying is true, then this Brody guy has known that your husband has been looking for you all this time, and has kept my niece not only away from her daddy but me."

"I'm so confused, because if you were to meet Brody you'd see that he's a great guy and would never harm anyone. I don't know what to make of all of this. I feel like I'm a pawn in some game and have no idea who the players are," I admit.

The bartender comes over and drops off a round of lemon drops and I spot Everly's ring finger.

"So you and Linc tied the knot?" I point down at the massive engagement rock on her finger, with a matching wedding band attached.

Everly looks down and twirls it around her finger.

"It was a long road but we got married barely a year ago," she says.

"What took you so long?"

"When everything happened at the hospital with Daniel and finding out what he'd done, Linc and I unintentionally took sides. At first, he was defending his dad and Levi and I were furious at what had been done to you. I knew you'd never harm Levi but everyone was so scared for Levi, and then you went missing. A lot of words were exchanged in the heat of the moment and I called off our engagement."

"Oh Everly, I'm so sorry," I reach over and hold her hand.

"I moved out and back in my apartment for a while. Dad and Adam went into mission mode, trying to locate you and find any leads through their contacts, but was hitting dead ends at every turn. Linc tried to contact me several times over the next month but I just didn't want to hear it. I was devastated that you were gone and that the person I wanted to spend the rest of my life with could think my best friend would try to kill her husband. It was a mess."

"I can't even imagine that all of us were so effected by some crazy madman who wanted revenge on Linc and Levi. Our life could be made into a Lifetime Movie." We laugh. "How did you work it out?"

"I know right. Anyway, Dad was the one who set us up. I went to a restaurant, thinking I was meeting him there, and it was Linc who showed up. Dad texted and told me to hear him out, and to either fix things or cut ties completely. So we started slow, *again*, and then eventually he popped the question and we married a month after him asking. He said he didn't want to take any more time away from our future than what had already passed. I had wanted to wait until you came home but Linc insisted that you'd never want me to wait."

"He is right about that," I tell her. She seems so happy. Marriage is a perfect look on her.

"How was it seeing Levi again after all these years?"

That is such a loaded question.

"He looks good," my inebriated-self blurts out, and I clamp a hand over my mouth.

"Those Thorne brothers sure are good looking," Everly stares off dreamily.

"I'm conflicted because I want to strangle him for making decisions about our life without including me in it. But then I also want to climb him like a tree and never let him go."

"Well, life is too short to have regrets," she slurs, and I think that lemon drop was the drink that pushed us over to the drunk side. "Is Grandma keeping our baby tonight?" she mentions as the bartender comes over with another round.

"Here is another round ladies," the woman places two lemon drops each in front of us and then two shots. "Thought you might like to try this shot, it tastes like a jolly rancher."

I pull out my phone and send a text to Grandma, asking her to keep Halo overnight and she gladly accepts. Before I lose my nerve, I send a text to the number Levi gave me letting him know about Halo being over at Grandma's house, in case he wanted to spend some time with her. I turn my phone on vibrate, not wanting to be disturbed. Just as I place it on the table, in case Grandma or Glammy might need me, Everly holds up the shot for us to toast.

"To maddening sexy men!" Everly cheers, and I repeat the same chant before our glasses touch.

Bottoms up!

CHAPTER THIRTEEN

Levi

Watching her walk out the door just now was like watching her do it two and a half years ago at the restaurant. I'm not sure what I expected, but I was hoping she'd stay. I'm sure it was a lot to process, but the thought of her going back to that bastard has me in knots. Something doesn't sit right about Buttons and Brody, and that entire situation.

A knock at the door brings my eyes away from the window, hoping that Saylor has come back to me, but it's Dr. Blake on the other side.

"I heard Saylor leave and wanted to know if you needed a session?" she offers with her notepad in hand.

I open the door wide to let her through and aimlessly walk over to the sofa to veg out. I was shocked that Saylor even showed up at the hotel. I feel like I didn't even get the chance to really talk to her. We only covered the threat and not the progress I've made being under Dr. Blake's care.

"Were you able to tell Saylor everything?" she asks, and it makes me roll my eyes.

"I told her most but not all. It was a lot to take in for her, so she left." I sigh and rub my hands hard over my face.

"And?"

"And, I hate that she probably is headed back to *him* for comfort when it should be me," I huff. "I know the role I played in this and take full responsibility, but it still hurts. Doesn't she understand what *his* role played in all this? I thought she heard what Mitch and Dean were saying but now I'm not so sure."

"Mr. Thorne—"

"Can't you call me Levi? I think after a year we should be on that level at least," I quip.

"Mr. Thorne, the reason you left Dr. Jordan was because you'd gotten too familiar with each other and thought she was more of a friend than therapist," she states, and I appreciate that about her but it still feels weird.

"Fine." I sound petulant but don't care right now.

"What goals are you wanting to accomplish while here in Montana?"

"Get my wife back and have my daughter never leave my side." I'm quick to answer. I've thought about this ever since we got off the plane here.

"And if your wife doesn't want to leave *him?*" Dr. Blake asks my biggest fear. We avoid saying his name out loud.

I know after speaking with my grandparents that Saylor and Brody are being intimate, and I hate the thought of her with someone else but as everyone reminds me, it's my fault.

"Then I'll just have to show and remind her why she chose me first. She has no idea what I've gone through to get here today and the changed man I am from it."

"That's good, Mr. Thorne. It's realistic and I think you have what it takes to get you there. Please remember that it's been over two years that Saylor has been away from you and a lot has happened to her as well. Even though she's had *his* help, she has been doing this on her own, essentially. It's not going to be 'a few flowers and chocolate' kind of situation to fix this."

"I know. Saylor hates getting flowers anyway; she thinks it's a waste of money since they die a few days later." I smile thinking how she's not like every other woman. Jewelry won't do either; she's an *actions speaks louder* kind of woman. Although, she did love it when I bought her new baking tools.

"Were you able to speak about seeing Halo? Or of all the things you've done to get you ready to be a father to her?"

"No, we only were able to discuss the threats that led to her leaving and the crash. We touched on *him* a bit, then she left when she learned we were still married and not divorced."

"Did she seem receptive in what you were saying?"

"I'd brought in Mitch and Dean to confirm when she had her doubts, but she seemed to take everything in stride."

"Well, it's a start, and hopefully after some time, she'll call you and the two of you can manage to have another conversation about the rest of it." She starts to gather her belongings.

"Thank you, Dr. Blake."

"Before I go, have you thought of the possibility that the end result is you and Saylor not getting back together, and only co-parenting baby Halo?" she asks.

"There is no scenario in this universe where that is going to happen or even become an option," I firmly state.

"Mr. Thorne, I understand that when you were in the attorney world you always got what you wanted, but when it comes to people there might not be an outcome in your favor."

"If, and I'm saying a big if, she and I aren't on the same page then I plan to tie her to the bed until she comes to her senses." I shrug.

"Mr. Thorne, I have to strongly advise against that." Sarah is getting herself all worked up and I can see that my humor didn't reach her. Although, I did tie Saylor up once after we got home from our honeymoon when she was being stubborn. That ended in the best sex ever, after we both calmed down and listened to each other. Some couples hold hands until the other partner is ready to listen and others tie their partners up. *To each their own, I say.*

After assuring her that I was only half joking, she leaves me and heads out for the rest of the day. A firm knock raps at my hotel door, and I make my way over to answer it.

"You look like shit," Linc greets me when I pull open the door.

"Thanks a lot," I tell him. "It's been a rough twenty-four hours. Come on in."

We walk toward the living space and I head over to the drink cart and pour us both a glass.

"Have you seen Saylor or your baby yet?" he asks as we both take a seat across from each other.

I can't help the smile that forms, "Yeah man, I saw both last night at Grandma's of all places."

"Grandma's? How?"

"I haven't got all the details yet but they've known where she was for almost a year," I fill him in. "I wish I'd told them about the entire situation and then we would've been reunited a long time ago," I say, then hang my head.

"Hey, we aren't going to do that. You've learned to a lot over these last few years and you aren't the same guy you were back then. Stop looking back."

"I know but I can't help but think that one decision altered so many lives."

"Tell me all about my favorite niece," Linc changes the subject, and I launch into every little detail I could remember seeing Halo.

"She's just… perfect. Saylor looks even more amazing than the last time I saw her," I can't help but say. "Did you come by yourself?"

"Everly went out to buy things for Halo while I took a call from Olivia about a case she's having trouble with. Reid said to tell you that he'll be here in two days after he's finished speaking at some dental conference across the world."

"Yeah, I got his text this morning."

"How are you feeling right now with everything?" he asks.

It takes me a minute to think of everything. "Relieved, anxious, stupid and mad."

"It's a lot to take in. I know you've been praying for this day to happen for a long time."

"She's moved on, from what little I've gathered." I say with a defeated sigh.

"In what way? You're both still married to each other."

"She thought Daniel pushed the divorce through. It didn't help that that fucker Brody was in her ear, I'm sure, feeding into whatever agenda him and Buttons were pursuing. Saylor basically said without saying that they were in a *real* relationship."

Linc starts to run his fingers through his hair and lets out a frustrated sigh.

"If that fucker wasn't already dead, I'd beat the shit out of his fat ass. I still don't understand why Buttons would basically kidnap Saylor and hide her away. I know he hated us for always winning court cases against him, but doing what he did is a whole new level of insane." Linc gets up from the couch and starts to pace the length of the room. "Okay, this can all be resolved as long as you both are willing to work things out. Surely, Saylor just needs a few days to process all this information, and then see you were just trying to protect her and the baby."

"That's the hope but we'll see."

My phone buzzes and I get a text from an unknown number, but realize who it is immediately.

Unknown: Halo is at Grandma's house for the night if you wanted to visit with her.

Even when I think I've messed up, Saylor has always given me a second chance. Or third, or fourth. I program her name into my phone and also send it to Mitch so that he can have it.

Levi: Thank you, baby. Will you be there?

Saylor: I'm busy and need some time to think.

I wonder if she's dealing with *him*. That smarmy lying bastard, who has been playing house to my family, knowing I've been looking for them.

Saylor: I'm trusting you to keep her there and not take off with her.

Does she think I'd kidnap our daughter? I'd never leave without her or Halo.

Levi: Never. I'd never do that to you, Saylor. When I leave, I plan on it being with the two of you by my side. Willingly, of course, unless you want to involve ropes!

Saylor: Don't, Levi.

Well crap, that didn't come off as I wanted it to. I guess my humor is best saved for Mitch these days. Maybe Halo will think I'm funny?

Levi: Don't what?

Saylor: You can't just expect me to drop everything and jump into your arms after everything that has happened. We are different people than we were two years ago.

Boy, don't I know it!

Levi: I know but I still plan on us being a family. I'll do and show you that I'm the man for you and earn it all back again.

Saylor: Spend some time with our daughter.

Levi: Yes Ma'am!

"If you're not careful you might split your face in half with that smile you have going on," Linc says, breaking me out of my texting haze.

"Want to go and meet your niece?"

"I'd love to since my wife has found your wife and are hanging out together," he informs me.

"Let's go then," I grab my wallet and hotel key, and walk towards the door. Off to Grandma's house we go!

After playing with Halo and tiring her out, she is beyond ready for a nap so I stay, rocking her to sleep. We had so much fun running and playing outside in the backyard. She is so fun and full of life. I can't believe that, even for a second, I doubted being a father. Everyone sat on the back porch and watched me and her as we played. She is everything I've dreamed of and more. I just hope Saylor will give me a chance to make this right. Our daughter deserves the best, and that includes both parents under the same roof.

My phone buzzes in my pocket, and I quickly reach to silence it before it wakes her. Placing her gently in her crib, I briskly walk out and into the hallway, to see who interrupted my time with my little angel.

"Hello," I snap answering the call, not seeing who it was.

"Mr. Thorne, I think it might be a good idea to come back into town," Dean states. He and the others stayed behind at the hotel. I didn't want more people than necessary around when I spent time with Halo.

"Why? What's wrong? If it's not life threatening, I'm not coming."

"Sir, after Mrs. Thorne left the hotel, I followed her at a safe distance, wanting to make sure she made it home securely."

"Okay, has something happened? Is she secure?"

"Sir, right now she is across the street from your hotel, and has probably drank her weight in alcohol, along with the other Mrs. Thorne."

"What the fuck are you talking about? Are they okay?" I ask.

"Yes sir, they've been sitting at the same table the entire time, pounding back drink after drink. I'm pretty sure the bartender has cut them off and has been putting shots of water in front of them for the last five minutes, with the ladies thinking it's still alcohol."

"Stay put and make sure they don't leave from the table," I order. "I'm on my way."

I hang up and look back at the closed door that leads to my

little angel. Placing a hand on the door, I make a vow to her even though she's too young to understand.

"I promise to fix this little one. I'll make things right between your mommy and me."

Striding down the hall, I spot Grandpa, Linc and Mitch shooting the shit.

"We need to go. Apparently your lovely wife and Saylor have been drinking at a bar across from the hotel this entire time."

"Ohhhh! So that's why we received a text from Saylor," Grandpa says thoughtfully.

"What do you mean, Grandpa?"

"Saylor sent us a text, asking us to keep the baby overnight earlier."

"Does she do that a lot? Let you keep Halo overnight?" I ask, pondering if my wife has somehow become a lush since we parted over two years ago. I wonder if I'm going to need to get Dr. Blake involved, if Saylor has become an alcoholic. I should probably Google if they offer AA meetings here in this little town. I wouldn't blame her, with everything I've put her through over the last two years.

He shakes his head.

"No, Saylor doesn't like to be away from Halo too long. Us and Sharilyn and Alan have to practically beg on our knees to get a full night with her." He chuckles, like we are all privy to his joke. "She's the best mother and always put Halo first, before anything or anyone."

I nod as we make our rounds of goodbyes before heading out to the car.

Less than twenty minutes later, Linc and I are walking into a place called 'The Watering Hole' and it looks like any other small-town bar. The music is playing low, pool tables are in the back corner and TV's are spread throughout the room.

We spot Dean in the corner, out of view, and he meets us half-way. Glancing over his shoulder, I see our little women with their asses at a wooden table. Saylor has her elbows on the table with her hands propping her head up. Everly isn't fairing much better.

"No one has approached them since they sat down. Only the bartender has spoken with the women," he informs us.

"Okay. Let's go and get my little firecracker before she falls out of the booth," I say and can't help the small smile that graces my face. Saylor has never been much of a drinker and when she does partake, she's the biggest lightweight, especially when it comes to drinking liquor. This should be fun. I've waited a long time to hear that sassiness come out in her.

I approach from behind and run my hand lightly up and down her back, and she shivers at the touch. The bartender stops making a drink and hurries over to us.

"Beat it buddy, she's not interested," he spouts. I have to give him credit for watching out for her.

Saylor slowly turns her head, but isn't shocked to see me there.

"It's okay Rusty, this here is my first husband," she slurs, and waves her hand in gesture at me.

"First? How many you got, Sweetheart?" He raises an eyebrow and looks at her with humored interest.

"Wouldn't you like to know." Her sass shines through and I have to muffle a laugh, but then hate that she even considers that asshole her husband. "This one likes to spank," she says and starts having a giggling fit. "Oh, and he can tie a knot better than any boy scout."

I've tied her up once and spanked her twice, before we were separated, and I love how she focuses on that. It gives me hope that she's been thinking of our time together and not the wife-stealer. Not wanting to spend our time talking or thinking about that fucker, or about my knot tying skills, Linc and I both dig in our wallets and pull out a handful of large bills and place them under their glasses of waters, then nod to Rusty.

"There's nothing wrong with a few smacks to the ass if you ask me." Rusty winks at Saylor, then takes her drink and money, along with Everly's before disappearing down to the other end of the bar. "Let me know if you're taking any more applications for future husbands."

She starts to have another giggling fit and tries to wink at him, but fails miserably.

"Baby, let's take a walk," I say, and help her from the wooden table. I watch as Linc sweeps Everly's legs up, bridal style, and carries her out the front door.

"Still bossy as ever, I see." I shake my head as she continues her sassiness. I learned at the beginning of our relationship that when Saylor drinks, her filter is nonexistent. She says whatever is on her mind. Most of the time, she thinks it still remains in her head but then her mouth opens and she lets it loose.

"If I remember correctly, you love my bossiness," I retort.

She lets out a dreamy sigh.

"Yeah you're right, but also your bedroom eyes. I turn to mush every time." I place my arm around her waist and she leans in to my touch. I relish the feel of her against me, and I pray that this isn't the last time I get to hold her.

We start to walk out of the bar and she's clinging to me, as every step is hard to keep her upright. I want to pick her up, but I don't know how she'd react, and the last thing I want is for her to push me off and we both go flying and she gets hurt. "You're still hard everywhere it counts," she murmurs, as I let her small, delicate hands roam freely. It takes all my will power to not sneak in the side alley and have my way with her when she's feeling me up. I just pray she stays above my belt. Slowly, we wobble across the street with the cool night air surrounding us to the hotel. Mitch and Dean are trailing us to make sure we're safely on our way.

Once we are down the hallway, I deliberate whether or not I should knock on Dr. Blake's door, to see if she wants to bunk with her, but my mind is telling me that she's my wife and I've been in need of her in the same bed for far too long. Even if it's just to lay next to. With my decision already made, Mitch gets my key card out and scans the door, opening it for us.

"Call if you need anything, sir," Mitch offers, then he and Dean both exit the room.

Saylor is still leaning on me and her weight on my body is sending me into overdrive. She smells like sugar cookies, the same as I remember, but with a hint of alcohol mixed in.

"I need a shower," Saylor states, and tries to walk over to the closed door by herself, only to find that it's the closet. "Oh—" she gasps, then giggles. That sound is what I've wanted to hear for so long. "I'm definitely bad at choosing door options, aren't I?"

I know she's referring to having to pick between staying in LA or leaving to keep Halo and herself safe. I hate that she even had to in the first place.

"Let me help you," I push, and lead her over to the next set of closed doors and turn on the light. The bathroom is a good size, with a large walk-in shower and claw foot tub. I turn the spout on in the shower and check the temperature to make sure it's not too hot. Maybe a cold shower will do us both some good.

"Why do they make them so hard to take off?" She whines with a huff. "No wonder people become nudists!"

When I turn around, I'm greeted by a sight that will be

ingrained in my brain. She is pulling off her bra while trying to kick her sneakers off. They find the rest of her discarded clothing as she moves to her jeans. I know I should let her have some privacy, but *damn*. My body won't move, and if it did, it'd be right in front of her, helping remove the remainder of scraps that hides her gorgeous body. I love that she's still comfortable with me seeing her like this. Her body has changed slightly. The stretch marks on the sides of her stomach, where she carried our baby, are beautiful. She's softer in her mid-section and it makes her all the more alluring.

She's having a hard time with her hands not cooperating correctly, so I willingly help pull her jeans and panties off. I'm on my knees, at the same, perfect level as her pussy, and I can't help but inhale her intoxicating scent. I let out a moan, and feel her fingers slide through my hair. My strings of control are being cut, one by one, and it's becoming harder not to just face plant right into her heaven.

Letting out a long breath, I force my body to stand. This is not how I want us to reconnect again. I tell myself, as an excuse, as to why I'm not ravishing her already.

"Let's get you in, okay," I say and step aside to let her pass. Something crosses over her face, and she looks almost disappointed at something. *Did she want me to touch her?*

I help her walk over to the shower and watch her almost hit the tiled wall once she's under the warm water.

"Shit, Saylor." I grab her to steady her, but she seems unfazed by my words.

"Aren't you going to join me?" Good heavens, this woman is going to be the death of me. "I'm sure you need a good scrubbing too." She giggles again, while wiggling her eyebrows and another string of control is severed. A man can only hold on for so long. *Lord, give me strength!*

Telling myself that I only want to make sure she's not going to hurt herself, I quickly strip down to my boxers, and my dick sighs in relief from being locked up in my tight jeans.

"My, my Mr. Thorne, I think you have a situation going on." She's eyeing my dick, that is poking out of the waistband, and it only makes me grow harder the longer she's eyeing me. "Has he missed me as much as I've missed his magical touch?" She licks her lips and I almost come instantly.

"Sh-shower Saylor." I grit my teeth, stumbling over my words because I'm seconds away from hauling her up to the wall and pinning her there for a long time; until I can get two years of cum released from my heavy balls.

"*Shower Saylor,*" she mocks me and finally turns away to wet her hair. "Don't you ever get tired of being so serious all the time? Life is short, Levi, live a little." She sways, and I place my hands around her luscious hips that have grown since birthing our child. Shit, the thought of my hands on her as I plow her from behind has me leaking cum. Christ, this was a bad idea. *Focus Thorne, now is not the time to be weak. She needs to trust you and you have a long way until that happens.*

She's staring at my chest and a wicked smile crosses her face. *Good God keep your mouth shut, you little vixen!*

"Your nipples are always so hard, it makes me want to lick and bite them." *Christ!* Another string cut and a groan leaves my throat at the thought of her touching me like that. That love I have for her sassiness, and her lack of filter I adore and think is cute, is coming back to bite me. "You should have them pierced. I read that it's an outstanding feeling when they're given a tug as you orgasm." *I beg your finest pardon, but what the hell has she* been reading? Porn? *Do not smack her ass. Do not smack that tight ass. This is not the time to encourage her.* "I've thought about doing it." She truly looks sad at the thought, and my heart melts that she has been missing me just as much as I have her. Even that fucker couldn't erase me in her thoughts and soul.

Everything she does is slow motion, so I take over and wash her body as my own pleads for mercy as I touch every inch of her silky skin. I do make sure her large tits have special attention, since they've grown from the last time I've held them. I may or may not have given them a squeeze. I also notice the marks on the sides of her stomach; evidence that I put a child in her belly. Carefully, I kiss each one when she's not looking down watching me. She couldn't be more beautiful or perfect. Once she is clean, and I hope sobering up, I towel dry her and she heads out into the room, hopefully a little more awake after giving her some meds and water to drink. I take my time drying off and will my dick to calm the fuck down. Removing my wet boxers, I toss a towel around my hips and go in search of some fresh ones for me and Saylor. I need to put some armor between us, or we are both going to be in trouble.

The moment I walk out of the bathroom, I should have walked right back in and called for backup, waving the white flag. There, sitting on the bed spread full eagle is my beautiful wife. She's propped up on her elbows and her eyes are giving me a *come-hither* look, as she pats the space next to her.

"Oh, lover boy!"

Christ, I'm in trouble.

CHAPTER FOURTEEN

Levi

"Levi," she seductively says my name and I fight back a groan. "Can you come and help me with something?"

I tell my body to stay the fuck put, but it's a traitor to my demands and starts to make its way towards her. She's a magnet for my body and it practically floats from the doorway to the end of the bed.

"What do you need, baby?" I ask the stupid question, hoping she's going to ask for some clothes, but I think I know what she wants. And I don't think I'm strong enough to deny her.

She gives me the most mischievous smile, which I've loved about her since we first met, and melt.

"I have this ache and I can't reach to soothe it out," the little minx seductively says.

Stay strong, Thorne. Don't fall for this now and have her hating you more in the morning.

"Where is it?" *Stop asking and throw a blanket over her ripe body.*

She pulls her knees up, exposing herself more and moans. *She fucking moans.*

"Everywhere." She pushes a finger in her mouth, and then pulls it back out. My dick jumps under the towel and almost pushes it to the ground. "But it really aches here."

Her wet finger dives down to her pussy, that I've tried not to stare at for my own personal sanity, and pushes in. Without thinking, I quickly lunge at her, to grab for her wrist, to stop her from torturing me.

"Oh my God, baby," I say as my eyes roam to her finger entering and exiting her pussy. She's drenched, and I can't remove my hand from her wrist as it continues to move in and out.

"You like that Mr. Thorne?"

"Stop, Saylor. Please, I'm begging you." My breath comes out in a pant.

It takes all my will power, but I release her wrist and take a step back.

"We can't. It would only make things more difficult."

She stops, pulls her finger out and sits up.

"You don't want me," she sadly accuses. "I thought you loved me?"

I have to close my eyes and take a heavy breath while counting. The smell of her arousal has tantalized all the senses in my nose, and I try to calm my urges to plow into her with my pulsing dick.

"Baby, I want you more than my next breath. And I love you more than my own life."

"Then what are you waiting for? I'm here. Isn't this what you've been waiting for?" She pouts, and I love her that much more.

How can she not understand that I'm trying to be a better man? To prove that I'm worthy of her.

"Because I want you to not regret this in the morning and

hate me even more. I love you so much, but I don't want to ruin this again."

"I knew I wasn't enough and you've moved on," she whispers as if she meant to only say it in her head, but her drunken self doesn't have a filter.

I drop my towel and show her just how much I want her, but regret it immediately.

"Does this look like I don't want you? I ache for you, and to be this close and not able to touch what's mine is killing me."

"Then touch me, make yours again." She spreads her legs wider, tempting me more.

"Please baby, I'm begging you," I plead again, but my words aren't even convincing me now. My body takes a step towards her before I even realize it.

For someone who's drank her weight in alcohol, she's quick and I've underestimated her ability. Or my mind is hazy having her naked in front of me. She jolts forward and captures my dick with her hands and mouth before I can blink.

"Oh, fuck!"

The last string of my sanity is cut and now I've lost all control of myself. I used to take pride in my self-control, but being with Saylor has thrown that out the window. And if I was smart enough, I'd jump out that same window to save myself, but like a man who hasn't seen or been with his wife in over two years, I yield and succumb to her.

"It's bigger than I remember." Her filter failing her again.

Maybe a little release will do us both some good? I think to myself as Saylor goes all the way down to the root of my dick. Jesus, I forgot how good it is with her not having a gag reflex.

We both are moaning, as my fingers find the back of her head, pulling her wet hair into a makeshift ponytail. The damage has already been done now, so we might as well enjoy it.

"That's it baby, take me in, suck me dry." I know I'm not going to last long as I pump in and out of her small mouth, loving how she sucks my dick. "God, I've missed you and your mouth. I love you so much, baby." I unleash and thrust my hips faster into her willing mouth. It doesn't take but maybe five more pumps, and my balls draw up tight against the base. "Take it, Saylor. Take every drop." I push her all the way down on my cock and hold her there, as rope after rope of thick cum shoots out and down her throat.

When I've depleted every bit of cum, she sits back on her haunches and wipes the corners of her mouth with a goofy grin. My breathing is coming out in sharp pants, making me light headed, but I can't help the smile surging from my face. *Did that really just happen? This feels like the many dreams I've lived off of over the last few years.*

Saylor gets back into her previous position and opens back up for me.

"My turn," she sings, and touches her big tits. "Can you do that thing that your tongue always does?" *I'm going to hell for this but what a way to go.*

I dive down between her thighs, and nuzzle her pussy with my face as I coat it with her juices. She tastes even better than I remember. I lick, kiss, nibble and bite all over her lower lips and clit. She's bucking under my mouth as she thrashes her hands on the bed. I move one hand and reach out for her tit and give it a squeeze. She's bigger than before the pregnancy and I love it. I love everything that it has done to her body. If it's possible, she's even more perfect.

"Ah, I've missed your tongue!" Saylor moans as her hips try to push up farther into my mouth, but I hold her down.

I know she's on the edge of coming, and I can't seem to slow myself to make this last longer as my mouth attacks her. With my other hand, I slide a finger into her soaked channel as she clamps down on me. I work in a second finger and if it's possible, she's just as tight as she was before, if not tighter. Focusing on her clit, I get to working my tongue when her legs stiffen and she screams down the house with my name on her lips. *Mine!*

In the heat of the moment, she snaps her head up from the bed and gives me a serious look.

Fuck! I knew I shouldn't have done this.

I shift from gulping up all her juices to my knees. My dick is telling me to shut the fuck up and dive in, but I need her to slow down. She's had a lot to drink tonight, and I think she's still in a foggy stage.

"Levi," she gasps, and pulls me closer to her so that we're side by side.

She trails her hands over my shoulder, as if she's inspecting me. Saylor touches the metal around my neck that holds her wedding rings. She stares at it for the longest time, then gently puts them down. I watch as she caresses each of my burn marks from the car bomb with her petal soft lips, and it makes my body shake. No one has touched me in years, and she is setting me on fire, making me ache to mold her to me and never let her go from my side ever again.

Her fingers trace over the scars where the doctors had to go in and stop the internal bleeding to save my life. From what the reports show, it was a miracle that I survived.

"Are these from the bomb?" Her eyes have turned sad, and lost their orgasmic bliss.

"Yes," I answer, but she doesn't lift her head to look at me.

Finally, she comes further down to my lower stomach where I have two new scars that are the newest to the collection.

"Crash?" She gives a questioning look, noticing that they are newer than the other ones.

"No." Do I want to tell her about them tonight?

"What are they from? They look like they happened not too long ago."

"They happened eight months ago."

"Eight months ago? Levi, they look worse than the other burns. What happened?"

"I'll tell you, but I have to tell you something else first," I say and she sits up straight and crosses her legs Indian style, leaving her naked body open and on display. I grab the small blanket at the end of the bed and cover her. There is no way I'd be able to focus on this if she is that exposed. I cover myself with a plush blanket to help focus on what I need to tell her.

"First, I want to tell you that you were 100% right about Blaire," I start, and see her cringe at that bitch's name. What a way to ruin a sexual moment, than to say that trolls name. "Everything you ever said about her was spot on. The morning before we had our epic fight at the restaurant, I went to see her at the police station. She tried to get me to help her and when she finally told me what she was in for, it hit me like a ton of bricks." I sigh and continue. "She had records and photos of everyone and every little detail. She kept files on all her clients and who she set up. Some of the photos were of underage kids."

"That bitch!" She yells, and clenches her hands into fists like she's ready to punch someone. "Boy, I'd like to get my hands on her and choke the ever-loving snot out of her." Saylor cups her hands together, making the choking visual as if she were doing it right there.

"The line is a mile long but no one got their chance."

"What do you mean? I'm sure between you and my dad there are some resources that will help make her prison stay very uncomfortable."

Christ, she doesn't know.

"Saylor, Blaire is dead. She died in a jail cell at the police station, waiting for her trial to begin."

"What? How?" I can see some of the haziness from her drunken stupor becoming clearer.

"She apparently hung herself with the bedding or something." I still have my doubts about it being a suicide, but could care less.

"Well, ding dong the bitch is gone! Hallelujah, at least there is one less horrible person on this earth." I couldn't agree more. "Damnit! I really wanted to kick her ass for what she did to me and Halo," she says as an afterthought.

The thought of what Blaire did to Saylor and our child makes me want to dig her up, pour gasoline all over her bones and set the bitch on fire.

"Like I said, get in the long line. Anyways, when she was arrested, she had files on me and every one of the models. She had some recordings of our time together, along with her time with Linc. I'm still not sure how, but my thoughts are that Kevin Jenkins and Blaire worked together somehow, and he was able to obtain those files."

She sits there, taking everything in as I continue.

"Somehow, after Kevin blew the building and himself up, he must've had the files sent to the families of my old cases that I helped keep out of prison, as an insurance policy if something were to happen to him. He'd given mine and Linc's home address, along with our entry codes to get into the buildings."

"Oh god, Levi."

"Yeah, well, eight months ago Mitch made me leave the apartment for some fresh air because I'd been holed up looking for you. We went around the corner for some sandwiches and on our way back, a guy was waiting for us outside of our building. When we got closer, he pulled a gun and shot me twice in the stomach."

She gasps and covers her mouth with both her hands, then reaches out for me, taking my hand, holding it in a tight grip like I might slip away. Tears fill her eyes and I want to cry along with her, but muster everything in me to stay strong through this and for her.

"Who did this to you?"

"One of the victim's fathers," I shrug, not wanting to talk anymore about the past.

"Was it bad? Any permanent damage?" She's wildly checking me out with her eyes like I might bleed out at any minute. "What is it with you and crazy people?"

"I don't remember much, but according to Mitch and Mom, I almost died on the sidewalk." I shrug like it's no big deal but in reality, I was minutes away from bleeding out on the concrete.

"No. You can't." I can see tears swimming in her pretty blue eyes and it makes my heart hurt. She might hate me now but she still cares about my wellbeing.

"Baby, I'm fine now and nothing is going to take me away from you or Halo. Ever."

She surprises me and flings herself over to me and lays me out on the bed, hugging me tightly to her. Her naked body now nuzzles up to mine.

"You could've died Levi!" She wails and the tears fall down her cheeks. I try to wipe them as they fall, but they come flooding down, dripping on my chest. I think she's had too much thrown at her in a short amount of time, plus the alcohol isn't helping matters.

"I'm here and I'm fine."

She rubs her nose and then shakes her head while trying to sit up.

"Wait, the last articles I looked up said that you were on the east coast, or something, for the last eight months or so."

"Linc had the firm send out that release so the paparazzi wouldn't try to hassle me and find out that I'd been shot and lying in a hospital bed, almost dying. The PR group thought it was the best way to continue business as usual, even though I haven't been back to work since the car bomb. I left the firm and haven't looked back."

She leans in and lightly touches the two bullet hole scars again, and then her mouth captures mine with a searing kiss. She opens her mouth and I take full advantage as my tongue dances along with hers. It's been years since we've shared a kiss, and it's just as explosive as it was our first time outside the bar we met at.

Saylor briefly pulls back and looks in my eyes, as if looking into my soul.

"You could've died, Levi," she says again and reclaims my mouth. We stay like that for a while until we're breathless and are forced to swallow air into our lungs.

"Give me your dick, Levi," she commands, shocking me. She grabs my hard cock in her hands and pumps it a few times. "Make love to me. Show me how much you've missed this."

"Saylor," My voice comes out as a warning, but I'd do anything she asked of me right now with her hands on me.

"Don't *Saylor* me. Give me your dick now and make up for the lost time. We've both been through so much and I think we both need this."

I really hate this. She's my wife and I should be able to enjoy every inch of her delectable body, but then there's a fine line that I don't want to cross and not return from.

She must see me battling with myself and continues.

"You said I'm still your wife, and aren't the duties of a husband to please his wife? Or would you rather I got it somewhere else?" She taunts, and knows exactly what she's doing.

Not thinking clearly, and pushing the thought of her and that fucker out of my mind, I make the decision.

"You want this dick, baby?" I grab my throbbing cock from her hand and give it a hard tug. "You want to be reminded of who you belong to?"

"Bout time you decided to join in." Her non-filter is shining through again.

I grab for those luscious hips and switch us so that I'm under her and she's on top of me. I really want to lay her down and worship her body for hours, but I know that I'm not going to last very long and with the way she's bouncing, we don't have much time anyways.

We both moan as I spear her all the way down to the base of my cock. *Home.*

"You always feel so good, Saylor. I will never get enough of this tight pussy for as long as I live." I grunt and grip her hips harder, meeting her thrusts. "That's it, ride me hard."

She bears down, making sure her clit rubs against my pelvic bone, and the orgasm from earlier starts to resurface again. I pick up my pace, pulling at her hard nipples, feeling my release on the threshold. Sitting up so that we're nose to nose, I bend slightly to wrap my mouth around her puckered nipple, causing her head to shoot back while she arches her back.

"Levi!" Saylor calls out as her orgasm takes hold.

"Come baby, cream all over my dick." My dirty words are her undoing, and her body shakes as her release takes over and she calls out my name again as it echoes throughout the room. I'm surprised that the front desk hasn't already called with a noise complaint.

I'm pulling her hips down harder and faster, as she leans her limp body against me, as I bounce her on my cock. Placing my thumb over her sensitive clit, I start to rub circles.

"One more, Saylor. Open up one more time for me and then I'll give you my cum."

"I can't." She moans, but there isn't any conviction behind it.

"Yes, you can." I change angles slightly, hitting a spot that makes her spine shudder. I know she's about to come again and work my dick even harder, deeper. "You like that?" She moans again and the beginning of another orgasm builds in her. "I know you do. Your pussy is gripping me so tight trying to milk me. It's missed its home."

"Give me your cum, Levi." She pants, losing her breath with each thrust and turning the tables on me. "Fill me up."

"Fuck!" I yell, then bite down on her nipple, making her clench around my cock even harder, sending us both over the cliff. I feel ropes of thick cum coat her walls as I wring out the last drop into my woman. I continue to bounce her slightly, until I'm sure she has every ounce of cum.

We both fall back against the bed with her laying on my chest, trying to catch our breaths. I rub her back, almost lulling us to sleep.

"You are the best thing to ever happen to me, Saylor. I love you so much and I'm never going to screw this up again," I promise after we've calmed our beating hearts.

Her breathing has evened out, and I know she's asleep. Gently,

I place her lower half to the side of me so I'm not tempted to enter her again once I've recharged, but leave her top half laying across my chest. I know that I should go to sleep, knowing that this will be the first time in over two years that I'll have a full night's rest, but I want to watch her for a while. To memorize her features again and to hold her like I used to. I'll never take her for granted ever again, and I'll show her every day how much she and Halo mean to me.

Hours have slipped by and I still haven't had my fill of watching her, but my eyes are heavy and my body is exhausted after we reconnected earlier.

"Love you," Saylor mumbles in her sleep and it's just another thing I love about her. When she's drunk sleeping, her truths come out. I never have to wonder because I know at night she'll always talk in her sleep and tell me things that she's keeping from me.

Leaning down to press my lips to her ear I whisper, "I love you too, Saylor."

I can't help it but for the first time in two years, I fall asleep with a smile on my face. I just hope when the sun comes up in a few hours that Saylor doesn't have any regrets about what happened here tonight.

CHAPTER FIFTEEN

Saylor

The sunlight burns through the window, hitting me across the face. Ugh! What in the world was I thinking yesterday, drinking so much? My eyelashes flutter open, but I immediately close them when the pounding in my head surfaces. Ah! Never again.

Turning away from the sunlight, my eyes slowly open and nothing around me looks familiar; the wall, pictures, furniture, nothing. Holy shit, where am I? I try to sit up but I'm suddenly not able to pull the strength to do it. I decide to wait it out and see if I can rest a little longer, then try again.

I wake with a startle, as there's a light snoring from behind me. What the hell? Brody better get all the sleep he can because when I'm done rimming his ass with my foot, he'll never want to sit down again. Gently, I pick his arm up from around me and slide out from under it. Scooting to the edge of the bed, I lift my body up to sit up and decide whether I need a throw up bucket or not.

There's a whine from behind me and as I turn to see what's wrong, my body flinches as I see Levi laying down in the same bed

I just exited from. Holy shitballs! Levi? What is he doing here? I take in my surroundings and see I'm nowhere near my bedroom, or in Brody's room at the house, but in Levi's hotel suite.

I jump up, like I've sat on a tack, and the room spins at my sudden movements. Balancing myself on the side table, I notice a bottle of meds with a cup of water next to them. Taking two for my headache, I never take my eyes off of his sleeping form. He's always been so handsome when he sleeps, so young looking. I had hoped when our paths crossed, he'd be balding or fat but once again, I never get what I want.

He rolls on his back and his hands go above his head, giving me the perfect view of his body as the sheet draws down past his waist.

Don't look Saylor. Don't you look at his dick!

Jesus, it looks even better than before. Everything on him looks better. God, I've missed his face and warmth, his arms wrapped around me never letting me go.

No, you hate him, Saylor. Stay strong and don't give in. This entire situation is his fault. Well, at least the restaurant part is.

Wait! Why is he naked and in the same bed that I just jumped out of?

I slide my blurry eyes from my toes to my chest and see that I'm just as naked as he is, and I let out a shrill. Oh no!

The noise must wake Levi because his eyes open slightly, and he reaches over for my body on the now empty space that I was occupying. He snaps his head over to me, and smiles when our eyes meet.

"Morning, baby!" He's still sleepy but his voice is smooth.

"Don't *morning baby* me, Levi Thorne! Where are my clothes? How did I end up in the same room as you?" I demand, then try to cover myself in front of him. "Naked! Levi, I'm naked for Saint Peter's sake!"

"Saint Peter? I didn't realize you'd taken up religion," he jokes, but when I don't laugh or even smile, he turns serious. "You don't remember last night, do you?" He sits up, and so does his hard dick.

Focus Saylor, don't let his magic dick distract you. Magic dick? Where did that come from?

Oh my god! Last night I told him that his dick had the magic touch in the shower. Oh my god!

Don't freak out, just find your clothes and leave, it will be like it never happened. A sudden gush of fluid runs out from between my legs and my hand cups it.

"Oh my god! We did it, didn't we?" I draw a short blank as I look at him in bed, then pull my fingers from my wet body. He opens his mouth, but I beat him to it. "Jesus, this is not happening."

My brain finally syncs up to the rest of me, and flashes of last night filter through my head like a slide show.

"Baby, don't freak out," Levi slowly says, but it has the opposite effect on me.

"This is bad. This is really bad." Throwing my fingers in tangled hair, I search the room for my clothing, but don't see one article that belongs to me.

Levi gets out of bed and makes his way over in front of me, naked as the day he was born. And in slow motion, I take in every muscle that flexes as he walks, even his bouncing dick.

"This isn't that bad, Saylor. It's okay what we did, we *are* still married after all."

I snap my eyes up to his and my eyes catch the chain floating around his neck. Rings. My wedding rings. I can't believe he still has them. He notices my gaze and looks down to where I'm staring.

"They haven't left my body since I woke up from the bomb." His fingers touch them, then fists them in his hand. "Mine was cut off my finger when I was brought into the ER after the car blew up. I had a new one made after your letter." His left ring finger boasts the exact same wedding band that I placed there on the day of our wedding.

"I—" My own hand reaches out automatically to touch them too, but a sparkle from the sunlight catches my hand and I see the two bands already on my ring finger. Oh God!

"Don't Saylor. They don't matter." Levi catches my left hand in his. "They aren't real, but these are. We are still man and wife," he pushes, but guilt has already seeped in. "The last two years were make believe and they don't count. We don't even need to talk about them if you don't want to."

"What have I done?" I gasp, trying to calm my heavy breathing.

"You've done nothing wrong, baby."

"How can you say that?" I step back and yank my hand out of his, but he matches my step with his. "I've..." The words get caught in my throat. "I've cheated." My body starts to shake.

"This whole situation is complicated Saylor, you can't look at it like that." He tries to reassure me, but I don't see it.

"You're right it's complicated!" I yell, not caring if I wake the entire hotel. "First, I married you, then you pushed me away, only for Daniel to file divorce papers on me making me believe you wanted them. Then, after years of waiting for you to come back, I finally move on with someone else only to find out two months later, that I'm still married to you and that he might've been deceiving me!"

I heave in a breath, but don't stop.

"I'm a cheater. I slept with someone who wasn't my husband. And now I've cheated on my fake husband with the real husband!"

I'm losing it. I'm dizzy and white spots flash before my eyes. I might pass out. Or throw up.

"Baby, we can get through this."

I shake my head and continue to back away from him. I need my space, and with him this close I can't think straight. Tears are streaming down my face when the reality of what I've done settles in.

"I've become the one thing on this earth I swore I'd never be." I look Levi right in the eye.

"Baby, no," Levi starts, but I don't want to hear it.

Swirling around, I see a door that I hope is the bathroom and retreat as quickly as I can, but get turned back around and roughly pushed up against the door.

Levi growls and his face is so close to mine our noses touch.

"You listen to me, Saylor and listen good." He holds my chin up with his fingers. "You are kind and loving and loyal. Those are the qualities that made me want to marry you so fast. You might have been with Brody but in your heart, I know that you were always still mine. Can't you see that you waited for years before you could even move on? You knew in your soul that we were always meant for each other. Don't let those thoughts seep into your mind and spread. I am yours and you are mine."

As if knowing what I need, Levi circles my waist and pulls my body into his for a bone crushing hug as I cry it out. I thought I was done crying over my marriage, but I guess I'm not. He whispers in my ears how much he loves me and how he'll fix this for us, but all I can do is hold on to him. Anchor myself to him, as if I need a lifeline right now.

"It's okay Saylor, we'll get through this," he says as I finally calm down.

"How can you be so calm? The Levi Thorne I knew would burn the whole town down by now and have Brody in an unmarked grave." Levi is the most laid-back guy I've ever met but he was always so possessive with me after we got married. This isn't the man I married. Not by a long shot. To be honest, I loved how obsessed he was with me.

"Saylor, when I lost you, I thought my world ended. I've lived the last two and a half years without you, and I don't ever want to experience that again. Dr. Blake and I have spent months and months dealing with the possibility of you moving on with everything that you thought had happened. I don't blame you for one second. Yeah it hurts to know that you're not only mine any more, but I'm the one who caused this and I have to be man enough to own up to it. Like I said before, this is a complicated situation and I'm not the same man as I once was two years ago."

"Wow," He truly has changed since I last saw him. Maybe this new shrink is really breaking down his deep seeded walls.

"But I do expect you to uphold your vows, now that you know we're still married," he quips.

And there is the caveman I knew.

"Excuse me?"

"I don't want that pencil dick anywhere near my pussy again. Is that what you wanted me to spell out?" This man has some nerve. "Especially, since he deceived you for over two years, knowing that I was trying to find you."

Rolling my eyes even though he has a point, I twist the knob and the door opens to reveal the luxurious bathroom. Before Levi can step foot in, I close the door in his face and lock it. I find my clothes in a pile on the floor and sweep them up and start to put them on.

Once dressed and after I brush my teeth, with Levi's toothbrush, I make my way out and find him on his phone, typing away. He notices me right away and puts his phone up. He's already dressed in jeans and a polo, looking like he just walked right out of a store catalog and not just rolled out of bed.

"I'm going to go over to Grandma's to get Halo." I avoid his gaze on me. I can't help but think that this is the most bizarre situation I've ever been in.

"Can I see her again?" he asks, and it's the second time I've ever heard Levi sound vulnerable. The first was when we had a showdown at Brody's house the other night. My heart sinks with him thinking that he has to ask to see his own daughter.

"Of course, she's your daughter. You have every right to see her," I assure him. "Levi, I'd never keep her away from you. This might be a crazy situation but you are her father and that will never change."

"Thank you." I nod and he lets out a breath. "I've got a session with Dr. Blake in a few minutes, would you like to stay and have one with me?"

I know that patience was never a strong suit with Levi, but this is one case that isn't going to be fixed overnight.

"I'm not ready to sit down with you and a shrink. The last few days have been a lot, and I need time to process that on my own before I do anything else or speak with someone."

He nods his understanding, but I can tell he's disappointed.

I move to leave, but turn to face him.

"Levi," I blush before I continue. "As great as last night was, it can't happen again. Drunk or not, it shouldn't have happened. I'll take the blame because we both know I can be persuasive when it comes to alcohol, but it can't and won't happen again." He smirks, and a giggle leaves my lips. "We share a daughter and right now she needs to be the priority. We have a lot of trust issues that need to be worked through to even become friends at this point," I say with finality. "I don't even know what the next steps are. Then there's the Brody situation, and I need time to work through all of this."

"I understand." He nods.

Walking into Grandma's house, the smell of breakfast fills my nose. I hear voices in the kitchen and make my way there. Greasy food sounds good and will hopefully help the slight hangover I've got.

"Good morning!" I say in my best cheery voice, but inside my stomach is in knots. Can they tell Levi and I had sex last night? I don't think I could handle Grandma and Grandpa thinking of me in a bad light, jumping from one man to the other.

Glammy and Granddad are here, along with Alice, Everly and Linc. I'm surrounded with hugs before I can make it three steps into the room.

"Good morning, dear!" Grandma returns with the same excitement. "Come have a seat and we'll all have breakfast together."

I nod and make my way over to Halo, giving her kisses all over her face. She's got a million cheerios on her tray, trying to line them up in a straight line. Halo hates been interrupted when she's concentrating hard and starts to fuss, so I walk over to the fridge to grab the jug of orange juice.

"Brody contacted the house last night," Grandpa whispers next to me so that the others don't hear our conversation.

"Oh." Crap, I didn't even think he'd try to come find me. Wait. Of course, he would but he was the furthest thing from my mind.

"I told him you were here with Halo and were already asleep, and that I'd tell you to give him a call when you woke up."

Does Grandpa know I was with Levi?

"I was there when Levi was called to come pick you up," he answers my silent question, and I can tell from his eyes that there isn't any judgement there.

"Thank you, Grandpa." I feel a little better.

"This is a horrible situation that my grandson has put us all in but I want you to know that we still support you and our angel baby, in any way that you choose." I give a slight nod. "But Brody has a lot to answer for, and I think he owes you an explanation. There is no excuse for him keeping a father and daughter from each other. I know that Grandma and I did, but we thought he wasn't looking for you and had moved on as well. In our eyes, we thought he'd pushed you and Halo away and didn't care where you landed. If we'd known that Levi was actually looking for you this entire time, then things would have been different."

"I agree. It seems that he has been keeping just as many secrets as Levi. But at least Levi was trying to protect us from a threat; Brody seems to have kept us for himself," I say.

"I'll tell you this because I love my family. I'll always fight for Levi and his happiness. If you make the choice to get back with him, at least make him work for it," Grandpa says and we both smile, because even though I'm not blood to them, they still like me better.

"I don't even know what I'm going to do at this point. Did you know that we're still married?" He nods and tells me that they found out the other night.

"You'll know, just follow your heart and let it lead you," he offers, then looks over to the sink where Grandma is washing fruit. "I did."

After breakfast, I take Halo outside before it gets too hot and play in the backyard when Levi, Mitch and Dean pull up. Security goes inside, while Levi comes over to us and starts to play at the water table that Halo is splashing at.

"Dada!" Halo shouts, then dumps a cup full of water on his shirt when she tries to hand it to him.

I burst out laughing, seeing his polo soaked.

"Something funny Saylor?" He has a gleam in his eyes and because I've seen it before, I know what's to come.

"Don't you do it!" I snap and move to get up and run away.

I don't get very far before a set of strong arms rope around me, hauling me back. Levi brings me back over to the water table, kicking and screaming, all the while Halo is giggling.

"Levi!" I shout as he grabs the water hose and wets me and him in the process. "Stop!" I'm yelling and screeching as the coldness soaks me to my panties.

Levi stops but doesn't release me. I feel little hands on my legs and stop kicking so that I don't knock into her.

"Help Halo! Get Daddy!" I cheer, hoping Levi will let me go and focus back on Halo.

"Oh, does my baby doll want to help Mommy?" he asks and my heart flutters at his endearment towards our daughter.

Halo starts to talk, but Levi swoops down and circles her around the waist and pulls both of us up into his strong arms. He lets off an evil laugh and brings us both over to the water. I know this is going to be crazy. I can see that we have an audience, as the whole family has gathered out and are sitting on the rocking chairs, watching us. Mitch and Grandma both have cameras out filming this no doubt.

This goes on for a while, until I hear the voice that I've been avoiding until now.

"Am I interrupting?" Brody says from the gate to the backyard.

All movement stops, and both Linc and Mitch come off the porch to get closer to us.

"Da!" Halo squeals, oblivious to the undercurrent happening around us. She takes off and heads over to Brody.

Brody lets himself in the gate and swings her up in his arms. I know this is going to be confusing to her, but just hope that both men will calm enough not to make a scene in front of her.

Levi is at his full height and clinching his fists as he watches Brody with Halo. I give him a pleading look, hoping he doesn't lose his cool.

Walking over, I get in front of the laser beam shooting out of Levi's eyes and greet Brody. He and I have so much to discuss, but not here and not in front of Halo.

"Hey," I greet, and shove my hands in my back pockets that are drenched from the water table so I won't touch Brody. Levi is barely hanging on by a thread with another man holding his baby, and I don't want to make it worse. "I was going to call you after I put this little one down for a nap."

"Let's leave and we can put her to bed at home," he urges.

I need answers from Brody, but I don't want Halo to hear if we get loud or it turns ugly.

"She's already here. It's not a big deal." Halo wiggles in Brody's arms and he promptly places her back on her feet. She takes off towards Everly and I see she's holding her favorite doll. *Sneaky bitch!*

"Sadie, what's going on here?" Brody asks, and I feel Levi approach now that our daughter is out of hearing range.

"What does it look like? It's a family reconnecting after being held apart for over two years, dipshit," Levi bites out. "And her name is Saylor."

"And whose fault is that?" Brody retorts.

"You, you motherfuck—"

This is going to get ugly if I don't step in.

"Enough! Not here in front of Halo," I say, and put up a hand onto both their chests.

"Sadie, let's get our baby and go home."

Oh, shit. Wrong thing to say in front of a possessive caveman who just found his family.

Gently as he can, Levi hooks an arm around my waist and physically moves me behind him and steps up to Brody. Both Mitch and Linc are within arm's reach, as Linc stands behind Brody.

"That's MY daughter, fucker, just like that's MY wife." Levi snares as he bumps Brody in the chest. I know they both work out hard and it'll be a bloodbath if it comes to blows.

"Stop! Don't do this," I yell and squeeze my way in between the two men. "Brody, you and I need to talk. Let's go back to your house and do it there."

"You're not going anywhere with this lying, scheming sack of shit!" Levi fumes and tries to maneuver me again, but I dodge him.

"Levi, you can't tell me what to do. Now go and put our daughter down for a nap," I order.

"Everybody shut up!" We hear a voice coming up towards us. I barely look away and see Grandpa and Granddad marching over to us. Halo, Glammy, Everly, Alice and Grandma are all missing, and I hope they've gone inside.

"Sorry Grandpa," we all three mumble as he finally reaches us.

"This is not going to happen here, do you two hear me?" Grandpa lectures us.

"Yes, sir," they both say.

"Brody, I'll meet you at the house. Let me check on Halo and then I'll head out," I tell him.

He nods, then turns to head back to the truck. Grandpa walks with him as they converse about something. I let out a breath, thankful that they didn't come to blows, then start to make my way to the house to check on Halo before I leave.

A hand wraps around my wrists, halting me from moving.

"Don't go over there with him. Please Saylor, you know I'm

not a begging man but I am now." He looks conflicted and I hate that, but this is something I have to do.

"Levi, so much has happened since I came here to Montana. Brody and I have been through a lot, and whether you like it or not, we have history together. He was the one to put the pieces back together when you broke me. I know he's played a role in all this, along with you, but he deserves to get to explain."

"So, what, you just go back to him? Where does that leave me? Us?" he asks.

"I don't know, Levi. Two days ago, I thought I'd never see you again and now I find out that not only have you been looking for me and Halo this entire time, but that we are still married. I need to process all of this. This isn't going to be fixed overnight, and you can't ask that of me."

He takes a deep breath, closes his eyes then reopens them. A look of resolve is there and he nods.

"Okay. I know this is going to take some time. I'll wait for however long it takes."

"Thank you."

We walk into the house and find Halo playing happily with her toys, but I can see it in her eyes that it's naptime. I give her a big kiss and show Levi our naptime routine. I love how he takes it all in, wanting to learn everything he can to help where Halo is concerned. After getting in the truck, I rub my forehead and temples to rid the headache threatening to come back.

Turning on the road towards the ranch, I can't help but dread what I'm about to find out.

CHAPTER SIXTEEN

Saylor

Brody is speaking with Patrick when I pull in and park the truck. I can't even wrap my head around the last few days, let alone comprehend that the person who I've leaned on for the last two years has been lying to me and keeping me from my family. *Why would he do that? He was not only the person who was supposed to protect me but he became my friend.*

After reopening my eyes and letting out a shaky breath, I open the door and make my way into the house with a slight wave to Patrick. Zeus is there to greet me and I'm thankful. I need all the comfort I can get right now, as I don't even know how to start this conversation. I'm mad as hell and yet completely sad that someone I thought of as my friend did something like this to me. The door opens from behind me as I'm seated on the sofa. My legs are void of shoes and drawn under me. Zeus stays at my feet, very aware of his surroundings and my mood. He lays his head on my lap, like he knows I'm feeling defeated after everything.

Brody comes over in front of me and drops to his knees, almost pushing Zeus over, who growls and nips at Brody's arm.

"Sadie, I know there is a lot going on in your mind with *him* coming back and I hate that. If I could make it better I would." He looks scared and cautious. "There are just some things that you have to understand…"

"My name is Saylor," I say, trying to hold back snapping at him. Starting the conversation with aggression won't get us any-where. "Why? Brody why didn't you tell me that the DA of Los Angeles was your uncle?" I question, raising an eyebrow. There is more than this to discuss, but I guess we need to start at the be-ginning. "We had hours on the road to Montana to talk, but you didn't think that was something I should know?"

"Saylor," his voice is pleading with me but he must see how sorrowful my face is. He takes a deep breath and continues. "I didn't think…no, I was told that this was a special case when my uncle called me. I was headed back to Montana, after a short visit with him, when he called and asked me if I would do him a favor. He gave me a rundown of the situation and said that he needed an answer straight away. My first thoughts were to decline but after Googling you and reading over your situation, I changed my mind and told him that I'd take the assignment." He shifts up from his knees to the seat next to me, keeping his leg up against mine and as close as he can be to me.

"I didn't think it would be a big deal that Uncle Burt and I were related, as long as I did what I was supposed to do."

"Maybe not, but when he died you should've told me Brody," I stressed. Wait, I remember something Mitch told me. "You went to LA and even spoke with Mitch," I accuse.

He nods, but doesn't give me an answer.

"Brody, you're going to have to tell me. I'm not going to try and pull everything out like pulling teeth." I feel my anger start to rise. I wanted to sit down and have a calm conversation about this, but if he doesn't tell me everything, I think I might blow a gasket.

He sits there for a long while, but doesn't move. He stares straight ahead and it's grating on my nerves.

"If you aren't going to start talking then I'm leaving." I go to stand and it must light a fire under his ass. He grabs for my wrists and holds me there. Zeus is on his feet, and in a protective stance, with his ears pointing straight up. I know that Brody was his owner but Zeus is very much my dog, and has been since I came here to the ranch. He ignores Zeus and focuses back on me.

"Okay, okay, I'll tell you but you have to promise that you won't leave me."

"I can't promise that Brody. I feel like I'm a ping pong ball being thrown from one life to the other, only to find out that the life I've settled on was never supposed to happen and that my first life has been trying to find me this entire time."

"I love you Sadie. My life would be empty now that you and Halo have filled it."

A sigh leaves me and I know that it will take some adjusting to, but this was always supposed to be a temporary home and life. It was never supposed to be forever. We've been each other's person for over two years and a bond has grown from that. It's only been the last two months that I've let myself open to the possibility of being with someone other than Levi, but I know that my heart will always be connected to Levi, no matter where we end up.

I'd always thought Brody was like a big brother when I first got here to Montana, to lean on and it was only recently that I've seen him as someone I could enjoy and try a relationship with. I want to give him the benefit of the doubt because Brody has been nothing but loving and the support I've needed through this time.

"Brody, please just tell me. I want to believe that there is some explanation to all of this."

"What do you want to know?"

"Everything. I deserve to know everything! And stop calling me by that stupid fake name," I almost shout, my patience running thin.

He scrubs his face, then leans back against the cushion.

"Yes, when Uncle Burt died, I went to LA. I lied to you and said that it was a business meeting for my scope and goggle design. The second trip was when Mitch summoned me to the hospital, to question me about Uncle Burt and if I knew anything about your whereabouts."

"Why didn't you tell Mitch where I was? And why didn't someone from the DA's office inform us that my case had been handed over to a new person to be our point man?"

He turns his eyes to his boots that are perched up on the wooden coffee table.

"Because there was no other person who knew about you."

How can that be?

"What do you mean, no one knew about me? I'm pretty sure the government keeps tabs on everyone they put into Witness Protection."

"That's just it, no one knew. My uncle and I were the only ones who knew you left and that I had you in my care."

"What the hell, Brody!" My blood pressure starts to spike and there is a loud pounding in my ears. "Were you ever going to tell me? Or was this some kind of sick game to keep me away from my family?" I accuse.

"It was never a game, Sadie. I've been in love with you from the moment we crossed over the state line, here in Montana. I did my research on Levi Thorne and I did you a favor by keeping you out of his clutches."

"What does that mean? You know nothing about my life with Levi!" I practically scream. How dare he try to even measure the life and connection Levi and I shared.

"It means I know all about his connections with that woman who he was involved with, Sadie. His family is nothing but poisonous and I saved you, even if you don't realize it right now. Your grandparents have been through enough with that family of his."

Oh, you judgmental prick!

"You know nothing about what Levi and I did in our relationship, and you have no right to judge someone or something that you obviously know nothing about," I yell and stop myself from clocking him in the jaw. "And I think that we can start calling me Saylor since the ruse is over."

"You're right I don't, but I do know that you needed to get away from him and I succeeded in that. Ask your grandparents about your aunt." I would squeeze his head off his shoulders if I could get my hands around his neck. "Look at the life we made here, Sadie. There are no threats of being blown up or shot at. No stalkers around the corner, or the press trying to take yours and Halo's photos. We can have a peaceful life here and just be us."

I take a deep breath, trying to calm my heartrate. I stand to put some distance between us because right now I'm pissed and am wanting to hit something. Once I have enough space, I face him, wanting to make sure I'm very clear with this next go around.

"Brody, you had no right to make that decision for me. ME! This is my life and I get to choose how I want it to turn out. How could you think that I wouldn't want to know that my husband was looking for me? You had no right!" I'm shaking with rage that is building up inside me. How dare he make this decision for me and my daughter.

"We have a life here; don't you see it. Halo is happy and you are loving the country living. You can't tell me that you honestly miss having a husband who works all the time and can't make your life easier? There are no worries here for that, you and Halo can run free and never have to worry. I love you Sadie, and I want to spend the rest of my life with you and Halo. Can't you see that's what I've been trying to build for us?"

This is the most fucked up life a person could live. With a firm resolve, I stand on my feet.

"You can't have something that doesn't belong to you!" I wave my finger at him. "Halo and I were never yours to begin with. We were only here because your uncle said that he could help protect me and my baby from the madman who tried to kill my husband."

"You would never be in danger if it wasn't for being with that asshole in the first place," he retorts. "We are together now and don't you see the difference in how your life is better now."

"I was never yours!" I yell. "I only started dating you because I thought my husband divorced me and didn't love me. I thought he had moved on and didn't want to be a part of his daughter's life." My chest is heaving and I'm short of breath. "How could you ever think it was okay to keep me from him and my family? I had a thriving business that I gave up, thinking this was going to be temporary. Brody, you can talk all you want about Levi being a monster but you are no different." I'm shaking with rage and Zeus is nudging me to sit down but I can't. I need to get some distance from him.

"So, what? You're just going to run back to him with open arms? What about me? What about what we shared here for the past two years? Two months?" He goes to stand. "And stop calling him your husband when he divorced your ass when you were placed under arrest."

I've never been driven to violence in my life, other than when I slapped Levi at the restaurant, but I could easily punch Brody in the face right now.

"Newsflash, Levi and I are still married. He had it stopped when he found out that his father did it against his wishes." I narrow my eyes. "And I never said that I would run back to him. He and I have a lot of issues that we have to work through, but even if I do that would be my decision." I point to my chest.

"And us? What about us?" Brody points back and forth between us.

"How can there ever be an us when I was manipulated into moving on with someone who knew my husband was turning the world upside down looking for me?"

He looks as though I've struck him, but what did he think would come of this once the truth was out, and that he played a major role in keeping a wife from her husband and a child from their *real* father.

Then it hits me like a ton of bricks. Levi has been looking for me like crazy since he woke up. All doubts of him not wanting me are gone. He didn't stand a chance to find me when DA Buttons hid me by not putting me in the real Witness Protection. Levi never stood a chance. If he didn't have the resources at his disposal then he might never have found me. I'd go on living my life thinking he hated me and never wanted our child. Would Grandma and Grandpa have kept my secret? I know that my grandparents would've.

Am I still mad at Levi for keeping me in the dark about the threats to me and Halo? Yes. But it does soften the blow knowing that he's broken down every door looking for me and Halo.

The guilt of what happened last night settles heavily on my chest, and I need to tell Brody the truth, or I'm no better than him.

"Brody, something happened last night with Levi," I start, and am having a hard time looking him in the eyes. "I… I didn't stay at Grandma's house. Instead, I got drunk at a bar with Everly in town and somehow Levi was there and took me back to his hotel. I'm not going to torture you with the details, but you can guess what happened."

He starts to pace the room and pulls at the collar of his shirt. He's mumbling things I can't hear but finally, he stops and turns back to me.

"Okay," he says and continues. "I can understand and rationalize that. A lot was thrown at you in the last few days and I can look past last night. But please Sadie, let's not rush any decisions right now when the tension is so high. I know I've kept things from you but…"

"Are you delusional? There are no buts, Brody. What did you think was going to happen when all this blew up in your face? You can't even call me by my real name. This isn't real, Brody. You put me and Halo in your real-life fantasy. My daughter has been calling the wrong man 'daddy' and *he* has missed so much of her life already."

"Honestly, I never thought it was. The more time went by, the more I thought we'd really become that married couple that everyone here thinks we are. You were finally in a good place, opening your heart again, and I know that I could've made you happy until we were old."

"Even if that were true, our relationship was based on a lie. A lie that you knew about from the start. No relationship could ever survive this kind of dishonesty. Just because you say the sky is green doesn't make it true, and telling yourself that you love me doesn't make that true either. You knew how I struggled with leaving Los Angeles and how heartbroken I was. How could you sit there and watch me cry for days, knowing my husband actually cared and wanted me back? I don't think I could ever forgive you for this. I couldn't care less about me but when my daughter is affected by this, you've closed your own coffin."

"So that's it. We're done and I'm never going to see you or Halo again?"

I haven't really thought that far ahead really, but I guess we are. How can I be with one man when I'm still married to another? I'm not even sure that I'd want to be with someone who deceived me for two years anyway.

Brody walks back over to me and holds my hand as he sits down.

"I'm sorry, Sadie—Saylor. I think after losing my last relative and realizing that I was the only family member left, I latched on to you. Halo came shortly after and I had the picture-perfect family wrapped in a bow at my fingertips." I can hear the sadness in his voice and my heart aches for him. I know he wanted a family really bad, but you can't just steal someone else's. "At first, I know we were playing a role but as time went on it felt right, and the more I let myself believe that this was real the more I wanted to make it happen in reality. Consequences be damned."

We sit in silence for a while, taking in everything with both of us lost in our own thoughts. Never did I think that this is how my life would've turned out when I moved to LA.

"Please don't hate me, Saylor," Brody pleads after a while.

"I don't hate you Brody, but I can't say that I'm not mad as hell. We all played a role in all of this, it's not just one person's fault." I lean forward and prop my elbows up on my knees and my head goes to my hands, hiding my face. "I need to get mine and Halo's things, we're going to be staying at Grandma and Grandpa's house or with Glammy and Granddad."

"What? No Saylor, you don't have to leave. This is yours and Halo's home," he pleads.

"It really is not, Brody. This is your home and I think that my husband finding me and our daughter has changed things completely. Especially, now that the truth is out."

He looks so sad and it breaks my heart that I'm the one who did that, but I can't be here with him after learning the truth from his own mouth. I really feel like I have no fight left in me after the last few days. When is there going to be peace in my life?

I've got several bags of our stuff and most of my clothes and bathroom items from my room, along with my birth control pills and Halo's vitamins from the kitchen. I didn't really have anything in Brody's room, even though he had pushed to move all my things into his. Brody helped carry everything out to the truck when an SUV pulled up to the front porch. Ryan steps out and I'm glad to see that he is alone. I don't think I could handle another pissing match again.

"Mrs. Thorne I can take you anywhere you'd like."

"Thanks Ryan, and can we go back to calling me Saylor?"

"Of course, Saylor." He smirks, and it feels nice to have him around again. He grabs the bags in my hands and places them in the back of the SUV.

Ryan was a nice guy when he was my security. Once we established a boss/friendship, it made it easy to have him around all the time. He kind of reminds me of the brother I never had.

"Saylor, you can take your truck, you don't need to be driven around," Brody spouts off.

I know I could but it doesn't belong to me; it belongs to him and I need to distance myself from him.

When the car is packed, I turn back to Brody and for the first time since meeting him, I'm nervous to be around him. We've acted like a married couple from the moment we met and now things are… different and I'm not sure how to be around him.

He starts before I can, "Please call me when you're ready to talk. I know I went about this the wrong way but I do love you and Halo very much. I'd love to still get to see and play around the ranch with her."

This is so hard because I want to say not a chance in hell, but I can't bring myself to hit him with another blow. I'm not one to revel in someone's pain, and even though he did what he did, I can't kick him while he's down. Halo already has a daddy, and I don't want to confuse her any more than she is going to be. But something is nagging me and I didn't want to add to this fire that is already separating us, but I need to know.

"What did you do with the photos I had you mail? The ones where you told me you sent them off."

I already know the answer because everything that Levi and Mitch said yesterday has been confirmed by Brody. But I want him to say the words so he understands how hurtful and wrong it was of him to do this.

He steadies himself against the front of the SUV and hangs his head.

"They're in a file in the lower cabinet in my office." He sounds as defeated as I am right now, but I don't have the capacity to help myself and him. My left hand feels weighted down as I catch the sight of his rings on my finger. Gently, I pull them off and drop them into his front pocket of his shirt.

How can someone you thought of as a true and loyal friend so easily be manipulating you and not miss a wink of sleep? Before I know what is happening, something comes over me and I lose it.

The last few days have come to a head and I can't take any more information. I'm like an active volcano erupting. My hand balls up into a fist and I wheel it back and snap it forward, connecting with his face.

"I think we've said everything we need to say." I shake my hand to alleviate the throb. He looks shocked and I can't believe I've just socked someone, but I think the last few days have me at a breaking point.

Brody tries to take a step towards me but Ryan thankfully steps in. Brody starts to say that he loves me and Halo over and over, and it's almost too much to handle.

"Haven't you ever been in love with someone that you'd do anything for them, even if it meant hurting them a little?" he pleads, wiping at the corner of his mouth.

I snort, thinking about what Brody just said.

"Yeah, I have but that doesn't justify the last two years. How could I ever trust anything out of your mouth again?"

We stand there looking at each other, and the more I look at him, the more betrayed I feel.

"Did you ever think of what this would do to Halo? Let's say your plan worked and years down the road she's old enough to understand, and thinks her own biological dad didn't want her. Feels abandoned and unwanted. I've been there and know how that feels!" I scream, thinking about my own dad and all his disappearing acts he's done. "How can you ever justify that? He missed *everything* while you swooped in and planted yourself right in that role. He never saw her birth, or first step or word. He didn't get to rock her to sleep in the middle of the night in a storm. You stole all that from him because you wanted a family that was never yours!"

"Ready, Saylor?" Ryan interrupts me, and I nod. He ushers me to the passenger door and blocks Brody. I can't deal with this anymore. I don't think I'll ever get past keeping a child from their parent.

I squeeze Ryan's hand, then climb in the front seat of the SUV while he gets behind the wheel. After a few minutes of being on the road, I can't help but ask the question that has been on my mind.

"So, the boss sent you here to get me?"

Ryan never takes his eyes from the road, but a small smirk plays on his mouth.

"No, he doesn't know that I came."

"Really? That doesn't sound like the Levi I knew."

"Last report was he was rocking baby Halo while she slept." I ponder over that. "He's changed a lot since losing you, Saylor. The boss has seen some dark days in the two years you've been gone."

I can only imagine what this must have been like for him, knowing we were out there in the world and not be able to find us. I'd be devastated if the roles were reversed.

"Why were you there at the ranch then?" I ask, only a few miles from the house.

"Because, believe it or not, I do care about your safety and wellbeing, Saylor. I know I should've done more back then to help when you got arrested, and this is me making sure that nothing like that ever happens again." He finally looks at me, and I know that Ryan and I are picking up right where we left off over two years ago. He has always been my sounding board when Levi and I had our disagreements, or if something came up at work. "I know you have some doubts about what was told to you yesterday, but I promise you that everything Mr. Thorne told you in the hotel was factual. We all have been looking night and day for you and baby Halo."

"Thank you, Ryan. That means a lot. And I believe everything that you all told me. As hard as it was to hear, I'm glad to know that life really isn't that cruel."

Hopefully, once I can get some alone time to think things over, I'll be able to figure out what the hell I'm going to do, now that everything has come to light. First thing I know for sure is that I need to talk with the grandparents and make sure Halo and I can stay for a while. I already know the answer, but still I don't want to put anyone out.

Pulling up to the house, Ryan helps me with my bags and we head in. We walk in the living room with both grandparents, Everly, Linc and Alice all sitting there, almost in a circle, holding onto the baby monitor. Suddenly, I think something must be wrong when I see tears in their eyes, but when I get closer, I hear the most touching thing I've ever heard. Levi's voice comes over the monitor and the screen shows him rocking our baby while singing *You Are My Sunshine*.

My heart picks up in pace. This, right here, is what I imagined him doing when we first found out we were pregnant. There is nothing sexier than seeing a macho, badass, hotheaded man showing his child how much he loves them.

And it's like falling in love with him all over again.

But this time, I'm going to take my time and not rush anything.

CHAPTER SEVENTEEN

It's been two months since I landed in Montana and found my family, and today is the day that we are all leaving to head back to Los Angeles. Dr. Blake has been in LA for a while and came back a few days ago. I haven't needed to have a session, but I'm making time for one today. Saylor thought it was crazy that I wanted to have Dr. Blake up here the entire time. She said that if I needed a shrink that bad then I was in far worse shape than she thought, or I still wasn't taking her advice. Either way, I needed to sort my shit out and start trusting in my judgement again, and the advice. With those words swirling around my head, I sent Dr. Blake home the next day.

"Mr. Thorne, tell me about how you're feeling today," she begins and starts jotting down words in her notebook.

"Happy, no thrilled but also nervous," I answer as I lay on the sofa, with my hands behind my head in her hotel room. I never felt that I could be relaxed speaking with Dr. Jordan in his office, because I was afraid he'd run and tell my brother about all my issues. But ever since I started seeing Dr. Blake, I've become one that lounges out on a couch and spills the beans.

"Why nervous? I thought one of your goals was to have your family back in Los Angeles fulltime."

"What if I screw this up again? But this time I really *do* lose her. We've grown closer, and not just as a family, but as a couple. What if we change when we get back to LA? What if she remembers the hurt being too much and decides to change her mind?"

"What has brought the two of you close these past two months?"

"Obviously our shared love for our daughter, but it's also the alone time we spend together when Halo's napping. Things are almost back to normal."

"You say almost? What does that mean?"

I roll my eyes this time and sigh.

"We have become friends this time around, instead of jumping the gun and cannonballing in the deep end, like last time." I pause and think back over the past two months. "We haven't been intimate since that first night and surprisingly, I'm okay with that. I don't want to rush her or make her feel like that's all I want from her. We just…talk."

"It's good to have a solid foundation starting out in a relationship. I'm glad you two are taking baby steps. The most devastating thing would be to jump in and then it not work out in the end. Halo would be the one who suffers."

We both sit in silence for a few minutes as I reflect on what she's saying, and both Saylor and I have already agreed that this was the only way for us to be able to move forward. Although, she didn't make the decision lightly. She didn't think we should even try to be a couple at first, and just work on my relationship with Halo. I quickly told her that there was no way that I would accept a world that she and I didn't belong to each other. So, we decided to start out as friends and maybe work towards dating, and then more. It's more than I imagined at this point, but I'll take whatever I can get at this moment. Saylor has had a lot of chairs taken away from her, just when she thought she was comfortable, and she needed time for us to rebuild that trust.

"Saylor and Mom are on better terms."

"That's good. Was it forced?"

"No, I think the more Mom and Saylor hang out, the more Saylor sees that Mom is nothing like Daniel, or excuses his behavior. It would make our relationship hard if she were to put Mom in the same category as that horrible man."

"Saylor is going to still have some trust issues with your family because of what she went through over two years ago."

"I know. Right now, it's important for Saylor, Halo and I to get reacquainted and build back the trust and relationship. We are looking to renovate one of our rental properties that I've acquired to make our family home. Both Saylor and I want Halo to grow up with some outdoor space and not an apartment. We know that it's going to be a little more challenging once we are back in the city and under a microscope."

"I agree. Once others start to come in the picture, then things tend to get a little more complicated. But as long as you and Saylor have a stable foundation, then it will be easier on both sides. Just remember that Saylor went through something horrible while you were in a coma. That is always going to stick in the back of her mind when she sees your family face to face, then remembering how they were so easily convinced to jump on the Daniel bandwagon. I'm sure it will take some time for her to adjust and trust them again."

I nod in agreeance. Both Saylor and I wanted it to be just the three of us for a while even though Mom, Grandma and Grandpa are staying here also. Halo seems to be adjusting well, living at Glammy and Granddad's place. I've been living with my grandparents so that we are able to get as much time together as possible, and I couldn't be happier about that. Even though Grandma and Grandpa love Daniel, because he's their last living child, they know his actions played a massive role in this, and have made sure to make this a safe place for Mom and my family.

"Should I bring up the elephant in the room? Or are we not going to discuss Brody?" She urges.

"Ugh! Why do we even need to waste our breath on the loser," I mumble and rake my fingers through my short hair. Saylor decided I needed a haircut a few days ago. When I looked in the mirror, I thought she had scalped me.

"I think that *is* something we need to discuss and see how your progress in taming your temper has been."

There are some days I really miss Dr. Jordan and after her bringing up Brody fucking Jackson, this is one of those days. She knew when to move on from a subject. Dr. Blake is like a dog on a bone and beats a dead horse until I've overcome it.

"Well, I haven't seen the guy but once when he showed up to Halo's birthday party, the day after you left to go back home to LA."

"And what happened at the birthday party?"

"I was on my best behavior," I quickly say. "I'd never want my daughter to see that side of me."

"That's wonderful, Mr. Thorne. I'm sure Saylor and Halo are both happy that they didn't see that side of you." *If she only knew how Mitch and Ryan almost had to tie my hands to my sides she wouldn't be praising me.* "And the other time that you saw Brody?"

"We beat the shit out of each other." I shrug.

"What!" she shrieks, and the notebook falls out of her lap.

"He was waiting outside my hotel a few days after Halo's party and things got a little heated." I shrug again, not wanting to relive it.

Brody thought he was going to intimidate me and make it known that he wasn't going to let Saylor go without a fight. He came looking for one hell of a fight and I delivered. Both Ryan and Mitch finally broke it up after both of us had some nasty cuts, busted lips and bruises across our bodies. My body may have been put through the wringer these past few years, but I worked him over and not once did I falter. I swear, and so does Ryan that I won and kicked his ass and it felt amazing, but facing Saylor the next day with my face swollen didn't make me feel like a winner. Halo kept touching my face and saying 'booboo'. Her and teddy bear were my nurse over those few days, and as much as I loved that, I know that it disappointed Saylor that I'd sunk that low. A week later, Saylor and I finally spoke and she understood how that interaction needed to happen after everything Brody stole from me. She didn't like that it came to blows, and made it very clear that better have been the only time it happens.

Saylor and Brody haven't had much contact since she moved in with Glammy and Granddad. She felt she needed time to recoup, and even shut me out for a week before we could even sit down in the same room. I know she thought of Brody as a close friend, and nothing more, which doesn't make the manipulation any easier.

It hurt to know that they'd had sex but I know that this is a sticky situation and we can't take back what happened in the past. I do blame myself for everything that happened and take full responsibility, but Saylor says I'm only responsible for keeping the threat against her and Halo a secret, plus the restaurant fight. The others were a string of unfortunate events that just happened to occur back-to-back. She really is amazing, and I try every day to show her with my actions instead of just words. We can only move forward and learn from our mistakes.

She gave *his* rings back and I was beyond overjoyed that day, but also hurt when she wouldn't accept her original wedding bands back. She said she still needed some time before she wanted to put them on, if ever. She knew how much I hated her not having something on her finger, so Grandma gave me a simple gold band that Grandpa gave her as a promise ring when they first started to date. I swear it's like they can read my mind. She loved the idea of a promise ring and also that it came from Grandma. I know she looks to them for advice on everything and I love it. They've lived through a lot and had some difficult times in their long and loving marriage, and I can only hope Saylor and I have the same love as those two have for each other.

Grandma and Grandpa have been my champions with Saylor, since I've told them all the dirty details about what really happened. I know I still have a long way to go to win her over completely, but they have encouraged every step. They've also thought it was great that Saylor distanced herself from Brody. She really needed some alone time, so I'd take Halo for a few hours during the day to give her a break.

My grandparents and I have sat down with Dr. Blake and had a long session about their role in keeping Saylor hidden. I understood where they were coming from because as far as they knew I wasn't looking for Saylor and Halo, living the single life. If anything, I respect that they stayed by Saylor's side and helped her when she didn't have any other family to turn to. I promised to be more involved in their lives and that secrets have no place in families. We love each other unconditionally, but we also need to let others in to help when someone is going through a terrible time in their lives.

"And now what?" Dr. Blake asks astonished, bringing me out of my thoughts.

"Well, I think he got the picture."

"Mr. Thorne, I think we can both agree that violence is not always the answer. What happened to channeling that anger into something productive?" she asks.

"I wasn't angry, I just put him in his place, then walked away and didn't think about him again," I defend, but she doesn't seem to believe me. "Honestly, I feel better that I got it out of my system and now I'm done. If it wasn't then, I'd seek him out every chance I got to have another round since this is a small town. Plus, I couldn't let Saylor be the only one to get a swing in."

Ryan told me about Saylor punching the shit out of Brody when he told her he withheld the photos that were to be sent to me. I couldn't have been prouder, but then I was a mess worrying about her hurting herself.

She swiftly writes something down in the notebook, then turns back to me.

"Now tell me about the move back to Los Angeles? Living arrangements and so forth."

This is where it gets a little tricky.

"Well, Saylor and Halo are going to be staying at Sharilyn and Alan's house until we can finish the renovations on the new place for all the family to live in."

Saylor didn't want to live in the penthouse when I offered to stay in a different location. She thought it wasn't a good idea to have Halo in an apartment when she has been running wild and free out in the country. Her grandparent's house is in a gated community and has a large backyard where she can run all that energy out. Saylor also thought it wasn't the right time for us to move in together yet. I hate that I won't be under the same roof as my girls, but I understand, and will give her the time she needs.

"How do you feel about that? It can't be easy knowing they won't be living with you."

"It fucking sucks. I hate that I can't just move them back in with me, but I understand we are not there *yet*. We've come a long way but I've waited this long, so a little longer isn't going to kill me."

We talk some more and I tell her that Saylor hasn't heard from her dad yet. When Saylor asked Sharilyn and Alan about why her dad never stayed in close contact with her or them, they had a shocking answer that blew both of our minds.

"I think it's time we finally told you about Amanda," Sharilyn and Alan both told us after we put Halo down for her afternoon nap. We'd just cleaned up the living room of all of her toys, when they asked us to have a seat.

"Who's Amanda?" Saylor asked, and from the sad looks Glammy and Granddad gave each other, I knew this was going to be a hard discussion.

"Amanda was your dad's twin sister," Alan said, clearing his throat.

"How come I've never heard about her until now?" Saylor asked.

Sharilyn gave a heavy sigh and pulled out a small worn photo and showed us. It was a picture of a young Adam, seated beside a girl who looked almost identical to him. Saylor was almost the spitting image of her aunt.

"Amanda was killed when she was right out of high school. She had started dating this college boy behind our backs, right after Adam had enlisted into the military. She'd told us that she was meeting up with her girlfriends, but apparently it was this crazy guy who came

from money. For months, they met and had a relationship. When she tried to break things off, he didn't take it too well and killed her."

Saylor gasps and I pull her into my side for support, as Alan clutches Sharilyn's hand for comfort.

"That's horrible, Glammy. I'm so sorry," she says tearfully.

"We were devastated, and when we told Adam that his twin had been killed, something broke in him. He was never the same toward us. He kept his distance, and threw himself into missions and anything that would keep him away. Adam blamed us for not keeping a closer eye on his sister, and said that we were partially to blame."

"He was just upset. Surely you know that the only person responsible is the man that killed her, right?" Saylor argues.

"We know that now but at the time all we could focus on was how we didn't do more. He went into these fits of rage and destruction, leveling everything in his path." Alan speaks up. "Years went by without a word from Adam. We'd send weekly letters that went unanswered, until one day he came home. He had a beautiful wife and little girl in tow," he smiles like he is remembering that day so fondly. "You were the perfect little angel and your mother was the sweetest woman. Over the next few years, things started to seem like Adam had come around and wasn't so angry with us anymore, and was truly happy in his career and life. And then your mother passed away. It was like Amanda had died all over again for your father. He became a shell of the person he was again. He stopped coming home to you, and left you with us for weeks without any contact. He took on more assignments and eventually signed over guardianship of you to us."

"Adam thought in his mind that everything that he had, and he touched and loved died, so keeping his distance from you was his way of making sure you lived." Glammy told me.

"How do you feel about seeing Adam again, after he attacked you in the hospital once you woke from the coma?"

"I'm not sure. I'm more concerned about how seeing Adam will affect Saylor, now that we know more about him abandoning her for such long periods of time. As long as he is cordial with me and doesn't do anything to upset my wife and little girl, then I'm open to a talk or have some level of a relationship."

"That's very noble of you, but I think you should really have a conversation with Saylor about her father. And I don't mean skip over one, but have a true and in depth talk about how Adam treated you at the hospital." Yeah, I'm not ready for that yet. "How about a discussion regarding Daniel?"

My eyebrows shoot up to my hairline.

"Why would we need to discuss that asshole?"

"Surely if you are going to tolerate her father, she should return the favor for yours."

"Have you lost your mind? I don't even tolerate my fath—Daniel."

"I understand but if you're going to try and make amends with Adam, then it's only fair that she makes an effort to reconcile with yours, right?"

"No way! I don't want her or my daughter anywhere near that guy. He did the most unthinkable thing a person could do, and I could've lost them both because of him. No, I don't think she should have to endure it. End of conversation, Doc."

"Okay, fine. We'll let it go, for now, but I do want you to have a conversation with her about Adam at some point."

"Maybe we can do a joint session and you can tell her." I cringe, thinking about having to speak to Saylor about her father. No one wants to hear what an asshole their father is. *Trust me, I should know.*

"I don't mind and welcome the suggestion." She pauses for a moment. "I have been instructed to tell you that Saylor and I have had a few sessions, but that is as far as I'm willing to speak on the matter. Saylor said that it was okay to mention it, and I wanted you to know that she is seeking counsel for what has happened over the past two years."

"Thank god!" I reflect for a bit, trying to gather what this could mean. "Does she hate me? Is she interested in staying married to me?" I pry. What if she gets back to Los Angeles and files for divorce after we land?

"Mr. Thorne, you know that I can't divulge my sessions with other clients unless they give permission to me in writing. What I can say is that what you and Saylor share is something special, and if she didn't want to make that leap with you again then she wouldn't."

That is the best news I've heard in a while and can't stop the smile from breaking across my face.

"Patience, Mr. Thorne. Remember, this needs to go at her pace," Dr. Blake reprimands me. "She is still processing everything, and wants to make sure that this is the right move for her and Halo."

Of course, she is. Saylor doesn't do anything half assed. Especially when it comes to our baby. I just want her to need me as much as I need her.

"I see your wheels turning. What are you questioning in your head?"

"I just…Saylor is like my next breath. I wake up for her and every choice I make I have her and Halo's best interest at heart. Sometimes I feel like she's not…like she doesn't need me as much as I need her. I guess I'm scared that she can walk away easier, if she doesn't have that same need as I do."

"Mr. Thorne, you still deal with a lot of insecurities about your relationship with Saylor, but from what I can see, it goes both ways," she says, shocking me. Did Saylor say that or is this just Dr. Blake trying to soothe me? "From what I've learned about you and Saylor's time apart, she waited over two years before she even tried to move on. Even then, she didn't want to but thought she had to and was just settling. Does that sound like someone who just throws away someone or doesn't need them as much as you do?"

She's right. Saylor and I have talked about her dating Brody. She felt like it was the only way for her to try and get over the heartache. But she never really thought of Brody like that but she was stuck because she was 'married' to him and it might blow the cover if she did anything different. I hate that she thought she didn't have any other options and I kick myself every day because of it. This was my mistake and one that I'll never make again.

"I think there is something wrong with my body. I'm a total mess, ever since I came here." I swear my body might not be able to endure country living much longer.

"What do you mean?"

"I cry. A lot," I admit. Five years ago, I would've happily checked myself into a facility if I even thought of ever admitting this but now, I can freely say it and not worry.

"It's called emotions, Mr. Thorne. Tell me, what brings it on?"

"Saylor. I blame Saylor for this." I start. "Just the other day I was over at Glammy's house around naptime, when Halo snuck out of her crib and found me sitting on the couch, reading over some potential houses that would make great rentals. I knew she was supposed to be in bed but it's hard to say no to her when she gives me those sad, pleading eyes. Anyway, Saylor came in from the backyard and saw she was up playing dolls with me and she punished her."

"Punished? How?"

"She made her stop playing and go back to her room and lay

down. Halo cried the entire time, calling for me to save her. It was the absolute worst. Then, Saylor and I got into an argument, and she practically sent me back to Grandma's house," I tell her. When I look up to see if she agrees with me, Dr. Blake looks to be holding in a laugh. She's laughing at me?

"Then what happened?" She barely is able to say without chuckling. I'm glad I pay her for this entertainment.

"I could hear Halo from across the hall, wailing for about ten minutes. That's when I realized that I was crying too."

"Mr. Thorne, I know it's hard but being a parent isn't always about having fun and playing. You have to show boundaries and set rules when it comes to kids, or they'll never learn respect or understand what the word 'no' means. You want Halo to be a well-adjusted child who grows up to be independent, and respectful of others and things, correct?" I nod but hate that she's making me have to be a bad guy like Saylor. "Then you'll need to follow Saylor's rules that she's set. Maybe you both can sit down and discuss what they are and how would be the best way to share the responsibility. It's not fair that Saylor has to always be the disciplinarian."

"Oh, trust me, we have. I'm fully under the *get in line or else* umbrella," I mock. "And that's not all. These Disney movies are just tear jerkers. I mean why does every movie have to have one of the parents die?"

I know that I still have a lot to work through with my own mother and father dying on me, but I can't think about that right now and decide to change the subject.

"I've become a dog owner." I perk up when saying so.

"Really? And how did this come about? I remember your reaction to being a dad, this any different except this is an animal?" she questions.

"Well, I didn't really choose to be an owner, I've inherited two," I tell her.

"Please elaborate."

"Saylor and Halo both have German Shepherds that are attached to them, Zeus and Ginger. They had them when I came here to find my family. The dickweed has both dogs trained to never leave my girls' side. Both Saylor and Halo love them, so that means that I have to love them."

"If you don't love the dogs that won't make you a bad person, Mr. Thorne."

"It will because then it's just one more thing that Brody will have with them that I won't."

"It's not always about competition."

"It is with that clown. And I don't even buy the whole act of him coming over to give my girls the dogs."

"What do you mean?"

"I think this was just a way to see them and try to plea with Saylor about giving him another chance."

"You think Brody has a different type of motive behind it."

"I had Mitch check both dogs and he confirmed that both animals are chipped."

"I'm not following, Mr. Thorne. A lot of pet owners have their animals chipped."

"I know that, but I wouldn't put it past him to do it so that he can always know where my girls are at any given moment." I huff.

"Have you expressed these feelings to Saylor?"

"I may have mentioned them, but Saylor seemed to brush it off with an eye roll."

"Is it possible that you might be overreacting, just a tad bit?" I stay quiet because then I really might have to answer it out loud. "Why not, when you get back to Los Angeles, take the dogs to a new vet and have them replace the chip with news ones? That way Brody won't be able to trace them, if you're this worried about it. I would recommend speaking with Saylor about it before doing it though."

Yes, because that is what your wife wants to see, you being insecure. Ugh!

I shrug then sit up on the sofa. I'm not here to discuss that asshole and don't want to waste my time even hearing his name. Dr. Blake must see my irritation and closes her notebook.

"Mr. Thorne, I know that you don't want to talk about Brody but he will be a present figure in yours and Saylor's life, until we all get back to Los Angeles for good. I think it would be better for you and Saylor if you just talked through everything that you hate so much about him, and then be done. Holding in animosity will only be more detrimental in the long run."

I hate shrinks. It's like God only gave them the voice of reason on Earth to piss us off.

"I'm good as long as he stays away from me and my family," I snap. "I don't want to talk anymore about that bonehead," I firmly say.

"Of course, Mr. Thorne." She concedes and removes her glasses. "Why don't we pick up when we get back to Los Angeles? Give my receptionist a call and we'll set up a time to meet."

"Sounds great."

"Safe travels."

I leave the room and make my way down the hall and out of the hotel, where Mitch is waiting to take me back to Grandma's house. Saylor and I have talked about getting a house where she and Everly grew up in Janesville. Linc bought a place there, and he and Everly travel there often to see her dad. I make a mental note to call and ask him about the area and the real estate out there.

Back at Grandma and Grandpa's house we've got just about everything packed up that is coming back with us to Los Angeles.

My phone rings, bringing me out from looking under the bed, and I smile when I see who it is.

"Hey, baby," I greet. "What can I do for you?"

"Hey Levi, I've got the last of our stuff packed but can't find Teddy Bear. Is she there at Grandma's?"

Teddy Bear is Halo's most beloved stuffed animal. It's a plain, soft, fuzzy pink bear with black eyes and nose. She sleeps with her most nights, or is attached to her hip when she's toddling around between both houses. Thank God the dogs know not to touch her or Halo would be so upset.

"When was the last time she had her?"

"I think yesterday when we gave her a bath after the ice cream debacle." Saylor laughs and so do I.

Yesterday we all went for ice cream, as a last time in town event, before heading back to pack. Halo had other ideas and when I wasn't looking for two seconds, she managed to get it all in her hair, face and body. I didn't fare too well either when I picked her up; she rubbed the ice cream that was on her dress all over me. My house was closer, so we brought her here to bathe before heading back to Glammy's house.

I check the bathroom one more time and find Teddy Bear under the towels.

"I've got her," I say, and I hear Saylor tell our daughter, who cheers and claps. There is no better life than this.

"Please don't forget her and don't pack her away. Halo will need her for the plane ride."

"Yes, dear!" I mock, making Saylor giggle. "I'll be there shortly."

We hang up and I text Mitch, to let him know that we are ready to head out. Mitch has been back and forth between Los

Angeles and Montana these last two months. Both Saylor and I agreed that it was too long for him to be away from his life there. We both know how it feels to be separated for long periods of time and so he has Ryan stay with us, and took the other two back with him. We aren't in any danger here, so it's only been him and Ryan these two months.

Once we made it to the jet, it took three men to load all of our things under the plane. I understand Saylor's load because she's had two years worth of belongings and Halo's things, but what Grandma is sending us home with is another story. She didn't want to leave anything that Halo might miss at their home. I feel as though Grandpa is going to have to add an addition onto the house with all of Grandma's things, if she keeps this up. Little do they know, but Reid has had a playground built in their backyard for Halo to play on. He's sent me pictures and even I'm excited to have a go at it.

After forty minutes, we are in the air, and I couldn't be happier to have my family with me heading back home. I've only dreamed of this, and it is finally becoming a reality for me.

Reaching over, I place a hand on Saylor's, and she turns away from looking out the window. She accepts my touch more and more, as time goes on. At first, she avoided all touching but as each day goes by, I'm able to freely brush against her or hold her hand. My body craves hers, and I find I'll do anything to be next to her. I do notice, when we go out in public with high traffic, that she touches and holds onto me just the same and I love when she does. It's a step in the right direction for us to becoming more of a married couple and finding our way back to each other.

"What are your thoughts on a home outside of the city?" I ask. I know we talked about living in one of the rental houses we have, or finding something further out, but I just want her and Halo to be happy, wherever we pick.

"I'm not sure, maybe something with some land to let Halo and the dogs roam easily." She looks forward at where Zeus and Ginger are crated with Ryan up front, then back at me.

"Do you want cows and horses like at the ranch?" I leave out *his* name as best as possible and Saylor understands. We don't discuss *him* anymore and I think Saylor is still dealing with his betrayal. I know what I did by keeping her in the dark about the threats, but what *he* did was deliberate.

"Good lord no. Can you imagine the upkeep of a place like that? No, but I would like to have plenty of space away from neighbors," she admits, and I feel some relief. I'm not too keen on having to hire a bunch of men to take care of the land and be there when I can't. "Is that going to be a problem with your commute into the city for work?"

I love that she still considers me in our decisions, as I will do everything in my power to include her in mine. No more secrets between us.

"Baby, I haven't been doing much work the last two years, and if it means I get to spend more time with you, then I'll continue to only take on a few renovating house projects a year. You and this girl of ours are my whole world, and nothing is more important." And I mean every word.

The flight attendant comes by and gets our drink orders. She brings me a black coffee, Halo gets milk in a sippy cup and Saylor orders a ginger ale because she's been having an upset stomach lately. She blames it on moving, and I don't blame her. Coming back to a city where she was treated horribly must be hard and nerve-racking. Not to mention, the press is going to have a field day when they notice she's back and with my baby.

"Will you stay with us at Glammy's house or are you heading back to the apartment when we land?" she asks.

"I'd like to stay, if that's okay with you. Being away from you and Halo is the last thing I want."

She nods and squeezes my hand, as Halo hands me her empty sippy cup. She's rubbing her eyes and I know it's almost naptime for our little girl. I check her buckles again for the fiftieth time since we've boarded the plane, and make sure Teddy Bear and blankie are near for her to snuggle with.

Once we land and the SUVs are loaded, we start our drive to Glammy's home. I hate that once everyone is settled, I'll be in a different place once again by myself. Alone. I can't wait for the day when I'll have my wife in bed with me every night. I might even have Halo share a room with us for a while, just so all of my family is together. I know that's not logical but man, I can almost taste having it all.

Halo sleeps through the entire ordeal of moving from the plane to car and then to her and Saylor's room at the house. Ryan put together the portable crib quickly, and my little girl let out a long sigh when she was able to stretch out and lay on her belly, with her cute little butt up in the air.

I watched for a long while as she slept and couldn't picture my life before having her in it. A gentle hand touches my upper arm, and I turn to find my wife standing there. She nods to the other side of the room and I follow where she pointed with her head.

"Levi," I turn my attention away from Halo, who just started to babble in her sleep like her mother. "I think I'm ready to try again. I'm not saying we jump in and become man and wife, but I think we can be more than friends. I feel like we've been through so much and have missed out because of one bad decision, and a line of gigantic misunderstands."

Saylor sounds hesitant and timid with her words.

"I'm not saying that what you did was right, and if you ever do something like that again then it's over, Levi. I won't be in a marriage where we aren't equals. Deep down, I can see where you thought you were making the right decision for me and our family but it can't happen again. If you can promise me to always be honest, then I would love nothing more than to try and rekindle what we had before."

"Oh, baby," my voice croaks and my knees buckle. I end up crouched down in front of her as I basically push her to sit on the bed, while grabbing for both of her hands. "I promise you won't regret this. Every day, you'll see how I'm not the same man I was when we first met. I love you more than I ever thought possible. You and this little one are my whole life and I plan to prove that." I start to lean in but stop. "Can I kiss you?" I ask because we haven't been intimate since we spent that night together.

Saylor smiles then nods, leaning forward towards me, giving me the green light. I don't hesitate in capturing her lips and sealing mine over hers. My body moves closer so my hips are between her knees, while my hands release hers and wrap around her waist. She gasps with the sudden movement, and I take advantage as I plunge my tongue in and dance with hers.

I think we've passed obscene and only stop when we hear a small squeal.

"Me, me!"

Saylor and I pull apart and laugh as Halo is bouncing in her crib, trying to escape, wanting the same attention.

"Does my baby doll want kisses too?" I ask in a sing-song to Halo. She cheers and I'm more than happy to oblige, never releasing my hold on Saylor. This couldn't be a better day if it tried.

Finally, all the pieces are starting to come together and I can see the light at the end of the tunnel.

A while later, Mitch barges into Alan's study, not bothering to knock, where I'm doing some research on houses and replying to some emails.

"What?" I question, Mitch never just bursts through a door unannounced.

"Sir, I need you to come with me. Now," Mitch urgently states and practically drags me out the door and outside, where Ryan is standing holding an opened package.

Once we are securely away from the house, Mitch speaks.

"Sir, I just received this and I don't think it is something we can ignore."

I look in the package and see a picture of Saylor, Halo and myself holding hands on either side of our baby, as we walk down the street from yesterday, heading into the ice cream shop. At the bottom of the photo is a message.

I told you what would happen if you didn't leave them. Did you think I'd make empty threats? I'm coming for them; you and your security won't see it in time.

CHAPTER EIGHTEEN

Saylor

I can't believe I just said that to Levi. *I think I'm ready to try again* was not what I was going to say when I touched his arm. What I was going to ask was whether he wanted to order takeout or have me make a small dinner. Boy, that went in a completely different direction. But every time we touch, I'm still that girl who is zapped at contact and loses all train of thought. I was planning to have a very long discussion with him, after we were settled here in a week or so, about moving forward. *Well, I guess there's no time like the present.*

I know in my heart that he and I belong together and nothing can break our bond, even years apart. When I was with Brody, I was still thinking about Levi; it didn't matter what was happening. I was always wondering what he was doing or what he would think about how Halo was growing. It's probably why I was pushing off and holding out to *date* Brody.

The last two months have been so hard on me, and speaking with Everly daily and not seeing her has been difficult, now that we have been reconnected. I ended up calling Dr. Blake, and with her encouragement after a week, and breaking down over the phone, we managed to skype our sessions. The more we talked, the better I felt afterwards.

We spent hours on the phone at times and even on weekends. Dr. Blake has been the ear that I needed to rant and rave to when I felt myself hit a brick wall with both Brody and Levi. She always makes herself available, even afterhours.

With Levi, it was easy sessions for some reason as opposed to Brody. Levi, I held so much animosity towards but it was all displaced. I thought he was behind everything that happened to me when in reality, he was only responsible for keeping the threat from me. That restaurant debacle didn't help but after some hard truths, I understood where he was coming from. I hated he kept it from me, and he better never do something like that ever again or else I'll smother him with a pillow in his sleep. But Dr. Blake reminded me of Levi's past and how even though he's worked through most of it, he still has a lot of insecurities when it comes to me. In his mind he thought that by not telling me, he was keeping me and the baby safe. As horrible as that sounds, is that really such a bad thing for a husband to want to protect you and your child? Yes, he kept something from me but according to him and Mitch, he was trying to find me to tell me about the situation. If all marriages ended when one spouse made a mistake, then no one would be married.

Levi has been more than forthcoming since he found me and Halo, and I have no reason but to believe he won't do it again. I trust he'll make the right decision next time, and that he's learned from his mistakes that caused us to be apart for over two years.

One thing Dr. Blake said to me was, "Now that you know the whole truth and situation, can you walk away from Levi and only be happy to see him when he picks Halo up or on her birthdays?" The answer was an immediate no. Some may think we have an unhealthy relationship but to us it works, or worked, I should say. Now we have a second chance to learn and grow to be even better than we were the first time around.

Like Dr. Blake reminded me, I knew full well what I was getting into when I married Levi. I knew of his insecurities and abandonment issues. We'd had a few sessions with Dr. Jordan, just so that I understood him and his line of thinking. I knew something wasn't right at the restaurant when he made a scene and if I'd been in my right mind, I'd known what he was up to. Levi never liked doing anything in the public eye when it came to our relationship, and having lunch in the middle of a restaurant should've been a red flashing warning sign. Had I not been so hormonal, I think things would've turned out differently; I think I'd still have slapped the shit out of him but things would've been clearer.

Brody, on the other hand, was a lot more complicated. I thought that we were friends and his betrayal cut deeper than Levi's, if you can believe that. Dr. Blake said that it was because I trusted him blindly, and he purposely kept me away from my family for himself. I don't know why, but I carried a lot of guilt when I found out that I was still married to Levi and had slept with Brody. Then, to only get drunk and sleep with Levi while I was in a relationship with Brody.

With Brody, he made me feel safe and I felt tricked that someone whose sole purpose was to protect me was there to deceive me. He made it to where Levi missed the birth of our child and all the beginnings of her life; he'll never get to have those moments back.

Brody had continued to try and contact me any way he

could, but I just couldn't be anywhere near him. It stings, and the bitterness is too fresh. When I gave him his wedding rings back, you'd thought I was ending a real marriage. I feel horrible because I know deep down that somewhere he thought he was doing the right thing, but I don't think I could ever look past it or forgive him for it. A few weeks later, he brought Zeus and Ginger over stating that they'd gone into a depression, not having Halo and I around, and asked if I'd please take them to keep. Levi swears it's just another attempt to keep tabs on me and something for me to remember him by. I gave him the hardest eye roll known to mankind. To my shock, Levi just smiled then took Halo outside to play with the dogs. The change I've seen in him over the last few months is nothing short of amazing, and a small part of me feels giddy inside like I did when we first met.

I think back to when I took Halo to the ranch, to tell Brody about us leaving with an army of security following. It seemed like something that needed to be done in person and not a conversation over the phone. It was a hard talk, but I'm glad I was able to say goodbye and thank him for everything he did for me and Halo, even though he hid the truth from us. Brody was still there when I needed someone to pick me up at the beginning.

"So, this is really it? You're leaving for good?" Brody asks, as he *pushes Halo on the swing.*

I know that he thought of her as his own, but I still feel that betrayal of him not being this close to her if he'd just told us the truth from the beginning.

"Yes. We leave in a few hours."

The silence is long and the only noise is Halo squealing.

"I think I always knew the moment he found you that this would never work," Brody finally says, as the conversation hit a wall. *"Even if I didn't lie about everything."*

"You did?" I ask astonished.

"Yeah," he pauses like he's debating if he should tell me. "You talk a lot in your sleep." I've always known that and hate it because I can't control what comes out of my mouth. "He was always a topic or a single word when you slept. It was like you still needed him, even when you had me next to you."

I can see the sadness in his eyes and even though Brody and I are at odds, I still hate seeing him this way.

"You'll find someone, Brody, to love you and only you. You deserve to have a happily ever after with someone who doesn't come with all this baggage."

We stand in silence again for a while as Halo feeds the chickens one last time, and I finally feel at peace. Brody and I had a complicated friendship but, in the end, I know that we are going to be leaving on good terms. We may never cross paths again, or speak, but I'm okay with that.

I let Halo tell all the guys on the ranch bye and give hugs. A part of me is so sad to be leaving this behind, but the other part is glad to get my other life back. To not live in fear of being spotted and my cover blown.

"Are you still giving Halo her vitamins and taking yours as well?" Brody asks out of the blue as we walk back to the SUV, where Ryan is waiting to load us up.

"Yeah, why?" I ask. What a strange question, but maybe he's just making sure we're taking care of ourselves.

He looks down at his shoes and tugs on his shirt collar like he's nervous.

"It's just—" Brody starts to say.

"Saylor, you ready to go? We can't miss our flight time," Ryan interrupts as we approach the car, and Halo is tugging on his pant *leg to make her fly. And of course, he scoops her up and throws her in the air.*

"Yeah, we're ready," I say and turn to tell Brody bye. The conversation forgotten, I find myself in the biggest hug engulfed in Brody's arms. His touch now feels foreign, but I try my best to let him have this one last thing.

"I truly am sorry Saylor. I love you more than you'll ever know, and don't want you to hate me."

"I don't hate you Brody." I finally give in, squeezing him back.

A throat clears and I know Ryan is ready to get out of here. I'm sure he's uncomfortable with Brody touching me and wants to step in, so I step out of his embrace.

"If you ever find yourself in LA or in Janesville, hit me up and we'll have a coffee or something," I offer but I hope it never comes. I don't plan on ever seeing this man again.

He nods and I walk to the car, where Halo is already buckled, and hop in the front with Ryan behind the wheel. We pull out and I wonder if I'll ever see Brody Jackson again.

My thoughts from earlier are interrupted, as Halo stands from the floor tossing her ball down the hallway then goes to chase it, as Ginger stays close by. I'm thankful that Glammy and Granddad are allowing us to stay here with them at their LA home and allowed us to bring the dogs with us. Following behind her to make sure she stays away from the kitchen, Halo bypasses that room and dashes out the front door, where someone left it cracked open. Rushing after her, I'm two steps out the door when Ryan sweeps her up.

"Thank you, Ryan!" I exclaim. "She's getting faster every day."

"No worries, Saylor. We're staying closer for now," he says, then tosses her up in the air to keep her from wiggling out of his arms. They are the best of buddies now and Ginger is slightly jealous of the attention Halo gives to Ryan.

I look out over the driveway, and find Mitch and Levi in a heated argument. I've never seen him be so aggressive with Mitch, and my legs move on their own accord towards them. The closer I get, the louder their voices carry towards me.

"You said he was dead!" Levi snaps and shoves a package into Mitch's chest. "And that this was all over."

"He is. I don't—"

"What's going on here guys?" I ask, wanting to break up this tense moment.

"Saylor—" Levi trails off, then wraps me in a bear hug, squeezing all the air out of my body.

"What's going on, Levi? What could be so upsetting that you'd speak and yell at Mitch like that?"

"Oh, baby. I thought it was over but it's not."

"Levi, you're not making any sense. What's not over?"

"Where's Halo?" he asks looking around, and I point over to the front door that is now closed and no sight of Ryan, Ginger or Halo.

"Please, listen to me. Nothing is going to happen to you or our daughter, I'd never let anything happen." Levi gives me the most pleading look.

"Levi you're scaring me," I plead, and take a step back to give us both some breathing room.

"Don't leave me, please," he sounds like a child all of a sudden, and I know whatever it is it's bad.

"Tell me. I can handle it, just tell me."

Levi never takes his eyes from me and reaches out his hand to the package that Mitch is holding. He holds it to his chest like a spoiled child who doesn't want to share his toys. Slowly, he lowers it and I look inside.

The first thing I notice is the perfect picture of the three of us walking hand in hand as a family. I actually think we should frame it. But then, the further down my eyes go, I see in big bold red letters a message at the bottom.

I told you what would happen if you didn't leave them. Did you think I'd make empty threats? I'm coming for them; you and your security won't see it in time.

The world spins and my stomach drops, but not before my knees buckle. I can hear shouting and the howl of Zeus in the background, but the black spots cover my eyes as my body goes limp.

BEEP...BEEP...BEEP...

The sound of yelling wakes me, but my eyes are heavy.

"Sir, you can't have animals in the hospital." A female voice finally rings out.

"He's not going anywhere but staying beside her."

"Sir, he's making it hard for the other nurses to do their job. It's against policy to have him here," the female states.

I hear the growl of Zeus, and feel a shift of weight at the bottom of the bed.

"Then get someone in here that he trusts and it won't be a problem! Zeus isn't going anywhere. Get your supervisor in here and don't come back unless you have answers for me. No, get the CEO in here, my family has given millions to this hospital in donations, and I won't have you upsetting my dog or wife when she wakes up," Levi booms.

The door opens and closes as my vision starts to clear.

"Thank god, you're awake!" Levi beams and rushes over to me, and Zeus turns so that his head is in my lap.

"What happened? I remember being in the front of the house, then you letting me see that package. Was it real?"

Levi nods and grabs for my hands.

"I promise that nothing is going to happen to you or Halo."

"Where is she?" I start to panic.

Levi places a hand on my cheek, "She's playing in an office down the hall. Ryan is in there with Everly, Mom and Mitch. We've got two other men stationed right outside the door. Linc is talking to the chief of police."

"Who would send that? I thought you said Kevin Jenkins was dead?" I lean in to his touch, as my heartrate starts to slow down.

"We don't know. Mitch, William and Dean are looking into it." He looks about as frustrated as I do. Maybe the saying *'igno-rance is bliss'* really is something to live by.

"Am I okay? How long did I pass out?"

Levi gives a soft smile, but it doesn't reach his eyes.

"Almost three hours." My eyes widen as he continues. "There is something I need to tell you, and I'm not sure how you're going to take it but I need you to know that I'm here and we'll do this together."

"You're scaring me Levi. What is it? What's wrong?"

Before he can tell me, the door opens and a man in a white coat is ushered in. Zeus is on immediate alert and sits up in a defensive stance. Right away, I remember him.

"Saylor, it's so good to see that you're awake," Dr. Hampton says, as he comes up beside the bed. Zeus calms and lays down, but keeps watch. "I hope your husband has told you the reason I'm here, and hopefully we'll have the results shortly."

"Results? Of what?" Dr. Hampton looks over to Levi, and he shakes his head.

"Well," he pauses then turns his full focus to me. "When you were brought in, I was in the ER at the time and took over your case. Your husband told us of your medical history and when I asked if you were on birth control, he had said yes. When I asked what kind, one of your security handed over the pill package to give us the name."

"Okay, but why does that matter?"

"It matters because there was a complete recall on that certain brand of birth control."

"Recall?"

"Yes, Saylor, that type was not effective at stopping pregnancy."

"What are you saying?" I pause, taking in everything he's telling me. "Am I pregnant?"

"According to the results taken in the ER, yes you are pregnant."

"Oh God! Are you sure?"

"Yes, the results were accurate." I feel my hand get squeezed, and remember that I'm not the only one in the room.

"How far along? This can't be happening, not with everything going on."

The door opens and a nurse comes in, pulling the sonogram machine and a folder with papers in her hand. She hands the paperwork over to Dr. Hampton, then starts to plug in the machine.

Dr. Hampton starts looking down at the documents, squinting his eyes at certain parts of the pages.

"What is it? What does it say?" Levi all but demands, and I can feel the sweat form in our joined hands.

This can't be happening. How is Levi going to deal with me having Brody's child? Now he'll always be in our lives. Will Levi want that? Will he leave me because I'm not having his child?

"Saylor, Mr. Thorne, it seems that when we ran your blood panels, to have it on record, that birth control being present in your system came back as negative."

"Negative? How? I take it every morning when I wake up. Like clockwork!" I turn to Levi. "I swear this isn't like the last time where I forgot. I take it every morning, and haven't missed a day since getting back on it right after Halo was born."

"I believe you." Levi gives me an encouraging nod, and kisses my forehead.

"According to the results, there is no evidence of any trace of it being in your bloodstream. That means that for at least the past twenty-one days, you have not been taking an effective form of birth control."

"Then what the hell has she been taking?" Levi demands.

"That's what I was getting to. My assistant had the pills in the package tested and with a security guy from your team, Mitch, I believe standing over them. The results are that every pill in the package are all sugar pills. But it also showed that the packaging had been tampered with."

"Sugar pills?" Levi says before I can speak.

"Yes, the entire pack." Dr. Hampton confirms. "Saylor, do you remember where this prescription came from?"

I try to think back at the name of the pharmacy in Helena, but come up blank.

"I don't remember. Brody always—" I stop and close my eyes.

No, he wouldn't. He couldn't have, could he?

"That motherfucker!" Levi yells, and Mitch comes rushing in at his scream.

Tears are flooding down my face and I'm having a hard time catching my breath.

"How could he do this? Why would he?" I wail as my heart is breaking at Brody's ultimate betrayal.

It seems like forever before both Levi and I calm down. Our hands are latched together, holding on for dear life.

"We'll get through this, baby. I promise."

"Would you like for me to come back another time to scan the baby?" Dr. Hampton asks from a corner, where he and a nurse are waiting patiently. I completely forgot he was even there.

"No, let's see the baby and make sure that he or she is healthy," I shakily say. No matter who the baby's father is, I'm a mother first and foremost and I need to make sure everything is going smoothly for him or her.

After several minutes, Dr. Hampton scans and takes the measurements. He asks several questions about when my last menstrual cycle was and after calculating, he turns back to the screen.

"I'd say that you're around eight weeks according to the measurements and dates of the last period."

Levi freezes, and I can see the wheels turning.

"What is it?" I ask him.

"It could be mine." His confidence shining through. "That's around the time we got together. It's possible that this baby is mine." He places a hand on the side of my belly.

I feel a wave of relief wash over me, but I don't want to get my hopes up.

"But it was just that one time. Brody and I—" I trail off, not wanting to think about that jackass right now.

"All it takes is just one time, Saylor. And we both know that I have very good swimmers!" We both burst out with a laugh, but then remember how serious this situation is.

"Levi," my voice trembles and my lip quivers, but then he's right there with his nose touching mine.

"We are going to be just fine. No matter what," he assures me, and I can only nod.

"But what about—"

He cuts me off again, like he knows what my mind is saying before I can finish speaking.

"You and me, baby. Against the world."

CHAPTER NINETEEN

Levi

"I don't care what you have to do, bring that fucker here! Hog tie his ass to a saddle and have him ride here on a black stallion for all I care, but get him here!" I blast to Mitch and Ryan.

It's been two days since Saylor was released from the hospital and we found out that she was pregnant. When Dr. Hampton told me the news, I was over the moon and couldn't believe that we were going to be giving Halo a brother or sister, but as a few moments passed, a flash of that asshole's face came into the picture and my world was thrown into a tailspin. I felt as though the Hulk was about to burst out of my skin at the thought of Saylor having another baby that wasn't half mine. It took Mitch putting me in my place to bring me off the ledge. I had so many emotions running at the same time; joy, heartache, rage, fear. Dr. Blake got an earful and after a long session, I finally realized that it didn't matter that the baby might not be mine. The baby was going to be a part of Saylor and that was all that mattered. She was my whole life, and I'd accept the child as I do Halo. But I wasn't going to accept that little smarmy fucker, who I know purposely switched Saylor's pills, in hopes of tying her to him for the rest of his life.

Saylor decided that staying at Grandma and Grandpa's house was too risky and didn't want to put them in harm's way, so we're holed up in the penthouse apartment on lockdown. I know she's scared, and I hate that I can't do anything right now but say words and not be able to take action. Once again, we're playing the waiting game to see if any other threats are going to arrive. Everly's dad has offered for them to come and stay at his cabin in Janesville for a little while, but I'm not sure if security would be able to monitor everything as well out near the forest.

The only upside to all of this is that Saylor is sleeping, not only under the same roof as me, but in the same bed. I could tell she was trembling when it came close to bedtime and so I scooped her up and led her to our room. Of course, Halo sleeps right between us because we didn't want her far from us, so the only logical way was to have her with us. I've never slept better in my life knowing my family is close to me, even when I catch a hand to the neck or a foot to the nose when Halo ends up turned upside down, with her head towards the footboard. I find myself with an arm over her body and my hand is securely resting on her stomach.

"Sir, Colbert and the team have landed and are heading over to the ranch to get Brody."

"Good, let me know when they're in the air."

A thud on the door interrupts our meeting and before I can reply, the door flings open and Halo comes toddling in on a mission, with Saylor right on her heels. The tapping sound from the dogs nails follow closely behind. They are always around, making sure to stay close to my girls.

"Halo Thorne!" Saylor lectures, but her voice says that even though she's trying to reprimand her, she doesn't really mean it.

"Hurry baby doll! Quick!" I shout and throw my arms out to catch her.

"Dada! Hep, hep!"

"I got ya." I twist in my chair to turn away from Saylor, like she's the big bad wolf.

"Ugh," Saylor groans and plops down on the sofa that I have in the office. "Tag you're it. She's all yours."

Saylor is definitely showing all the signs of being pregnant; I think we all thought it was the stress of our fucked-up situation, or the move. She looks tired, and I don't think that it has anything to do with the threat.

"You feeling okay, baby?" I ask but don't look over to the area she's in, because my little doll has my pen, trying to scribble all over my desk. I think I'll order Halo her own desk filled with colors and books, just for her. She might want to be a lawyer one day too and will need her own little space to flourish. *No, she can be whatever she wants, no pressure.*

"Just tired," she pauses, and I see her throw her arms over her face out of the corner of my eye.

"You have a nap and this little girl and I will solve world peace." I quickly distract Halo and swipe my pen from her hands before she pokes her or my eye out.

"I spoke to Dad before we came in here," Saylor mumbles.

"And?" I knew it would happen eventually. I'm channeling all my inner Dr. Blake techniques so as to not show any harboring dislike towards the man. "I'm sure that was exciting to hear from him."

Halo wiggles out of my grip and rushes over to Ryan, wanting him to pick her up. He bends down and she yanks on his tie to make him eye level with her. We all know what she wants and he immediately tosses her up in the air, giving us a moment to talk before she's on to the next amusing adventure. Saylor was right;

an apartment is a horrible idea for a little girl who's had acres and acres to roam freely.

"He wants me to swing by Glammy's house with Halo in a couple of hours. Dad wants to meet his granddaughter."

"Did you tell him about the threat?"

"I mentioned that someone had sent something targeting us, but not in any detail. He was pushing that it was safe there with him, and more room to roam for a two-year-old than in a stuffy apartment," she says looking over at me. "He's not wrong. Kids need fresh air and to run all that energy out."

"Do you want to go?" *Please say no!* I hate that Adam has so much animosity towards me and we haven't even had a proper introduction. He is her father, and I think it'd be healthy for her and her dad to rekindle their relationship, if it can be managed. I just hope we can let the last few years be water under the bridge and move on from all of that. If not, then it is something I'm going to have to deal with for the rest of my life, so I need to just suck it up for her sake.

"I'd love to see my dad but don't you think it might be dangerous to be out in public?" I can see it in her face that she'd love to go and her body perks up. I'd do anything to see her happy.

"Mitch? Can we get a team together and have it work?" I ask after picking up the phone and calling him into the office.

"You're going too, right?" Saylor questions, then sits up. Halo makes a break for the door, where Tina has milk and cookies, and Ryan is hot on her tail with Ginger following right behind them. That man is worth his weight in gold. I didn't think it was possible for a person to have as much energy as a toddler, but Ryan seems to be on the same level as her.

"Mitch and I'll swing by later. We've got something coming in that needs tending to." Her face drops and I get up to make my way over to her. Lifting her up and placing her in my lap, I cuddle her tightly to me with my hand over her slightly raised bump. I missed a lot when Halo was growing in her belly and my baby or not, I plan to be there every step of the way. "I promise to only be a couple hours behind you. You know I can't be that far from you and Halo, now that I've got you back."

"I know, I just hate that we have to go separately. It's weird, I've been away from you for over two years and now, I can't think about being away for even a few minutes."

"It's not weird, it means you're just as obsessed with me as I am with you. Besides, you'll only be across town." I kiss the end of her nose and move to her lips. It was supposed to be a light peck but fuck it, we're back together finally and I'm not wasting any more time. As soon as one of us moans, a throat clears and I remember Mitch is still with us.

"Sorry, Mitch," Saylor says as she buries her face in my neck, but I can tell she doesn't mean it.

"I think we can work something out if you want to go and see Adam." Mitch never looks over at us on the sofa, but continues to type on his phone.

"Really?" Her voice goes up an octave in excitement.

"Why don't you go and pack a bag for you and Halo, while I talk out the plan with Mitch. Maybe I can convince Linc and Everly to go out to Janesville for a few days and look at a few properties out there to buy. Let Tina watch the baby, so she doesn't unpack everything you put in the bag."

"Are you sure?" she asks with a huge smile. I know she loves being outdoors just as much as I do. Being back in the city just doesn't feel like it used to and I think we, as a family, would flourish more being out of here.

"Yeah." I give her a nuzzle on the neck and plant a kiss right under her ear in the spot I know drives her crazy. "Maybe we can have a few minutes alone before you leave," I whisper.

Standing with her still in my arms, I place her feet on the ground and swat her fine behind, then adjust my dick.

"Why Mr. Thorne, are you saying you can only go a few minutes now? Maybe it's time to trade you in for a new and younger stud who can last longer." She giggles.

I growl then lunge, but she manages to whip around Ryan, who comes in at that exact moment blocking me. *Damn that woman! I'll show her how long I can really go and she'll be begging for mercy.*

Once she's gone, the room goes back to business.

"What's your thoughts Mitch?"

"I'm sure you don't want to bring Brody here to confront him under the same roof as Saylor right now; I think letting her go would be the ideal situation." He's right, I don't want my wife anywhere near that asshole at the moment. One sniff of her and he'd think she's the one who requested him here. Plus, one mention of the baby and he's never going to leave us alone. He'll think he has a chance to worm his way back into their lives.

"You're right, what are the plans on getting her and Halo there safe?"

The three of us spend the next forty minutes going over and tweaking their visit to Sharilyn's house, and who is going with Ryan and my girls. We also discuss the trip out to Janesville, and I message Linc about our last-minute idea. He's on board to get away for a few days. Reid can't make this trip, due scheduling conflicts at his office, but wants to have everyone over when we get back. Once we all feel comfortable with the plan, I go in search of my wife but find her asleep on the bed next to our baby, who's also making light snoring sounds.

My phone vibrates with a message from Mitch, letting me know the *package* has been secured and is taking off from Helena, Montana soon. That gives me almost three hours to spend with my girls. Instead of wanting to interrupt naptime, I strip down to my boxers and slide behind Saylor and reach over her body to snuggle Halo closer with my hand. As much as I wanted some alone time with Saylor, I'd never trade a moment of the three of us being this close. Soon, it'll be four and I want to soak up as much time as I can before we change to a larger family.

Saylor and Halo have been gone with a group of security to watch over them for just a little while now, which means that they should be at Sharilyn's house meeting Adam now. There were a few detours, as my wife wanted to stop for Mexican food, but so far so good. I hate that I can't go with them but right now, I'm waiting for a little pissant to get here so I can squash him like the annoying insect he is. The flight was delayed, due to weather, and the plane was grounded for almost an hour before taking off. Mitch has been instructed to not intervene unless necessary, because I really want to get a piece of him.

I'm sitting in my office when I hear the ping of the elevator, letting me know that my company has arrived. Mitch knocks three times, then opens it with him and Colbert striding in with Brody.

"So, this is how the other half live. Must be nice to have people at your beck and call at the snap of a finger."

"I have no complaints." Mitch and Colbert both press on Brody's shoulders, planting him in the chair across from my desk. The fact that he was in the military and doesn't show any signs of putting up a fight has me a little on edge. Why would he come willingly? Unless he has an ulterior motive.

"What do you want Levi? You won the woman, so what could you possibly take from me or have to discuss?"

I'm sure my smirk could rate as evil, but I came prepared for this meeting. Shoving two files across my desk, I wait and watch for him to accept them and see just what I do to people who cross me or harm my family in any way. Being well connected and representing the right people does have its perks. Plus, having the best attorney in the nation for a brother doesn't hurt either.

Curiosity getting the best of him, he takes the bait and opens the first one. It doesn't take him long to figure out what I've done.

"You can't," he fumes but pauses, never taking his eyes off the paperwork and continues to read each line. "How did you do this?"

Brody throws the file back on the desk as his pretty boy face turns menacing.

"It was real simple, I just snapped my fingers and it happened." I make a show of snapping, just to give it the added effect. "This is what happens when you fuck with me and my family. You not only crossed a line when you lied to Saylor about your uncle dying, but keeping me from my daughter, thinking you could claim and raise her as yours is something I'll never forgive or forget."

I slam my hand on the file he just tossed down.

"This is just the beginning you little fucker."

The file under my hand is the government contract that Brody has that is providing to our military. The paperwork is a termination agreement; I've got a buddy who owed me for handling his messy divorce that oversees the contracts to be written up. I haven't had them cancelled but it's just one simple call and it's a done deal.

Brody hesitantly opens the other file, and his fingers dig into the papers.

"You piece of shit!" Brody yells, and tries to stand but finds Mitch and Colbert pushing him back down by the shoulders into the chair.

"The only one who fits that bill is you, asshole."

Brody rereads the papers and closes his eyes. That file contains his patents for his goggles and scope; the two products he created and is distributing to the military.

"You and your family truly live up to your name. I've read all about you and your law firm, and unless you see it in person, I guess people really wouldn't know the real you and how ruthless you all can be."

"You haven't seen anything yet," I bark. "I know all about what you did to Saylor's pills." I let that sink in and from the pale color that crosses his face, he knows what I'm talking about.

I can see the scrambling that is going on in his head, trying to find his next words. Finally, he doesn't say anything but instead crosses his arms over his chest, a smug grin across his face.

"If you found out, then that means Saylor is pregnant." The fucker actually smiles at his words.

This isn't how I wanted this conversation to go. I'd much rather he didn't find out until after the baby was born and we find out if it was mine or his, but he causes me to lose my cool at the drop of a pen.

"Well, is she?" He pushes, and I want to put my fist through his face.

"*We* are pregnant again," I admit. A flash of disappointment crosses his face and I enjoy it for a split second. It's wrong of me to revel in his discomfort and disappointment, but it is nothing compared to what he and that bastard uncle of his put me through for over two years.

"How far along?" It's like he's trying to grasp at straws.

"Around eight weeks." I can tell he's counting backwards to the week to see if he fits in the equation and when he gets to that week, he splits his face in two with a smile.

"Don't you mean Saylor and *I* are pregnant," he smugly says, and a growl leaves my chest. I launch myself across the desk and have a tight grip on his collar with both of my fists.

"You deliberately stole her free choice and decisions from her. I've got my brother and associates looking into the legal ramification of your actions, and I hope to God that they throw the book at you, *if* by some slim chance my baby doesn't share the same DNA with me."

I know that it is possible the baby Saylor is carrying is his but, in my mind, that baby has my DNA and blood, not his.

Brody shoves my arms away, and quickly gets up and starts pacing the room. He's mumbling under his breath, having an entire conversation with himself. He stops abruptly and turns towards me and security.

"Where's Saylor? I need to see her. This is fantastic, I'm going to be a dad."

Is this fucker delusional? If he thinks I'm going to let him within a hundred yards of my wife, he's crazier than I thought. Mitch must be thinking the same thing as he moves closer to him, keeping a watchful eye.

"She's not here and even if she was, she wouldn't want to see you and have to look at your deceitful face."

He frowns, but it doesn't last long.

"I know that I went about this the wrong way but I really need to speak with her, to explain."

"Yeah, there *is* a lot of explaining to do, you prick."

"Look, not that I owe you anything, but at the time Saylor and I were discussing Halo getting older and I had asked her if she wanted more kids. Of course, she said yes but that it didn't look like it was in her future. We discussed how she was an only child and wished she had siblings, and how lonely she had been. I thought you were out of the picture, and it seemed like the best solution. Being with Saylor made me want things I never wanted before. She has this way of making you see your life through different glasses, and it really spurred me on to reach out for a family of my own."

"But you took my family!" I yell and stand closer. "She wasn't yours, and Halo is definitely not yours. Try to justify it all you want but at the end of the day you stole, lied and deceived your way into having Saylor trust you. She'll never forgive that."

"But this little one might be mine. Saylor and I could be having a baby together."

"Not likely." This isn't getting us anywhere, and I need to wrap this up so I can go and be with my wife and daughter. "Look, right now the last thing Saylor needs is stress. It's not good for her or our baby."

"I want to be there for her," he starts to say but stops, his eyes go over my shoulder and widen. I turn my head to see what caught his eye and all I notice is my bookshelf with law books and some family photos. Saylor and Halo make up the majority of it.

I move back to look at Brody, and his face his scrunched in disgust.

"You lying hypocrite! I knew you had to know where we were this entire time. You knew that Saylor had finally moved on and was happy and you couldn't just let us live our happy life without your pathetic face in it."

Is this guy demented? What the fuck is he talking about? I came as soon as we found out where my family was.

"What the fuck are you talking about?" I look over to Mitch

and watch as he moves quickly over behind me, with his hand tucked behind him. All security carries weapons. We don't take any chances after everything I've been through over the years.

"I'm talking about you having your guys in Montana this entire time, watching our every move. I thought he was just a local, but now I know differently."

"We didn't have anyone in Montana unless you count my grandparents, who I might add, kept Saylor and Halo hidden from me for the last year."

He scoffs and I'm about ready to knock the shit out of him. I don't have time for his drama right now.

"Then how do you explain him being around town for months?"

Brody shoves his finger over my shoulder and points to a photo on the shelf. Mitch and I both turn to see who the fuck he's talking about.

"Who?"

He moves closer and points to a group of photos on my shelf. One is Saylor's pictures of her parents, from when she was a little girl. Next to that photo, is one of them that include her grandparents, with Saylor resting on her dad's shoulders. Then, I have a photo of Saylor with my two brothers and Everly. There is also a photo of Adam and his military buddies, with all their kids surrounding them. And the last one is of Daniel and Mom, with me and Saylor.

Brody points the person out and I hear Mitch gasp. Or maybe it's me, but I don't spend any time thinking about that.

"Brody, you better not be fucking with us. Are you sure you saw *this* person over the last few months there in Helena?"

He swipes the photo off the shelf and points to the person once again.

"I have no reason to lie. I saw this person and I'd be able to pick him out of a line up. He's always been at a distance but I've seen him all around town."

"Holy fuck!" Mitch breathes out, while he whips his phone out and starts typing.

My mind is reeling at this and I can't believe that *he* would do this. This entire time we've been looking for an outside threat when they've been right under our nose.

"Mitch, alert security that's with Saylor and tell them to lock her and Halo down in Glammy's house until we can get there. Nobody in and nobody out." I pull at my hair and my knees feel weak. "Christ, we have to get to the house before something happens to them. I think he's been waiting to get her alone before he makes his move."

Mitch nods, and we start to storm out of the office.

I'm shouting off orders about getting the cars ready and to have men on the ground. This fucker was just waiting for us to separate before making his move.

"Wait! I'm going with you," Brody shouts and chases after us. Colbert tries to block him but Brody shoves him out of the way.

"We don't need your help," I snap

"If Saylor is in danger then the baby is too. I'm not going to leave it to chance, besides I can help if need be. I do have military training."

I hate that he is even in my presence but right now, we don't know what we are dealing with.

Mitch comes running out of his office in full tactical gear, and has a grim look on his face.

"Sir, we can't reach any of the men from security."

"Not even Ryan?"

He shakes his head.

"The house phones aren't working either."

"Fuck!"

"Who is this person to you, obviously he's kin to you in some way?" Brody pipes up as we load in the elevator to take us up to the roof.

"He's someone who apparently wants to ruin my life and take everything from me."

CHAPTER TWENTY

Saylor

We finally pull up to my grandparent's house and the place looks the same as it did a few days ago, before the bottom fell out.

Once Ryan punches in the code to the gate, we were granted entry. Out on the porch, Dad stands from the rocking chair and is waiting for Halo and I to get out. He's bouncing on the balls of his feet and looks more than excited to see us.

"There she is! Oh, Saylor, she looks just like you when you were a baby," he gushes and it's as if no time has flown by and we haven't seen or heard from each other in almost three years. The moment is a little surreal, but I chalk it up to being tired.

"Hey, Dad," He engulfs me and Halo but she squirms in my arms wanting down.

"Hello, pumpkin, I'm your granddad or Papa," he introduces to Halo but she toddles off towards Ryan, who has her teddy bear and pink blanket in his hand.

"She takes a while to warm up to people," I say and give him another big hug. "How've you been?" I ask. "Where have you been?"

"I've been looking for you. Took off on some leads. It was only recently that I received word from Tommy that you'd been found and were here," he shrugs, not looking at me but watches as both Zeus and Ginger climb out of the car and head straight for us. "When did you become a dog lover? And why do you have so many guys here with you?"

"Zeus kinda just stuck to me one day, he's the best," I tell him and give my dog some scratches behind his ears. "Ginger was given to Halo for her first birthday and they're inseparable. As far as the guys, Levi thinks it's best right now until Halo and I get settled back into our lives," I vaguely answer, not wanting to tell him about the threats that just started back up.

I can see an odd look in his eye, but then he turns back to me.

"Well, let's get you and my granddaughter nice and comfy." He walks to the driveway, towards the guesthouse that Glammy and Granddad had added for him years ago. Whenever he did come in for visits, he'd stay out there or in the shop he built to tinker in. "Your muscle can all stay out in the shop if they want; I've made a room to relax in out there."

"Oh, okay."

After letting the guys know about the shop, Halo, the dogs and I all follow Dad in the guesthouse. It still looks the same as it did the last time I was back here; absolutely nothing has changed. My room was always in the main house and none of us stepped foot back here. Dad has always been a very private person, since I can remember, and loved to have his space.

Once Halo is set up with some toys in the living room, Dad and I sit on the couches and catch up with everything that's happened. I've brought photos of Halo and myself over the last two years, living in Montana. Brody gave me those photos that were supposed to be sent to Levi, and I made copies to give to the family.

It's late afternoon and Halo is starting to rub her eyes, letting me know that her quick nap before dinner is ready to start. Dad and I have been talking for what seem like hours, and I've lost track of time. I leave out that I'm pregnant again because Levi and I want to wait and see how things turn out with Brody before we let others know about the baby. Also, I wanted to have a very elaborate discussion about what Levi has said regarding how Dad treated him when he was in the hospital, but I want it to be when Halo isn't in the same room. I have no doubt in my mind that Levi is telling the truth and I want some honest answers as to why my dad would attack a man in a hospital bed. My dad can seem rough around the edges but he's never seemed like the type to be so violent. Yes, he has left me most of my life for my grandparents to raise but after hearing about him losing his twin sister, and then my mom, I can start to understand where he might be coming from.

I love my dad more than anything, but Levi is my whole life. If for some reason he can't accept that, then we are going to have a problem. Levi isn't going anywhere so if Dad can't seem to get along and be civil with my husband, then I can't see how we're going to get past this. I'm hoping after Dad sees how great Levi is with Halo, and how he's moved heaven and earth to find me and his daughter, that Dad has a different attitude towards him.

"Hey, Dad, let me put Halo down for a quick nap and I'll start some dinner for everyone. Levi and the others should be here any time and I'm sure the guys out in the shop could use a meal."

"How much time do you think it'll be before they get here?" he asks, looking over at his watch.

"Not sure but soon."

"Okay, you can use the spare room, next to the office, down that hall. I'll go and check on the guys outside, and see if they need anything until then. A storm's coming and I want to make sure everything is secured and locked up too. If little Halo is anything like you were, then naps are essential to her happy life." It makes me giggle when Dad reminiscences about my time as a child. "I'll let the dogs out to do their business." I nod, but know that Ginger won't go if Halo is going down for a nap. It's like she's programed to stick with Halo and when she sleeps; Ginger is 'On Duty'.

We both go our separate ways and I carry an almost asleep baby down the hall. It's been a long time since I've seen these walls and entered his home here. Ginger, of course, is trailing behind, as it took some convincing to get Zeus to follow Dad outside.

I make quick work at putting the portable crib together that goes everywhere with us and I place her in it, along with Teddy Bear and blanket. She snuggles right up to it and I turn on the small lamp in the corner. Ginger is planted in front of the crib, and she lays facing the door.

Closing the door, I take a few steps down the hall towards the kitchen to get dinner started, but a loud thud then a shatter slams against the wall in Dad's office. Opening the door, I see that the window is slightly open. Papers are scattered on the floor from the wind blowing in, so I quickly move to close the window and latch it. Turning, I bend down and start to pick up all the papers and receipts, then place them on the desk and try to organize them the best I can.

Thinking I'm done, I move to leave the office but see one more piece of paper sticking out from under the closet door. Wanting to make sure everything is picked up, I walk over to pick it up, but my foot pushes it completely under. Twisting the knob, I open the closet door and place my hand against the inner wall to steady myself to grab the paper. But what I find couldn't prepare me for everything that happens next.

The wall gives and slides open, revealing another room off the closet. What's strange is that I don't remember ever seeing this room when I was here years ago. Maybe Dad needed a place to store his guns, or maybe he put a safe with valuables in it. Curiosity gets the better of me and I take a peek in. There's a light switch on the wall right when you enter and I flip it on.

"Oh. My. God!" I whisper.

It's not a safe room, or a place to hold guns or valuables. It's like somewhere you hold a command base meeting. What is Dad doing in here that he had to have a secret room? Maybe he has a customer who wants a more private consult? Is this part of his work that keeps him gone for months on end?

There's a large table in the middle of the room and the walls are covered with papers and diagrams. On one side of the room, he's got four laptops and what looks to be three satellite phones. What is going on? Is Dad back in the military and working on a special mission? If that is the case, I know I shouldn't be in here. I need to leave but as I start to walk out, something in the far corner catches my eye and my legs move on their own accord, to see if my mind is playing tricks on me.

The closer I get the more I'm positive that my eyes are seeing it and I'm not imagining this. Not only do I see a diagram of a car that looks to be the exact replica of my husband's pride and joy, but there next to it is a handful of pictures of me and Halo in different stages of being in Montana.

This can't be happening. The photos look to be taken from far away. Was he watching us? Did he know where we were this entire time? My confusion is short lived, as Zeus starts to bark up a storm outside and from the sound, he's on high alert. Something inside of me knows that this doesn't sit well, and I'm not sure what to do with all of this. I quickly look over the other papers on the walls and see many different locations. There's the LAPD building layout, the blueprints of our penthouse in LA and Thorne Law Firm, another diagram of a warehouse, and maps of Los Angeles and Montana.

My mind starts to wonder and look at the other papers but Zeus's bark is getting more frantic, then goes eerily silent. Something's happened. I abandon the room and go to the window in the office. Dad is stepping out of the shop and briskly walks towards the house. He's got his phone in his hand, talking to someone.

I'm not sure what to make of this room, or what to do with it. If it's nothing, then I've just violated my dad's privacy. But why does he have all that information on Levi's work, home and car that blew up? Should I speak to Ryan about it, or face my dad first? It might be nothing and then I'd be making a fool of myself. Maybe I'm just being paranoid because we just received a threat? Surely there is a reasonable explanation for all of this. Maybe he was helping find out who the threat was that was targeting our family? That would seem like the logical choice, right?

I hear the back door shut and I hightail it out of the office, then towards the living room. Dad is stuffing his phone in the back pocket of his jeans when we come into the same room together. He looks as though he's sweating from the moisture on his forehead and the beginnings of a sweat ring under his arms.

"Hey, Dad," I say, but it comes out like I've just run a marathon. "Want some coffee or tea? Halo is down for the count for a while." I try to calm my heartrate.

"Sure, honey, coffee would be great. I've got some things I need to look at that need my attention for work."

"Okay," I say and turn to walk to the kitchen. "Oh, the window was open in the office and papers got blown everywhere. I tried to pick them up and organize them for you," I say over my shoulder.

I watch in my peripheral as he stops right before the entry of the hallway.

"I'm going to go out and ask the guys if they need anything to drink while I brew your coffee." My legs work their way to the back door.

"They all went to walk the perimeter," Dad says sharply.

"Oh." I finally turn to face Dad and find him in the middle of the room standing tall. "Well, I'm sure Zeus is itching to get back in here."

"Zeus went with them."

I know something isn't right because Zeus would never just go with someone else and leave my sight. Not to mention, Ryan would never allow us to be separated when there is a threat on us. Zeus and Ginger are our last line of defense, in the event that something happens to security. The hairs on the back of my neck start to stand at attention.

"You saw it, didn't you?" he asks calmly. Too calmly.

"What?" I question, but everyone knows I'm a shit liar.

"Sweetheart," he says in warning, like I'm a little girl again who just marked up one of his books with a highlighter.

"Why do you have a hidden room behind the closet of your office? Why is there all this paperwork on Levi? His house? Work? How do you have photos of Halo and me for the last two years when I just gave you some for the first time?"

Dad's stance goes rigid, like he's about to go to war.

"I did what any other father in my position would do," he defends.

"What does that mean?"

"It means that I've been trying to clean up the worst decision you ever made. And to resolve what my parents should've done decades ago."

"Clean up? Dad, Levi is the best thing to ever happen to me. There isn't anyone else I'd want to spend the rest of my life with."

He gives a slight mocking laugh, and I have to wonder where the hell this is coming from.

"Saylor, listen," he steps closer, eliminating the distance between us. "I know you think you might love him, he is your first real boyfriend and all, but he and his family are not what you think they are. I should've put a stop to this over twenty years ago and then we'd never be put in this position. When I found out you started dating the chump, I thought it would sizzle out. I never thought you'd marry the guy and then have a baby with him in such a short amount of time."

"Is this real right now? Are you really having this conversation with me about my husband and the father of my child?"

"Yes, Saylor, I am."

Everything that Levi said about my Dad hating him comes to the forefront.

"Did you really threaten Levi by saying that if you found me first that you'd hide me away and never let him find me?"

"Of course." He snorts. "Honey, the man was marked for failure the moment his parents stuck those needles into their veins and killed themselves. I wasn't about to let you fall into that pit. Not after everything you went through with watching your mother die. I know what a disappointment life can be and I wasn't about to let that happen to you. I'd do everything in my power to prevent that from happening to you ever again. His family is nothing but poison, and I won't have my daughter attached to that. Not when I could prevent it this time."

"Dad, Levi loves me and would never do something like that. I have always been his main priority."

"Tell that to all the families of the victims, where he and his brother let murderers go. Tell Daniel, the man who raised him and molded him to defend guilty criminals, who plow down innocent lives. He lived the fast life and was catered to, all because he wanted to make a name for himself, and didn't care who he was hurting. Look at Blaire Hutchins and what she did to you. She almost cost you Halo, all because you and Everly wanted to have her held accountable for what she was doing." My eyes widen as I realize that Dad knows about the escort business and possibly Levi and Linc's involvement. "That evil woman was more than forthcoming about his ways and how he liked to treat women who he paid for."

My world is reeling and I can't focus on anything at the moment.

"Are you saying that you and Blaire were friends? Talked?"

"I made it my business to know my daughter's boyfriend, and pursued her after finding out you'd started hooking up with the one *family* that I despise more than anything. I knew she was holding more back so I decided to befriend her, and the more I found out, the more I was determined to get you away, even if it meant you some heartache for a little while."

"Blaire Hutchins is bitch. She lured them in with the promise of fame and riches. She was the head person in the prostitution ring in LA for God's sake!" I can't even believe that my dad would befriend a woman like this.

"Oh, I knew exactly who she was after a while, but I needed hard proof before I made my move. I just didn't think you would be such a sucker and marry the asshole so quickly. Out of all the men in this big city, you and Everly had to go and pick a Thorne."

I can't believe what I'm hearing. This has to be a nightmare, and I'm going to wake shortly.

"What hard proof did you need?"

"Blaire was so stupid and had files in her vault, in her office behind some bookshelf. When I was sure I had all the copies of all the files and recordings, I made a call to a buddy of mine and had her turned in to the police. She never saw it coming; that bitch thought we'd work together and break the two of you up."

"You're the reason she was put into jail? She was the one who beat me to a bloody pulp and could've made me lose Halo!" I scream, forgetting that my baby is down the hall sleeping. I thought Everly and I were the ones who put in a tip to get her caught.

"I know." He looks somewhat regretful, but then it's gone. "Don't worry she got what was coming to her in the end. And so did Linley, though I didn't expect that bitch to go as crazy as she did on Everly."

"Did you cause Everly to almost die?"

"I planted seeds for Blaire to have Linley make a scene to scare Everly away. I didn't plan on her going fatal attraction at the spa, but don't worry Linley is living in hell for her actions. You and Everly will never have to worry about that lunatic, or Blaire ever again."

A gasp leaves my lips as I remember the diagram of the Los Angeles PD blueprints.

"Did you have something to do with Blaire dying in jail?"

"I may or may not have pushed her to do it. She didn't need much convincing, after a visit from me.

"Oh my God!"

"Don't be upset, the world is a much better place now that she's no longer prancing around here."

I can't believe this is my dad, the man who raised me to love and be kind to others. The man who would kiss my booboos and hold me when my mother died.

If he was this hungry to break us up, what else has my dad done?

"I know you think it was harsh but it wasn't," he tells me.

"What else have you done?" I stare, laser focused at him. There is a lot more to this than what he's saying.

He shrugs like he's bored with this conversation, but we are far from done.

"Tell me," I demand and my mind goes back to the hidden room. "You sabotaged his car, didn't you?" He stares back at me, not budging. "Didn't you! I saw the diagram of the car in the room back there, tell me," I yell, shaking to my core.

"Yes. Is that what you want to hear? I did. That man has a horrible past and bloodline, and it was going to bleed over onto you. That was something I wasn't going to allow. Do you even know the type of people he represents? He takes on murderers and gets them off scot-free with some loophole. All it takes is the right dollar amount and he'll do anything."

"Allow? Why would you do something like that? Why not just come talk to me and tell me what was going on with you? He doesn't even do that anymore and never really wanted to, but felt he had to follow in his brother's footsteps. Levi is kind and loves to work with his hands rebuilding homes and being outdoors like me. He does great things for the community but doesn't want the publicity for it—"

"Because you were blinded by all the hearts and grandeur he had. I knew when I found out who he was that he had some spell weaved on you, and you wouldn't have been very receptive to me saying anything."

"Thanks for the vote of confidence, Dad," I sneer. "I've always had my head on straight, even when you abandoned me for months, leaving my grandparents to raise me and not you," I spit.

"No, you weren't in the right frame of mind, and after watching my daughter be publicly humiliated for all the world to see, I knew I had to fix the problem sooner than planned."

"Sooner?"

"Yes."

"Are you crazy? I could've been in that car with him!"

"I knew where you were the entire time. I've had eyes on you ever since the news announced you being married to that asshole."

Now I do feel my knees weaken. My own Dad has had me followed for months before he tried to kill my husband. How did my security not notice someone else watching me?

"Wait, they thought Kevin Jenkins was behind the car bomb."

Dad crosses his arms over his chest and rests back on his heels.

"I told you that the Thornes had a past. Kevin just happened to be part of it. It was like two birds one stone kinda thing."

"Kevin was a Senior Associate at Levi's law firm that was fired for falsifying documents at work against Linc. He made sure he lost his job and we didn't hear anything else from him after that. Levi would've said if he had a connection to him."

"Would he?" Dad questions.

I know what he is trying to do; make me question Levi and our bond but I won't play into his hands. Levi and I have worked extremely hard to build our trust back and leaving something like this out would be devastating.

"Levi's dad, Daniel, and Kevin's dad used to be in the same law firm when they started out of law school. They both were rising to the top when Daniel did some underhanded shit and blamed it on Kevin's dad. His dad got disbarred after the firm turned him over. Let's just say the family feud didn't end there. Kevin thought he could pull the same on Linc and have him lose everything, just like his old man."

"How do you know all of this?"

"Because, unlike you, I don't walk around with my head in the clouds. I did my homework, then started to tail Kevin and get close to him. He turned out to be the biggest scapegoat of all. I think he might hate the Thornes more than me, especially after the beat down his security gave him."

"Did you kill him too?" I can't even believe I have to ask this question to my father, but now I'm not sure what he's capable of. "The building blew up before they were able to get to him."

"Now that was all him. He was a lunatic, genius, but one crazy motherfucker." He almost sounds proud.

"I can't believe you're just standing there like we're talking about the fucking weather. When did you become so callous?"

"The moment I learned that the world didn't care about doing what was right, but only what money could buy you. I had to sit and watch as my child felt like she didn't matter, and was humiliated for the entire world to see. I promised to never have her experience that again," he defends. "So I decided to enact something that had been festering in my soul, and should've been taken care of a long time ago."

"I don't understand where all this is coming from. Why are you so against the Thornes? What did they ever do to you?"

"Because that bastard let my sister's murderer walk free and didn't bat an eye to the destruction he caused!" Dad yells. I've never seen him lose his cool before and fear starts to climb up my spine.

"Your twin, Amanda? Is that who you are referring to?" I ask. "Levi wasn't even around at the time all that happened."

"No, but Daniel was. He was on the legal defense that got

him off. He was the one who found the piece of evidence that got the bastard set free." Dad zones out, looking off to the other side of the room. "He let that man walk free and my sister was rotting in the ground. She was the best person in the entire world. She was kind and loving and would never even think to hurt a single soul. She didn't deserve what happened to her and it's all because of that money-hungry scumbag."

My heart drops and a wave of sadness forms over me. My dad has been holding a grudge all this time, and biding his time to strike out at those who hurt his twin. I understand his frustration and anger, but I can't believe he'd go to all these lengths. This isn't normal.

"I'm so sorry that Amanda was killed but—"

"I wasn't going to let you be part of that family's collateral damage. Then I find out that Everly was involved with the other brother, so I decided to take action. There was no way I was going to let their claws get into you girls. I stayed away for your own good, and look at the path you chose."

"Oh, Dad, how could you do this?" I palm my forehead in despair. So many lives have been destroyed.

His phone goes off and he quickly answers it, keeping an eye on me. But just as fast as the call came through, it ends.

"Our ride is almost here."

"Ride?" Now he's thrown me for a loop.

"We're leaving. I need to get you safely away, now that Levi and his goons have found you. I really thought Brody would've done a better job of keeping you hidden, but beggars can't be choosers. I thought the asshole would've found you before two years, especially being so close to his grandparent's place, though."

"Was Brody in on this with you?" I can't believe this.

"No, but I had been watching for some time, making sure you and Halo were fine."

"You knew where we were but didn't say anything, or come by to see me?" I can't stop the hurt in my voice, even though I'm mad as hell at him.

"I couldn't risk Levi finding you so I kept a low profile."

A ping from his phone goes off.

"It's time, go get Halo. Leave everything here, I'll make sure you two have the things you'll need at our next stop."

"I'm not leaving with you and neither is my daughter."

"See. This is why I couldn't sit you down and have a discussion about Levi Thorne. He has you brainwashed and you're not thinking clearly."

"No one has brainwashed me!" I yell. "I love that man and he's everything to me and Halo. He'd walk through fire for me and Halo."

Dad looks even more bored. The door down the hall creaks open, and my heart stops. Halo. She must've heard us yelling and woke up. I hate that she has started crawling over the railing now that she's a little older. Ginger helps her over the side a lot of the times too. So she doesn't hurt herself. Dad is between me and the hall, making it difficult to make it to her first.

"There she is!" Dad gushes as Halo comes into view, holding her teddy bear and pink blanket with Ginger on her heels. She is thankfully oblivious to the storm brewing in here.

Before I can move, he's got her scooped up in his arms and put on his hip. This is a nightmare of epic proportions. There is no way I'm leaving here with him to some unknown place, but now that he has Halo, I can't help but to comply for her sake.

"The dog stays," Dad says as he rocks her back and forth, as her tired form lays her head on his shoulder. There is nothing more

I want than to snag her from him. Never in my life did I ever not want to be around him. All those years of wishing he was more in my life is coming back to bite me in the ass.

"Dad, we can't go with you. Levi is not what you think. He'd never hurt me or Halo. Ever." I take a step towards him slowly, making my way to reach Halo. If someone would've asked me yesterday if I trusted my life with Dad, the immediate answer would've been a *hell yes*, but now I'm not sure what this man is capable of.

"It's not up to you anymore. I thought you'd gotten your head on straight in Montana, but clearly Levi still has his hooks in you." Lights from a car flash through the living room window. "My guy is here and we leave now."

Just as I'm about to reach him and rip Halo out of his grasp, the front door opens and Levi and Mitch barge in. Dad stumbles back from the shock, and I lose my chance to grab Halo.

"Put our daughter down or hand her over to Saylor, Adam," Levi demands, as he comes to stand by me. Mitch is evaluating the situation in the room by standing off to the side, as if to box him in.

"Not a chance Levi. I wish you'd just died in the bombing, then we wouldn't have to go through all this," Dad states, and pulls something out of his back.

A gun.

"Oh god, Dad! Don't do this in front of her!" I'm panicking and try to lunge at him, but Levi holds me back.

Halo is fully awake now and starting to cry, while reaching for her daddy. I'm a nervous wreck, shaking. Ginger seems to be taking in the room, and starting to crouch down in a defensive po-sition, not liking her cries. Halo is wiggling, trying to be released from Dad, because he's holding her too tight.

"Adam, let Halo down and we can talk all you want," Levi

says in the calmest voice ever. How is he not as panicked as I am? But then I see his hands trembling, and know that he is anything but calm.

"I've heard and seen enough to know that no amount of talking will change my mind. My daughter and grandbaby may be caught under your spell, but I'm not. Your charms don't work here. I know all about your past and what your family puts people through first hand. The apple doesn't fall far from the tree, does it? I refuse to sit back and watch my daughter be the next one in line to being a victim of the choices you've made."

"Please don't do this Dad," I beg, as I sob along with Halo. Ginger is getting more irritated, but then Dad raises the gun up to point it at Levi. "NO!" I scream and try to move my body in front of him.

All at once, not only does Ginger make a move but Zeus comes out of nowhere, from the other side of the room from the kitchen, and they both attack him. Ginger's jaw sinks into his forearm and Zeus aims for his thigh, making Dad drop Halo. Thankfully, Ginger is right there to soften the fall. We hear a small whimper from Ginger, but she battles through it and grabs Halo by the clothes and drags her over to us. Zeus is still on Dad, not letting up.

I scoop Halo into my arms and hold her tight to me.

"Get her out of here," Levi says as he checks us over quickly. Ginger is sniffing Halo and licking every inch of her.

Just as I'm about to run out of the living room, Brody makes his appearance from the hallway and sees Dad and Zeus fighting. Dad is hitting Zeus with the butt of the gun to knock him off his leg. Levi shields us, and tries to guide us over to Mitch, who has his gun out yelling at Dad to put the gun down.

I glance back one more time and watch as Dad points the barrel of the gun at Zeus.

"NO!" I scream, and Brody jumps from behind Dad to push the gun away from Zeus and Dad.

In a matter of seconds, the gun goes off. Something passes by my head in a whiz, as Levi tenses behind me and heaves out a loud gasp.

"Baby," Levi's eyes are wide and it's as though he's struggling to breathe.

I turn fully around and see his shirt spotted with the color red but it only takes moments before the spots are covering most of the white shirt.

"Oh my God! No!" I yell, shifting Halo to one side and placing a hand over the blood-soaked clothing.

Two more shots ring out, then a wail follows, but I can't bring myself to pull away from Levi.

"Ginger retreat!" I scream a command at our dog and she comes over to us, grasping Halo with her mouth latched on the back of my baby's clothing and takes off with her crying out of the guesthouse to safety, like she has been trained to do. I'm frozen in place and can't take my eyes off of Levi's eyelids, as I watch them slowly getting closer to closing.

"Saylor," Levi gasps for a breath.

"Don't talk, just focus on me." We sink to the floor and I immediately move his shirt up to see the damage. "I love you so much."

Blood is seeping out of a hole in his chest. Leaning over, I reach for anything I can to put some pressure over the gaping wound. Mitch comes over and tears off his shirt, turning Levi on his side to keep pressure on the back exit wound. The room is eerily quiet, but I can only focus on my man right now.

"I love you, baby. I love Halo," He's panting for air, but I can only see his eyes lowering more and more.

"We love you too. So much. Please stay with us. Focus on me. Stay with me. Stay with us." I move one of his hands to my stomach, and whisper for him to focus on me and my voice.

There are sirens in the distance and then a whirl of people are in the room. Levi gets loaded up on a gurney and rushed out. I'm rushing out the door, when I happen to look back over the living room to see Brody on the ground and the paramedics are performing CPR on him. *Oh my God, when did he get hurt?*

"We have a pulse," one of them says, and they load him up and move to rush him out.

Dad is over by the couch with a paramedic, checking his shoulder, as it looks like he was shot in the arm. Police have him circled and cuffed.

I'm numb. It feels like the events in the room are playing out in slow motion and I'm rooted to the floor, watching as everything moves around me.

I can't even grasp what just happened here. Every good childhood memory is now tainted by the events of today. Everything I thought my dad to be was nothing more than an illusion. How could he have done something like this?

"Saylor, we need to get you to the hospital," Mitch grimly says, and ushers me out to where Zeus and Ginger have circled Halo, as a pair of police officers try to entertain my daughter, but both dogs are making it impossible to get near her.

In a flash I'm running over and as she sees me, she does the same with our dogs following, growling at everyone to stay back away from us. I can't even put into words how I'm feeling as I hold her little frame to mine. What if Halo had been the one to take a bullet? I shake off the thought and try to focus on the love of my life, who's fighting for his life right now.

Somehow, we arrive at the hospital but I'm in a haze. Mitch escorts me to a conference room, and has Halo and I set up with Zeus and Ginger there for comfort. I vaguely heard a protest about our animals, but it was shot down when they found out who was brought in. I'm certain Mitch made sure to reveal the donation that this hospital will receive if we're kept comfortable and not disturbed. He also made the horrible phone call, that no parent or relative wants to get, to the Thornes, who should be arriving soon. My grandparents are on the way, along with Everly and Linc.

It feels like hours have gone by and not a single doctor has made it in here to update us. Ryan came in not too long ago after being released from the ER. Dad had injected security with a high dose of tranquilizers to put them out until he was able to get us out of the house. Zeus was also given some but thank God he was able to come out of it and make his way in to save us from Dad.

Save us from dad.

The words seem funny to say in the same sentence, in reference to my dad. The man who raised me and taught me how to tie my shoes and played ballerina with me in elementary.

I'm lost in my thoughts, watching Halo sleep next to Ginger and Zeus, as Everly and Linc go to get everyone some food and more coffee. A vet came in when we first got here to check them out. I'm sure Mitch scheduled that and I'll thank him later for it, when I can bring myself to speak.

Finally, the door opens with Mitch, Ryan and two doctors in blue scrubs coming in, both holding their surgical caps in their hands. Their faces are unreadable and I think I might vomit.

"Mrs. Thorne," one starts. "I'm Doctor Vincent."

I nod but don't speak, too terrified of what he's about to tell me.

"I'm so sorry but we did everything that we could." All the air leaves my body, and Ryan is there to catch me. "We weren't able to stop the bleeding and once we were able to get in, there was too much damage. I'm sorry but he didn't make it."

CHAPTER TWENTY-ONE

Saylor

6 Months Later

I'm staring down at the headstone and wonder how things could've been different. If I'd made a better decision, or didn't approach the sexy man at the bar that night. I think I'll always wonder now but I have to move on and promise that, from here on out, I'll live each day to the fullest without any regret. One thing I've learned from all of this is that you're not guaranteed tomorrow, so live today as if it's your last.

Dad's trial had come to an end last week and I'm thankful that I'll never have to experience something like that ever again. Having the Thorne name helped push it along quickly, and his defense didn't put up much of a fight and asked for a speedy trial. Taking the stand was the hardest feat I've ever had to endure. Knowing that I was giving testimony that would put my dad behind bars was hard. No, it was horrible. A nightmare. His attorney tried to blame PTSD for the cause, and I hate that they tried to use a scapegoat to get him off. Mine and Levi's entire relationship was put under a microscope.

"Mrs. Thorne, can you please describe the time of your mother's death?" Mr. Russell, dad's lead attorney, asks.

I sit there for a second, never wanting to revisit that part of my life.

"It was not a good environment for anyone, much less a child, to live through."

"Was there any type of abuse in the household?"

"I don't see how that is relevant to this case," I snap at him.

"Mrs. Thorne, you going through that horrible time just further proves that my client was trying to not let that situation ever happen again."

"I'm not sure how losing a parent to cancer would be trying to justify his actions; by bringing up my past is the worst possible thing he could do. He did this on his own and he was in his right mind when he followed through with it. No one could formulate a plan so calculated and not be sane."

"Mrs. Thorne, did your husband ever try to manhandle you or do something to you that you protested or didn't like?"

"Never." There is no way I'm going to let what happened to my dad's twin sister have any weight in his actions regarding what he plotted and planned.

"Is it true that your husband publicly humiliated you in a crowded restaurant and declared he wanted a divorce?"

"What does that have to do with the price of beans?"

"Objection!" The prosecution yells, stopping me from answering.

The trial is closed to the public but I still don't want our private life out there for others to scrutinize. It's really none of their business and it has nothing to do with this trial.

It only took the jury three hours to decide that he was guilty, but the kicker was that they bought some of the PTSD. They sentenced him to life in a mental hospital that is run by the state. He killed two people and he's now getting to stay in a place where he'll get unlimited TV and bingo nights, while the others are buried and are never going to see another day. At least he has no communication with the outside world.

It's not fair but then again life isn't either.

"Saylor? You ready to head back?" Ryan asks, coming up from the car.

"Sure." I place the flowers in the vase beside the headstone and kiss my fingers, then place them on the top.

"I'm getting married today. I know that you're probably turning over down there because of it, but I hope that you'd be happy for me. He's a good man and loves me with his whole heart and has from the moment he saw me. You'll always hold a special place in my heart, even though I'm mad as hell at you." I think back to the first time we met and smile.

I can't believe I'm getting married today. This is my second time, or is it my third since I had the paperwork to show that Brody and I married, even though it was fake?

Anyway, after the shooting and the speedy trial, I was the one who pushed for it. As I said, life is too short not to live each day to the fullest and I didn't want to waste any more time in being happy. This is the right choice for me and Halo. She's super excited because she gets to wear a beautiful dress.

Pulling up to the small ranch, I feel a calmness rein over me. We decided that we wanted to stay close to Los Angeles but find a place with some land, so that Halo could continue to have her animals to feed and play with. After the trial, I couldn't get out of the city quick enough. We found a beautiful twenty-acre lot with a gorgeous house already on it, ready to move in. It belonged to a Senator who was looking to down size after losing an election.

"There she is!" I hear Everly yell down from the upstairs.

The house is huge and has plenty of room for our growing

family. Six bedrooms, nine bathrooms, game room, gym, theater, and an awesome library. The kitchen is amazing and Tina has practically lived in there since we moved in. I'm so glad she is here to help me through everything. Tina has always mothered me and she treats me more like a daughter than employer. The property also has several living quarters and three barns. Glammy and Granddad sold their LA home and built a small house here on the property, and so did Grandma and Grandpa. They are neighbors and share a driveway from the main house. Everly and Linc bought the ten acres next door and are officially moving in two months.

"I'm here, I'm here," I say as I walk my happy self over to the kitchen, where Tina is killing it in there preparing the meal for later. I told her that I'd have the small reception catered but she wouldn't hear of it.

My stomach roars, announcing me, and Tina immediately opens the fridge to hand me cup of salsa, as I already have a bowl of chips in hand. This little one wants nothing but salt. With Halo, I wanted nothing but sweets; it's crazy how one pregnancy can be completely different from another.

"Are you ready for this evening, Saylor?" Tina asks as she pulls out some food from the oven.

"More than ready. I don't think I'm as nervous as I was when I got married the first time."

"Really? How so?"

"Well, marrying *LA's Golden Boy* was a lot of pressure and I felt like one wrong move and I was going to be crucified. Now, I'm just me and everything seems more laid back. No pressure at all." I smile as I chomp down several chips at once.

"Have you heard from my groom?" I ask, once I've eaten half the jar of salsa and rub my five-month pregnant belly.

Glammy strides into the room and gives me a look I know all too well.

"I know you're not happy about this decision, but I really know what I want; I wouldn't have proposed to him otherwise."

"It's not that I'm not happy, just cautious. You've been through a lot over the last few years, and I want you to do what is right for you but also make sure you've had time to heal. There's no rush," Glammy tells me.

"I understand where you're coming from and love you for it. Thank you for being amazing these past few months." I do appreciate and value her opinion, but I know I'm making the right decision. She and Granddad have had a hard time dealing with my dad's insane decisions over the last few years. They keep blaming themselves, but I won't hear of it. Everyone is responsible for their own actions, as well as the consequences.

"I only want the best for you and to see you succeed in whatever it is you want, even if it's rushing into marrying that man today," she says and we both burst out in giggles. "We are just glad that we get to be part of it this time."

"Hey, I need the bride to do her hair up there. Halo is trying to put bows on the dogs and paint their nails. Zeus is not having it and going crazy trying to escape," Everly says, coming in the kitchen and swiping a cookie from the plate by the oven. She eats three in rapid succession then rubs her pregnant belly. They found out right in the middle of the trial that she was pregnant and we love that our babies are going to be so close in age.

"I'm coming." I hop down from the stool and start to walk that way.

"We only have two hours before the wedding starts and we have so much to do," Everly stresses.

"Can't we just wear pajamas? And my hair up in a bun?" I whine at having to get all dolled up.

"Have you lost your mind? Saylor you only get married once…" She pauses and then clamps her mouth shut. "I mean twice?" She pauses again, only for us to bust a gut laughing.

Once we get our fits of laughter under control, the beauty squad does their magic and works me over.

Shortly after that, Halo comes in wearing her beautiful white, lace tea length dress. She has a pair of brown cowboy boots on, with her hair up in a curly ponytail and a matching headband. She looks adorable and is the most beautiful flower girl ever.

As I put on my matching lace dress, Halo and I look like twins. The groom left me a perfect pair of baby blue earrings, with diamonds around the outside. They match the bottoms of my heels that are the same color, but were specially made and dipped in baby blue glitter.

Halo loves having our picture taken together and I think we have a little ham on our hands. After we take a million photos, Everly comes in all dressed with Glammy behind her.

"Oh Saylor, you look so beautiful," Glammy gushes.

"Picture perfect," Everly interjects.

"You sure?" I turn back to the full-length mirror and place my hand on my protruding belly.

"Absolutely," they both say and we make our way carefully down the stairs with the help of Ryan.

"You can turn back now. I've got a getaway car ready and we can have the jet ready to go with one phone call," Everly says as she stops me from opening the back door to head out to our ceremony.

"I promise this is what I want. Thank you for helping me do all of this."

"Hey, I'd do anything for you. That is what family does," she says, then wraps me in a hug where our bellies bump together.

My relationship with Alice, Levi's mom, is even better now after the shooting. We aired a lot out after the funeral, and are almost back to the way we were before all this mess happened. Although, Daniel is still not a welcome sight. I know in my heart that he was doing what he thought best for his son, but the hateful names and not helping me out when I was pregnant was the straw that broke the camel's back. He could've helped, and then I'd never been placed in the jail cell where that evil bitch and her lackeys beat me.

"Momma!" Halo squeals, and it brings me out of my thoughts.

She's looking at the lit-up barn, with the candle lanterns that lead the path to the barn doors. I wanted something simple here on our property. As soon as I proposed to the groom, he made sure this barn was the perfect fit for our wedding, and he didn't disappoint.

"You ready, baby girl?" I take her hand and we walk down the path towards the entrance.

Soft music plays on the other side of the lace curtain that separates the inside from the outside. I can see the entire barn is lit in candles, and there are strands of clear lights around the wooden poles throughout the barn. He made sure to put in new flooring so I wouldn't trip over the unleveled wooden planks that were there before.

The aisle is divided down the middle, and there are a few rows of chairs that occupy our closest friends and family; nothing like my first wedding where there was only myself, the groom and the Justice of the Peace.

Two men dressed nicely stand on either side of the door and carefully draw back the lace curtain. The music changes and my eyes meet my groom as Halo and I take the first step inside, as the Wedding March plays. Everything else fades away, and only he and I are there. My pulse starts to race, and it's like the aisle is a mile long.

Our two dogs, Zeus and Ginger who are at the front, perk up and move to us in a matter of seconds. Halo jumps up and takes off to meet Ginger halfway, but I stay put and take in everything that is about to happen. Our lives will never be the same after this, and we plan to move forward and never look back at the past. We've learned a lot but promised to never experience those mistakes again.

My groom, impatient as ever, moves from the front of the aisle and meets both Halo and I in the middle. He picks up Halo, giving her a sound kiss on the cheek, then circles my waist placing a hand on my protruding belly, giving me an almost inappropriate public kiss. Only the sound of the Pastor clearing his throat makes him stop. He blushes pink, and it only makes me love him more. We've come a long way over the months, and I have to say that I made the right decision after picking up the pieces, after that fatal night several months ago.

As we make it to the front, he places Halo down and fixes her dress before her attention is back on Ginger, and they move over a few feet away from us and Pastor Reynolds.

"Shall we begin this beautiful ceremony?" Pastor Reynolds asks, and we both nod.

The Pastor starts by reading a few verses but my hearing is muffled by my groom's whisper. We're only inches away and if I wasn't five months pregnant, I'm sure he'd be molded to me.

"You look stunning," he whispers.

"Thank you," I mouth.

He leans his body into me, and I know he's about to seal his lips to mine but once again the Pastor speaks up.

"I know both the bride and groom want to say their own vows..."

My eyes focus back on my groom and I can't help but start to tear up, looking into his beautiful eyes.

"Levi, if you will start your vow renewal." He nods to the Pastor, then turns back to me.

"Saylor, my love, my life. Words fail me every time I opened my mouth when I was practicing this. I know we've been here before, but this time it's different. We're different. You came into my life when I needed you the most and turned me upside down and inside out. For the longest time, I thought this was a fluke and that at any moment, I would wake up and it would all have been a dream. That I was destined to be alone for the rest of my life, but from day one you wedged your way up to the bar and changed all of it. Three months later, we married and I swore to be one with you and walk through this marriage as an equal partner. I failed that because on day two-hundred and forty of our marriage, I lost you to my foolish pride. Never did I think that one mistake would cost me my entire world for over two and a half years. But it did, and in a way I'm thankful. Thankful because I was able to grow up and become the man you needed. The man who you deserve."

I squeeze our joined hands, and will the stinging in my eyes to let up. We've both cried enough over the years, and now I want nothing but happiness from here on out.

"Today, I stand before you and our daughter, and pledge that for as long as I'm breathing that I'll be the man you both want in your life. I promise to be the best role model for our daughter and the best husband that you could ever want. I promise to love, honor and cherish you, to include you on every aspect of our lives and walk hand and hand together until we can't walk any more. I love you Saylor, with my whole heart, and promise to keep you safe and warm on chilly nights, to help make you the best person that you have always wanted to be. I love you and promise these things until death do us part."

Levi takes his monogramed handkerchief out of his front pocket and dabs my soaked cheeks. How can anyone follow those words?

Pastor Reynolds turns towards me and nods, letting me know it's my turn. Steeling myself, I take a deep breath and try to calm my emotions to get through this.

"Levi, I didn't really know what living was until I saw you for the first time. The moment I stumbled into that crazy bar, it was like you had turned on a switch and my life began. You have given my world color and I don't think I could ever go back to living the way I was before you."

Our daughter walks over and circles her daddy's legs, giving him a big hug, making us all laugh.

"You have shown me what it's like to have a true partner and even though we've had some rocky bumps in our time, I think we both can say that we are better people because of them. It might've taken us years to get where we are now, but I'm glad that you never gave up on us. Our daughter and I love you more than you'll ever know and I hope that every day I can show you exactly that."

I can see the tears welling up in his eyes, and I know he's trying his best to keep them in because seeing him cry is going to make me lose it.

"Kiersten White said it best, *'I'd choose you, in a hundred lifetimes, in a hundred worlds, in any version of reality, I'd find you and choose you.'* Never in my heart was there another for me; you are it for me Levi Thorne."

"I promise to love, honor and cherish you. To keep you and your heart safe, to be a sounding board when life is too tough, and even a warm place for your cold feet. I pledge my love and life to you, and only you for, as long as we both shall live."

We don't wait for Pastor Reynolds and surge forward to seal our promises to each other. We're already married so we can do as we like. I can hear cheering and clapping in the distance but tune them out. It's only when I feel a tug on my dress that we pull apart.

"My daddy!" Halo stomps her little boot.

"Of course, baby doll." Levi swoops down and brings her between us as we both kiss a chubby cheek, sending her into fits of giggles as she's the little ham of the party.

The reception is what I had hoped it would've been the first time around. I think back to the girl I was then and the woman I am now, and can't help but be relieved that I've changed. At least for the better, I think.

My lower back has a pinch to it so I'm sitting down to relieve some of the pressure. My mind drifts back to three months ago, and I can't help but remember when the doctors came in to tell me that Brody didn't make it. At first, I thought it was Levi and my entire world stopped for a few brief moments. Ryan, Everly and Linc had to hold me upright until they assured me that it was in fact Brody, and not Levi, who had died.

"Wha…what do you mean, he didn't make it?" I sway and several hands catch me.

"We did everything we could, we're sorry for your loss," one of the doctors says, but I can't focus on anything right now other than the fact that the love of my life didn't make it.

"This can't be happening," I look over to my left and see Ryan. "He promised me forever. He said he'd never leave me and Halo!"

"Saylor…Saylor please listen."

I think I went into shock because the next thing I knew, I was in a hospital bed. Something was holding my legs down and when my eyes focused, it was Everly with her head laying across them. She was sound asleep. I heard beeping and when I turned my head, I saw a man lying in a bed next to me, making my heart stop.

"Levi!" I shouted as if I was dreaming and wanted to wake us up.

I heard his familiar grunt as Everly sprung up from her seat.

"Shh." Everly grabbed for my hand. "He needs all the rest he can get."

"But…h-he's here? The doctors?" I stuttered.

"They were talking about Brody, Saylor. Levi is in bad shape but they think he will be just fine, as long as he rests and gets through this first night."

"Oh, thank god!" I reach over the rails and grip his hand in mine. "Please don't leave me."

I thought my heart died that day, and it took a long while before I felt as though we were going to be okay, after everything that had happened with Dad. We buried Brody, here in Los Angeles, next to his family. Brody had changed his will and left everything in my name. I didn't feel right taking it, so I decided to leave the ranch in Montana in the hands of Patrick to run. With Levi's help and his resources, Jackson Ranch is a safe harbor for women and children in Witness Protection. Patrick loves the idea, and they just had its first guests last week. Levi is helping with all the other details, and all the profits from Brody's goggle and scope designs is going into a fund to maintain the ranch and all the help there. He's licensed it out to a client who specializes in that field, and with a few tweaks from their R&D, they have been able to create an even better product for our military.

"You feeling okay, baby?" I hear my man's voice. Levi saddles up next to me, then picks me up as though I'm not pregnant and places me on his lap.

"Just thinking about the past and how we got here."

He places a firm hand on my belly, then kisses my neck.

"We only need to think of the present and future," he whispers, sending shivers down my spine that leaves me squirming on his lap. "How's my boy doing?" He rubs me, and a small kick follows his hand.

"Starving for cake." I giggle when Levi bites my shoulder.

We found out that we're having a boy a few weeks ago and couldn't be happier. Although, Halo is not on board yet. She doesn't want anyone taking her daddy's attention away, especially me. We are still unsure if the dad is Brody or Levi but as Levi has stated before on many occasions, *DNA doesn't matter*. I'm still planning on getting a paternity test done after this little guy comes out, for peace of mind though. I'll love him no matter what but health wise, I want to be prepared for anything. And, he will also have the right to know if he doesn't share the same biology as his sister, or the dad that raises him.

"Well, we can't have that." He stands with me secured in his strong arms.

"Wait, it's not time for cake yet!"

"Baby, we can do whatever we want. It's our party, these people are the intruders."

A loud squeak rings on the dance floor as we make our way over to the cake table. Knowing that voice, we both freeze but when we see what's going on, we laugh along with everyone else. Ryan has Halo in the air, tossing her high, as Mitch tosses her teddy bear the same height at the same time. We really couldn't have asked for a better family than this.

Without thinking, I gather a dollop of icing on two fingers

from our cake as Levi is distracted with watching Halo having fun. An evil grin forms on my face, and I launch my fingers torwards him and smear a line of icing down the side of his face. His eyes bulge as he realizes what just happened.

"You know, being pregnant won't save you, right?" he tells me smiling and reaching over my shoulder. I love his playful side.

Zoning out the guests, Levi and I have a food fight with our wedding cake. Halo comes over at one point but only to swipe a few pieces to eat. Once we've had enough, Levi bends and picks me up bridal style and whistles to get everyone's attention.

"We'd like to thank you all for coming and sharing this time with us, but as you can imagine, we have somewhere where we need to be." Not leaving any room for arguments, he heads out the door of the barn as Reid is yelling.

"But I haven't given my speech yet!"

Levi ignores him and takes long strides towards our house. Halo is staying with Alice tonight and will join us tomorrow, as we go on a trip to Disney World. I've never been and Halo can't wait to see all the princesses.

"You are so beautiful," Levi states as he sets me down in our bathroom, then pulls the zipper down the back of my dress.

"As are you," I retort and start to unbutton his messy white shirt. I'm pretty sure our clothes are ruined but I couldn't care less.

Levi starts the shower and pulls us both in. He fingers out all the pins in my hair and we clean each other. After toweling off, we make our way back to the bedroom.

"Lay down, baby. I want to devour you."

And he does just that. What seems like hours, and after several orgasms, Levi makes his way up my body and I feel his thick erection probing my entrance.

I let a moan escape. "You like that, baby?"

"More Levi. No more teasing. Please!" I whine. I'm all for foreplay but for the love of God my hormones are all over the place.

"Yes, baby." He thrusts and buries his fat cock to the hilt. We groan with satisfaction. "Is this what you wanted? Huh?" He starts to pump in and out, being mindful of my stomach.

"Yes!" I scream as I'm on the edge.

Levi grabs one of my legs and places it over his shoulder as he continues to pound into me.

"Come for me, Saylor. Cream all over my cock."

His words are always my undoing, and I explode. My body convulses with each thrust, as a shiver ripples up my spine. "Levi!" I call, but I'm not sure if it was in my head or if I really did scream his name. I'm floating on a cloud and don't want to leave my spot. There isn't anything better than being in his arms.

"Again," he demands, pushing right up on my clit, sending me into a frenzy.

"I can't."

"Yes. You. Can." He pounds in after each word. "You are my home. I could live in here for the rest of my life."

He places his thumb to my lips and I open automatically. "Suck."

I do as he asks, sucking on his thumb as if it were his dick. Swiftly, he pulls it out and like a magnet it finds my bundle of nerves that pulses like a heartbeat. Levi applies the right amount of pressure, then gives it a pinch. That's all it takes and I'm done. I moan his name and dig my fingers in his arms.

"Saylor, baby!" He groans, and I feel him throb inside of me as he stretches and fills me to the brim with his seed.

Slowly, his pumps stop and we both are unmoving as we catch our breath.

"There will never be a day that I'll ever tire from seeing you come."

He gently places my leg down, then turns me so that he can spoon me. Levi wraps an arm securely around me to hold my belly in place. I can feel my eyes growing heavy after the long and exhausting day we've had.

"I love you, Levi. And I can't wait to spend the rest of my life with you."

If possible, he moves closer to me and gives me a small squeeze.

"You are my entire life, Saylor. Nothing and no one will ever change that. I love you with my whole heart."

I'm so glad we were able to find each other again. I will be forever grateful that he moved heaven and earth and battled all his demons to find his way back to me. My life would never be complete if he was not in it.

"You and me, baby, against the world."

EPILOGUE

Levi

FOUR YEARS LATER

"Halo Landry! You leave your brother alone!" I yell across the backyard, as I watch our six-year-old daughter taunt her four-year-old brother, as he decides if he wants to jump off the diving board.

"But Daddy," she whines as she tries to play off the fact that she was about to push him in. Ginger is waiting at the top of the steps as my son takes his sweet time.

Even though Ryan has the day off, he offered to take the kids swimming for a few hours to give us a chance to pack our bags. He has truly been one of the best employees that we've got, besides Mitch and Tina of course. We've blurred the lines a long time ago and now our children think of him as an Uncle just like Linc and Reid. In fact, Ryan and Reid have to compete for time when the weekends come.

A lot has changed since we renewed our vows four years ago.

First off, we welcomed our perfect baby boy who came into the world screaming like a banshee, four months after our ceremony.

He was just beautiful and the entire birthing was an amazing experience. I had missed Halo's birth and had the worst guilt in the days leading up to the due date. Of course, Saylor wouldn't let me dwell on it for too long but I did lay there almost every night by Halo's bedside, and promise to never miss another important milestone of her life ever again. And I haven't.

Kason Axel Thorne came into the world. He was wrinkly and red but perfect in every way. I was in love the moment the doctor pulled him from Saylor. I knew that nothing in the world would separate us and that our family was whole again.

Saylor had asked for a paternity test as soon as she was settled into our hospital suite, but I said no. It didn't matter whose DNA he had. He was mine. But like most of the time, Saylor won. We had Kason's mouth swabbed and blood drawn, then mine as we waited twenty-four hours for the lab to run the test. We were getting ready to leave the hospital when the doctor came in with the results. We both stared at the envelope, for what seemed like forever, when Ryan and Mitch came in to carry our bags down to the car.

"Either open it or trash it, but either way we have a very hungry little monster, down with Tina, wanting her brother and wanting to eat." Ryan nudged us both before they both left us and a sleeping newborn alone.

"Do we need to know?" I asked. "We could just put it in the safe for later."

"No, I need to know. We need to know for health reasons and to sleep better at night," Saylor stated. I know that she's the one who needs this.

"Okay."

I reached down and pulled the tab on the back, then reached in and grabbed the single paper.
Los Angeles Hospital Paternity Labs

It is concluded that the sample given of Patient A (Kason Axel Thorne) and the sample given from Patient B (Levi Thorne) have been tested and the results are as follows.

Patient A (Kason Axel Thorne) and Patient B (Levi Thorne) are 99.99%…

My heart stops beating and I crumple the paper. Tears flood my eyes. I wasn't expecting this to have such impact on me. I already claimed him as mine either way, but to know that both of my children share mine and Saylor's DNA is something unexpected.

Saylor grabs both of my arms and must think I'm upset, but it is further from the truth.

"Oh God, Levi, I'm sorry—" She starts to wail, then wraps her arms around her body, retreating within herself. "Why was I so stupid? How could I have let him manipulate me so easily?"

"Saylor, baby—"

"I understand if this changes things for you and you want to leave. Have nothing to do with my baby—"

"SAYLOR!" I scream to get her attention and in doing so, I wake Kason.

We both hurry over to him in his carrier but I almost shove her out of the way, forgetting that she had just given birth not so long ago. Carefully, like Saylor and the nurses have shown me, I cradle him against my chest.

"He's mine," I say to her, and hum in his ear to soothe him back to sleep.

"I know you said that it didn't matter about DNA but after seeing your reaction, you don't have to if you don't want to Levi. There is still time to have the birth certificate changed."

"Saylor, you're not listening. He. Is. Mine." I lean over the bed and pick up the crumpled piece of paper handing it to her.

Her eyes scan over the words several times, as if not believing what she's reading.

"He's yours," she says in disbelief.

"He's mine," I proudly say and pat his little back.

"I was so worried…"

"I told you I had awesome swimmers!"

Her smile could light up a football stadium and that's how it should be for the rest of our lives. She comes over and hugs me, careful to not wake a now sleeping baby.

"I didn't think it was possible to love you more Levi, but every day you surprise me and I fall in love even deeper."

The second thing that has changed for us is that I only work buying and renovating houses for rentals, or flip them. I've hung up my law degree and haven't looked back. We live on the ranch and love our little country life. I still get paid for being a partner at Linc's law firm but I don't actively work on cases anymore. In fact, Linc and I have put the best team in place to help the firm grow and let Olivia, our other partner, run the entire firm. He mostly goes in and signs off on things in the middle of the week and holds all meetings on those days. If it can't be done during those days, then it gets pushed back to the next week. He worked his ass off getting the firm where it is, so now is the time to reap the spoils of his hard work and enjoy his life with his little family who lives next door to us. Linc is still the face for the firm but deals with fewer cases.

The best part of all of this is that I love being at home with the kids all day. Yes, there are days when I want to rip my hair out, but nothing is more rewarding than watching them grow up right before your eyes.

So, that brings me to the third thing that has happened in the last four years. Three months after Kason was born, we found out that Saylor was pregnant again. Like I said, my swimmers are awesome. Let's just say that the pull-out method was not in our cards, or I may have stayed in a little longer than necessary, but hey, when a man's in the moment with his hot wife naked begging him to fuck her harder what's a man to do?

Nine months later, we welcomed Addison Haley Thorne. She was just as perfect as her brother. She has my beautiful eyes like her older sister and Saylor's hair color. Her and Halo could be twins in how their features match up. Although, she has my scowl perfectly perfected.

Reid has surprised us all with his settling down. Never did I think it was in the cards for him but one day he came over with a woman who he'd helped on the side of the road. She was short with dark hair and glasses, a straight up bookworm like my wife. It was a huge contrast from his tall, blonde, long-legged women from before. She was just as cute as a button and apparently perfect for my brother. They married six months from the time he saved her from the road and are expecting their first baby this spring.

Linc and Everly have two sets of twins. I'm not sure how they manage them all at once, when trying to juggle one at a time is still challenging to me. They have their little compound on the property next door and we see them almost every day. Saylor and Everly have playdates with the kids.

Our grandparents are starting to slow down as more time passes. They say the kids keep them young, but we can tell by the way they are all traveling less. Linc and I have hired some help to come in twice a week to do all the menial jobs, so that they can focus on the fun things that they want to do.

Alice works part-time at Linc's law firm, and has been helping out at our houses with our brood for the last few years. She's the best grandmother to our children and couldn't be more pleased. Her and Daniel reconciled eighteen months ago. At first, I wasn't happy about it and refused to understand why she'd take him back but then Dr. Blake quickly reminded me that even I made a mistake and was forgiven. Don't think that it was an easy process, but Saylor was the one who offered the olive branch first. She amazes me at every turn. I also think that not having either of her parents present in her life had a lot to do with it too. That doesn't mean that security leaves the room when our kids hang out over at their house, but we are slowly mending the bridge. Daniel apologizes every time we see him but I think it's going to take a long time for all of us to build a relationship, where she feels comfortable with being in the same room alone together. He is an amazing grandfather to all our kids, but it doesn't mean all is forgotten.

"Levi? Is that you?" I hear my angel calling from in the walk-in closet.

"Yes, baby." She's packing herself a bag even though Tina said she would take care of it.

"I can't find my pink slippers. Have you seen them?" she calls out.

I look over at the end of the bed and see Zeus hanging his head. It's like he knows how she gets.

"Have you looked on your feet?" I say sweetly, hoping to ease the blow that's about to erupt.

"Ugh!" she groans and pops out of the closet. "This is the last time Levi Thorne! No more!"

She is even more beautiful than when I met her all those years ago. Saylor comes barreling out with a rolling suitcase, wearing only panties and a bra. Her nine-month pregnant belly on display, making me harder than ever.

"Baby, that's what you said with Addi and look where we are

now." I place a firm hand on her belly and feel a hard kick. "If I remember, you were begging for my cum nine months ago when the discussion of another precious baby was brought up."

"I know but this one is it. Any time you're naked, I lose all rational thought," she whines. "I think you should get snipped." She snuggles against me as I sit her on my lap.

"Snipped?" I question, and my body flinches. She giggles and lays her head on my shoulder.

"Is Addi still napping?" She nips my earlobe, sending my body abuzz.

"Mhmm."

"So maybe we have a little time to get this little girl out the old fashion way instead of being induced?"

"Oh, you naughty devil." I bite her shoulder right under her ear where her neck is. "Zeus door," I command and he does as he's told, shutting our bedroom door.

I place my wife at the end of the bed, with her arms on the bed and her feet spread open firmly on the floor. Being ready to pop is a challenge when having sex and finding the most comfortable positions for her. "I think I'm up for the challenge Mrs. Thorne."

Six hours later, we welcome Mallory Wren Thorne into the world. She was quiet as a mouse and her cries were barely heard, with her striking strawberry blonde hair. Like all the other births, I cried harder and louder than our children, as they placed them in my arms.

Never did I imagine my life would be this full of happiness and love. I've always thought that I'd end up alone but all it took was one tiny brunette woman to bring me to my knees and change me in ways I never thought possible. She is the light to my darkness, the moon that brightens the dark skies. She is the love of my life and nothing, and no one, will ever change that. We've been through hell and back to get to where we are today and, strangely, I wouldn't change it for anything. In life, you have good with the bad and even in our bad times, we shined through and came out better people for it. When push comes to shove, she is my number one person. It truly is us against the world. She leans on me and I lean on her. Where my weaknesses are, she is stronger and vice versa.

There's a whimper coming from the small bassinette in our hospital suite, and I quickly bolt from the recliner so that my sleeping wife can have a few more moments of rest.

"Hey, pretty girl," I sing in a whisper, as she coos back to me. She truly is a quiet baby. "Did you have a good nap?" She stares at me, or at least I think so. "How about a quick change and then we'll wake mommy, huh?"

I cradle her in my arms and lay her down at the changing station here in the hospital. I've become a pro at this over the years and love it. Most men refuse to change a single diaper, or getting their hands dirty, but I find that it's the best time to have some daddy-baby time. I get to tell them all about life and how they are going to be the best at everything. With Kason and Addi, we even had secret hand bumps during our late-night changings. I was meant for this life; I just didn't know it until it was right in front of my face. I'm just hoping I can get one more from Saylor before she puts her petite sized foot down and we stop making the world's best babies.

Once I'm finished, I'm surprised to find my beautiful wife awake, watching me and Mallory.

"How're you feeling, baby?"

"Sore but good," she says, shifting in the bed. "You really are the master at diaper changes, you know."

I shrug while swaddling her in her soft purple blanket that

Halo picked out. Apparently, I was destined to be a father to mostly girls. Kason and I are completely outnumbered in our house.

"I didn't push out a baby so I'd like to think this is my contribution."

"Well, I think it makes you even sexier for it."

"Careful, or I'll impregnate you again before we leave the hospital," I tease, but I wish I could.

I know we have a houseful of healthy, wonderful kids at home but there is something about Saylor being pregnant that sets me on fire. She is the most beautiful, glowing woman I've ever witnessed, and she's the best mother a child could hope for.

"Can we revisit this after Mallory is out of diapers?" she suggests, and hope blooms in my chest at having another set of little feet toddle down our hallways.

"You can have anything you want, baby."

I place Mallory on the half circle pillow under Saylor's breast and she latches on without any problem. It seems all our children take to the tit like their dad.

"I don't want anything but our children and you," she says, looking up from the baby. Sometimes I think this is all a dream, and that I'll wake up one day and be alone in my large office. But each day I'm reminded that tomorrow is never promised and that we need to live each one to the fullest.

Cupping her face, I lightly kiss her lips as the smacking from our daughter reminds me that we aren't alone.

"Love you, baby," I whisper against her lips.

"Love you more."

"Impossible."

THE END

Thank you so much for reading Levi! I hope you loved it and will leave a review. I wrote this book back in 2016, when I first started to dabble in the writing world. At the time, I had no intention of ever releasing it or letting anyone read it. Originally, this was going to be a very long book but once I read over it again, I knew that it would be better to split it up between the two brothers, Linc and Levi. Which formed the Thorne Brother Series. They were so much fun to write and to dive into their world of love and faults.

Join my newsletter for sneak peeks and
special project opportunities:

Follow me along this journey for updates on
the current and next projects.

www.AmberAllee.com

Goodreads:
www.goodreads.com/author/show/48624101.Amber_Allee

Facebook Page:
www.facebook.com/AmberAlleeAuthor

Facebook Group:
www.facebook.com/groups/655580198616583

Instagram:
www.instagram.com/author.amberallee

TikTo:
www.tiktok.com/@author.amberallee k

ALSO BY AMBER ALLEE

Las Vegas Mafia Series
THE PRINCE
HIDDEN QUEEN
BISHOP

Thorne Brother Series
LINC
LEVI

ACKNOWLEDGMENTS

Kevin, you are my favorite person in the world! Thank you for pushing me to publish all my stories. I never would've done this, had you not held me accountable for a promise I made. You are the peanut butter to my jelly!

Mom and Dad, thank you for always showing up and being my biggest champions.

Misti K, thank you for wearing so many different hats so that I can make these dreams come true. You are the most organized person and my life would be chaos without you!

Stacey B, you amaze me with each and every book that you touch. They always turn out better than I can ever imagine. Thank you for all that you do and for always working me in because something crazy always seems to come up!

Stacy G, I swear each cover gets better and better! You have such a talent and I love all the work you do! Thank you for bringing my visions to life and making them so perfect.

Andrea B, thank you for fixing all of my mistakes and giving the best advice with editing. You are truly a gem and I love all of our calls and texts! Thank you for working tirelessly to make this perfect!

M.E. Carter, your guidance with the story and characters are invaluable. Thank you for making sure each part flows and I don't miss or leave anything out.

To the Readers, thank you for taking a chance on me and reading my crazy books. I truly hope that each of you love them as much as I loved writing them. Your support through this journey means everything to me. Your reviews and kind messages fuel me to be a better writer.

To the Promoters & Influencers, thank you for getting my book out there and seen by the readers. You guys make such a difference for indie authors like me and I am so thankful for each and every one of you.

ABOUT THE AUTHOR

 Amber Allee is the author of two sizzling romance series—*The Las Vegas Mafia Series* and *The Thorne Brother Series*—blending suspense, drama, and swoon-worthy alpha heroes. Since releasing her first book in 2024, she's hooked readers with stories full of heart-pounding twists and unforgettable love stories.

A proud Texan, Amber still lives in her hometown with her husband and two kids. When she's not writing, you'll probably find her buried under a pile of blankets with a good book, playing games with her family, or planning her next beach vacation. She loves to travel, wears leopard, adores everything that sparkles, and never turns down a cold Coke over nugget ice.